D0632954

LOVE
at 350°

LISA PEERS

THE DIAL PRESS
NEW YORK

Love at 350° is a work of fiction. Names, characters, places, and incidents are the products of the author's imagination or are used fictitiously. Any resemblance to actual events, locales, or persons, living or dead, is entirely coincidental.

A Dial Press Trade Paperback Original

Copyright © 2023 by Lisa Peers

Dial Delights Extras copyright © 2023 by Penguin Random House LLC

All rights reserved.

Published in the United States by The Dial Press, an imprint of Random House, a division of Penguin Random House LLC, New York.

THE DIAL PRESS is a registered trademark and the colophon is a trademark of Penguin Random House LLC.

DIAL DELIGHTS and colophon are trademarks of Penguin Random House LLC.

Library of Congress Cataloging-in-Publication Data
Names: Peers, Lisa, author.
Title: Love at 350 degrees: a novel / Lisa Peers.
Description: New York: The Dial Press, [2023]
Identifiers: LCCN 2023004549 (print) | LCCN 2023004550 (ebook) |
ISBN 9780593595183 (trade paperback; acid-free paper) |
ISBN 9780593595190 (ebook)
Subjects: LCGFT: Romance fiction. | Novels.
Classification: LCC PS3616.E334 L68 2023 (print) | LCC PS3616.E334 (ebook) |
DDC 813/.6—dc23/eng/20230419
LC record available at https://lccn.loc.gov/2023004549
LC ebook record available at https://lccn.loc.gov/2023004550

Printed in the United States of America on acid-free paper

randomhousebooks.com

2 4 6 8 9 7 5 3 1

Book design by Debbie Glasserman

FOR DANI—

I am only here

because you are always there

LOVE
at 350°

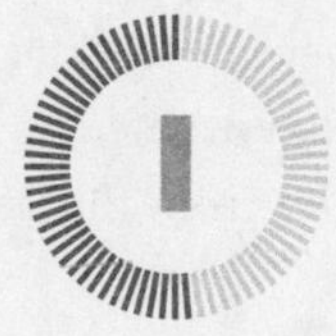

Tori Moore scanned her classroom, checking her fifth-period Biochemistry of Baking students' progress. Three of Sequoia High's star football players were pulverizing dry ice in a blender ahead of mixing it into their strawberry and chocolate bases to fast freeze the ice cream. Another team hovered around a saucepan, willing a cup of caramel sauce into existence out of white sugar, water, kosher salt, and immense patience. Some students were candying walnuts; others were making marshmallow fluff. A pair of ambitious sophomores were attempting to make a homegrown version of M&M's. Each student had already written a term paper describing the chemical reactions and biodiversity that conjured the magic of dessert. At the end of today's class—if all went well—they'd get to eat their homework. All that stood between them and summer vacation was making ice cream sundaes. With all the ingredients made from scratch.

"Oh, sugar," she heard one of the football players mutter as his blender stalled. Whenever Tori heard an outburst like that, she smiled. It meant that the fifteen teenagers, who could have easily spent the period gossiping or chucking chocolate chips at one another, were concentrating completely on their final exam.

It also meant her students respected her enough to follow her rules; namely, that when they got stuck, literally or figuratively, they could swear as loudly as they wanted as long as they used baking terms. Her personal favorites from this semester's class were *Lamination!* and *Choux!*

Crouching down to use the classroom's paper towel dispenser as a mirror, Tori took a minute to freshen up. She adjusted the green-and-gold paisley scarf she'd received as a present from a student last Christmas, which she wore often because it amplified her hazel eyes, and corralled her thick hair into a ponytail, making a mental note to book a cut and color appointment since the gray hairs were infiltrating the strawberry blonde again. She also confirmed that she didn't have cocoa powder mixed in with the freckles across the bridge of her nose. Standing back up, she brushed a smudge of brown sugar off her hip and turned her attention to her students.

"Ten minutes, folks!" Tori's co-teacher, Della DeMarco, warned the students. Her update was met by a chorus of groans and barked orders to fellow teammates.

"Dude, we need more CO_2. The strawberry ice cream is soup!"

"No, no, no, don't let the sugar crystallize!"

"Hold the candy still, Katy. The *M*s are blurry!"

Tori caught Della's eye: They were both beaming with pride. Della was the Skills for Living teacher, and they'd developed this curriculum together a few years back based on a conversation they'd had during their shared lunch break.

"I'm sick of kids thinking my class is the same old-timey, prim Home Ec where their grandmothers sewed aprons decades ago," Della had said, taking a bite of her peanut butter and jelly sandwich and leaving a ring of coral lipstick on the white bread. "I got into this field because I want kids to learn how to take care of themselves. Be self-sufficient, manage their money, set some goals." She'd adjusted her cat-eye glasses and leaned in. "You know, they used to call this Domestic Science for a reason. Now, kids blow it off as an easy A and barely try."

"I know what you mean," Tori had said, unwrapping her caprese sandwich. "They take my chemistry class to get into college, but a lot of them think they'll never use the information again, so they do the bare minimum. I wish we weren't so tied to the textbook."

Della's dark eyes focused on Tori's sandwich. "Wow, that looks delicious."

"Here," Tori said, tearing off a piece to share.

"Did you make the focaccia?"

"Last night."

"And the mozzarella?"

"Saturday."

"And the basil and tomatoes . . ."

"From my garden."

"Now you're just showing off." Della picked up the remains of her PB&J and frowned. "This was the best I could come up with this morning. Most mornings."

"Della, it's not a contest," Tori reassured her. "You're a great cook as well as a terrific teacher."

"And you're a fantastic cook. I mean, you should teach my class sometime."

"Same."

At that moment, they had looked at each other, and the penny dropped. Over a weekend brunch of homemade lemon ricotta pancakes and a glass or two of prosecco, Tori and Della came up with the Biochem of Baking lesson plan. They'd pitched it to the administration and arranged their schedules so they could team teach. Five years after it launched, it was still one of the most popular courses at Sequoia High. It not only breathed some fresh air into Tori's career as a science teacher; it also cemented her fast friendship with Della, a teaching vet with three decades of experience under her belt who'd provided advice and ego boosts when Tori needed them most.

"Five minutes," Della called from the other side of the classroom. This was Tori's cue to text Mr. Alonzo, the principal, to taste the final projects. The Pacific Ocean breeze wafted by the windows, which were open on a rare June day when there wasn't any Northern California fog and the sun hung in the sky like a poached egg. Tori took a deep, satisfied breath, and along with the eucalyptus and salt air, she inhaled the unmistakable scent of incinerating sugar.

Tori walked over to a group of girls, one suspending a saucepan inches above the stove top and hyperventilating. "How's the caramel sauce going over here, Brianne?"

"I swear the temperature was right," the girl said, frustrated and apologetic.

"It was 338 degrees!" her teammate Jacqueline added. "We're almost out of time! We are so fu—" She paused briefly midsentence, then finished, "fudged!"

"Well, here you are anyway," Tori said. "What can you do?"

"We don't have time to start over," Jacqueline said.

"We could add a splash of vanilla to even out the flavor," said Dakota, the third girl on the team.

"Hurry up and do something!" Jacqueline said. "It's cooling!"

"Okay," Brianne said, squaring her shoulders. "Let's add the vanilla, cream, and butter and hope people think burnt caramel is a culinary delight."

"Go to it, ladies," Tori said. "Good luck!"

As the girls got back to work over their saucepan, Tori joined Della at the back of the room.

"How much time?"

Della looked at her stopwatch. "Two minutes left."

"Want to give them an extra minute?"

"Not fair to those who've figured out how to stay on schedule," Della replied. "Besides, I want to get out of here on time, take advantage of the half day, and grab some tacos. Want to join me?"

"I can't," Tori said, only half regretting it. She was fond of Della, but inevitably when they socialized, her colleague would drop names of ladies she knew in hopes of setting up a blind date, not so delicately suggesting Tori should get back on the scene. "I'm taking the twins into the city for lunch," she explained. "It's our last-day-of-school tradition, and now that they're graduating and it's their *last* last day of school, I definitely can't miss it."

"I can't believe they're going to college already," Della said, shaking her head. "I remember when they were freshmen in my fifth-period class. Milo was a head shorter than Mia back then."

"I still think of them as babies, wrapped in their blankets like burritos. They couldn't fall asleep without being side by side in the same crib," Tori said wistfully.

Della squeezed Tori's arm. "But here's the silver lining. Once you're an empty nester, we'll be able to get together more often. At least until you meet that special someone."

Tori braced herself. *Here comes the pitch.*

"Speaking of which," Della went on, "you would *love* my cousin Linda. She's really outdoorsy, always posting photos of her hikes with her chocolate lab. Oh, and she's vegan."

Tori cocked an eyebrow. "You know I can't live my life without butter, eggs, cheese, yogurt, cream . . . and did I mention butter?"

"What *I'm* worried about is that you can't imagine life without Mia and Milo," Della said firmly. "You've been back on the market for what, three years now? You're beautiful, thoughtful, and smart, and you have a lot to offer to some lucky woman out there." Della paused before pulling closer to whisper, "And while you're not old, you're also not getting any younger."

Before Tori could figure out how to respond, Della clicked her stopwatch and called out, "Time, everyone!"

Following whoops, sighs of relief, and scattered applause, the students brought their projects to the main table, which was set with scoops, bowls, and spoons. Mr. Alonzo walked in just as the last topping was plated and presented. As formidable as he looked in his navy suit and steely brush cut, Doug Alonzo was a reasonable administrator and a good guy. Tori had appreciated his support of the Biochem of Baking idea from the start, as well as his empathy throughout her divorce.

"Very impressive work, folks, and it smells delicious," he said to the class. "So take me through all this."

After each student explained the science behind their sweets, Tori shot them smiles and thumbs-up. They had learned so much.

"Great, great job, everyone," Mr. Alonzo said, grabbing an ice cream scoop. "Now, who can I serve first?"

By the time the bell rang, there wasn't so much as a lick left of anything. Even the "Nouveau Burnt Caramel Experience" had been consumed. The students cleaned up their stations, turned in the textbooks they hadn't needed to open, and waved goodbye to Tori and Della before laughing their way down the hall and out into the summer sun.

"Well, that's that," Della said as she slung her purse over her shoulder. "Another year done, another year closer to retirement."

They hugged goodbye, and as Della headed to the parking lot, Tori sat down for the first time in hours, exhausted after marinating in the students' stress all morning. Looking across the chairs and stoves, she acknowledged that she wasn't just tired. She was burned-out. Twenty years in, she hadn't stopped loving the kids, but she felt stuck in a never-ending loop of standardized test prep, lesson planning, and budget restrictions: Her creative spark was burning dangerously low. Maybe summer break would energize her enough to face the fall semester with a smile. Hopefully.

Tori got up and walked from stove to chair to table to make sure no one had left behind a cellphone or notebook. She checked her own desk then took her apron and lab coat off the hook on the back of the door and folded them into her bag. She scanned the classroom a final time, keys in hand.

"Anything here you can't live without until Labor Day?" she

asked herself with a twinge of regret. She used to say that to Shelby on the last day of school before they'd collect the twins and start their summer vacation as a family. At least she did before Shelby cheated on her, quit teaching, and moved to New York with her new girlfriend to start living the life she'd always dreamed about.

Tori sighed. "Nope, nothing at all."

Even though the twins had chatted all through lunch about prepping for their move to Boulder to start classes at the University of Colorado that fall, the ride home was oddly quiet. Neither of them was head down in a phone. Instead, they were staring out the window at the sun glittering on the ocean and the waves swishing across the beach as they drove south down Highway 1 toward Eucalyptus Point. Tori sensed there was something they wanted to say but maybe didn't know how.

"Penny for your thoughts?" she offered.

Mia, sitting in the front passenger seat, hesitated before answering. "Are you going to be okay when we're at college?"

That was not where Tori thought the conversation was going to go. "What do you mean?"

"Living without us around. Being all alone."

This brought her up short. They shouldn't have to worry about her. That wasn't their job.

She checked her rearview mirror, avoiding Mia's gaze. "You two haven't spent a solid weekend at home with me for months, and I've done fine."

"This is different," Mia said. "We'll only be home for Christmas break."

"And spring break, right?" Tori asked.

Milo snorted. "Not me. I'm going to stay at my insanely rich friend's place in the Caribbean."

"Who's that?" Tori asked.

"Yeah, who are you talking about?" Mia asked over her shoulder.

"Don't know yet," Milo said blithely. "It's my goal to find someone who fits the bill during Freshman Week."

"I'm not going to be alone," Tori said a little too loudly. "I have lots of friends. There's Cassie and Lee Anne . . . and Della, too, sort of."

"They don't live with you," Mia pointed out.

"Joey and Johnny then."

"That's what we're afraid of!" Milo piped up, leaning in from the back seat. "Without some actual human beings at home, you're going to mutate into this homebody who spends all her time baking muffins and knitting sweaters for the cats."

"Why did you jump straight to cat sweaters?" Tori countered, deflecting his earnestness. "Besides, I could make them look supercute."

"I'm worried that you'll try to live out your hopes and dreams vicariously through us," Mia said.

"And you'll text us way too often," her brother confirmed.

Tori was touched, and a mite flustered, to realize that the twins had been harboring all these worries about her future while they were on the brink of their own. She sighed and braked for a red light. "Do you actually think I won't survive without you two at home? Don't worry. I'll do just fine."

Mia shot a look at her brother. "Mom, we know that you'll cope. You're the expert at coping. You've been doing that ever since Mommy moved out."

Milo nodded. "No lie."

Mia continued. "It's just . . . well, we just want you to know . . ."

Milo picked up where his sister left off. "What she's trying to say is, we think you should start to date again."

The light turned green, but it took Tori an extra second to put her foot on the gas.

Tori looked at her son in the rearview mirror, his eyes sharp and serious. She then glanced at Mia, her somber, heart-shaped face an echo of her own. They weren't joking anymore, and given they rarely talked about their mothers' split, this was clearly something they'd been mulling over.

It wasn't that she didn't want to fall in love again. She just didn't know if she could.

She'd fallen hard for Shelby at San Francisco State. Tori had been an introvert majoring in education because her mother had pressured her to go to college to get a "good, practical job" instead of going to culinary school like she wanted. In contrast, Shelby was a poet, a magician with words, and the center of attention no matter where she went. The fact that Shelby even gave her the time of day seemed like a miracle. Even though their aspirations were diametrically opposed, they were convinced they could create a future together.

Shelby dropped to one knee shortly after their graduation from State, promising to fulfill Tori's dreams of having a family and opening her own bakery someday. At the beginning, their domestic partnership was in perfect balance. Tori's teaching salary seemed like it would be enough to float them both while Shelby got established as a writer and Tori saved enough for the bakery. But it wasn't long before the plan was overrun by the cost of eight rounds of artificial insemination, then Tori's medical bills before, during, and after carrying two babies at once, then their buying a house south of the city when the San Francisco apartment got way too small to raise a pair of high-energy kids, not to mention the adoption costs for Shelby and a long-overdue wedding in 2013 when same-sex marriage was finally legal in California.

Saving for the bakery, much less for the kids' college or retirement, became more and more remote, and Tori had gotten sick of shouldering the financial burden alone. After multiple blowout arguments and months of couples therapy around the time the twins were eleven, Shelby reluctantly took a job teaching English at Sequoia High. But the pressure of practicality and putting her creative goals aside to focus on what was best for the family—and Tori—ate away at Shelby like the steady drip of a rusty faucet. Three years ago, Tori had woken up to find an envelope on the kitchen table containing divorce papers and a letter outlining Shelby's unwillingness to set her dreams aside . . . especially since she had found someone new.

These days, Shelby lived in New York with her girlfriend and taught poetry at the New School. She was living her dream.

Tori, clearly, could not. After all this time, she had made her peace with that. Most days, anyway.

Tori turned left onto their street, and soon they were in their driveway. Before the kids got out of the car, she turned to face them. "Listen, I love that you're so concerned about me," she said, "but you ought to focus on yourselves. You are getting ready to start the best part of your lives. You're going to college! That's all you need to think about. And hey, I appreciate that you're okay with me dating again, but I'm not interested right now, and that's nothing to worry about either. I will know when the time is right . . . and I won't be playing dress-up with the cats in the meantime. Okay?"

"Okay," they said in unison.

"Will either of you be here for dinner?" she asked as they walked up the driveway.

"Rick's picking me up in an hour to go to Scott's pool party, so no for me," Milo said.

"And I'm spending the night at Tanesha's. We'll be deep into *Alien Distraction* until really late," Mia added.

"Okey doke," Tori said, unlocking the side door, finally home. "I'll be all alone, then, I guess."

The kids stopped in their tracks.

"I'm kidding," Tori said, grinning. "Go have fun!"

. . .

Once Milo and Mia had taken off with their respective klatches of friends and she was pulling together a meal for one, Tori was willing to admit that Della and the twins were right: She was going to be awfully lonely on her own come the fall. Looking down at the remains of her chicken Caesar, she was kind of lonely already. Maybe some calories could cheer her up. She queued up her "Best of CBGB" playlist and went into the kitchen.

Baking helped her clear her head. The basic ingredients were so simple but so versatile:

Flour
Sugar
Butter
Eggs

Nearly every recipe she could choose to make, no matter how complex, had these elements at their core: the carbon, hydrogen, oxygen, and nitrogen of baking. Mix them in equal measures, and she'd get a pound cake her English great-great-granny would have been pleased to have for tea. Introduce them to cocoa, baking soda, milk, vanilla, and salt, and a chocolate birthday cake might be in the offing. Swap butter for olive oil and the zest and juice of an orange, and like Italian home cooks on the other side of the world, she could create an unbelievably moist cake just aching for strawberries macerated with balsamic vinegar. Invite cinnamon and nutmeg to the table and toss them into a bowl of sugared, sliced Granny Smiths while flour and ice-cold butter were bonding on the marble pastry board, and soon there'd be the scent and taste of a thousand fall afternoons.

The variations were countless, the experience sublime. She could add or subtract ingredients, go elegant or rustic, but within a few hours, all five senses would be satisfied, and she would have food to share with those she loved.

Tori was due at Cassie and Lee Anne's the next morning for breakfast, so this evening's mission was making a chocolate chip sour cream coffee cake. She gathered the ingredients into a tidy line on her counter and measured each one into its own small glass bowl, setting up her mise en place to be sure she had everything she needed and was ready to go; there was such security knowing everything was where it was supposed to be.

"These numbers look awful."

Kendra Campbell glared at her older brother, Alden. He sat on the other side of her kitchen table, his expression apologetic yet firm, dozens of charts and spreadsheets fanned out in front of him. Kendra had come home from the restaurant around three that morning and fallen asleep on her couch, too exhausted to change out of her chef's jacket. Alden had called at 8:00 A.M. to remind her he was coming over in an hour to go over her books, but she'd fallen back to sleep and missed her chance to shower. Then, waking with a start a few minutes before nine, she'd twisted something in her back getting off the couch, which was happening more often now that she'd passed her fortieth birthday last fall. She'd barely managed to feed her French bulldog, Julia, slug back a cup of coffee and some day-old brioche, and pull her jet-black hair back into a low bun before Alden knocked on the door. She was tired, she was cranky, and she was in no mood to be told her finances were on the fritz by her manager/accountant/pessimistic older brother.

"That's impossible," Kendra said, pushing her bangs off her face and rubbing the back of her neck. "Gamma Raye's been open three years, and people still wait a month to get a reservation. I'm one hundred percent booked more nights than not."

"Your rent went up in January, remember? There's so little commercial real estate left in Sonoma, the landlord can charge a fortune."

"We ought to buy him out," Kendra said, folding her arms so her crepe pan tattoo faced outward like a shield.

"That might have been possible if you hadn't used up your line of credit to open so many Chippy Chunk locations," Alden said.

"There are only ten," she protested, "and they're spread out from Seattle to San Diego. They're doing well in their markets."

"Each one had start-up costs you're still paying off, staff turnover is just as high as it's ever been in this industry, and those rents are creeping upward as well. They're not exactly money trees, Ken."

"But people love my cookies, Den. They're what got me noticed when I was pastry chef at Chez Ma Soeur a decade ago. Chippy Chunk is what helped me get financing for Gamma Raye."

Alden nodded. "Yes, I know. That's why bankers, and pretty much everybody else, call you the Cookie Queen."

"You know I hate that!" she growled. "It's so simplistic, not to mention misogynistic—like all a girl can do is bake cookies because it's so easy. I'd like to see them try it sometime!" She poked her index finger into the tabletop for emphasis and immediately regretted it; her hands were still achy after yet another long night in the Gamma Raye kitchen.

Alden, who'd heard this tirade many times before, barreled ahead, his voice level yet sympathetic, his demeanor even-keeled and patient. "We both know that a restaurant is a low-margin business even when you have a steady stream of customers, and the bakeries take years to break even, no matter how fantastic the food. Therefore, I have a recommendation."

He paused, apprehensive. Kendra waited for him to continue but couldn't contain herself for long. "Spill it!"

Her brother cleared his throat. "You need to consider renewing your *American Bake-o-Rama* contract."

Kendra shot to her feet. "Come on!"

Alden cut her off with a grimace. "For another three years."

"We talked about this," Kendra said, rising up to her full six-foot height. "Den, I'll be way over forty by then!"

"Forty-three, to be exact." Alden hung his prematurely balding head.

"All that prep work and so many long days of shooting during every weekend for two months straight," Kendra said, counting each protest off on her fingers. "All that dialogue to learn. All those recipes I have to develop so I'm not giving away my best-kept secrets. On top of everything else I have going on?"

"Yeah, but—"

"And Buddy? He doesn't care how well the contestants bake as long as they look good on camera."

"I know it's a lot to manage," he said quietly.

She kept going. "Not to mention those wannabes—excuse me, 'home bakers'—who burst into tears when I tell them to add a little more salt next time."

"That may be more your fault than theirs, Kendra. You can come off kind of . . ."

Her lake-blue eyes narrowed. "Kind of what, dear brother?"

"Stern."

She let out a bitter snort. "They should be grateful. Most of the chefs I worked with coming up didn't offer critiques. They'd just start swearing."

Alden sat back in his chair. "They say you're ruthless . . ."

"No, I'm honest," Kendra corrected. "I'm telling them the truth, whether they like it or not. They need to understand the high standards they'll have to live up to in the food industry."

"And confrontational," Alden added with a wry smile.

"Hey!" She wasn't chuckling now. "If they can't stand the heat, you know what they say: 'Get out of the kitchen!'"

"Look, I'm on your side, as are your many fans," Alden said with his hands up in surrender. "Constructive criticism is necessary, and it provides dramatic tension for the program. But you need a lighter touch. It's gotten to the point that the network is worried you're frightening the contestants."

That brought Kendra up short. "What on earth do you mean?"

He pinned her gaze. "Remember Becca from last season?"

Kendra shuddered. "Yes. The 'rainbow cream cheese' lady."

"That's the one. Remember what you told her, on camera no less?"

She hedged. "Something like, 'If you pronounce *asiago* like *ah-saggy-oh* one more time, I will . . ." She trailed off, muttering the rest, ". . . 'blowtorch your bagels'?"

"Exactly that," Alden said flatly. "Becca had to breathe into a paper bag for ten minutes just to do her on-camera interviews after that. The network wants a more collaborative, feel-good vibe than you've been doling out. I mean, your Twitter hashtag is #TheChopper."

She snorted. "At least that's better than #CookieQueen."

Her brother folded his hands and leaned in. "The thing is, *Bake-o-Rama* pays well, it promotes your brand, and the money from the show and other related appearances is floating the other parts of your growing empire that are cash poor right now. Reupping is a smart move, and dialing down the disgust is even smarter."

Kendra held her brother's gaze for a moment, then looked away, feeling defeated. She left the kitchen and flopped facedown on the living room couch, moaning into a sofa pillow. Alden followed her, sitting down at the other end.

"Hey, sis, are you okay?" he asked.

"I'm fine," she said into the pillow. "Can't you tell?"

"Kendra Jane, I say this as someone who loves you: You smell like rancid butter. You need a shower."

She sat up and noticed for the first time that raspberry coulis was splashed across her front like blood spatter. "I know," she said. "I stayed late at the restaurant, and time got away from me this morning."

"Why did you stay so late? You own the place, and you can get Patrice to run night service some weekends. You're not a line cook anymore."

Kendra picked at the raspberry coulis, only managing to spread the stain wider. "Den, sometimes I wish I was on the line again. I miss making the magic happen side by side with the team, you know? I love watching the customers enjoy their meal and have a great night out. I like getting my hands dirty."

"And getting your uniform dirty, too."

Kendra smiled for the first time since he'd arrived. She wiped off a smudge of last night's eyeliner with the back of her hand. "Besides, it gets pretty quiet here at home by myself."

"You know you're welcome at our place anytime," Alden offered, putting his arm around her shoulders. "With two kids under five and a trombone player for a wife, it's never quiet at my house. You still coming for brunch in a couple of weeks?"

"That's the plan," she said.

"Good. Would you mind if I invited a friend to join us?"

She froze. "What kind of friend?"

"A nice friend. A *single* friend."

Kendra put her head down in her hands and groaned. "Alden Ross, I say this as someone who loves you: You've got to stop trying to set me up."

He shook his head. "You can't have the family you want without putting yourself out there."

"I am too busy to make a relationship work," she said. "I'm at a crucial point in building my business and my brand. Besides, no sane person wants to date on a chef's schedule."

"So date another chef. Or a sultry maître d'. Or a really cute baker at the Chippy Chunk on Fisherman's Wharf."

"Are you kidding? The last thing I'd want is to date someone else in the food industry."

Alden laughed. "Yeah, what could you possibly have in common with someone like that?"

Julia gave a soft bark from the corner of the living room, where she was curled up in a bed decorated like a frosted donut. Kendra got up to hold the dog's face in her hands and stroke her wrinkly brow. "Okay, my little sticky bun, I'll take you on a walk. Just give me a minute."

"I'd better get going," Alden said, standing. "So, to sum up, you need to renew your contract and try to be more empathetic toward the contestants. Or at least pleasant."

"Understood, boss." Kendra sighed in resignation. "When are we back in production?"

"You'll have to sit in for the final rounds of auditions in a couple of weeks. They're sorting through the applications now. More than four thousand this year."

Kendra whistled.

Alden shrugged. "Clearly, there are a lot of people who are eager for you to intimidate them." He stopped at the door. "Ken, I'm really proud of you. You've earned every bit of your success."

She was touched. "Thanks. Back when we were kids baking for Mom when she was working weekends, who would have thought I'd end up here?" She motioned toward the French doors and the view of the rolling Sonoma hills, gold in the summer sun.

"Thing is, your work/life balance is one hundred percent work and zero percent life, and that's a bad path, hon. There's nothing I want more for you than to find someone to share this with."

"I know. I want that, too."

"Maybe you need to put your focus there, and just maybe that'll make it easier to lighten up on the show, too. Or vice versa." He hugged her. "See you in a couple of weeks if not sooner. And I'm not asking for permission: I'm inviting a guest."

"Fine," Kendra said, waving him off. "Safe home."

Once Alden's car pulled out, Kendra put Julia in her harness, attached the leash, and started down the long dirt road away from her property toward her neighbor's farm. The air was dry and warm.

Julia snuffled at the grass, occasionally surprising a grasshopper. Kendra yawned, knowing she really should take a day off. Alden was right: Patrice could run the restaurant in her stead for a night or two, and she didn't have any Chippy Chunk duties until Wednesday's monthly manager conference call to introduce her new flavors. The blog could wait, as could the review of the galleys for her second cookbook. Even with *Bake-o-Rama* on the horizon, she didn't have to start doing recipe research today. She could just appreciate the extra daylight of a beautiful June Saturday.

She just wished she wasn't doing all this appreciating by herself, on her own.

She'd known friendships would be tough, and dating near impossible, while she was coming up through the restaurant ranks, but she didn't expect she'd still be alone at this point in her life. Her most recent romantic relationship lasted four months and was over two years ago, with her tech exec former girlfriend carping that Kendra was the only person she knew who spent more hours at work than anyone in Silicon Valley. Now that she had a level of fame and visibility, she was getting unsolicited attention from some fairly eager female fans. But even the few who passed the sniff test were not destined to last for the long term, because inevitably there'd come a time when Gamma Raye was understaffed or Chippy Chunk had a summer cookie debut coming up, and when Kendra finally came up for air, her dates had usually moved on, often questioning her priorities. More than once, she'd heard the words, *It's just food!*

But it was never "just food." It was her livelihood, her artistic temperament, her ambition, and her personal history baked into each baguette and every snickerdoodle. She took every bite very seriously, and no one seemed to understand that well enough to tolerate her, much less fall in love.

She looked into the cloudless blue above her and exhaled. Her situation couldn't be that hopeless. Maybe all she needed was to balance her workload with a more active social life. She could join a book club or a bowling league or . . . delegate at work.

Kendra shook her head. "Who am I kidding?"

Julia had stopped and wouldn't budge. Kendra tugged on her leash.

"C'mon, puddin', let's keep going."

The dog turned back toward the hill leading to their house.

"Julia, we've only been out here five minutes." Julia sat down, staring fixedly up the hill.

Kendra sighed. "Okay, fine, lead the way."

The Frenchie nearly galloped, anticipating a biscuit and her bed. Stumbling a bit in her chef's clogs, Kendra followed, attempting to keep up with the only woman in her life.

Tori was humming along with Chrissie Hynde and mixing pancake batter for a leisurely Saturday breakfast when she heard Mia shriek.

She wasn't overly concerned. That sounded like her daughter's run-of-the-mill reaction to exciting but non-life-threatening news, like her favorite musician breaking up with his boyfriend. She continued whisking in the buttermilk, hearing Mia's footfalls overhead as she scurried to her brother's room.

When she heard Milo whoop, Tori wiped her hands on her dish towel, turned down the music, and walked to the foot of the stairs.

"What's going on up there?"

She barely had enough time to step out of their way before the kids bounded down to her.

"Mom, Mom, Mom!" Milo exclaimed, his green eyes dancing. "You've got to sit down!"

"What? Why?"

"He's right!" Mia echoed, guiding Tori over to the middle of the sofa in the living room, sporting a huge grin beneath her glasses. The three of them sat, Tori sandwiched between the two ecstatic teenagers.

"Okay, what is it?"

Mia composed herself. "You know *American Bake-o-Rama*, right?"

"Do I?" Tori asked, racking her brain.

"It's the televised baking competition we're obsessed with," her son said. "You know, the show that started my obsession with candied ginger?"

"Uh . . ."

"There was also that episode that started that epic fight between Mia and me about whether shortening is better for chocolate chip cookies than butter? Remember that?"

Seeing the blank look on Tori's face, Mia added, "The show with Kendra Campbell, that hot lesbian judge who owns Chippy Chunk Cookies."

"Ah—the hot lesbian judge," Tori said. None of this rang a bell. "So?"

"So they had a call for contestants about a month ago," Mia said. "And Milo and I nominated you . . . and you made the top one hundred!"

The twins' faces shone with delight, but Tori was totally confused. "Wait, back up. How did you nominate me? Wouldn't I have to sign something since you're not eighteen yet?"

"We'll be legal in a few weeks," Mia said.

"You mean a few months," Tori said. "You lied about your ages?"

"They don't care, and that doesn't matter right now," Mia continued, exasperated. "Did you not hear that you made the top one hundred?"

"What does that even mean?"

"It means they selected you out of thousands of entries," said Milo. "And, um, it also means you have a technical exam and a meet and greet at the *Bake-o-Rama* studio in Sonoma on Monday morning."

"*What?*" Tori's stomach dropped. "Who am I meeting and greeting?"

Milo checked the message on his phone. "The casting director, the producer, and the judges. It's really more of an audition than a meet and greet. I just didn't want to freak you out."

"Well, that didn't work," Tori said.

"Relax," Milo said. "I've seen some of the exam questions online, and I know you'll ace them. I mean, you know the chemical formulas for most of the ingredients, so you already have a leg up. And the audition should be easy. You've lived through enough parent-teacher conferences to be able to handle anybody."

"Will I have to bake something?" Tori asked, the blood returning to her face.

"Uh, yeah, Mom, it's a baking competition," Mia deadpanned, grabbing Milo's phone to look at the email. "You have to bring two different examples of your baking with you on Monday. If they like you and your bakes, you go back on Wednesday to make something on the *Bake-o-Rama* set for a final, on-camera audition."

As the kids practically vibrated with excitement, Tori's brain finally caught up. "Look, this is a really sweet thing you've done, but I am no TV personality. I can't even look good in a selfie, much less on a game show."

"Televised baking competition," Milo corrected. "And none of that negative self-talk! We raised you better than that."

Tori smiled despite herself. "How many contestants get on the show?"

"Seven," Mia said.

Tori persevered. "How many episodes?"

"Six," they answered together.

"They tape in Sonoma at Three Vines Winery, where the audition is," Mia hurried on, anticipating her mother's next concern. "You can drive up there in about ninety minutes."

"*And*," Milo said triumphantly, "the show tapes in July and August, so you don't have to worry about taking time off from school."

"But that's right when we have to get you ready to fly out to Colorado!" Tori protested.

"We. Don't. Care!" they said over the top of each other.

Tori stood and went back to the kitchen. "This doesn't make any sense."

"It makes perfect sense," Milo said as he and Mia followed her. "First of all, you won't have any time to feel lonely or sad or have an existential crisis about being an empty nester."

Mia picked up the thread. "And bonus: You can make new friends and get out of Eucalyptus Point for once."

"Besides," said Milo, "you might win the top prize."

That got Tori's attention. "What's the prize?"

"An engraved cookie sheet," Mia said.

"Oh."

"And one hundred thousand dollars," she continued. "Plus starring in a future Food & Drink TV Network show."

"What do you have to lose by auditioning?" Mia said. "Just do it!"

Tori leaned against the kitchen island to collect her thoughts. First off, kudos to Milo and Mia, who had gone to all this trouble to show her how much they loved her baking—and loved her, too. Next, they rightly called her out on the fact that she had followed the same pattern every summer: Natter around the house, read a bunch of books, bake a lot, and hang out with the same small circle of friends she saw throughout the year. Restful? Sure. Adventurous? No.

Then there was the prospect of the prize money. When the twins were born, she and Shelby had joked that while they got a two-for-one deal on maternity bills, they wouldn't be so lucky when it came time to pay college tuition. With financial aid, they could just make it work, but $100,000 was a game changer. It could even be seed money for her own bakery at last—the dream she'd put on hold these past many years.

Hosting a TV show, though? Sure, she had some skills, but she was no expert. Viewers would see she was a sham in a heartbeat.

Besides, who in the world would want to see Tori Moore, of all people, on television?

But this was all hypothetical anyway. She only had a 7 percent chance of getting on the program, much less winning.

Then again, she'd already beaten the odds to get this far.

And maybe, just maybe, it would be . . . fun.

Milo and Mia were standing in her personal space, eager-eyed and unyielding. She looked at one, then the other.

"Well," Tori said at last, "I do need a new cookie sheet."

The cheering sent Joey and Johnny flying off the window seat and skittering down the hall.

On Monday morning, Tori checked in at the registration desk at the Three Vines Winery and was handed a lanyard with a tag displaying her first name and her audition number: lucky 13. She then followed the *American Bake-o-Rama* signs to the main tasting room. Carrying a chocolate gateau de mille crepe cake in one carrier and three dozen assorted macarons in another, she walked in with all the determination she could muster.

The tasting room was large enough to accommodate an exorbitant wedding and was set up as a series of stations for the different tasks of the day. Toward the end of the circuit, production assistants with headsets and tablets were circulating among the clumps of contenders, taking people one by one into what looked like the main kitchen, the round-windowed metal door swishing closed behind them. That had to be where the judges were waiting: a room full of knives and fire.

Shaking off her nerves, she handed in her cake and cookies at the first table. A staffer labeled them with her audition number, stacked them on a cart, and whisked them off to another part of the room. Tori felt as if they were being wheeled into surgery while she could only pray they'd survive.

"Wow, a crepe cake and macarons? You aren't messing around."

Tori turned to her right to find an affable, silver-haired man in a western shirt and cowboy hat.

"I figured I needed to pull out all the stops while I could still bake in my home kitchen," she said, smiling as she scanned his name tag. "Mel? Nice to meet you. I'm Tori."

Mel put his bakes on the table and shook her hand. "Good to meet you, too."

"Those cheddar biscuits look delicious," she said, trying not to let the fact that they were, in fact, utterly perfect get to her.

"Thanks. I hope they'll get the job done. And if they don't, I hope they like coconut cream pie as much as my grandkids do. It's been bubble-wrapped in a cooler since my red-eye from Austin this morning. I hope it's holding up."

The pie looked as if he had placed every toasted flake individually on top, probably with state-of-the-art chef tweezers. "I'm sure they will," she said, impressed. "That's gorgeous."

Mel motioned toward the next station. "Ready for the written exam?"

She shook her head. "I need to walk around first. Clear my mind."

"I get it. Best of luck, and hopefully we'll see each other on the show." Mel tipped his hat then walked toward the exam table.

Tori took a swig from the water bottle she'd picked up at registration and began to stroll around the room, intent on staying calm. Milo and Mia, bless them, had devised a *Bake-o-Rama* boot camp and drilled her all weekend so she'd be prepared for meeting the judges. Pacing by the various tables and the other contestants, she ran through some of their key points.

Trevor Flynn is the senior judge and has been on the show since it began. He's a San Francisco restaurant institution and is an expert in breads, custards, and liquor-infused anything. Contestants love him because he is supportive and charming, but he's not a pushover. Like a favorite British uncle with high expectations.

Then there's Kendra Campbell. Also known as the Cookie Queen—but don't say that in front of her—and #TheChopper—don't say that either. If Trevor is the sugar, Kendra is the spice. She has incredibly high standards and zero tolerance for weakness. Mia said she could count the number of times she's smiled on the show on one hand.

"Hey!"

Tori had been so lost in thought, she didn't realize she had collided with someone until her water bottle flew out of her hand and splashed them both.

"Sorry!" Tori blurted, feeling around in her purse for some tissues. "I am so sorry. Are you okay?"

The other woman had to be at least six feet tall. Tori had to step back to make eye contact. Her own apologetic expression was met by a pair of exceptionally blue eyes, a frame of coal-black hair, and a distinct lack of a smile. It was like taking in the power of a volcano from a foot away, ready to erupt.

"Just watch where you're going, number 13." The woman brushed by her and headed into the kitchen, the door flapping closed behind her.

Exhaling at last, Tori picked the now empty water bottle off the floor.

"Ah well," she told herself. "Since I am clearly not going to be chosen for the show now, at least I can give the kids a souvenir: the water bottle their mother dumped all over Kendra Campbell."

Zak, the production assistant, ushered contestant number 12 out of the kitchen then came back in to call a fifteen-minute break.

Kendra stood up from behind the rough wood table and rolled her shoulders. "That was painful. He should have boned up on metric measurements before he applied."

"And figured out how to keep fruit from sinking to the bottom of a sponge cake," Trevor huffed, finishing his write-up about hapless number 12, his purple reading glasses at the end of his nose. "How many more are we seeing, Zak?"

"You have fifteen more today, then twenty tomorrow," he said, checking his clipboard. "Just be glad not everyone in the top one hundred passed their written exams."

Kendra grunted her displeasure, and Trevor shot Zak a weary look. "As they say in the States, 'Awesome.'" He clicked his pen closed and handed the paperwork to the production assistant, who left to hand off their notes to the casting director. "Sometimes I can't help but feel sorry for these people," he said, placing his glasses atop his tastefully graying head. "They come from all over the country to audition, with stars in their eyes and batter under their fingernails, their hopeful hearts beating beneath their apron bibs. Then we toss them out for not knowing some obscure cooking fact most folks will never use in a lifetime."

Kendra shook her head as she wandered over to the counter for more coffee. "Amateurs make mistakes, a lot of them. And hey, nobody begged them to audition."

Trevor raised an eyebrow. "Professionals make mistakes, too—at least I do. And I'm sure you've seen how many of our less-than-perfect amateurs have great potential and go on to excel during the show. Don't you agree?"

Her stomach tightened. Trevor was a true legend in San Francisco restaurant circles, and his approval—or disapproval—mattered to her. She didn't want to come off as a brat, not when she hoped she'd one day be considered a peer. Now seemed like as good a time as any to try taking Alden's advice.

"You're right," she backpedaled, not looking up from the cream pitcher as she doctored her coffee in case she was blushing. "We have to focus on their potential. Give them a chance to do their best." Those words were harder to say than Kendra had expected. It wasn't like anyone had given *her* a chance like that when she was starting out, since the male chefs were certain women like her would never have the creativity or temperament to survive in the business. Come to think of it, her past girlfriends really hadn't given her much of a chance either: They were mostly type A's who also wanted to be catered to . . . and she wasn't a caterer, in any sense of the word. Self-reliance and keeping a distance between herself and those who could take a bite out of her self-worth—that strategy had worked pretty well most of her lifetime.

Until Alden made her promise to be less tough on the contestants, and here she was, blowing it before the cameras rolled.

Zak stuck his head in the door. "Buddy is on his way."

Trevor and Kendra groaned. Buddy Walters was Food & Drink TV Network's programming vice president. Kendra first met him with Alden when she'd interviewed for *Bake-o-Rama* four years ago, right after she won her James Beard Award for Chippy Chunk. Once they had taken a seat in his oversize office encrusted with signed sports memorabilia, Buddy didn't come up for air for twenty minutes, blathering on about the "gamification of the food industry" and "marrying art and commerce" and "earning viewer eyeballs with genuine storytelling while the clock is ticking." To keep from falling asleep, Kendra counted how many times Buddy said the word *basically.* She'd reached eleven by the time Buddy turned to her and said, "So what I'm basically saying is, we want you to be a star judge. Good with you?"

She'd let out an accidental "Ha!" by way of a reply, having scored a full dozen. Thankfully, Alden had enough composure to frame her outburst as enthusiasm, then asked for time to confer with his client, at which point he had told her to put a sock in it and sign.

"Howdy, chefs!" Buddy strode in wearing an outfit that had clearly been chosen to present a noncorporate air, which it might have if it weren't so obviously calculated: purposefully mussed brown hair, carefully barbered three-day beard, a network-logoed fleece vest zipped over an Italian dress shirt, and vintage basketball shoes that Kendra figured probably cost as much as her mortgage payment.

"Good morning, Buddy," Trevor said.

"Hello," Kendra added. For her, that was almost effusive.

"Mind if I sit in on the next candidate or two?" Buddy asked, pulling up a chair. "I always like to see who's interested in joining our merry band for the next season."

"No problem," Kendra said, though it hadn't really been a question.

"How have they been so far?" Buddy asked.

"Delightful people, all told," Trevor said, at the same time as Kendra said, "They're light on the basics and easily frightened." She flushed. Being compassionate was hard.

"Nobody is perfect enough for our Cookie Queen," Buddy said, punching her arm. "But hey, the audience loves to root for a good-looking baker who's a disaster. We could probably use more of them; they're ratings gold." He turned to the list of candidates. "Next up is Tori Moore?"

"Yes," Zak confirmed, rolling the cart over to the table, showcasing a plate of jewel-toned macarons and a mirror-glazed chocolate gateau de mille crepe cake.

"Those look gorgeous," Trevor said. "Very well presented."

"They look übercomplicated," Buddy said. "Will anyone be able to bake these at home?"

"She did, so I'm sure others could do the same," Trevor said. "Kendra, want to do the honors?"

Kendra circled the table and picked up a cake knife. "Anybody got a blowtorch?"

Zak rummaged through a couple of drawers then placed what looked like a sci-fi ray gun into Kendra's outstretched hand. She pulled the trigger and used the blue flame to heat the knife blade before cutting into the cake. Slicing four narrow pieces, she put them on biodegradable bamboo plates and handed them around to the team.

"A spotless mirror glaze you can see yourself in, and nice, clean layers," Kendra observed, counting the number of crepes separated by millimeters of vanilla frosting. "She used thirty crepes, and they are consistently thin and not overwhelmed by the buttercream. And the cake cut really well; it's quite tender." She tasted a forkful. The fusion of bittersweet chocolate, eggy crepes, and feather-light icing was extraordinary. "Wow. Just wow."

Trevor concurred, nodding and mmm'ing. There was more to sample, however, so they halted after a bite or two.

"On to the macarons," Kendra said, passing the platter from person to person. She selected a green-flecked cookie and gave it a good sniff. "This smells like basil," she announced. "Could these be savory?"

"You are correct," Trevor said, reading over the recipe in the audition packet. “Seems like we have three flavors: pesto, chestnut, and sweet potato.”

“These are going to either be surprisingly tasty or totally gross,” Kendra said. “Here goes nothing.”

The basil in the meringue paired well with the burst of pine nuttiness of the creamy middle layer. After some clunkers from previous contestants, these were a luxury. “So, so good,” Kendra said, reaching for the sweet potato option next.

“It’s practically perfect,” Trevor said. “Macarons aren’t easy, and they often are prettier than they taste. The chestnut flavor is a marvel, and the hint of bourbon is genius.”

“Hang on,” Buddy said, eyeing his green cookie without tasting it. “This macaroon— ”

“Macaron,” Kendra said quickly. “Macaroons are coconut cookies made with egg whites and condensed milk. That there is a macaron, which is a French meringue sandwich cookie.”

“So it’s basically another pretentious French pastry,” Buddy said, tossing the macaron to Zak, who took a large, satisfied bite.

“That’s not a problem in my book,” Trevor said lightly.

“This is *‘American’ Bake-o-Rama,*” Buddy said. “Basically, most of our viewers have kids and jobs and chores and not a lot of time to be in the kitchen, yet every season we choose a bunch of culinary nerds baking complicated European desserts our viewers would never want to make in a million years.”

“But, Buddy, didn’t you tell me once that we are in the aspiration business?” Trevor asked the producer. “It’s not that our viewers *will* bake these amazing pastries. It’s enough that they believe they *could* bake them if they just spent a little more time or paid more attention.” He smiled at Kendra, hinting with his eyes that she should join in.

Kendra couldn’t answer immediately. She was finishing her slice of Tori’s gateau, in spite of having already sampled twenty different pastries in the space of a couple of hours with dozens more to come;

it was that phenomenal. Eventually she nodded, wiping a wisp of icing off the corner of her mouth.

"Okay, okay," Buddy said, tossing his barely bitten slice into the trash. "As long as your ratings stay high, I'll keep my mouth shut. But when someone makes a killer brownie, you all owe me a Benjamin."

Trevor and Zak chuckled on cue. Kendra gritted her teeth.

"Are we ready for Tori?" Zak asked.

"Sure," Buddy said. "Bring her in."

Kendra took her seat between Trevor and Buddy and reviewed Tori's contestant file. She did a double take at the Polaroid headshot. "Lucky number 13," she said under her breath.

"What about her?" Trevor whispered.

"I ran into her earlier. Literally," Kendra whispered back. "She wasn't looking where she was going and sloshed most of a bottle of water on me."

"Lucky number 13 indeed," Trevor murmured.

The door swung open, and as Tori walked in, only one word came into Kendra's brain: *sunshine.* The afternoon light filtering through the windows illuminated the copper woven through her thick hair and made her smile shimmer. The room even seemed to warm up a little. Or was that just Kendra? She mentally fumbled for another word—any other word—but only came up with *whoa.* Flustered was not a state of mind she was accustomed to, and it had to stop. Now.

"Hello again," she said, extending her hand. Her voice was lower and gruffer than she'd intended.

"Yes, hello, and again, so sorry about earlier," Tori replied, her handshake firm, her hand . . . soft.

Kendra cleared her throat. "No harm, no foul," she said, relieved that her tone was more casual and, maybe even, *pleasant.*

The rest of the team introduced themselves, and Zak escorted Tori to a piece of tape on the floor at the center of the room.

"Stand here with your toes on your mark," he directed. "I'll be in the back recording the interview, but you should talk to the panel instead of into the camera. Okay?"

"Got it."

Zak went behind the camera, and Trevor got the ball rolling. "Tori, it's a pleasure to have you with us today, and let me start by saying you are an amazing baker. Your submissions are delicious."

"I'm so glad you like them," Tori said, her eyes lighting up. Her hazel eyes, Kendra noticed.

"You also did an impressive job on your exam," he added with a smile, glancing at her file.

"All those years as a chemistry teacher turned out to be good for something," Tori said with a self-effacing laugh.

Trevor turned to Kendra. "Do you have anything to add?"

Kendra, who'd been watching how Tori's smile made her nose crinkle, snapped back to attention. "Uh, no, we can get started on the Q&A." She squared her shoulders and folded her hands on the table. "Tori, we have a few standard questions that we ask everyone. Let's start with an obvious one: Why do you want to be on *Bake-o-Rama*?"

"Actually, I didn't want to."

Kendra blinked in surprise. Most of the folks who auditioned could monologue for hours about how much the show meant to them.

"And yet you're here," Trevor said in baffled amusement. "Why?"

"Well, as you probably learned from my application, my kids nominated me. The fact that they think that highly of my baking is a reason all by itself."

Trevor chuckled, but Kendra was sure there had to be more to it. "What makes you think you'll be a good contestant?"

Tori considered the question. "I used to think that baking was just like a scientific experiment: measure the ingredients, set the heat at the right temperature, mix to allow the chemical reactions to take place, correct for environmental phenomena like humidity or having to substitute an ingredient, and then the dish will come out perfectly. Breaking news: I was wrong. It amazed me that even if you do all you're supposed to do, the recipe might still taste a little off, like something's missing. My theory is that to have the best results, I have to focus on who I'm baking for: my kids or my best friends, a wedding or a birthday party. Maybe I could simply make some stranger's day brighter because they ate something I baked. Whatever the occasion, I believe that connection, that *why,* is what catalyzes the ingredients and makes something not just good but utterly delicious. I want to test that theory as a contestant."

After all these years in the business, Kendra wasn't sure she believed what Tori was describing. But it was an answer she hadn't heard before, and she had to admit—it was charming.

"If you win *Bake-o-Rama,* what would be your next step?" Trevor asked.

Tori hesitated a second or two before saying, "I'd like to open a bakery." Her cheeks flushed as she smiled a brave smile. Kendra had the impression Tori had never said those words aloud in front of anyone else.

Kendra leaned forward. "Based on your submissions, you seem to know what you're doing. Why aren't you running a bakery already?"

"I've asked myself the same question a lot lately," Tori said quietly. "Teaching has been incredibly rewarding. It's been a steady presence in my life for two decades, one I really needed when my marriage imploded a few years ago. And don't get me wrong: I love my students to death, and some days that is enough. Then my son and daughter told me I was selected for this audition, and I finally realized that for way too long, I'd been teaching others to do what I wanted to do myself. It's not that 'those who can't do, teach.' For me, I teach . . . and that means I can't do what I really want, which is to bake for a living. Still, it's terrifying to think about changing careers after all this time. I know that a professional bakery is nothing like a home kitchen, and I'll have a lot of competition from accomplished chefs like you." She gestured toward Trevor and Kendra with a smile. "Long story short, I want to be on *Bake-o-Rama* because I want to learn what I'm capable of."

That resonated with Kendra, recalling that scary, thrilling day she took a leap of faith and created her business plan for that first Chippy Chunk location. She nodded as she made notes on Tori's audition form.

"With that in mind, let's talk technique," Trevor said. "How do you handle the butter when making a rough puff pastry?"

"I cut cold butter into cubes and mix it in with the flour and the wet ingredients in a mixer," Tori said, not missing a beat.

"Do you know your way around a French puff?" the judge continued.

"I sure do!" Buddy interjected out of the blue, clearly expecting laughter.

Trevor ignored him and continued. "Tori, how do you handle the butter in a French puff pastry?"

"I use the book fold method."

"How many turns?"

"Six."

"And how long in the fridge?"

"While I could get it done in an hour, I prefer overnight."

"As do I." His glasses perched on his nose, Trevor made some notations on Tori's audition information then looked at Kendra. "Any other questions we need to put this poor woman through?"

Kendra cocked her head and scrutinized Tori's body language. The contestant was still standing tall, her arms at her sides, her face relaxed. She hadn't been rattled at all—a good sign, given how intrusive the cameras would be during the long hours of the shoot days. Yet her apparent ease could mean she wasn't taking this seriously enough, especially since she'd said she hadn't intended to audition in the first place. "What scares you about being on the show?" Kendra asked.

"Making a truly stupid mistake," Tori said.

"Like what?" Kendra pressed.

"Oh, you know, mixing up salt and sugar. Slicing off a finger on camera. Letting my cake catch fire in the oven and burning the set down. Poisoning a judge." She laughed and rolled her eyes. "You probably think I'm a nutcase."

"No, not at all!" Trevor said genially. "What would you do if one of those freak accidents actually happened?"

"I'd do what I tell my students to do: Accept what's happening and improvise."

"Even if I've been poisoned?" Kendra asked with a slight frown.

"Especially once the cops showed up."

That earned a laugh from the room.

"And on that note, that's all we need for now," Trevor said. "Thank you, Tori."

"Thank you so much," Tori said. Zak turned off the camera and followed the contestant out the door.

"She's delightful," Trevor said as the door clicked shut.

"Those were some killer bakes, too," Kendra said, privately agreeing that Tori was delightful, not only because of her baking. "Savory macarons—that was a new one for me."

Buddy shook his head. "Cookies are supposed to be sweet. My mouth was so disappointed."

Trevor smiled sympathetically.

"And that wasn't a cake," Buddy continued in exasperation. "It was basically a pile of flapjacks!"

"That's what a mille crepe cake is," Kendra said. "It's a cake made of crepes . . . basically."

"Another French thing?" Buddy asked.

"Japanese, actually," Kendra said, her mouth tightening.

Buddy turned to her, smirking. "Well, Cookie Queen, what did *you* think of her not-sweet macaroon-a-rons and her stack of not-flapjacks?"

"They were exceptional," Kendra replied, looking Buddy square in the eye. "She's the best we've seen so far. If she does as well during the on-set audition on Wednesday, I'd definitely want her on the show."

Buddy stood up and headed for the door. "You're the experts," he said. Before leaving, he faced them and grinned, although Kendra thought it looked more like a leer. "That one was pretty. You won't hear any complaints from me if she makes the cut."

Kendra and Trevor waited until they were sure Buddy was out of earshot then shared a joint shudder.

"What a tiresome human being," Trevor said.

"You're being way too kind," Kendra said.

Zak poked his head in. "Can I get your notes before I bring in the next contestant?"

Kendra filled in the remaining blanks on Tori's audition sheet to document her critique then stood and handed over her paperwork to the PA. "Put this one on top. She's a keeper."

"Folks, please keep the noise down. We're almost ready. I promise this time." Cal, a wiry man with a stopwatch around his neck and a Food & Drink TV Network hat on his head, put his bullhorn back onto his director's chair and paced over to a cluster of crew members. On the other side of the room, Tori opened and closed her hands in an attempt to stay loose and be ready to go at a moment's notice. It wasn't working.

Along with thirteen other finalists, she was back in the tasting room at Three Vines Winery. Since the initial auditions a couple of days ago, the space had been transformed into the *American Bake-o-Rama* stage. The front third of the set featured an enormous midnight-blue sideboard flanked by lavender china cabinets showcasing prim white plates, milk pitchers filled with silk flowers, and a variety of brightly hued coffee mugs hanging on hooks. Suspended over the sideboard was the circular *Bake-o-Rama* logo outlined in white lights, with patriotic bunting threading through the *B* and *R* and an arch of stars across the top. Seven neat rows of workstations, ovens, and appliances filled the main floor, with refrigerators along the outer edges. The sidelines were cluttered with camera rigs, light trees, computers, and crew ready to jump into action. The overall effect was a cheerful, odd combination of country kitchen, Fourth of July picnic, and NASA.

Milo and Mia, overjoyed that their mother had cleared the penultimate hurdle to being chosen for *Bake-o-Rama,* had spent the last twenty-four hours prepping Tori for this final round of auditions. They'd ransacked her closet to select a camera-ready outfit (a light green short-sleeved shirt printed with pink and white peonies, olive-toned capris, and cherry-red Chuck Taylors) and coached her on hairstyle (a no-fuss high pony) and makeup (minimal). They'd taste-tested and timed her choices for the bread and pie recipes she was expected to bake and helped her assemble the ingredients to take with her. They'd even gotten up early to see her off before the sun came up so she'd be in Sonoma ahead of her call time of 6:30 A.M., offering her last-minute advice like, "Be confident!" "Don't let the judges psych you out!" and "Whatever happens, don't cry until you're in the car."

They didn't say why she might be crying. Perhaps that was for the best.

What they couldn't prepare her for was the exasperating hurry-up-and-wait atmosphere of shooting a TV show. As the general hubbub burbled on around the room, she and the other contestants had been standing at attention for well over ninety minutes. Tori wondered how it could possibly take so long to get this show on the road.

Cal raised his bullhorn again. "Folks, we'll get started promptly at 8:30, for real this time. Thanks for hanging in there. Ten minutes."

Tori exhaled, relaxed her shoulders, and sat on the stool behind her. Then she felt a tap on her shoulder and turned to see a friendly face.

"Hey, Mel!" Tori stood and hugged him, feeling awkward. "I'm sorry I didn't say hello earlier. This whole thing has been so nerve-racking."

"No worries. I've been trapped on the other side of the stage until now myself." Mel was beaming in his bright white Stetson with a silver studded band.

"You look sharp!"

"Thank you," he replied, shyly looking down at his ostrich leather cowboy boots.

"How are you holding up?"

"All I can say is, good thing I got my hip replaced last year," he said, patting his side. "When I was running my tile business before I retired, the last thing I wanted was to have my crew wasting half the morning hanging out like this."

"This is nothing like teaching high school either," Tori agreed. "We have to be in the classroom early and ready to go right when the bell rings at eight."

"That's showbiz, I guess. If this is what George Clooney has to go through, I can, too," Mel added with a chuckle. "How does the competition look on your end of the room?"

Tori looked around at the nearby contestants, considering. "They'd surprise you," she said. "One guy I met during registration is an architectural grad student. That lady grabbing a scone at the snack table? She runs a dog-sitting business. Then there's Jayden, the one with the beard in the striped sweater over there. He's a stay-at-home dad with four boys under twelve. It amazes me that any of them have the time to bake, much less be this good at it."

"We're no slouches either!" Mel said encouragingly. "I gotta tell you, though, the gal I'm sharing a baking station with is a tough customer." He pointed toward the far side of the studio. "She's the one in all black."

"I haven't met her yet," Tori said.

"When I introduced myself this morning, she looked at me like a spooked cat, said, 'I'm Natalie,' then turned her back on me," Mel said. "I tried to make small talk, and she barely said anything. I'd get a better conversation out of her rolling pin." He shook his head. "I know everyone is nervous, but the way I see it, there's nothing wrong with being friendly and getting through this together. Otherwise, why go through all this tension and stress?"

"For the hundred thousand dollars?" Tori suggested.

"That's not enough to make it worth being miserable, if you ask me. But hey, I'm just doing this for the fun of it. If I wasn't here, I'd be on my boat."

Liam, the assistant director, approached the two of them, Zak trailing behind him. "Hey, there," he said. "Good to find you both together. Cal wants to switch your baking stations. Mel, you'll be at Station 4. And Tori, you'll be at Station 1 next to Natalie. Zak here can help you move your things."

Mel shot Tori a knowing look. "Looks like someone caught Cal's eye."

Tori waved him off. "It's probably for some silly reason, like they want a floral shirt next to an all-black getup."

"Or maybe Cal knows a star when he sees one," Mel said with a grin.

Tori didn't know if she believed that, but she couldn't help hoping he was right.

Tori and Zak scooped up her ingredients and recipes and took them to the front station. Mel picked up his basket of flour, sugar, and spices then gave Tori a wave. "Good luck. You'll do great."

"You, too!" she said. "See you at lunch."

Tori arranged her canisters and jars of ingredients in the order she had them in her home kitchen and put her recipes on the stand. She double-checked the bowls, knives, and other equipment she'd need to have at hand. Then she smoothed her hair back off her brow and tightened her ponytail.

"Places, everyone," Cal commanded through his bullhorn.

As the sound tech tested the microphone at their station, Tori turned to whisper, "Natalie, hi there. I'm Tori. Good luck!"

"Shh!" Natalie hissed without looking at her.

Chastened, Tori turned toward the stage, hoping Natalie would get a chance to take a deep breath at some point.

The lights brightened at the front of the set, and Anika Charles strode to the center. Milo and Mia had told Tori that Anika had been a contestant on a reality dating show before she landed the *Bake-o-Rama* hosting gig, even releasing a successful pop song along the way. On set, she looked like the epitome of good vibes in her yellow gingham sundress and coordinating headband that framed her tumble of black curls.

"Hi there, everyone! I'm your host, Anika Charles. Welcome to the final round of auditions for *American Bake-o-Rama*! Give yourselves a round of applause!"

Tori and her fellow challengers joined in, clapping and cheering.

"That's some great, positive energy coming from fourteen amazing bakers!" Anika continued. "We're relying on you to keep that up throughout the shoot. I know the day might seem like it'll never end, but remember, the camera may be on you at any time, so let's keep it upbeat. Are you ready?"

The room replied with a chorus of "Yes!" and "You bet!" and "Let's do this!"

"All right!" Anika said, clapping her hands together. "Now, let's reconfirm what we'll be doing today. We will run this audition just like a regular episode, with our judges observing and interacting with you and the cameras recording the baking process. You can also expect to be pulled away for individual commentary during breaks in the action. Got it?"

After another round of yeses, Anika continued. "Each of you should have come prepared to bake a savory bread and a fruit pie using your own recipes and ingredients. But as you know if you've watched the show—and I'm sure you've watched the show a lot!—before each bake, the judges will let you know if you'll make your recipe or if you'll set it aside to make one of theirs instead. That's what we on *Bake-o-Rama* call a Bake and Switch!"

Anika walked over to the contestant standing at the workstation behind Tori and scanned her name tag. "For example, we have Charlotte here. Turn around and say hi to everyone, Charlotte."

"Hi, everyone!" Charlotte, a silver-haired woman in her late sixties, swiveled to greet the crowd.

"What are you ready to bake today?" Anika asked.

Charlotte waved a hand over her station. "I plan to make two dozen soft pretzels for my bread, and I have a great boysenberry pie as well."

"Those sound delicious," Anika said. "If Trevor and Kendra do a Bake and Switch, which of your recipes do you hope you'll still get to make?"

"Ooh, I'm real proud of my pretzels, so I hope I can stick with them," Charlotte gushed.

Anika walked over to the baker at the other end of the counter, a young woman with an explosion of blond curls. "And here's Brenda. Everyone, say hi to Brenda!"

"Hi, Brenda!" the room shouted back.

"Hello, everybody!" Brenda responded with an enthusiastic smile.

"Brenda, what are you ready to bake?"

She pointed to her fruit basket. "I've got a cherry and blueberry galette and a rosemary focaccia."

"And which one do you hope to bake?"

Brenda hesitated. "The focaccia. Trevor wrote the book on baking bread, and if I mess up one of *his* recipes, he'll never forgive me."

The room tittered, and Anika returned to center front. "We'll just have to wait and see, but keep that optimism flowing, Brenda. Is everyone ready to say hello to our *Bake-o-Rama* star judges?"

"Yes!"

"Me, too! Please join me in welcoming our two amazing celebrity chefs, Trevor Flynn and Kendra Campbell!"

Trevor and Kendra entered from behind the wall at the front of the studio to a round of cheers and whistles from the contestants and crew, and Tori steeled herself. While Trevor shared a charming smile with the group, Kendra looked regal and impenetrable. The kids had shown Tori some of the chef's famous takedowns of past contestants to prepare her for the worst. Various photos of Kendra's disdainful glare had been turned into memes, too. The GIF of Kendra dropping a burned loaf in front of a startled contestant with the quote, "Is this *bread* or a *brick*?" had been downloaded tens of thousands of times.

Suddenly Tori understood why the twins had advised her to wait to cry in the car. Her mouth went dry and her palms started to sweat.

"Welcome, bakers!" Trevor said with the polish and demeanor of a British lord in a Netflix drama. "On behalf of the Food & Drink TV Network, Kendra, and myself, congratulations for reaching the final round of auditions for *American Bake-o-Rama.* You can take pride in being fourteen of the finest amateur bakers this country has to offer."

"That's right, Trevor," Kendra said. Her expression was stony as she then addressed the contestants, "You have worked very hard to get to this point, but you're not done yet. There are two more baking challenges ahead of you before we decide who will join us for our seventh season."

"Yep, all eyes are on the pies—I mean *prize,*" Anika declared. "Let me ask you: Who here wants to be crowned Best Baker?"

The room erupted with a chorus of "I do!"

"Who wants to star on their own show on the Food & Drink TV Network?"

"I do!" the crowd yelled in unison.

"Who wants to win one hundred thousand dollars?"

Tori silently mouthed *I do!* along with the others, worried that if she said it out loud, she'd jinx herself.

"I thought so!" Anika said. "Kendra, what's your advice for our awesome contestants?"

"You're not in your home kitchens," Kendra said. "So be aware that the knives might feel different in your hands, the bowls may be a different weight, and the measuring cups may not have the tick marks or labels in the same place. Stay sharp."

"I'll add that you always must keep moving forward," Trevor offered. "While you certainly know what you're doing, anything can happen. No matter what, you have to have a dish to show us when time is up."

"And, if worse comes to worst," Kendra added, "accept what's happening and improvise."

Tori was surprised: That was exactly what she'd said in her audition. She'd clearly made a good impression.

"With that, let's begin our first challenge," Anika said. "This morning, we will start on the sweet side. You will be baking your best fresh fruit pie using any fruit or combination of fruits you like. You can use pie dough or pâte brisée—that's shortcrust pastry, if your French is a little rusty. One crust, two crust, or something in between: just as long as it fits in the pie plate."

"Pie plate!" Brenda blurted. "But I'm making a galette!"

Natalie whirled around to shush Brenda, just like she'd shushed Tori. Tori turned to give Brenda an encouraging smile, but she was looking down at her hands, her cheeks reddening. Why was Natalie wound so tight? Maybe she needed a lot of quiet to focus, Tori reasoned, or she wasn't great at taking in oral instructions or had trouble concentrating; any number of kids in Tori's classroom had the same issues. Or maybe it was a whopping case of stage fright. Tori could relate to that.

Anika continued. "You have two and a half hours from start to finish, and I know you can do this—I crust you! Let's. Get. Started!"

Tori exhaled, scanned her recipe, and got to work. First up was the crust, which could use some time in the fridge while she peeled and sliced more than seven cups of apples. She measured out the flour, using the flat edge of a chef's knife to skim the top of the metal cup before dumping it into the bowl of her standing mixer. Next in was a half teaspoon of salt. She whisked the dry ingredients together, and with that squared away, she rushed over to the refrigerator to her left. Opening the door, she searched for the sticks of butter with her name written on the label in bright blue marker. Adrenaline flooded her body. She knew she'd put them in when she'd arrived, but now they were nowhere to be seen.

She closed the door, took a deep breath, and opened it again. Her butter did not magically appear.

As her heart rate skyrocketed, she felt a gentle nudge. It was Charlotte. "I think you're in my fridge!" she whispered.

"Sorry!" Tori shifted one fridge to the right and found a videographer a couple of feet away, capturing every second of her confusion. She looked straight at the lens and offered a rueful smile, saying, "Well, I'm getting off to a great start, aren't I?" She opened the refrigerator in front of her and, with a heady sense of relief, pulled her quarry out from the back of the top shelf. She turned again to the camera, holding the sticks up. "Found the butter!" She scooped a couple of ice cubes into a measuring cup and hustled back to her spot.

The videographer followed her. "Heads up, here they come."

Before Tori could ask who was coming, Kendra was standing on the opposite side of her workstation, flanked by Trevor and Anika.

As she unwrapped the butter, Tori took in what Kendra was wearing: a long-sleeved gray-and-black-striped T-shirt with a skull and crossbones across the chest. The bones were a whisk and a carving knife, and the skull wore a chef's hat. She was clearly taking no prisoners.

"Hey there!" Tori said as casually as she could, concentrating on slicing a stick of butter into cubes.

Trevor leaned in. "Tell us what you're making for us today."

"I'm making a paper bag apple pie," she said.

"Paper bag?" Kendra asked curtly. "What do you mean?"

"It's a one-crust apple pie with a crumble topping that I bake in a paper grocery bag."

"I've never heard of that method before," Trevor said, seeming intrigued. "What does the bag do?"

Tori began cutting the butter into her flour. "It keeps the fruit from burning on top, for one thing, and the spices get infused deep into the filling as it bakes," she explained. "It's really tasty."

"I'd expect the crust to get soggy if all the moisture is locked in a bag." Kendra sounded unconvinced.

"I brush the crust with an egg white before putting in the apples," she said.

"And how many cups of apples?" Kendra pressed.

"Seven and a half."

Kendra whistled in surprise. "With all that fruit, I'd expect you'd end up with apple soup."

Before Tori could reply, Trevor asked, "Are you doing any decorations or ornamentation?"

"No," Tori said, feeling a prickle of panic. "The crumble is all it needs."

Kendra's mouth was a flat line. Trevor spoke up before Tori could feel even more uncomfortable. "Well, we can't wait to see how this turns out. Thank you, Tori."

Kendra murmured her thanks as well, and the judges and host moved on to Natalie's end of the workstation, with the videographer and sound guy moving along with them. Zak took his place in front of Tori's workstation. "How're you doing, Tori?" he whispered.

"Oh, you know, just getting into the swing of things," she replied as she blended ice water into the mixture. "Having a camera up my nose is new to me."

"You'll forget they're there soon enough," he assured her. "Whenever you've got something in the oven for more than a half hour, take a break in the kitchen. There are no cameras there. Pace yourself; you've got a long day ahead. Good luck!"

About thirty minutes later, once her pie was fastened in a Safeway bag with several paper clips and stowed in her oven, Tori took Zak's advice and went to the kitchen. She grabbed a bottle of water and a banana and took a seat on an overstuffed plaid couch, setting her timer on its arm and double-checking how long she had before her pie was ready to emerge. She hadn't realized how much tension she was carrying in her hamstrings until she flopped her feet out in front of her. If she made it through this to the show, she was never wearing these sneakers again: They were cute but had utterly no support.

"Mind if I join you?" Jayden, the baker with four young boys, managed a smile while crunching on a granola bar.

Tori smiled and Jayden let out a short groan as he eased onto the couch. He took off his Atlanta Falcons cap and rested his close-cropped head on the cushions. "I thought getting the boys off to school was stressful," he said. "I'm a wreck, and we're only a couple of hours into this."

"That's exactly why I'm hiding in here for a moment," Tori said. "What pie are you making?"

"Peach almond lattice," he replied, pointing to an orange stain on his apron. "I wanted to represent Georgia pride at the contest today. I also brought in a bottle of my homemade peach schnapps as a side aperitif."

"That's smart," Tori said.

"It's insurance," Jayden chuckled. "If the pie doesn't turn out, at least Trevor will enjoy getting a cocktail before five P.M."

Tori laughed. "Wouldn't anyone?"

"What do you have in the oven?" he asked.

"Paper bag apple pie."

"Huh." Jayden wiped a granola crumb from his beard. "Sounds rustic."

Tori was beginning to think that wasn't a good thing. "It's delicious and supersimple to make, but I'm not telling them that," she confessed. "Otherwise, I'd probably be shown the door."

"There's no rule saying good food has to be complicated," Jayden said. "I mean, if I made nothing but grilled cheese sandwiches for my kids on a daily basis—and I don't mean some bougie, three-cheese combo on artisan bread with imported mustard, grilled with EVOO, and plated with a cornichon; I'm talking about taking a slice of American processed cheese food product and slapping it on a couple of pieces of white bread with the balloons on the wrapper and frying it in mayo—they'd think I'm the next Anthony Bourdain."

Tori grinned. "I know, right? We spend all this time worrying about whether it's okay to use the Mexican vanilla instead of the more expensive stuff from Madagascar, yet sometimes I'd give anything to eat pancakes from a box mix," she said. "It's crazy what we're doing here."

"But it is fun, right?"

"It had better be. We've got twelve more hours of this, then if we're really lucky, six more weeks of it after that." Tori looked at her timer. Even though she had plenty of time, sitting around so far from the set was making her antsy. She swallowed her last bite of banana and stood. "I'd better check on the baby."

"I'm right behind you," Jayden said, tossing his wrapper in the trash. "I'm sure nothing bad's gonna happen, but I've watched enough episodes of this show to worry anyway. Good luck!"

"Same to you."

The door had barely closed behind her when a videographer tapped her on the shoulder. "How much time do you have left before your pie comes out of the oven?"

She looked at the timer. "About forty-five minutes."

"Great. We'd like to get a stand-up with you real quick. Come with me."

"What's your name again?" Tori asked.

"Ted," he said then motioned to his right. "And this is Mike. Easy to remember: I'm Ted the Talking Head, and Mike has the mic."

Ted and Mike led her outside to a brick-paved terrace off one side of the main building. The tables and chairs normally set for wine tasters and tourists had been cleared, and there was a taped *X* on a spot on the patio. Ted pointed and said, "We need you to stand here as we mic you up."

Tori hit her mark, and Mike clipped a tiny microphone on the lapel of her shirt and handed her the wire. "Could you please drop that down inside your shirt? We don't want it to show."

"Sure." She shimmied until the long, thin cord hung down below her hem. Mike plugged it into the mic pack, flipped the tiny power switch, and handed it back to her.

"Could you clip this on the back of your waistband please?"

"No problem. Is this what I'll have to do for every interview?"

"When we do stand-ups, yeah," Mike said.

"So, if I wear a turtleneck dress, you're going to need a really long cord."

Mike grinned. "If you want to wear that in the middle of the summer, just let us know ahead of time."

"We don't use the lavaliers indoors since we have the built-in mics on the set," Ted said, pointing to his camera. "But when we're outside, the wind can mess up the sound quality with a boom."

"I'm just going to act as if I know what you're talking about," Tori said.

This got a smile out of the two-man crew. "Hey, I don't know anything about sautéing or simmering or whatever else you geniuses do in there," Ted said, "so we're even."

They adjusted the tripod and checked the light levels, and Mike had Tori count to ten as a sound check. Ted stepped over to her and put a reassuring hand on her shoulder. "Here's how this works. We'll ask you a couple of questions, and you look at the lens and start talking. No more than a couple of main points, mind you, since we've got a bunch of people we're going to have to edit together. Be sure to answer in complete sentences. Don't think too much about your answers; straight from the hip is what we're looking for. Repeat back what I just said."

"Look at the lens, keep it short, speak in sentences, and don't think. Did I pass?"

"With flying colors," the videographer said. "Here we go." The light on the camera turned from red to green. "What are you baking, and why did you choose it?"

"I'm making a one-crust apple pie with a crumble topping," Tori said, pleased to hear that her voice sounded calmer than she felt. "I like this recipe because, baked in a paper grocery bag, it comes out extrajuicy and delicious."

"Can anything go wrong?" Ted asked.

"I've made this pie dozens of times," Tori said. "It's pretty much idiot-proof." As she said the word *idiot,* her blood turned to ice. "Oh, no!"

Ted looked out from behind the camera. "What's the matter?"

"I need to get back to my station. Right now. I'm sorry." She tugged at the wire at her neck. "Mike, can you get me out of this—quick? After Kendra grilled me about my crust getting soggy, I decided to blind-bake the pie shell at 350 degrees instead of just filling and baking it all at once." She said this calmly even as alarm bells were clanging in her head. "Thing is, the pie itself needs to bake at 425 for an hour, and I forgot to turn up the heat. It's been in there for twenty minutes in a cool oven."

Mike rushed over and disconnected her. Tori tore back into the winery and onto the set, heading straight for her oven. She looked at the temperature setting and gasped.

Ted was on her right, camera in hand, panting a little from running after her. "What's going on? Explain it to us."

She turned the knob up to the correct temperature and checked her timer. "Sugar, sugar, sugar . . ." she muttered through her teeth.

This was a careless mistake, and she was going to pay for it.

"Okay," she said to herself, barely registering the camera still rolling, "The oven will heat up to 425 in less than five minutes, so that gives me about forty minutes at the right temp. If I give it an extra five minutes more than usual, I should be fine. That'll work, that'll work, it'll be okay." Ted and Mike, having captured her error in great detail, moved on to another station.

For the rest of the baking time, Tori either perched on her stool with an eye on the oven or sat cross-legged on the floor in front of the stove peeking at the pie through the window. Every time a *Why didn't I?* or *How could I?* came into her head, she stared at the oven even harder as if the energy from her eyeballs could make it cook faster. There was no time for a redo. She would have to wait and see how it turned out. And hope that some of the other thirteen bakers might have made worse mistakes.

Not Natalie, however. Throughout her vigil, Tori would catch a glimpse of her tablemate and marvel at her precision. Each of her pear and plum slices was exactly the same width. She'd made her crust with finely chopped pecans and even fashioned a few extra pieces of dough into neat leaves, placing them just so at the center of the tart as an accent. She moved from ingredient to measuring spoon to bowl and back like she was programmed. In any other circumstance, Tori would have been impressed by Natalie's meticulousness. At this point, though, it only compounded her misery.

When Anika came back to the center to announce, "Five minutes!" Tori took her pie out of the oven and started snipping away at the grocery bag. Over her shoulder, she saw that Natalie had brought her tart out already, placing it on the end of her station and adding a tiny, darling pair of marzipan bumblebees on florist wire to buzz above the pastry. It looked exquisite.

The camera was back, but Tori willfully ignored the intrusion. The time had come. Using a pair of red, white, and blue oven mitts, Tori pulled the pie out of the bag. Thankfully, it hadn't burned or bubbled over onto the cookie sheet, so it lifted out easily. Until the pie had cooled, though, it was anyone's guess if the crust was a sodden mess or the apples were crunchy. As it sat there steaming like a train engine, she stood back. There was nothing more she could do.

"Time's up, everyone!" Anika said. "Your pies should be at the end of your stations now. Hands off, Jayden! You're done!" Tori swung around to see him give the host a high sign. At least he seemed good-natured about it.

"And cut!" Cal came from the far side of the stage to join Anika at the center. "Great job, everyone!" he said through his bullhorn. "You made it through the first half of the taping, and it smells utterly amazing in here." The crew applauded, but most of the contestants were too stressed-out to join them.

Assistant director Liam took over the bullhorn, calling out, "Since your pies have to cool before they can be served to our judges, we are going to take an hour for lunch. The food is out on the western terrace, so please go and help yourself. You can also walk around the grounds if you want to stretch your legs. The overall rule still applies, though: We'll keep your phones and other devices at the security desk. We don't want you to be looking up bread-baking tips ahead of this afternoon. We will give you a five-minute warning before the lunch break is over. One hour, everyone. Back at 1:15 P.M."

Tori trudged out to the terrace and winced as she passed the tape mark where she'd had her gut-churning *aha!* moment. The catering team offered her a boxed lunch containing a turkey wrap, broccoli salad, and sliced fruit. She walked toward an empty table, planning to sit alone and stew in self-pity, but before she was halfway there, Mel and Jayden waved her over to their table.

"Why so down?" Mel asked as she took her seat.

"I forgot to turn the temperature up once my crust had finished baking," Tori said miserably. "For all I know, my pie could be a bowlful of raw apple slices and a glob of dough."

"Oh, I'm sure it's just fine," said a cheerful young woman in a bright blue hijab who was sitting across the way. "I'm Halla, by the way."

"I'm Tori," she said, unboxing her lunch.

"Besides, I did something even worse," Halla commiserated. "I had to start over because I wasn't used to their measuring cups. I used a half cup that turned out to be a full cup, so my piecrust turned into concrete. Then my filling burned on the stove. I think my pie was only in the oven for ten minutes total. It's a mess."

"At least we can have another crack at it when we do bread this afternoon," Mel said.

"But you know they're going to do a Bake and Switch, right?" Jayden said between bites. "They want to see how we do with a mystery recipe."

"Wonderful," Tori sighed. "I botched making a pie I've been baking since I was in high school. Who knows what I'll mess up cooking a bread recipe I've never seen before."

The four contestants ate and chatted, moving away from the morning's events toward getting to know one another better. Mel talked about the other creative pursuit he'd picked up in retirement: playing guitar in an Austin mariachi band. Halla was also a teacher, although she wrangled kindergartners in a public school in Dearborn, outside of Detroit. Atlantan Jayden had been getting more and more interested in making distilled spirits, and he was in the process of getting a liquor license to open a taproom in Buckhead. Tori listened and nodded, relieved to focus on anything other than her mistakes.

Once she'd finished her meal, she checked her watch. "I need to take a walk for a few minutes before we have to go back in for judging," she said. "Trevor and Kendra are going to be brutal."

"Look, the judges may not know anything went wrong," Mel said, patting her arm. "And if they take off a point or two, you have another chance to shine this afternoon with the bread bake. Keep the faith—you're still in the running."

"Thank you," she said, finally able to take a deep breath. "I'll see you in there."

Tori walked down the hill and hiked a circle around the property, keeping the main building in sight. Even though she was happy to put distance between herself and the studio for a few minutes, the last thing she needed was to get lost.

One pie, she kept telling herself. *One stupid pie, and it might be all over.*

This was the inherent danger of *American Bake-o-Rama.* Bakers were not judged on their previous work, and they didn't accumulate points week to week. The judging always centered on what was done that day. The best bakers in the world all have bad days, but if that happened during an episode, it could send someone home empty-handed.

Why had she agreed to audition? Because she wanted to see how she measured up against their high standards. Tori shook her head, thinking, *I should be more careful about what I wish for.*

She stopped short when she came upon a clump of California poppies. It had been drilled into her as a kid that as the state flower, these plants were protected and never to be kicked, crushed, or picked. A little checkerspot butterfly lighted on one of the apricot-colored petals, its brown wings bedazzled with white dots. It rested in the sun then fluttered off to find more beauty elsewhere. Watching it fly by, Tori knew she wasn't being honest with herself.

Okay, she told herself, *I also auditioned because I want to be a professional baker, even if it's just for one day on a TV show. I'm doing that right now, and I'm not going to give up.*

Brimming with fresh confidence, Tori restarted her hike, only to freeze a few steps later. Up the hill on the east side of the building was a smaller patio area. There, Anika, Trevor, and Kendra were eating their lunch. It looked like Anika was leading the conversation, with Trevor smiling and nodding. Kendra had pushed her chair away from the table so her long legs could be fully extended. Her arms were crossed, and she was watching her colleagues' chatter from under her bangs. Kendra's body language reminded Tori of students who sat sullenly in the back of the classroom, putting a lot of effort into looking tough and defiant when instead they were too self-conscious to join the conversation.

Anika spotted Tori standing among the scrub and wildflowers and gave her an enthusiastic shout-out. Kendra glanced over her shoulder and looked right at Tori: not friendly but not glowering either.

Tori gave a small wave, turned on her heel, and sped back toward the studio.

"Let's take a look at this paper bag apple pie, shall we?"

As Tori focused on smiling no matter what, Kendra lifted her pie above her head, peering through the glass plate. "The crust looks dry, not soggy. I'm surprised."

"I decided to blind-bake it," Tori said, hoping Kendra would appreciate that she'd listened to her concerns and adjusted her recipe.

Kendra brought it to eye level. "The topping is too light and looks underbaked: It should be golden brown. And there isn't any visual interest either. You could have made something out of extra dough or thrown in some walnuts or cranberries to liven it up. Why you used a paper bag is beyond me."

Smile, smile, smile, Tori told herself.

Kendra set the pie back on the workstation, carved a sizable slice with a chef's knife, and used a pie server to place it on the plate close to the camera. "That came out clean," she observed, "and the chunks of apple are fairly uniform. At least you have that." She cut the slice into three pieces and served them to Trevor and Anika before taking a bite herself.

Trevor took over the critique. "I agree with Kendra about the topping. It could have used a few minutes uncovered; it's a little pale. But I understand why you used the bag: Your filling is quite flavorful."

"I like my apple pie with a bit more nutmeg," Kendra huffed.

"Well, that's *your* apple pie," Trevor countered with a bemused expression. "In *Tori's* pie, there's a nice balance. The apples are a bit al dente, however."

"I had the oven set too low at first," Tori admitted.

"Good thing you changed your mind and blind-baked the crust," Kendra said dispassionately. She set her plate down and looked Tori straight in the eye. "Overall, this is a decent attempt at a standard apple pie baked with a novel approach. Thank you, Tori."

"Yes, it's quite lovely. Thank you, Tori," Trevor echoed.

"You're welcome," Tori said, trying to parse if there was any universe in which Kendra's comment could be considered a compliment. Before she could torture herself further, the camera moved on to the other end of the workstation, and the team stood in front of Natalie's spot.

The first words out of Kendra's mouth were, "That is one spectacular-looking fruit tart, Natalie."

There was her answer: Kendra had dissed Tori's pie, damning it with faint, instead of golden-brown, praise.

As their critique of Natalie's plum and pear tart continued, words like *near perfect, delightful presentation,* and *utterly delicious* were like blows to Tori's chest. It was clear she'd chosen a recipe that was way too basic and traditional for *American Bake-o-Rama.* It might have succeeded if her results were flawless, but they weren't. Against her will, a stanza of one of Shelby's poems echoed in her brain: *easily awestruck, not essentially awesome.*

Then again, Trevor thought the filling was lovely. That was something to hold on to, Tori reminded herself as she attempted to drown out Shelby's poetry.

As the team moved on to the other contestants, Tori leaned

over to Natalie. "Great job!" she whispered. Natalie, laser focused on the rest of the critiques, didn't answer. Her head shifted from contestant to contestant like a cat watching a squirrel, gearing up to pounce.

Tori sat back without saying anything else. It was going to be a long day.

"Five, four, three . . ."

As Liam counted off the last two numbers with his fingers in silence, Anika strode to the center with Kendra and Trevor following close behind. There was no applause this time around. The bakers had burned off most of their earlier enthusiasm and, save for a couple of people who sailed through the Pie Challenge, they were wary and nervous.

Kendra turned her attention to Anika as she welcomed everyone back for the second bake of the day with even more eagerness than first thing in the morning. Anika had a knack for bubbliness Kendra knew she could never possess. Thinking back over her comments to contestants during the morning round, Kendra realized she hadn't toned down her bluntness about mistakes one iota. As easy as it was for Anika, being supportive was not coming naturally to Kendra, which frustrated her. She wanted to be good at it. Now.

"As we move into our bread challenge this afternoon," Anika said, "it is probably no surprise to you all that our star judges are pulling a Bake and Switch! Instead of the bread recipes you brought with you, you will be using one from Kendra Campbell herself. When I give you the signal, you can turn the recipe over and get started. You'll have four and a half hours to complete this bake. Kendra, what should our lovely contestants know about this challenge?"

"If you want a flavorful, crusty loaf of bread, you need to use a starter," Kendra said to the group. "That gives the yeast time to ferment ahead of making the dough. Starters need time to come into their own, sometimes days or weeks. But, since we have to make this today instead of next month, I have already made the starter for you. In fact, I've made three starters: pâte fermentée, biga, and sourdough."

As she spoke, Kendra watched as many of the contestants picked up the containers or held them up to the light. Some even opened them and took a big whiff of each, their expressions ranging from apprehensive to panicked. Diving in instead of listening to her instructions was a rookie mistake. She'd learned that lesson the hard way the first week of culinary school, when her Introductory Kitchen Techniques instructor caught some students rooting around in their brand-new knife set before he'd finished his safety lecture. He'd pulled a cleaver off his table and thwacked it clean through a carrot lying on his cutting board, startling them into stunned silence. "Listen to me, or that'll be your finger someday," he'd said before returning to his lesson. Kendra had paid attention to every word of every lecture after that.

Two contestants at the front table were paying attention, though: Natalie, who stared at Kendra unblinking through her black-framed glasses, and Tori, who stood relaxed and receptive, as if she was listening with her entire body.

Good for them, Kendra thought.

Anika kept the patter going. "Three bread starters? Will our bakers need to use all three in this recipe?"

"That's up to the baker," Kendra said. "You'll need to decide which one—or which combination—is best for the bread you'll be making."

"Ooh, it could be a *biga* problem if you use the wrong one," Anika said with a sparkle. "Anything else?"

"The recipe is more of a guide than step-by-step instructions," Kendra said. "This is a test of your bread-baking know-how."

"Got all that, contestants?" Anika asked the room. "Okay, folks. Let's. Get. Started!"

The auditionees flipped their recipes over with a communal flutter. Kendra scanned the room for reactions as they discovered they were tasked with baking two identical loaves of New York rye studded with caraway seeds. Kendra could already hear worried mutters from around the room: "How long is this supposed to rise?" and "There's no temperature setting!" and "What in the world is a biga?"

Kendra had little patience for contestants—like Becca the rainbow cream cheese lady—who breezed through auditions by baking recipes they'd made before then flopped once they were on the show because they didn't have expertise beyond their tried-and-true dishes. She felt they took a spot away from someone who was more qualified for the rigors of competition. Buddy called them "ratings gold." Kendra called them "disaster factories."

But Trevor called them "less-than-perfect with great potential," and deep down, she knew he was right. The game show setting was unbelievably high-pressure. They were doing their best, and their best was pretty impressive for people who were self-taught. As she scanned the room, she reminded herself that, bottom line, they all wanted the same thing: great baking. And truth be told, back when she was starting out, she would have sniffed the starters instead of waiting for instructions. She had to cut these folks some slack.

How's that for empathy, Alden? she thought.

"Kendra?" Trevor whispered, a clipboard under his arm. She followed him offstage to reconnoiter. "I'll take the left side, and you take the right. How long do we have until they start the first rise?"

"About a half hour."

He looked at his watch. "Got it. We'll switch sides in twenty minutes." With that, Trevor put on his glasses and went to observe the seven contestants on the left side of the room. Kendra grabbed her clipboard and walked down the center to watch the other seven. During this phase, the judges had to scrutinize and document each baker's technique. Did they choose the pâte fermentée as their starter? Were they overmixing the dough? Did they try to knead it, which was a no-no for this recipe? Did they read the recipe as they went along, or did they plan things out before they got going? What was the likelihood they'd create some semblance of Kendra's chewy, robust rye loaves in the time allotted? This assessment, in addition to the flavor and texture of the bread, would give them a better idea of who had the skills to do well on the program.

Whenever Kendra complained to Alden during her off-hours about the *Bake-o-Rama* concept, which was frequently, she usually harped on the artificiality of the challenges. There was not a single kitchen in the world she'd ever worked in that set timers for finishing dishes or had bakers go head-to-head in some ridiculous contest to get a job. Chefs hired people with a strong work ethic and a willingness to adapt to that chef's particular way of running things without causing trouble. No stopwatch was needed: The food always had to be done right and be ready—now.

But this type of *Bake-o-Rama* challenge, with few instructions and no guidance from anyone else: That felt familiar. She had walked into the local Italian restaurant when she was fourteen and, needing a job and a place to escape after summer school let out, asked if she could help in the kitchen. She was handed a mop and a pair of rubber gloves and was told to keep the place clean. The only way Kendra had known she was doing a good job was if no one yelled at her for doing a bad one. By the time the owner realized she wasn't going to quit, no matter how many crusty lasagna pans they tossed in the sink, he allowed her to learn how they made the food. She had watched the chef, who was the owner's wife, as she tossed ingredients together without measuring cups or scales then worked them together with a heavy wooden spoon or her own two hands. This was undoubtedly how her mother and grandmother and every other ancestor had made pasta, focaccia, and cannelloni for centuries. Experience and deliciousness outweighed academics and refinement—and this early experience had inspired Kendra's desire to become a chef herself someday.

Giving someone a series of instructions could enable them to make a serviceable bread. Presenting them with the ingredients and expecting them to transform them into two loaves of the ultimate New York rye based on experience? That would separate the best bakers from the wannabes.

With Trevor starting in the back, Kendra began with Station 1, standing a few feet away from Tori. Given how sophisticated her initial entries had been, Kendra had been baffled by her choice of an unadorned apple pie with none of the bells and whistles other contestants slapped together to catch the judges' attention. It was yummy, even if it wasn't at all fancy or letter-perfect, and she was willing to concede the difference of opinion about the nutmeg. She even understood the paper bag in retrospect. The hominess of pinning it up and ripping it open to allow the steam to escape, the woody scent of the hot grocery bag on top of the cinnamon's bark, and the apples' autumn tartness made the pie coziness on a plate, creating a mood as much as a flavor profile.

Yet Kendra had immediately turned into #TheChopper, using a disdainful tone with Tori that skipped right over constructive criticism into just plain critical. She'd gotten that sort of treatment throughout her career—a slam couched as "a piece of advice"—but that wasn't how she ought to treat other cooks, especially someone with a lot of talent . . . and such kind eyes.

Why had she done that? To show her superiority over a batch of home bakers? *Or,* a quieter voice in the back of her head wondered, *to keep Tori at arm's length?* Kendra shifted uncomfortably. Why in the world would she need to do that? Bothered anew by how hard it was to put her cynicism aside, she promised herself to be more positive the next time they spoke.

Kendra refocused on the task at hand. Both Tori and Natalie were in the zone and didn't seem to notice the judge's presence at all. Tori's ingredients were divvied up in small bowls ready to dump into the standing mixer—including the pâte fermentée, which was the correct starter for the exercise. She had turned on the oven to preheat, and while it was a little lower than Kendra would recommend, it could still work. Tori had also apparently found the pizza stone: It was no longer on the shelf of the workstation, so it was likely in place on the middle rack of the oven, getting good and hot to help the bread crust up. As Kendra watched, Tori secured the bread hook onto the mixer, dumped the rye and wheat flours into its bowl with a couple cups of water, and turned it on.

So far, she was following the recipe. The next step, which was not written down, would tell Kendra if Tori really knew what she was doing.

Tori turned off the mixer . . . and sat down on her stool.

Kendra was impressed.

Stepping away indicated Tori knew that the flour needed time to soak up the water. Managing the hydration was vital.

If she really, *really* knew what she was doing, Tori would wait about twenty minutes before adding the starter, salt, and yeast, so Kendra moved over to observe her station partner. Natalie had finished blending the flours and water and turned away . . . to pick up the container of biga and plop it into the mixing bowl.

Kendra inwardly winced. Based on her interview and audition, she knew Natalie took a lot of pride in being a perfectionist. She'd told the judges how much she despised making mistakes . . . and she'd just made two. She'd have a hard time forgiving herself for that. Kendra knew what that was like.

As a judge, Kendra had to be impartial and evaluate each baker according to their results that day. While Natalie had aced the morning and could still end up with a couple of good-tasting loaves that would outshine the majority of her competitors, Kendra was concerned that her drive to be perfect could prevent her from being innovative and rolling with the punches, both critical to winning *Bake-o-Rama.*

In contrast, Tori didn't seem thrown by her previous setback and was leaning into her experience without hesitation. Resilience was a good trait to have on the show and would serve her well if she ever did turn pro. Because even though she wanted to make connections through baking for others, sometimes it was just about getting the dish out of the oven and onto a plate.

Unfortunately, love didn't always have a role to play in the kitchen.

It was creeping past 9:00 P.M., and Tori was completely spent. The bread challenge had wrapped up a couple of hours ago, and she was thrilled—and relieved—by how her rye had turned out. Trevor had seemed delighted with the "chew" and "alelike caramel" of her loaves and smiled at her warmly throughout his assessment. Even Kendra seemed less terse than earlier, and she complimented Tori's thorough knowledge of the bread-making process. She'd also taken an extra second to look her in the eye when saying, "Thank you, Tori." She may have even smiled slightly. That was heartening.

With the dinner break over, the judges were cloistered in the kitchen making their final selections. The contestants waited on the terrace, chatting in groups that merged and broke off as the hour got late. As agonizing as it was to hang around, knowing there was at least a 50 percent chance she'd be going home empty-handed, Tori was enjoying herself. The fourteen of them had been in the trenches together under weird and nerve-racking circumstances, so they had a lot to talk about. Mel was a social butterfly, moving through the crowd and ensuring everyone was included in the conversation. He even finally got more than a handful of words out of Natalie by complimenting her technique, although when he asked her about the bread recipe she didn't get to make, she closed up again, her lips sealed like a bank safe.

"Hey, everyone, listen up!" It was the casting director Tori had met at her initial audition at Three Vines Winery just two days ago. "We'll be meeting in two groups. Group 1 will follow me, and Group 2 will go with Zak. Listen for your name as I read off the groups."

Tori was listening so carefully for her own name she didn't realize Mel was also in Group 2 until he tapped her on the shoulder. "I guess we'll sink or swim together, huh?"

She nodded but couldn't say anything. Her mind was whirling. Group 1 was going to meet with the casting director: That had to be good news for them and bad for her. Mel was with her at the front of the Group 2 line, and she didn't dare look back to see who else was following Zak. He wasn't taking them into the kitchen or the tasting room, which seemed like the logical place to announce the winners. For all she knew, Zak was leading them straight to the parking lot to hustle them off the property.

Zak opened the door to a small dining room, and the seven contestants—Tori, Mel, Halla, Jayden, Natalie, Brenda, and Charlotte—were greeted by cheers and the popping of champagne corks. Anika, Trevor, Kendra, Cal the director, and the rest of the crew stood applauding in front of an enormous banner with CONGRATULATIONS, AMERICAN BAKE-O-RAMA BAKERS! printed in patriotic colors.

"We did it, kid!" Mel said, hugging Tori tight. She squeezed him right back, her eyes shining with tears of surprise, relief, and excitement.

The news was so overwhelming, and she was so fatigued, Tori felt like she was floating from person to person in a joyous chain of hugs and high fives. When she got to Natalie, however, she hesitated.

"Great job, Natalie," Tori said, offering her hand. "You are an amazing baker, and you're going to crush it on the show."

"Thanks," Natalie said stiffly, giving Tori's hand a quick, fierce shake.

As Natalie walked away to score a piece of the massive sheet cake, Tori gratefully accepted a flute of champagne from a strolling server. She still had a long drive ahead of her to get back to Eucalyptus Point, but she could handle a sip or two first.

"Congratulations, Tori," came a voice from behind her. She turned to find Kendra, flute in hand.

Summoning all the self-confidence she could in a split second, Tori tapped her glass to hers. "Thank you. I am so excited."

"You did a great job today," Kendra said, her tone measured. "Also, your gateau de mille crepes was one of the best things I've ever eaten. You earned your spot."

This was not at all what Tori expected to hear from the judge who groused about her nutmeg choices earlier that morning. "Wow, thank you! I'm so glad to hear that, especially from you." Tori heard herself say that last phrase and died a little. She began again. "I mean, I really respect your professional opinion since I'm just a home cook, and you're judging me. On the show." She knew her face was bright pink and wished she could turn her mouth off. No such luck: She was a chatterbox when she was nervous. "Nice shirt, by the way."

Kendra looked down at the grinning skull in the chef's hat and nodded. "The Gamma Raye staff gave this to me after doing three seatings for Thanksgiving dinner last year. We all kind of looked like this after the holidays." She glanced at her watch. "Actually, I have to get over there before dinner service wraps up, so I'd better get Trevor to start the toast now before he piles into another piece of cake." She clinked glasses with Tori again. "See you soon."

"Yep," Tori said, mystified. While Kendra hadn't exactly been friendly, she had been cordial, maybe even a little awkward. Where was the #TheChopper the twins had warned her about? As Kendra walked away, Tori remained a little befuddled, even though she hadn't had a drop of champagne yet.

Trevor tapped his glass with a dessert fork. "Everyone, may I have your attention? I know I speak for Kendra, Anika, and the team when I say this is one of the strongest slates of contestants we've ever had. I hope you're proud of the terrific work you've done so far, and I cannot wait to see what you'll do this season. Kendra, want to add anything?"

"I wish you all the best during the competition," Kendra said.

"Goodness me, Kendra, stop gushing!" Trevor teased before continuing to address the assembly. "I would like to propose a toast. To our *American Bake-o-Rama* Season 7 contestants, we raise our glasses to you. May your meringue always be peaked, your chocolate well-tempered, and your fruitcake rich and boozy. Cheers!"

As she raised her glass, Tori gave Mel a wide smile. Whatever happened next, her kids already seemed to be right about one thing: She just might make some new friends.

More than a week later, as the fog rolling in off the Pacific started to dissipate, Tori's longtime friends Cassie and Lee Anne arrived at her place for a Sunday morning confab, part weekly tradition, part celebration of Tori making the cut at auditions, and part consolation, as Milo and Mia had flown to New York the day before to see Shelby before they started their summer jobs.

"Cassie, she made my favorite!" Lee Anne exclaimed to her wife as she walked into the kitchen. Lee Anne had pulled a Saturday shift at the behavioral health clinic on Castro Street and looked ready to make the most of a relaxing day off, dressed in her yoga togs and sandals, her chestnut hair down her back, and a scrunchie on her wrist. "You usually only make babka for my birthday because it's such a hassle. What's the occasion?"

Tori hugged Lee Ann then Cassie as they entered the kitchen. "I wanted to time myself making it to see if I should use this for the Bread Challenge in a few weeks."

"How did it turn out?" Cassie asked, pointing to the twisty loaf on the kitchen table.

"You tell me," Tori said, flashing a large bread knife. "Do you want me to slice it for you, or are you just going to rip it apart with your hands?"

"You should know me well enough to answer that," Lee Anne said, stripping a sugary hunk off one end and dropping it into her mouth. She chewed slowly and dramatically, rolling her eyes to the heavens. "That is so amazing! You have to bake this on the show."

Cassie unwrapped the bowls of strawberries, crème fraîche, and brown sugar they'd brought and set them on the table. She was dressed for gardening in a faded denim shirt, smudged khaki cargo shorts, and a blue baseball cap to keep her braids in check. "How much chocolate is in this again?"

"Three whole bars," Tori said, bringing three mugs and a coffee carafe to the table then taking a seat. "And there's more than a stick of butter in it, too."

"No wonder it's the best thing ever," Cassie said, tearing off a hunk for herself and taking a bite. She shivered with bliss. "Oh, yeah, this should definitely be on the show. It's incredible, even though it's a little underdone in the middle."

"What?" Startled, Tori peeled away a couple of layers and poked the center. "Oh, no!"

"It's not that bad. I wouldn't worry about it," Cassie said, selecting a less doughy bit. "Everyone has a bad bake once in a while."

Tori frowned. "But that's my second try! I overbaked the first attempt. All that fine chocolate down the tubes."

"Please tell me you didn't throw the other one out!" Lee Anne said. "I'll eat it even if it turned into a pile of charcoal."

"It's over there," Tori said, pointing to a forlorn loaf wrapped in plastic wrap next to her microwave. "I might keep it on the counter throughout the competition as a warning in case I get too ambitious."

"You can do this," Cassie said with an assuring pat on the arm.

"I dunno," Tori said. "At the reception when they let us know we'd been selected, they'd put all the pies and the bread we'd baked on display before the crew got to take what they wanted. I had made rye bread before, so my loaves looked pretty good compared to the other ones. But then I got a good look at everyone else's pies. They had braided tops and decorations and all kinds of frou-frou. My apple pie looked like something Milo baked in kindergarten. It was pathetic."

"That's your perception. It may not be reality," Lee Anne said, dropping into therapist mode.

"I'm a bread and cake person, but when it comes to pies, custards, and even cookies, I'm winging it most of the time. Not like the rest of the people they chose," she said, Natalie's pristine fruit tart looming large in her mind.

"You have just as much right to be in this contest as anyone else who made it through the auditions," Lee Anne assured her. "You are talented, you're experienced, and you're rock solid under pressure."

"You had to do well to be selected out of all those thousands of people, too," Cassie added. "From what I've seen on the show, that Kendra Campbell doesn't put up with poseurs."

Tori could attest to that.

"Well," she said, "after the winners were announced, she did come over to tell me I earned my spot."

"See?" Lee Anne crowed.

"And she said my gateau was one of the best things she's ever eaten."

"Whoa, that's extremely high praise coming from her," Cassie said, dipping a strawberry in the crème fraîche then rolling it in the brown sugar. "Seems like she likes you."

"Then she wished me good luck," Tori added, feeling a little better about herself.

"Personally, or as part of the group?" asked Lee Anne.

Tori thought back. "Just me," she said.

"Ooh, maybe she *liiiiikes* you!" Lee Anne said in the same tone she'd used since she and Tori were in middle school together, gossiping about cute girls during gym class.

"That is impossible," Tori stated. "We've barely even met, much less talked. Besides, she's not allowed to 'like' a contestant. It's against the rules."

"When has that ever made any difference?" Cassie said, rolling her eyes.

"Besides, she probably has a girlfriend," Tori said. Immediately, her mind went into overdrive. Did Kendra live with someone? What was Kendra's type? Why was she herself even wondering about this?

Lee Anne watched Tori's face with all the shrewdness of a childhood friend. "Probably?" she said, grabbing her phone and beginning to type. "Don't tell me you haven't googled Kendra Campbell yet. Here we go: Her last romance ended two years ago when she broke up with some software executive. See?"

Tori took the phone and scanned the article. Sure enough, a recent interview with the *Chronicle* confirmed that Kendra was not currently in a serious relationship. It also indicated, if the photo of the tech exec's negligible body fat and laser-cut facial features were any indication, Tori was not her type at all.

"She seems like a grump, but gotta admit, she's hot on camera," Cassie added appreciatively, looking over Tori's shoulder at the photo of the chef standing in the gleaming Gamma Raye kitchen, self-assured and sexy in her crisp white jacket. Tori flashed back to the moment she'd locked eyes with Kendra during their celebratory toast. She was hot off camera, too.

"Somebody's blushing!" Lee Anne singsonged.

Tori resolutely shook her head. "I'm not going down this road, ladies. I have to stay focused and get my recipes ready to go ahead of our first day of shooting next week."

"Wait, I thought *Bake-o-Rama* starts in late October," Cassie said.

"That's when it airs," Tori said. "The show shoots until mid-August."

"Aren't you supposed to be back at school by then?" Cassie asked.

"No, we finish taping well before we have our first teacher in-service. But even if we did shoot later into the summer, it wouldn't matter. I probably won't make it past the first episode."

"Why are you saying that?" Lee Anne asked, exasperated. "You just beat out thousands of people to get to this point. And only six more stand between you and getting a hundred grand. You can do this!"

Tori folded her hands on the table and leaned in. "I'm not so sure," she confessed. "I have no idea what recipes they're going to surprise us with, and a lot of the other contestants are practically professional." Once again, Natalie's pear and plum tart flashed in her memory alongside her plain old paper bag pie. "It's like Shelby used to say about me: I'm 'easily awestruck, not essentially awesome.'"

Cassie and Lee Anne exchanged a glance. "That was just a line in a poem she wrote—a work of fiction," Lee Anne said.

"No, 'Rocket Blast' was definitely written about me and how boring she thought I was," Tori said with a sigh. "And of course, that had to be from the one book of her poems that got kind of famous."

"Stupid *New York Times Book Review*," Lee Anne sniffed. "I haven't read it since."

"Shelby's opinion isn't worth listening to," Cassie said, perturbed. "Look, I love her as a friend, but she never gave you enough credit for everything you've done with your life. She had a bad habit of trying to feel successful by making you feel small."

"I pity her fiancée," Lee Anne added, grabbing a strawberry.

It was as if all the oxygen had been sucked out of the kitchen. Tori stared at Lee Anne. "Her *what*?" she said.

"Oh, great," Cassie said, folding her arms and scowling. "You hadn't heard. Typical Shelby."

Lee Anne eyed her wife then turned to Tori. "She and Barb are getting married this December. She called us this weekend to let us know. We thought she told you already."

Even in the summer warmth, Tori felt bone-cold. "The twins are with her right now. They haven't said anything about it to me."

"Shelby told us she was waiting for them to arrive before sharing the news," Lee Anne continued. "She said she was going to talk to you, too, but . . ." She sighed heavily. "She didn't say when."

"How is this news hitting you?" Cassie asked gently. "You can tell us. It won't get back to her, unless you want us to convey a message."

Given that they had parted on barely civil terms, Tori knew she wouldn't be high on Shelby's call list. Still, if Shelby was expecting their children to break the news to her, that was a new low. "I'm surprised," Tori said honestly. "She made it pretty clear during the divorce that writing was going to be her top priority after our split, and she didn't want to be beholden to anyone else anymore. I never expected she'd want to settle down again."

"This can't be easy," Lee Anne said, squeezing her arm with a consoling hand. "It's a lot to take in."

All Tori could do was nod. Over the last three years, she'd attempted to process the pain of their divorce by considering their marriage to be an artifact from a former life, like a painting she'd made in high school that she could stow in the attic and ignore. At first it had felt alien to be on her own after so many years with Shelby, but given how much their relationship had degraded in those last months, she knew it was easier than living together one minute longer. Tori had no desire to reunite with her ex. Yet she couldn't help feeling stuck and pathetic by comparison.

But stuck didn't describe someone who was about to compete on a major television show. A baker who'd been praised by two of the top chefs in the country was in no way pathetic. And Shelby wasn't the only one with dreams and desires and drive. Tori had an opportunity to change everything now. *American Bake-o-Rama,* with its prize money and national airtime, could be the nudge she needed to grow into her own without the ghost of her former marriage haunting her anymore. Nothing was stopping her, except herself.

"Cassie, may I ask you for some legal advice?" she said, pulling a manila envelope from her bag.

"Of course," Cassie replied. "You already paid my retainer in breakfast pastry."

Tori put the envelope in front of her. "This is my *Bake-o-Rama* contract with the network. Could you read through this to make sure there are no surprises?"

Cassie adjusted her glasses and scanned the documents. "Well, they make it clear you aren't getting a dime unless you win the whole shebang. They'll put you up in a hotel for Friday nights of taping weekends and will reimburse your mileage and gas. Still, they're saving money on airfare since you're local. Cheapskates."

"I'm just grateful they'll pay for my ingredients once the show starts," Tori said, gesturing to the babka. "I don't think I could afford to make this again without financial aid."

"They also have a pretty tight nondisclosure agreement," Cassie continued, flipping pages. "Their media relations department will tell you how and when you can talk about your experience on the program, and you can't say a word to anyone about the outcomes of the weekly contests outside of immediate family until the season has aired in its entirety."

"And we're practically your immediate family, so we expect regular updates," Lee Anne said.

"No smart devices on the set," Cassie read on. "No posts about how you're doing on the show on your personal social media unless the content has been reviewed by their team: You'll have to walk through the world as if you competed all six weeks and have no idea who won."

"I can keep a secret," Tori said. "That shouldn't be a problem."

"And there's a nonfraternization clause here, too," Cassie said. "That means no hanky-panky between the judges and the contestants for twelve months after the contestant's last episode."

"Well, that could be an upside of getting cut early," Lee Anne chuckled. "Then there'd be nothing to stop you and the Cookie Queen from getting to know each other better a year from now."

Tori didn't quite know what to do with that idea.

Sixty-five miles north of Eucalyptus Point, just off Highway 101, Kendra had a lot to do and not much time to do it. She had to be on the road within the hour to discuss Trevor's choices for this season's recipes at his place in Tiburon, with a hope he'd entertain an idea or two from her in the process. She also wanted to vacuum the dog bed and nab some coffee before she got there.

Which was why she was lying on her couch instead, Julia snoring on her stomach, as she conducted an internet search on Tori Moore.

It had been more than a week since she'd looked Tori in the eye and congratulated her on being selected to join the show. Since then the willowy redhead and her radiant smile had crossed her mind a few times. Then her image would dissipate, replaced by one of long-suffering Alden with his balding head in his hands, pleading, *Don't get a crush on a contestant, I am begging you, Ken! You can't afford to lose this gig!*

Alden would be right about her needing the show to offset her financial precariousness. Her revenue from Chippy Chunk rose as soon as the first commercial for the season aired each year, and the show would undoubtedly bolster her cookbook sales as well. If she got the boot because she favored one baker over the others, particularly if it was because of the combination of said baker's baking skills and delicate freckles, Kendra's reputation would never recover.

There was only one thing to do: research *each* of the contestants. That deeper understanding would be helpful to the *Bake-o-Rama* team as they chose rigorous challenges to test them as individual bakers, she assured herself. And if she started with Tori and didn't have enough time to do the rest? Well, she had to start *somewhere.*

Kendra had memorized the limited personal information in Tori's audition packet, including her educational background, her professional history, and her birthdate. Other than deducing she was a forty-four-year-old Virgo—which, given Kendra was a forty-year-old Scorpio, was fantastic news—that didn't give her many useful tidbits to go on.

Unfortunately, there was not much to see online. Kendra found Tori's teacher profile on Sequoia High's website, which featured a friendly school photo of "Ms. Moore." It didn't seem like she had any relevant social media accounts, which Kendra could not fathom in this day and age. Tori did pop up on her teenagers' feeds here and there, identified as "Mom" in photos of school events, college tours, and a couple of birthday celebrations. Interestingly, her children also had some photos of another woman called "Mommy," but none of the two women together. This must be the ex—a *female* ex—which was encouraging. For background. That's all.

Kendra's alarm went off, jolting her back into reality. She had to leave the house in ten minutes. She shut off her phone and frowned. She didn't want to be a creep and shadow her across the interweb, so she'd have to get creative and find ways to get to know Tori through their interactions on the show. Rules were rules.

. . .

Kendra drove down to Marin County then put her SUV's clutch to the test, looping back and forth past increasingly expensive mansions to arrive at Trevor's monumental home. Not that Kendra's spread wasn't impressive in its own Spanish-tile-and-stucco way, but Trevor had the most spectacular view of the bay she'd ever seen.

Once she got to the front door, she found a sticky note directing her to go around to the backyard. There, Trevor was seated on the patio at a large glass and wrought-iron table scattered with papers and cookbooks.

"Halloo there, Kendra," he said with a delighted air, pointing at the food on a table near the pool. "Grab yourself a cuppa and a croissant and let's get down to business."

Mug in hand and croissant on plate, she sat down then dropped her bag. "Well, Trevor, whatcha got for Season 7?"

Trevor looked toward the house to ensure the coast was clear then leaned in. "I have nothing," he whispered conspiratorially.

Kendra looked at him, unsure of how to reply.

"My mind is as empty as a church on Monday," Trevor said with a strangled laugh. "So," he added, brightening, "it's going to be up to you to set the tone for this season."

Kendra hesitated. "But you usually take the lead."

"I've been buried in this for days, but after so many years of this formula, I am completely bereft," Trevor said. "I'm relying on you, dear. You're more than capable."

Kendra was floored. Their relationship had always been cordial, but this was the first time that he, the elder statesman of *Bake-o-Rama,* had let his guard down and showed her anything less than perfect polish, poise, and preparation. It was a relief to see he didn't have all the answers and was comfortable enough to admit it. But she wasn't sure she had as much confidence in herself as he clearly did. She'd followed his lead from day one. Now he was handing her the reins, and just like every day of high school, she was barely awake, much less prepared. So, she told herself, just like in high school, she was going to have to fake it.

She opened her bag and pulled out a mishmash of notes. "I do have an idea to run by you."

"Thank goodness," Trevor said, sitting back. "At the rate I was going, we'd be having them making deep-fried Twinkies or some such." He put on his glasses. "What do you have here?"

"You won't believe this," Kendra said, "but I think Buddy may be onto something."

"Buddy?" He took his glasses off again. "I find that extraordinarily hard to believe."

She shrugged. "Hear me out. This is *American Bake-o-Rama*, but because you and I went to culinary schools, which still focus on the French style of fine patisserie, we're expecting our amateur bakers to showcase those techniques and flavor profiles in order to win. That kind of baking takes a lot of skill and produces amazing work, but a lot of times we get great-looking bakes that taste like cardboard. And the French tradition leaves out a lot of amazing culinary influences that took root in the United States—African, Latin American, Eastern European, Middle Eastern, and so many others. Now, I love me a finely turned-out French pastry, don't get me wrong, but I started Chippy Chunk because there's a heart connection to a more homestyle kind of baking." She hoped Trevor couldn't tell she was thinking about Tori's paper bag apple pie and pressed on. "It can be just as demanding and take as much expertise, but the food stays accessible and delicious. Face it, not many kids are begging their parents to make them a tartelette aux noix."

Trevor took this in. "So I wasn't that far off about the deep-fried Twinkies?"

"You are one snobby Brit, Trevor," Kendra said without thinking. For a split second, she panicked. She usually kept her snippy sense of humor away from Trevor and wasn't sure if she'd gone too far.

Before she could apologize, he chuckled good-naturedly, his eyes crinkling with genuine affection. That, more even than him asking her to take the lead this season, made her feel like an equal rather than a junior partner. Maybe she really could do this.

"A culinary tour of American home baking it is, then," he said, nodding. "I only have one request."

"Name it."

"Promise me, on the life of that little bulldog of yours, that you will never tell Buddy that he inspired this. Otherwise, he'll 'basically' never let us hear the end of it."

She smiled wide. "Deal."

It was a bright Saturday morning, and the first day of taping was finally at hand. Tori stood at her pristine workstation, wearing a starched, cream-colored apron with her name stitched in cursive under the red, white, and blue *American Bake-o-Rama* logo. Each contestant was encouraged to have a signature style of dress that included footwear: Charlotte wore golf skorts and running shoes, Mel had his parade of western shirts and cowboy hats and boots, Natalie's attire was black-on-black all the way down to her Doc Martens . . . and Tori stuck to floral cotton shirts and colorful Chuck Taylors, which turned out to have utterly no arch support.

She could barely feel any part of her body, what with so much caffeine and adrenaline coursing through her veins. The seven contestants had been brought in a couple of days before to shoot publicity photos and intro videos for the network website as well as to start Social Media Boot Camp to learn how to build their "online personal presence," which was a new term for her. Even though she was staying at a nearby hotel and had gone to bed shortly after dinner the previous night, she had slept only a couple of hours before today's early start. The tension was just too much. After all, even though it hadn't been her idea to enter this contest, much less get to a point where she had to impress two of the best chefs in the country, the news of Shelby's engagement made Tori feel she had something to prove. The stakes felt unbearably high.

Tori stood in the middle row between Brenda and Charlotte at the center of the stage floor. She was grateful they each had workstations to themselves, now that there weren't as many bakers to cram into the limited space. She was also thrilled she was nowhere near Natalie; she had a feeling that today she'd need to be surrounded by people who were a lot more easygoing. Tori had set up all her ingredients, put her recipes in easy reach, and laid out a couple of key implements to be right at hand once the clock started ticking.

Provided she knew what she was baking. Which she was about to find out.

Anika got into place at the front, dressed in a darling sundress with a square, sailor suit collar. At Cal's signal, Liam stepped in front of the host with an electronic clapboard and slated the take (a term Tori had learned during her orientation). Instantly, Anika brightened as if the clapboard had flipped her "on" switch. Tori took a cue from her and smiled as well; who knew when the camera might catch her own reactions?

"Welcome, welcome, welcome everyone to Season 7 of the *American Bake-o-Rama*!" she began. "I'm Anika Charles, and it is my extreme pleasure to be here as your host. You're about to meet our seven contestants who, over the next few weeks, will take us to the heights of home baking by sharing their recipes and demonstrating their amazing expertise. And one talented baker will have a lot to show for their hard work at the end of the season, when we crown our Best Baker, earning them a starring role in a future Food & Drink TV Network program and prize money totaling one hundred thousand dollars! Our judges told me backstage that this season's contestants are some of the best bakers they've ever encountered—and speaking of judges, let's bring them out now! Let's give a big *Bake-o-Rama* welcome to Chef Trevor Flynn and Chef Kendra Campbell!"

Even though Tori would have clapped on cue for whoever came out from behind the stage, she felt an unexpected jolt of excitement when she saw Kendra. After Cassie and Lee Anne's visit, Tori had continued to look up the celebrity chef online for more background and, she was embarrassed to admit, a few more photos of those striking eyes of hers. Her research turned up a couple of professional bios from restaurants where Kendra had worked earlier in her career, numerous press photos, a few enigmatic candid shots, and several interviews in which the writers described the chef as "brusque," "taciturn," or even "overconfident." Now she was here in the flesh, commanding the *Bake-o-Rama* stage in a gem-blue turtleneck embroidered with blackbirds bursting out of a pie. But rather than feel intimidated, Tori was curious. So much energy must be going into maintaining this impenetrable persona: What was that about?

"Greetings, bakers," Kendra began. "Trevor and I look forward to learning more about you and seeing your best work over the next six weeks as we get closer to naming our overall winner. You've done some impressive baking to get this far, and we are here to test your talents and challenge your assumptions on what makes a baker truly great."

"That's right, Kendra," Trevor added. "And this season, we will examine your baking expertise with American classic recipes for cakes, pies, cookies, and more. During our weekly challenges, we will be looking for creativity, craftsmanship, and tastiness. Whether you make one of your own recipes or one of ours, we ask for nothing less than your best—and we know each of you is capable of utter perfection."

"Absolutely!" Anika said, nodding to her colleagues then looking into the center camera. "Now then, for those of you tuning in who are unfamiliar with the rules of *Bake-o-Rama,* each week's challenge will focus on a particular type of baking featuring one sweet and one savory example. Our contestants are prepared to bake either of these options using their own tried-and-true recipes. But there's a good chance that one of our celebrity chefs will pull a Bake and Switch, asking our bakers to use one of their recipes instead. By the end of each program, the judges will name the week's Best Baker based on the results of the challenge—and we'll have to say goodbye to one contestant. So every bake counts, people!" She stepped slightly to her right so the star judges could take center stage. "Tell us, Kendra: What is today's challenge?"

"Pies," said Kendra.

"Ooh, I love a good pie: cherry pie, apple pie, pork pie—wait, that's a hat, right?" Anika joked. "And what are our bakers starting with today: sweet or savory?"

"Savory," Trevor answered. "We are asking each of you dear contestants to use your own recipe to bake a savory pie that could be a main meal. While we require that it has at least one crust, the type of crust and the filling are up to you."

"Delish!" Anika said. "And how long do they have?"

"Two hours," Kendra said.

"Ooh, that's going to go by fast." Anika turned to the contestants. "You got that? Keep your eyes on the pies everyone! Let's. Get. Started!"

With that, Tori put her recipe into the holder and trotted to the refrigerator—she knew which one was hers this time—to pull out her ingredients and haul them back to her station. Running through the key steps of her recipe in her head, she switched on the oven then turned her attention to creating her mise en place. With numerous bowls set out around her cutting board, she was ready to measure, peel, chop, and prep all her ingredients before getting into the thick of assembly and baking. Her first priority was the crust: She was making a sturdy pastry with vegetable shortening instead of butter so it could stand up to the meat and vegetable juices without getting saturated. In a matter of minutes, she had wrapped two balls of dough and set them in the fridge to stay cold as long as possible.

Next up was prepping the filling, which involved a lot of washing and chopping. She was in the midst of cutting a handful of pitted prunes into quarters when the judges entered her peripheral vision, followed by Ted the videographer and his ever-present camera. This was her cue to look up and smile.

"Hello, Tori," Kendra said. "What are you making for us?"

"Cock-a-leekie pie," Tori said, scooping the dried fruit into a bowl and moving on to peeling a couple of substantial carrots.

"Oh, I love a good cock-a-leekie pie," Trevor said as if he was tasting every syllable. "How are you making this recipe your own?"

"I'm using chicken thighs because they have a much richer flavor than the white meat," Tori explained, pointing to the package of chicken on the counter, "and along with the leeks, I'll add some carrots to give the filling some color and offset the intensity of the prunes."

"Why did you choose this dish to make today?" Kendra asked.

"I like this better than a traditional chicken potpie," Tori said. "It's a little elegant without being too fancy, and it doesn't have all of that gloppy white gravy. Besides, sautéed leeks are the best thing ever, delicate and slightly sweet. Am I right?"

"I have to agree with you there," Trevor said. "So, given what you told us during your audition, I have to ask: Who are you baking for today?"

The question startled her. She barely remembered what she'd said during that anxiety-ridden interview, and now she was being quizzed on it. The answer was obvious, though. "Oh, I'm baking for you and for Chef Kendra today. I hope you love it."

That conjured the barest hint of a smile from Kendra. "Sounds great," she said. "Thanks, Tori."

The troupe moved on to Brenda, who, Tori realized as they interviewed her, seemed to be making precisely the type of white-gravy chicken potpie she had just criticized. She mentally wished her good luck and got back to slicing her carrots, idly wondering what it would take to earn a full-on grin from Kendra in her lifetime.

It wasn't long before she was inhaling some of the best scents in the world: bacon, butter-fried chicken, sautéed leeks, and fresh thyme. For Tori, the aroma conjured a storybook grandmother serving dinner to her snow-frosted grandchildren after a day of sledding: a hearty plate of warmth and comfort. She'd brought porcini mushrooms but decided at the last minute to nix them, not wanting to mess with the balance of meat and vegetables. The filling complete, Tori took her oversize saucepan to the freezer so it could cool quickly before being spooned into the pie shell.

This is going well, she thought to herself. Pulling the pie dough from the refrigerator, she walked back to her workstation and spotted Kendra off in the wings. She was watching her. Tori felt her heart skip a beat and told herself she was just glad the judge had caught her doing something correctly for a change. She was about to wipe down the cutting board when she spotted a four-ounce glass bowl, filled with neatly quartered pitted prunes. Which were supposed to be in the cooked pie filling. And clearly were not.

"I don't believe this," she said under her breath.

She considered her options. She could sauté them for a couple of minutes and throw them in the freezer while she got the crust ready, or she could just stir them in with the rest of the mix before baking and take her chances that they might be a bit chewy.

"One hour left for the savory Pie Challenge, friends," Anika called out. "No matter how you slice it, you have one hour."

That made her decision for her: toss in the uncooked prunes and let them fend for themselves.

As she rolled the dough, Tori attempted to clear her head. Forgetfulness wasn't her usual MO. Maybe she was getting too wrapped up in impressing the judges. Maybe she was trying too hard to impress one judge in particular. Frowning, she made a pledge to be extra careful from here on out.

A few minutes later, the cock-a-leekie pie—internally studded with uncooked prunes and topped with an egg-washed crust decorated with knife cuts in the shape of chicken tracks to vent the steam—was in the oven. At last, Tori took a seat and had a drink of water. She rubbed the soles of her shoes over the rungs of the stool to restore some feeling in her arches and scanned the room to see how her compatriots were faring. Charlotte was also taking a break, seated on her stool to Tori's left.

"How did it go?" Charlotte whispered rather loudly.

"It's in the oven. I'm glad for that," Tori whispered back.

Charlotte smiled then got up to switch on her oven light. Tori looked to her right. Brenda looked a little worse for wear, her brand-new apron spattered with flour and raw chicken juice.

"You doing okay there, Brenda?" Tori asked, walking over to her.

Brenda shook her head in shock. "I have made this pie at least once a month for ten years. I get onstage, and it's like I've never seen the recipe before."

"I know what you mean," Tori said.

"What is that all about?" Brenda asked, looking at the ceiling. "I mean, did the hot lights bake all the common sense out of my head?"

"It'll be okay," Tori reassured her, giving Brenda's shoulder a squeeze.

Ted appeared, tapping his camera. "Brenda, do you have a couple of minutes for a stand-up?"

She wearily checked her timer. "Sure. I'm not touching that sucker for at least half an hour." She followed the videographer out, asking if her hair looked okay, and Tori was on her own again, staring through her lighted oven window.

Less than an hour later, Anika called time just as Tori placed her pie on the cooling rack. Liam, the assistant director, called for a fifteen-minute break, and Tori made a beeline for Mel and Halla, whose workstations were in the back row.

"So am I the only one who feels completely unworthy to be here?" Halla asked.

"Why?" Tori asked. "What happened?"

"When I told the judges I was making spanakopita triangles with *store-bought* phyllo, Trevor looked like he swallowed a bug," Halla replied. "We only had two hours! What did he expect?"

"It looks great," Tori said, lying a little. Some of Halla's triangles had split, the innards oozing onto the plate.

"And Kendra interrogated me about whether spanakopita is even a pie because it doesn't have a crust," Halla fumed. "They're called 'spinach pies,' for crying out loud!"

"I'm sure it'll taste amazing," Tori soothed. "Mel, what did you make?"

"Shepherd's pie," Mel said. "I had to fiddle with the recipe this week to make it with a bottom crust. Usually, I just pile it into a casserole pan with the mashed potatoes on it. My family demolishes it." He shrugged. "The word *pie* is in its name, too. I don't know why they're insisting on a crust."

"Hey," Jayden said, joining the group. "What's wrong with Brenda?"

The four contestants looked straight ahead. Brenda was sitting on her stool at her workstation, hunched over, sniffling into a dish towel.

Tori hurried over. "Hey, what's wrong?" she asked quietly.

"My pie is a disaster," Brenda said, looking up from her towel. "It boiled over in the oven, and the crust burned in places."

Tori looked over her shoulder to see Brenda wasn't exaggerating. She turned back and put a hand on her shoulder. "Look, who knows what the judges will think? Maybe that's the way Trevor's dear old mum used to make it."

Brenda chuckled, wiping away a tear. "Maybe."

"And this is only the first bake of the day," Tori went on. "You have another chance to wow them this afternoon."

"That's true," Brenda said, looking a little more hopeful.

"Remember, all you have to do is be better than one other person to stay in each week," Tori said. "This may work out just fine."

"Thanks; you're right." Brenda took a cleansing breath. "How's my mascara?"

"Flawless," Tori said, giving her a hug.

"Places!" Liam called out. Tori looked back at Halla, Mel, and Jayden and gave them an okay sign. They nodded and went back to their stations. As Anika started her spiel to kick off the judging, Tori's mind was toggling between worrying about Brenda's pie and worrying that she was worrying more about Brenda's pie than her own.

Tori watched Jayden, then Natalie, take their works up to the front for tasting and evaluation. From her vantage point, she could hear what the judges and contestants were saying but couldn't see the pies themselves. The contestants had their backs to her, so she had to read their body language to assess their mood. Jayden presented a tamale pie with a masa crust: He stood straight and proud as they praised its flavor then slumped a bit when they deemed the crust as too dry. Natalie's entry, an asparagus tart with fontina and shallots, seemed impressive based on the judges' comments. Tori watched Natalie's arm movements from behind as she demonstrated how she'd braided a slender four-handed plait of dough to finish off the edges. Tori wondered why Natalie seemed so tense when all she did was succeed. After all, even though Trevor and Kendra had differing opinions about whether Gruyère would have been a better choice than fontina, they were still very impressed with her tart.

Charlotte went next. Tori had been so focused on her own baking that she didn't know what her neighbor had been working on until it was revealed at the judges' table: a classic quiche Lorraine. As soon as they cut into it, she heard Charlotte gasp: The crust was soggy, and the filling was slightly runny.

"Have you ever made this quiche before?" Trevor asked.

"I made it for the first time this week," Charlotte said. "I don't usually make this sort of thing. See, I like to make pie for dessert, not dinner."

"A quiche is less complicated than a lot of dessert pies," Kendra told her flatly. "You chose a classic dish without a lot of ingredients or frills. Being so simple, it has to be perfectly executed, and this is not. Not by a long shot."

Trevor echoed Kendra's evaluation with a more empathetic tone, and Charlotte thanked them before returning to her station, her eyes wide. Tori was sending a reassuring smile her way when she heard a small squeak to her right. She turned in time to catch Brenda whispering, "I still have a chance!"

Anika was back on mic. "Okay, Tori, please bring your savory pie to the judges' table!" she called.

Tori was determined to behave as if nothing could faze her: head high, big smile, and complete confidence with every step. "Here is my cock-a-leekie pie with chicken, sautéed leeks, carrots, and prunes," she said, setting the pie in front of the judges.

She scanned their faces. Trevor looked as open-faced and pleasant as ever. But Kendra's exacting expression seemed to say: *Don't you dare disappoint me.*

Trevor cut a sizable slice onto a glass plate then held it up for inspection from below. "The crust is nicely done, and the innards are staying put, as they should. Let's dive in, shall we?" He divvied the slice into three pieces, and the judges and host each took a bite.

"That's got a lovely flavor," Trevor rhapsodized. "This kind of pie could be dressed up for company by using pheasant or some other game bird instead of chicken, but then you'd miss the subtlety of the leeks."

Expressionless, Kendra was quiet for a moment—the longest moment in recorded history—then said, "I really don't like dried fruit."

Of all the reactions she'd expected—or dreaded—this hadn't been on Tori's list. "Well, that's unfortunate," she said, forcing out a small laugh.

To her surprise, Kendra laughed, too. "Especially raisins or anything that resembles raisins," she elaborated. "That said, the prunes complement the flavor and add some chewy texture that's a nice contrast to the silkiness of the chicken and leeks. I agree with Trevor: It's quite delicious." She gave Tori a small nod. "Nice work."

While the contestants dove into a mystery Bake and Switch pie recipe after the lunch break ("You have just three hours, people—and the time is going to *pie* by, so . . . Let's. Get. Started!"), Anika, Trevor, and Kendra stepped backstage into their green room and were immediately swarmed by the hair and makeup team.

Before *Bake-o-Rama,* Kendra hadn't thought of herself as good-looking; years of teasing in school about her height combined with her dislike of dresses and her unusual eye color had done a number on her body acceptance. Plus, she'd always told herself, it wasn't worth her time to try to be pretty, even if she'd wanted to: Why get all made up when she was going to spend fifteen hours in a hot kitchen? More than two years into the show, though, the ongoing touch-ups and brushstrokes and clouds of hairspray had become a kind of a spa experience. At first, she was afraid the show wanted to make her over into some sort of femme Chef Barbie loaded with contouring and false eyelashes. Instead, the team focused on making her look like herself on a really good day. She particularly appreciated being fussed over by the goth makeup artist who coveted her black hair and made her eyebrows look like Angelina Jolie's. They and the guy from Wardrobe adored Kendra's penchant for graphic tees and distressed jeans and found additional pieces that made her look fantastic and fierce. Instead of feeling like a dork with all those cameras trained on her, she'd begun to believe she deserved to be there—and looked good doing it.

Anika double-checked that her microphone was turned off then let out an irritated groan as she sat in her makeup chair. "I am sick to death of puns!"

"I could never do your job," Kendra said with real respect.

"I'm surprised *I* can some days," Anika said with a slight frown as a makeup assistant powdered her T-zone. "Trevor, what recipe did you give those poor people for the Bake and Switch? They looked completely freaked-out."

"It's a classic lemon meringue pie with a chopped almond crust," he replied with a note of defensiveness as the hair assistant spritzed his sides. "It's really not that difficult, especially these days. When I first made that recipe there was no such thing as food processors, and I had to chop the almonds by hand." He wagged a finger at Kendra, a sly smile on his face. "And Kendra, before you say anything, I can also confirm that I had to walk five miles in the snow to pick the lemons."

As she laughed, Kendra realized that for the first time since she'd debuted on *Bake-o-Rama,* she was having fun. Her morning at Trevor's home a couple of weeks ago had turned into an afternoon of the two of them banging out recipes for the entire season, then an evening exchanging culinary war stories that had brought them closer on a personal level. Kendra had had employers, she'd had staff, she'd had competitors, but she'd rarely had a work friend. Trevor was treating her as such, and it felt great.

Easing up on the snark pedal was still really tough, though. Kendra was trying to be gentler with her critiques, but she didn't want to candy-coat the truth, either, and hadn't found a happy medium yet. Then again, Tori had managed to make her laugh, which had been nigh impossible during Kendra's reign as #TheChopper. Tori was a woman of many gifts.

Before long, it was time to check on the cock-a-leekie cook and the others. "Trevor, you ready to go lurk and observe?"

"Anika, are you doing your rounds first?" Trevor asked.

"No, I'm having an eyelash emergency," she replied with her eyes closed, a makeup assistant doing their best to adjust the placement of her false lashes.

Clipboard in hand, Kendra followed Trevor out and circled around to the back of the group. The whipsaw drone of seven food processors rumbled around the studio as the bakers prepped the nuts for the crust. She took notes as Mel added in the dry ingredients, pulsing a few seconds before adding chunks of cold butter. He lightly greased the pie plate before pressing in the dough and set the crust in the freezer—required tasks that hadn't been spelled out in the instructions. He was doing everything correctly so far, reflecting the no-nonsense approach to baking she'd appreciated in him from the start: Rely on experience, do what needs to be done, and good things will follow.

In Mel's audition, he'd said he'd started to bake because he was trying to make sure his children, then grandchildren, ate better than the junk they'd pick up at the convenience store. Yet what started as a way to get a few more servings of wholesome food into his kids had turned into a hobby, then a passion for the former tile salesman. What Kendra found particularly interesting was how he seemed just as happy when a project totally failed as when it turned out perfectly. His rye bread had been dumpy, yet he'd taken it in stride and told the judges he was grateful to learn something new.

Kendra struggled to imagine what it would feel like to have such a lighthearted approach to the kitchen. As a teenager, she'd hungered to find something—anything—she could excel in, given her lackluster grades, unfavorable comparisons to her brother the math whiz, and inability to act on her interest in girls in a small Vermont town. Becoming an exceptional cook had been her ticket out of mediocrity, and holding herself to stratospherically high standards every time was the only way she knew to maintain her sense of self.

Kendra moved on to Charlotte, who was rereading the recipe aloud with Ted and Mike capturing her worried expression and hunched shoulders. She put the recipe down and raised her hands in surrender. "I have no idea what I'm supposed to do with this instruction: 'Make crust with ingredients above then blind-bake.' Bake for how long? Any particular way we're supposed to mix the ingredients? Give me a clue here!"

Kendra's theory from this morning's sad quiche Lorraine was confirmed: While Charlotte knew certain types of baking incredibly well, others were a mystery to her. Messing around until she figured things out would be fine if she was experimenting at home. On this show, though, there wasn't time for that. Her lack of pie expertise was a red flag. Right as she was about to write "disaster magnet" in her notes, though, Kendra stopped herself. Charlotte had not given up. She was doing her best with what she had. Her best might not be enough—but it was too soon to judge for sure.

Next up was Jayden, whom Kendra liked for his no-nonsense approach while always being quick with a joke to break the tension. She watched him stir the sugar, lemon juice, and cornstarch for the filling, keeping an eye on his crust in the oven. His other ingredients were unmeasured and still in their canisters and bags, and there was a thick layer of flour and nut dust on his cutting board. That kind of creative mess was not an issue if he was cooking for his wife and four little boys, Kendra thought, but if he had any serious plans for bringing his talents to a professional level, he'd need to learn how to keep things neat for efficiency's sake, not to mention the health department's.

Kendra looked around the studio to see where Trevor was in his circuit. He was near the front, just out of Natalie's line of sight, his glasses low on his nose and his hand covering his mouth to avoid telegraphing his reactions to what he was seeing. This meant there was no reason to delay any longer: It was her turn to observe Tori.

The camera was right at her elbow as Tori whisked the egg yolks in a bowl. "Making the filling is all about managing the heat," she explained, pouring in a bit of her sugar and lemon mixture. "Whisking in only a little of this hot stuff at a time allows the egg temperature to rise slowly. That's also why I'm mixing them in a glass bowl instead of the saucepan, which is still really hot. If you dump them together all at once, you end up with sugary, lemony scrambled eggs." She continued whisking then poured the thickened liquid back into the saucepan and put it on the stove. "It'll just need a couple of minutes on the heat, and after I toss in the lemon zest and butter, I'll put it in an ice bath to stop the cooking process all together."

Kendra was rapt. Tori was a natural at narrating her process, and her technique was spot-on. There was more to it, though. Watching her talk through the steps, Kendra followed Tori's ballerina-like hands, lithe and expressive with slender fingers and narrow wrists. She moved from one task to the next like it was choreographed, scooping the butter and lemon zest into the filling and stirring it together with an effortlessness that was mesmerizing. Tori also had a warmth to her voice that drew Kendra in; even though she knew the instructions for lemon pie filling backward and forward, she found herself hanging on Tori's every word.

Jotting down some notes, Kendra thought about the people she'd been attracted to in the past. Kendra's type was usually more hard-edged and outwardly ambitious, and Tori seemed completely different. And then there was the fact that Tori was a teacher, which was not a point in her favor since Kendra had a hate-hate relationship with public education. Yet there was just something about Tori that made Kendra feel . . . welcome.

"Your turn on stage left, my dear," Trevor whispered in Kendra's ear as he walked past.

Kendra dutifully observed the rest of the contestants, but her mind kept wandering over to Tori's station. She wanted to have an actual conversation with Tori, discuss topics way more interesting than tempering an egg mixture, watch her illustrate her opinions with those elegant hands. But something as innocent as going out for coffee would go against their contracts, which wasn't fair to Tori or a wise business move for herself. As she watched Natalie's precise measurements, Kendra wondered why she was letting herself imagine going down this road. She didn't even have Tori's phone number, and she couldn't ask for it without cameras popping up over their shoulders. Plus, what about her neutrality as a judge? She was already getting distracted while assessing Tori's performance, and that was a dangerous sign.

Even as she told herself to snap out of it, Kendra's attention wandered back to Tori's station. The baker was sweeping a rubber spatula back and forth over the pie filling to even it out before baking, her hips swaying slightly. Kendra wouldn't have been surprised if Tori was humming to herself. She was delightful—full of delight.

Kendra looked down at her clipboard to collect her thoughts. She needed this whole *Bake-o-Rama* gig financially and to boost her reputation and visibility. It was ridiculous to compromise any of that. She silently reupped her commitment to evaluate Tori, and everyone else, based solely on merit: Each episode, the bakes had to be more important than the baker. Still, she had to wonder, *What if?* What if this confusion she was feeling was actually a sign she should pay attention to because something amazing was about to start? What if Tori felt a similar spark between them, and Kendra just let that slip away? *American Bake-o-Rama* was Kendra's job—but what about her life?

There had to be some way to get a message to Tori. Something casual and private to let Tori know Kendra thought she was doing a great job and that she seemed to be a great person. A way to plant a seed that maybe, just maybe, could blossom well after the season was over.

"Have you finished your notes?" Trevor whispered behind her. Kendra started, jolted from her swirling thoughts back to set.

And then a lightbulb went on.

Notes.

Kendra smiled. "Not yet."

"Bakers, come forward," Anika called out from Kendra's side.

The lemon meringue challenge having wrapped before dinner, Anika, Kendra, and Trevor were back onstage, ready to announce the week's Best Baker and the contestant who would not return. The show would be edited to make it look like Kendra and Trevor made their decision within minutes of sampling the second dishes. In reality, they documented scores after each tasting. Then, with those numbers as a starting point, Trevor and Kendra sat in the green room to hash out who was in and who was out, sometimes adjusting their scores in light of the other judge's perspective. Sometimes their opinions ranged widely; there had been times when they'd debated for more than an hour before coming to an agreement and handing off their score sheets to the production team for verification. Only then could they stand in front of the tired, anxious bakers and deliver their fates.

"We start with Best Baker, which is one of the best parts of the show for me," Anika said, scanning the weary, hopeful faces of the seven contestants standing before them. "This week was the Pie Challenge, and one baker aced her savory bake and gained a braided edge over the competition. Her lemon meringue pie stood sky high as well. Natalie, you are this week's Best Baker!"

Natalie offered a coy smile as the rest of the bakers applauded. There had been no question in either Trevor's or Kendra's mind: The blonde in black deserved to win this round.

"Unfortunately, along with the good, we also have some bad news," Anika said, her tone turning from cheerleader to newscaster.

"Even this early on, it's hard to see anyone go, but that's how we have to do things at *Bake-o-Rama.* I am sorry to say that this week, we must say goodbye to . . . Charlotte."

The line of contestants quickly turned into a mob of support around their fallen comrade. Though this happened each episode, it surprised Kendra every time. Each contender, no matter how tenderhearted, had to know that they couldn't win unless other people left. It could be because they'd been well trained by reality television: A loss required a bittersweet goodbye, since that's what the audience at home would expect. Maybe the bakers understood their roles in this fake little drama and were playing them out for the cameras?

But looking at the group today, Kendra had to admit that she was witnessing something much more genuine. She watched Tori speak to Charlotte, and while Kendra couldn't hear what she was saying, Charlotte was smiling through her tears by the end of the conversation. That didn't seem contrived at all. Tori was doing what she'd done earlier in the day when Brenda was having a meltdown: sharing genuine kindness and concern, probably seasoned with a dash of hope. It was the opposite of what Kendra had experienced in her lonely early years as a chef. She, and many of the chefs she knew, chalked up the toxic atmosphere of a lot of professional kitchens to hazing: What didn't kill them made them stronger. What if she'd met someone like Tori back then instead?

What about now?

Trevor tapped Kendra on the arm. "Time to dive in." The judges joined the melee to congratulate Natalie and offer positive final words to Charlotte as Anika taped her outro to wrap up the episode. To demonstrate she was turning over a new leaf as a nonchopping judge, Kendra even made the effort to hug Natalie, who was as awkward about it as Kendra felt, and Charlotte, who held on too long and sniffled in her ear. Kendra was relieved to step away.

Following Anika's final take, Cal picked up his bullhorn. "Cut! That's a wrap. Thank you, folks! Great show!"

"And everyone, be sure to pick up your take-home gift before you head out," Liam chimed in. "They're courtesy of Kendra this week. Enjoy!"

The stage lights shut off as the white ceiling lights turned on, bathing the room in stark fluorescence. Kendra turned to find Tori standing behind her, untying her apron. She had only a split second to take advantage of a legitimate opportunity to say something unscripted.

"Hey," Kendra said, her voice cracking, which was freakishly embarrassing.

"Oh, hi!" Tori said, smiling in apparent surprise. She corralled a couple of strands of strawberry blonde behind her ear that had worked loose from her ponytail.

"Good work today," Kendra said as neutrally as she could, given there were dozens of witnesses milling around them. "You're getting more at ease with every round."

"Thank you," Tori said. "I feel like I'm going a mile a minute most of the time."

"Well, I look forward to seeing you—seeing *what you'll do*—next week." Groaning inwardly over her Freudian slip, Kendra began backing away toward the green room but not before looking back and calling out, "Safe home, and don't forget to get your gift box before you go."

She didn't want to overdo it, but she had to make sure Tori got the message.

"Joey and Johnny, how could you shed in my mixing bowl from way over there?"

Tori held up a long, brindled hair and shot her Maine coons an accusatory look. The enormous felines, sprawled on the dining room floor like a pair of shag throw rugs, blinked apathetically. They'd had the same reaction earlier that afternoon when Tori had asked them why her cheddar tarragon wafers tasted like sand.

In two days, she'd be back in the studio for the Cookie Challenge. The brief for this week's taping was to be prepared to make two types of savory cookies to serve as appetizers as well as four sweet recipes to be presented in a festive holiday box. It was not lost on her that Kendra had made her fame and fortune with cookies; the pressure would be a thousand times worse than the Pie Challenge. If Tori were a betting woman, she'd wager there would be no Bake and Switch: The contestants would make their own recipes for both challenges to test their creativity and skill in a field ruled by the Cookie Queen.

After the prune predicament, Tori had set aside any recipe with raisins, cranberries, dates, or any other squishy offenders. She'd also made a field trip to the Chippy Chunk on Fisherman's Wharf earlier in the week to see what the celebrity chef considered a great cookie. She bought the assorted baker's dozen, paying about three times more than for any cookies she'd ever purchased, and took them home to analyze. The box was divided into two sections. The one labeled "Fancy Schmancy" featured unusual ingredients and masterful execution. The strawberry black pepper bar had razor-sharp edges, and the top of the pomegranate Linzer cookie was slightly offset to showcase the vivid fruit filling. Curry macaroons, chili chocolate shortbread, and sesame seed sandwich cookies were some of their bestsellers according to the staff, which told Tori that there was a market for sophisticated sweets at a high price point, at least in the Bay Area.

None of the obvious craft and innovation could sway Tori's personal opinion, though: The best cookies in the world required chocolate chunks, walnuts, brown sugar, and enough eggs to make high-strung parents worry about their children contracting salmonella if they ate the dough raw. Apparently, Kendra agreed with her, because those gooey, delicious options were in the box section labeled "Kids' Klub." According to the colorful little card that came with the order, they were perfect for "however old you are today." Tori agreed, eating those first.

How Tori was going to live up to Kendra's gastronomical standards was a mystery. She had several tried-and-true recipes her friends adored, but she continued to worry whether they were going to be impressive enough. Her paper bag apple pie from the early audition still haunted her. She also had to get out the glue gun and art supplies to create a holiday box in which to present the cookies. She was still finalizing a design but was certain that there would be no glitter involved; otherwise, she'd be picking it out of the cats' fur until Christmas actually came.

And along with those two puzzles, there was one more to figure out: Kendra.

Now that she'd survived two sets of competitions evaluated by the celebrity judge, Tori could understand how Kendra had gotten her intimidating reputation. Plus, she'd been watching old *Bake-o-Rama* episodes as research while she was practicing in the kitchen. During a Cake Challenge last year, a guy named Paul had chosen petits fours as his sweet recipe, explaining at the top of the show that he'd never made them before but, "since cakes are my jam, I know I've got this!" Unsurprisingly, he had struggled at every turn, and he'd come to the judges' table with what looked like hunks of melted candle wax. When Kendra asked why he chose such a complicated dish, he shrugged, saying, "I don't know. I thought they were like cake pops, only square."

The camera had immediately cut to Kendra. "What is a cake pop?" she asked Trevor in miffed confusion.

"I believe it's a frosted ball of cake on a stick, like a lolly," Trevor offered.

"Cake on a stick?" she asked Paul, her voice even, her eyes like lasers. "What does that possibly have to do with a petit four, Paul?"

"Well, they're both dipped in icing and can be decorated and, uh . . ."

"You can't just whip up a plate of petits fours," Kendra had cut in, her tone icy. "They require a lot of skill and practice. How much did you practice, Paul?"

"Uh . . ." The cameras moved in for a close-up of the hapless baker, who'd said nothing as a large bead of sweat made its way down the side of his face.

That earned a *humph* and a raised eyebrow from the judge. "I'll answer for you," Kendra said. "Not enough."

As relentless as Kendra was, Tori understood her point. Paul had been cocky and cavalier about technique, something Kendra took very seriously. Although her delivery was curt, she was calling him out, not calling him names. That had been true when Kendra questioned Tori about her apple pie, too. Kendra was speaking from her position as a highly regarded chef. She did not suffer fools gladly.

Maybe she didn't want to coddle contestants because that wouldn't prepare them to succeed in the food industry. Maybe, because she was a female in power, people confused her assertiveness with aggression.

On the flip side, that meant a compliment from Kendra had to be earned. And, given what was in her gift box from Saturday's show, Tori may have just earned one.

With a nod to the challenge ahead, the cast and crew had received gifts personalized with their names: a gold silk brocade version of a Chinese take-out box, complete with a four-flap interlocking top and a wire handle, with an oversize fortune cookie inside. Curiosity nearly got the better of her during the commute home, and she'd cracked the cookie open as soon as she'd pulled into her driveway.

There were two fortunes. One was folded inside the cookie, with lottery numbers printed on one side and *Way to go today! Don't let your confidence crumble!* on the reverse.

The other fortune was crammed into the side of the cookie. Its message, unsigned and handwritten with a Sharpie in block letters on a torn scrap of paper, read, *You're a talented, compassionate baker. I admire that. Good luck next week.*

All week, Tori had been asking herself what in the world she was supposed to make of this second fortune. Had every person on the show received the same handwritten message? She'd stopped herself before texting Mel to ask; something told her this fortune was just for her. Had Kendra written it—and was that why she'd encouraged Tori to pick up her gift before she left? Obviously, there was no way she could ask Kendra. That would be too weird and possibly against some rule or regulation for the show. Besides, she didn't want to give any indication that, well, she was fighting off a crush on Kendra after being around her the past few weeks—a crush that had not been helped once she'd had her Chocolate Slab drop cookies, courtesy of Chippy Chunk. Anyone would fall a little in love with Kendra after eating one of those.

Tori's phone buzzed. It was the twins, right on schedule for their video chat from New York. She turned off her Talking Heads playlist, propped up her phone, and hit Accept.

"Hi!" Milo said as Mia situated herself in front of their screen.

"Wow, Mia, you look like a superhero," Tori said. "Did you dye your hair?"

"Affirmative." Mia turned left then right, showing all angles of her navy-blue angular cut with scarlet undertones. "Barb took me to the salon she goes to in Chelsea. I told her and Mommy that I wanted to try out a different look before classes start. New school, new me."

This was news to Tori, who would have happily taken Mia (and Milo, who she saw could really use a haircut) to her stylist in Eucalyptus Point.

"Barb said that's where we'll get our hair done for their wedding, too," Mia continued.

All this talk about her ex-wife's fiancée detonated a tiny rage bomb deep in Tori's stomach. She wanted to be the Cool Mom who took her kids for superhero haircuts; instead, the stepmom-to-be was snatching the crown. How dare Barb try to buy her way into Mia's heart right when Tori was adjusting to the reality that her little girl wasn't going to be at home anymore.

Thankfully, being on camera for a few weeks had taught Tori how to smile when she felt like screaming. "You look great, honey," she said.

"How's the show going?" Milo asked. "We have all kinds of questions."

"I'm sure you do. Can you close your door?" Tori had intended to brief them about her progress each week, but they were calling from her ex-wife's place with their iPad on speaker. She didn't want to deal with the fallout if Shelby was eavesdropping.

Mia closed the door then plopped back in front of the screen. "What challenge are you working on this week? Is it the Cookie Challenge?" Tori wasn't sure how to respond, and the twins, interpreting her hesitation correctly, cheered and high-fived each other.

"It *is* the Cookie Challenge!" Milo crowed. "We *knew* you wouldn't be eliminated this early on. Yay, Mom!"

Mia's tone turned businesslike. "You're going to be competing against Kendra more than the other bakers. Whatever you do, no dried fruit."

Milo nodded. "Kendra hates that."

"Especially raisins," Tori said, grimacing. The twins' eyes widened in horror. "Any other helpful hints?"

"Focus on flavor over form. It's got to taste amazing, or she'll take off points," Milo said.

"Don't go so extravagant that you get out of your depth," Mia added. Tori nodded, thinking of Petit Four Paul.

"But don't be too basic," Milo warned. "She's going to want a variety of textures and flavors and styles, and each one needs some flair."

Mia jumped in. "Oh, and you have to practice your royal icing work, Mom. When you tried decorating sugar cookies last Christmas, it looked like toothpaste."

"And tasted like it, too—way, way too much mint!" Milo stuck his tongue out and wretched.

The twins paused, probably because Tori looked as overwhelmed as she felt. Mia tilted her head and smiled. "Don't overthink this or try to get into Kendra's head. Just relax and be yourself, Mom."

"You're going to do great," Milo added. "We wouldn't have nominated you if we didn't know you could win this thing."

Tori was touched.

The following Saturday, though, Tori was glad just to survive until the lunch break. She and her fellow contestants had spent a grueling morning on the savory portion of the Cookie Challenge. There'd been no Bake and Switch, as she'd predicted, and the bakers had used every last second to make two dozen each of two varieties of cocktail-party-ready savory cookies, each perfectly alike, each alike in perfection.

As during the Pie Challenge the previous week, there was some disagreement about what exactly qualified as a "cookie." Trevor said Jayden's Parmesan twists skirted the rulebook since they were made from puff pastry. Mel got pushback for creating bland cookies that only came to life when he put salmon roe and crème fraîche on them; they had to taste good on their own, according to Kendra. The judges hadn't exactly gushed over Tori's rolled sesame wasabi wafers and Pecorino Romano thumbprint cookies with garlic jam either. Even after making three batches of each for practice at home, it'd been rough going in the studio. Tori had to wrap each incredibly delicate wafer around a wooden spoon handle while still warm, let them cool and set into a cylindrical shape, then slide them off without any cracks, breaks, or complete disintegration into crumbs. Kendra was quick to note that only twenty of the required two dozen were completely intact, which Tori knew lost her points. When it came to the thumbprints, Trevor's take was that her cookies were too salty and her jam too sweet.

She was exhausted by the time she got into the lunch line on the terrace. On top of the morning's stressors, Tori had invested a lot of energy into forcing the Kendra conundrum to the back of her mind to concentrate on her cookies, though she hadn't been entirely successful. Every once in a while, her attention would drift over to Kendra, who was hard to miss in a tomato-red, silk-screened long-sleeved tee with NOM NOM NOM written across the front below a dinosaur munching the San Francisco skyline. Her hair was swept off her face in a twist held in place with a tortoiseshell barrette, making her bombshell cheekbones even more unavoidable.

Tori plopped onto a picnic bench and tore into her sandwich. She needed carbs and protein stat, followed by sugar and salt, which were waiting for her at the bottom of her box lunch in the form of a brownie and a bag of organic corn chips. The fruit cup, with its noble commitment to nutrition and health, was going to have to wait its turn. Mel, Brenda, Jayden, and Halla soon sat down at her table, equally ravenous.

For a couple of minutes, they ate in silence. Then, in a quiet voice, Brenda asked, "So, am I allowed to say I did really well?"

"Absolutely!" Tori said. "That's terrific."

"Good for you," Mel agreed.

As Brenda described the judges' reaction to her cheddar cheese coin cookies, Natalie walked toward their table. Mel smiled and slid over to make room for her to join them, but she kept going without so much as a hello.

"That was weird," Halla said.

"That was typical," Brenda said. "I'm stationed next to her this round, and every time Mike and Ted come over for her commentary, she glares at them. I don't know if she's said a word on camera yet."

"I'd give her a pass," Mel said, waving them off. "We're all under a lot of pressure. Maybe she's just really shy or needs time alone to prep for the next challenge."

"Right. We don't know what her story is," Tori added. "And you have to hand it to her: She knows her stuff. She hasn't had a challenge go wrong yet."

"What's *that* like?" Jayden said with a frown.

They went back to eating and chatting for a few minutes, then Tori felt a tap on her shoulder. "Hey there, got a couple of minutes for Q&A?" Ted and Mike were geared up and ready to go.

"Of course. Good luck this afternoon, everybody!" Tori followed the video team to take her place on the *X* on the patio.

"Can we move so I'm not squinting so much?" she asked.

"We need the direct light," Mike said. "Squinting is better than a shadow across your face."

Once the camera light turned green, Ted gave a hand signal and prompted her first response.

"For the sweet part of the Cookie Challenge," Tori said, "I plan to make four of my family's favorite Christmas cookies: Russian tea balls, espresso shortbread hearts dipped in chocolate, mixed nut bars, and lemon rosemary macaroons."

"Any worries about getting them all done in time?"

"It'll be tricky to get them all finished in time," Tori said. "The good news is that while one is cooling, I can bake the next one. Plus, they're all pretty straightforward."

Ted asked a few more questions about her experience making each cookie, her technique, and who Tori thought was doing well this week (Brenda, whose bacon cheddar coins looked and smelled amazing), then said, "Before we let you get back to the kitchen, how are the judges treating you today?"

That caught her up short. "Why do you ask?"

"Because we ask everyone," Ted said, cocking his head to the side. "Kendra enjoys being tough. She's made people cry."

"Kendra has high standards, and I respect that," Tori said. "She's earned her reputation in the baking world, and she expects a lot from us, especially if we ever want to do this professionally someday."

"What do you hope Kendra says to you this afternoon?"

Several options popped into Tori's mind. *Hey, Tori, I can confirm I wrote you that note—and hey, I think you're pretty special.* Or, *I caught you staring at me—but only because I can't keep my eyes off you.* Maybe even, *If you're as sweet as your gateau, I'd like a little bite.*

She cleared her throat. "I'd love for Kendra—and Trevor—to enjoy my cookies. But my hope this afternoon is more about what they *won't* say. I just don't want to hear the words, 'You have to go home.' " She smiled as broadly as she could without grimacing, hoping she looked less flustered than she felt. "Okay, guys, I need to go set up."

She barely had time to shake off the interview before the team was called back from the lunch break, and soon Tori was back at her station, her recipes and ingredients at the ready. She checked to confirm that her presentation box, which she'd created in the shape of a red sleigh with silver bells and crocheted snowflakes, was still set on the shelves behind her. The sleigh was there, next to a set of cookie cutters, a few bottles of food coloring, some toothpicks, and a couple of pastry bags she hadn't seen before.

Tori let out a deep sigh. "Oh, sugar."

"What's wrong?" Halla asked as she arrived at her station next to Tori's.

"They're going to do a Bake and Switch," she said, pointing to the similar supplies on Halla's shelves, "and I think we have royal icing in our future."

Halla's eyes widened. "I think you're right."

"Places, everyone!" Liam demanded through his bullhorn.

Tori hated sugar cookies. No matter who baked them, no matter how beautifully iced, she thought they had a texture and taste profile akin to Play-Doh. As a result, she hadn't made them but a handful of times, and without much experience to build on, Tori's decorating practice sessions over the past week had been utter failures. She had yet to make royal icing that wasn't the consistency of spackle, no matter how many YouTube demos she watched. She also hadn't gotten the hang of flooding a cookie with thinned royal icing either: Her overly gooey concoction tended to slip off the edges instead of staying put and making a clean, shiny surface. If Kendra expected her to do better with less time and fewer instructions, she was going to be disappointed.

And that was the last thing Tori wanted.

As the Cookie Challenge Bake and Switch began, the bakers turned to size up the ingredients and review the mystery recipe. By the looks on their faces, Kendra could practically read their minds:

1. The instructions say, "Using ingredients listed, make sugar cookies using a cookie cutter. Decorate with royal icing in the pattern of your choice. You must use the flooding technique as part of your design."
2. There has to be more to the recipe than this—a temperature setting, or what order to mix the ingredients, or if these need refrigeration—something else.
3. There isn't anything else.

At this point, they'd fall into one of two camps:

The first group would be thrilled: *I make sugar cookies all the time. This is like getting extra credit. Hooray!*

And the second group would not: *I have no idea how to make sugar cookies. I'm doomed.*

She scanned the room, congratulating herself for coming up with a challenge that was both simple and diabolical and still rooted in the kind of work a professional baker would have to be able to master. Natalie smiled first; it was no surprise she'd be in Camp 1. Soon afterward, Halla, Mel, and Brenda were grinning as well. Jayden even did a fist pump in the air.

The only one in Camp 2? Tori—and she was not a happy camper.

This was unexpected.

Kendra's first impulse was to rush over to Tori and find out what the issue was, or even call out, *Just kidding, everyone! No Bake and Switch today!* Instead, she followed Trevor and Anika to Jayden's station, where Ted and Mike were already set up to record.

"I hope you like eating spiders," Jayden told the judges as they approached his station.

"That sounds disgusting," Trevor said.

"Only if you hate coconut," Jayden clarified. "I'm making Chocolate Coconut Spider Bites."

"Great name," Kendra said, noticing that his ingredients were scattered haphazardly across his work surface. "What else is on the menu?"

"Witchy Lady Fingers and Eyeball Meringues," he said, measuring flour and dumping it into a mixing bowl, kicking up a small, white cloud in the process. "And as luck would have it, I was planning to make Black Cat Sugar Cookies already, so I can stick with my plan even with the Bake and Switch."

"I bet your boys love Halloween," Anika said. "Do you make these cookies for them come October?"

"Yes, and then I bake another round of treats the first week of November," Jayden admitted. "With four of them bringing home so much candy, I raid their stash to bake M&M cookies and peanut butter cup cupcakes. Then I make extra batches for my wife to take to work. Gotta get it cleared out before the next wave of chocolate hits at Christmas."

"Splendid. Thank you, Jayden," Trevor said.

The group moved one station over, to Brenda's. Kendra had been surprised she'd done so well in the morning round, not having been all that impressed during her Pie Challenge. She was feeding the dry ingredients into the bowl with the wet in the standing mixer. "Hello, Brenda," Kendra said, trying not to break her rhythm. "Tell us about your holiday cookies."

"Welcome to Hanukkah Central!" Brenda said. "I am making Apricot Rugelach, Black and Whites, and Dreidel Surprise cookies."

"What's the surprise?" Trevor asked.

"Gelt," she said proudly. "I slip them between two cookies, seal everything together with frosting, and surprise! It's a sandwich cookie."

"Are you ready for the sugar cookie challenge?" Anika asked.

"Oh, yes," Brenda said, taking the dough from the mixing bowl and flattening it on a piece of plastic wrap. "I was all ready to make Sugar Stars of David anyway. It was like you read my mind!"

Next, Natalie took them through her First Day of Spring spread, Mel presented his suite of Valentine-themed cookies, and Halla showcased her Eid sweets. Like Jayden and Brenda, each baker had planned to make decorated sugar cookies as part of their original lineups. By the end of the circuit, Kendra was thoroughly disappointed with herself for not coming up with a more challenging challenge.

Then they arrived at Tori's station, where she was brutally chopping walnuts with none of the lyric choreography Kendra had admired the previous week.

"What are you planning for us today?" Kendra asked.

"I have a sleighful of Christmas cookies coming right up," Tori answered, her holiday cheer laid on thick. "I'm making Russian tea balls, espresso shortbread hearts dipped in chocolate, and lemon rosemary macaroons, which are all family favorites."

Kendra waited a beat, then asked, "What about the sugar cookie?"

"I'm waiting for inspiration to strike," Tori said, now sprinkling espresso powder into her mixing bowl. Kendra thought she could detect a pinch between Tori's eyebrows and a hint of desperation in her voice. Kendra's stomach sank. Had her note freaked Tori out?

"You're winging it?" Anika asked.

"Pretty much," Tori said with a shrug. "I've only made sugar cookies a couple of times before this week."

"How'd it go?" Kendra asked tentatively. She hadn't seen the baker off-kilter before, and it wasn't a good look.

"If I were tiling my bathroom, really well," Tori quipped. "The cookies were tough, and the icing was like grout."

As Trevor asked Tori about her other cookies, Kendra fought off the urge to remind Tori that she'd made enough cookies to know the secret to keeping these crisp, uniform, and strong enough to decorate: refrigerating the dough for at least thirty minutes to allow the flour to hydrate and the butter to stabilize. She imagined how Tori's face might light up if Kendra were able to demonstrate her own pro tip for keeping royal icing from drying out before decorating the cookies: push the extra air out of each piping bag once it was full of icing, then seal it off with a bread tie. Kendra could compliment her cool head and steady hands (those hands again—she couldn't not notice them). And while she was at it, she wished she could apologize for throwing Tori off her game with that stupid note. Why had she thought that was a good idea again?

Kendra's anxiety grew as she considered the possibility that Tori might lose this round. Of course, she wanted to keep seeing Tori week after week. But also, Kendra definitely didn't want *her* challenge to be the reason Tori was sent home. Still, she was surprised that Tori didn't have fluency with sugar cookies, which were fairly elementary. Looking at this as a judge, she was curious to see how

Tori would perform when she wasn't in her comfort zone. Especially with her knowledge of chemistry, Tori should be able to rise to the challenge if she thought it through and stayed calm. Could she come through?

"Well, we look forward to seeing how things turn out," Kendra heard Trevor say.

"Tori, you got this," Anika assured her. "Just relax."

"Keep a cool head and you'll do fine," Kendra said, thinking fast and hoping that was an innocuous way to give her a hint.

That got Tori to look up from rolling out her shortbread. "Will do," she said, smiling.

Kendra followed the team toward the green room, her heart racing. She had never given encouragement to bakers in the past. That was Trevor's role. Hers was to be strict, hard to please, and superprofessional (and a meme generator, apparently). She usually didn't care if a baker ran aground on camera, much less say anything to turn the tide. Was it obvious to anyone else that she'd tried to offer a clue to the prettiest baker on set?

"Hey, Cookie Queen!"

Deep in thought, Kendra nearly smacked into Buddy at the rim of the stage. The studio exec occasionally came on set to watch the taping, but usually the judges were given a heads-up, so this was an unwelcome surprise. "Hi, Veep," she said, hoping he'd remember how many times she'd told him to call her Kendra instead of that loathsome nickname.

"Rumor has it you gave everyone a gift last week," he said, with a conspiratorial smile. "A fortune cookie."

"Trevor and I came up with the idea to send everyone home with a token of our appreciation each week," she explained, wondering where the conversation was leading. "I brought them for the first week."

"Nice touch," the exec continued. "I wish I'd gotten one. How unfortunate."

"That was my oversight," she said, eager to placate him if it meant he'd leave sooner. "I'll have one sent to your office on Monday."

"No, no, I'm just joking with you," he said, grinning. "*Fortune* cookie? Un*fortunate*? Get it?"

Kendra forced out a chuckle, dying a little inside.

Buddy tapped his earpiece. "I've been listening in on your convos with the bakers this afternoon. You're really turning on the charm."

"I am?" she asked, willing her expression to stay neutral even as her pulse started to race.

"No," Buddy said. "Basically, you were cut-and-dried with everyone. Well, until you got to the end there, with that pretty little lady, Tori."

Now her emotions were ping-ponging between being annoyed at Buddy and worrying about what he was getting at. All she could think to say was, "Oh?"

"And if you're willing to take a note from me," he continued, "you should treat everyone like you do Tori."

"What do you mean?" she asked, her mouth dry.

"I like that you're showing your soft side after all this time," he said. "It basically shows you're evolving into a more supportive judge, maybe even a better person."

Kendra exhaled: Oblivious as he was, Buddy hadn't picked up on her secret crush. Still, she was aggravated that she was getting personality advice from this guy, of all people. "A better person?" she repeated.

"Our latest analytics show that your attitude has been tough on ratings. At first, people liked the drama, but now it just stresses them out," he said. "Our show's demographic tunes into *Bake-o-Rama* for a fun, uplifting experience. They don't want to see people *crumble* week after week—get it?"

"Yep," she said, hoping Buddy was finished. He wasn't.

"So, basically, what I'm saying is, keep it up. Keep giving out presents, keep giving people supportive comments, and keep trying to smile. You'll learn how one day, Cookie Queen!" He playfully tapped her arm with his fist.

"Copy that," Kendra said. As much as it annoyed her to hear it from Buddy, she was glad that her efforts were paying off. She tapped Buddy back in an imitation of team spirit.

"Atta girl!" Buddy said, removing his earpiece and heading to the tech table to return it. "And with that, peace out!"

Four hours later, Kendra, Trevor, and Anika were seated on the terrace, surrounded by various half-eaten holiday boxes. Once the cameras were rolling, Anika said, "Let's talk about our best bakers for this week's Cookie Challenge. Who did well?"

The contestants had learned their fates in person an hour ago and been sent on their way. This segment was always filmed later for efficiency's sake, but the host and judges had to speak as if they were still making up their minds. Getting this recorded was all that stood between Kendra and the late dinner waiting for her at Gamma Raye, so she was eager to get it right on the first take.

"This was a week where some bakers did well during one round then floundered during the other," Trevor began. "Success came to those who could manage their time to finish many different batches simultaneously before time ran out."

"That's what I saw, too, Trevor," Kendra said, her tone matter-of-fact. "For instance, Brenda did an impressive job during the savory challenge. Both her cheddar coins and rosemary tea biscuits were terrific, but when she had to do the four sweet recipes at the same time, she got way behind. Some cookies weren't even baked all the way through."

"Her Dreidel Surprise sandwich cookies were too hot to keep the gelt from melting, as well as the frosting and the other decorations," Trevor added. "Those were a disappointment."

"Then you had Jayden, who had a so-so morning but really came through with four clever and delicious Halloween treats," Kendra said. "When you're used to cooking for young kids, sometimes you think the sweeter or sloppier, the better. He hit the balance of taste and appearance just right. And his presentation was incredible. He's got some mad jack-o'-lantern carving skills, too."

"Natalie and Halla did solid work in both bakes," Trevor said. "Natalie's work is always neat as a pin, but sometimes I wish she'd let her flavors take a front seat over execution."

"I agree," Kendra said, experimenting with smiling a little as she delivered her assessment.

"And while a couple of Halla's batches were rough around the edges," Trevor continued, "her pistachio kahk and other cookies had complex flavors and lovely textures. I was very pleased with her work."

Anika spoke up. "Speaking of flavor, you have to give Mel a lot of credit after this morning's savory work, which tasted great—"

"Even if that flavor came from the toppings and not the cookies," said Trevor.

"He went in several delicious directions with his Valentine's Day spread, though," Kendra said. "As with Halloween, most cookies for that holiday are supersweet and gimmicky. Mel added in flavors you wouldn't expect, like toasted black sesame seeds in his chocolate wafer sandwiches, that were just amazing."

"We haven't talked about Tori," Anika said. "How did she do? When we announced the Bake and Switch, she looked like a kid who'd just dropped her ice cream cone."

"I noticed that as well, although she put her science teacher smarts to work and figured out the secret to superior sugar cookies," Trevor said. "That said, her Christmas cookie collection wasn't very innovative, and she didn't have the most original presentation compared to the others."

"But that's not necessarily a bad thing," Kendra said steadily. "I love making cookies more than any other dessert in the world, and I make a wide range of flavors and styles. But a simple shortbread heart with just the right thickness of semisweet chocolate, or a sugar cookie that has flavor and snap beneath a flood of sharp royal icing, can be the best eating experience around. And Tori delivered that today. In my opinion."

"Well, it seems like you may have some work ahead of you to pick our Best Baker," Anika said. "I'm glad we're leaving it to you two experts. I wouldn't know who to choose."

"Cut!" Cal said. "That should work, folks. Thanks, and have a great night."

With that, the sound engineers retrieved their microphones, and the video team started to clear out.

"Glad that's done," Anika said, getting to her feet. "I am outta here."

"Do you have dinner plans?" Trevor asked.

"With my agent," Anika said, grabbing her purse. "I've got contract negotiations coming up soon, and I have a list of suggestions for next year."

Kendra and Trevor exchanged a look.

"What sort of suggestions?" Trevor asked.

"Becoming a judge instead of just a host, for one thing," Anika replied. "Equal billing, more pay—even singing the *Bake-o-Rama* theme song. I can do so much more than read puns off a cue card, you know. Bye!"

The chefs watched her head off to the parking lot. "*Bake-o-Rama* has a theme song?" Kendra asked.

"Not now, not ever." Trevor shook his head.

They reentered the building to retrieve their things, and Kendra's stomach growled. She wasn't sure if she'd last until she got to the restaurant. "Is there anything left over?"

He scanned the side tables, where the remainder of the contestants' cookies were scattered for anyone to take. "There seem to be plenty of underdone rugelach and overdone dreidels."

"That's a hard no." Kendra joined him at the tables. "Brenda worked her butt off, but there wasn't any way around how bad her bakes went this afternoon. Ooh, there are two Chocolate Coconut Spider Bites left. Want one?"

Trevor nodded. "They were my favorite this round." He popped one in his mouth and sighed. "There is nothing wrong with chocolate and coconut together, ever. Thank you, Best Baker Jayden."

"Yes, thank you, Jayden," Kendra said, grabbing one for herself. She looked around for Tori's cookies, but they were gone. The crew had eaten enough entries over the years to identify and wipe out the best-tasting options each week. Kendra was glad they liked Tori's work as much as she did—especially the sugar cookies, which worked out better than those of some of her competitors who'd had a lot more experience with them.

That said, she was still hungry. There were some extra to-go boxes with no names on them near the doors, embossed with Trevor's Bay View Bistro logo. "Hey, Trev, what did you make for today's take-home gift?"

"A chocolate baby Bundt with cream cheese frosting," he said.

"Perfect," she said, taking a second box. "By the way, Buddy *basically* told me he likes that we're doing these gifts."

"I 'basically' don't care what he thinks, but how nice that he approves. Oh, could you check the message inside the box? The printer was supposed to correct a typo."

She opened the box and removed a square of light blue card stock with scalloped edges. "It reads, 'Good work, everyone! Next week will be a piece of cake!' then it has our names in italics," she said.

He looked over her shoulder at the card. "Thank goodness they fixed it. Originally it said, 'Next week will be a piece of *cane*!' Why can't anyone take their jobs seriously anymore, I ask you?" He picked up his leather portfolio off the sweets table. "Have a pleasant rest of your weekend, Chef."

"You, too, Chef." Before she followed him out, Kendra took one last look at the gift boxes, confirming that Tori had picked up hers, meaning another handwritten note was on its way home.

After a near sleepless night, Tori had gone to Cassie and Lee Anne's place in Bernal Heights for Sunday brunch. Now that they'd eaten their weight in omelets and sourdough and their plates had been cleared, she only had enough energy to stare out their back window at the jumble of houses farther down the hill.

"Hey, Tori, you still with us?" Lee Anne asked, poking her shoulder. "One too many mimosas?"

Tori stretched her arms in front of her, her spine releasing a series of loud pops. "Sorry, yesterday wore me out, and I didn't sleep well."

"Couldn't turn your mind off?" Cassie asked.

"Something like that," Tori said.

Exactly like that.

Once the winner and loser had been announced Saturday evening and she knew she was coming back for another week, Tori had screwed up her courage to find a way to talk to Kendra. Even if they only exchanged a few words, maybe it would be enough to confirm whether the judge had put that extra note in her fortune cookie—and why.

She'd planted herself where Kendra would have to walk past her after congratulating Jayden and consoling Brenda amid the post-competition hubbub. Sure enough, when Ted and Mike had taken Brenda aside to film her final spot, Kendra came right up to her, greeting her with a simple "Hey."

That one word had launched a migration of butterflies in Tori's stomach.

"Are you off to Gamma Raye?" Tori had said, surprised she could string that many words together. Up close, away from the cameras, Kendra's face was softer than when she was center stage. Perhaps it was because she could relax a little when talking to someone one-on-one. Or when she was talking to someone like her?

"Later, after I shoot one more scene," Kendra had said with a weary sigh. "We have a new manager doing his first weekend dinner service, and I want to make sure we don't have a line of angry patrons banging down the door. I need to go home first, though. I have to let Julia out, or she'll scratch a hole in the door."

"Julia?"

"My French bulldog," Kendra said quickly. "Sorry. That sounded like I have a great-aunt cooped up in my attic or something."

"I did wonder," Tori said, laughing. She couldn't help noticing how warm Kendra's smile was when she laughed.

"I have this kid drop by to take care of her on shoot days," Kendra went on, "but he can't come this late, and Julia gets pretty grumpy if she doesn't go out one last time before she conks out for the night."

"My cats give me an earful when I come home late," Tori said, grinning. "I don't know why they're so upset. When I'm home all day, they barely notice I'm there."

Out of the corner of Tori's eye, she saw Brenda, who was quietly gathering her cooking supplies to leave for good. Tori imagined that if she were in Brenda's shoes, she'd try to be invisible, too. She wouldn't want to say goodbye yet again to everyone. She'd rather just disappear.

Kendra followed Tori's gaze and they both watched Brenda slip out the door. "That has to be the hardest part about being a judge," Tori said. "Saying goodbye to a contestant every week, especially as you get to know them better."

Kendra faltered. "I mean, it's my job. The show doesn't work if I don't."

"Still, it has to be difficult," Tori said. "I don't think I could do it. I'd feel like I was crushing their dreams."

"It's the exact opposite," Kendra said earnestly. "I'm not doing a baker any favors by coddling them. I'm giving people honest feedback and telling them what it takes to succeed. You must know what I mean. You're a teacher. You don't tell a kid who's flunking that they're doing fine, right?"

"No," Tori admitted. "I tell them the truth. Still, I feel for the kid and what they're going through."

Kendra shrugged. "It's not personal."

Tori didn't buy that. "This job never gets personal for you?" she asked. If Kendra really admired her for being a "compassionate baker," she had to have some empathy mixed in with her pithy professionalism.

Kendra's mouth curled into a private smile. "It's not supposed to." As if she'd been caught doing something illicit, she immediately straightened up, her face impenetrable once more. "Don't forget your take-home gift," she said. "Have a good week." She gave Tori's arm a gentle squeeze before walking off to the green room. Tori watched her go, her hand covering her elbow to keep Kendra's touch from evaporating.

That smile and that squeeze: They had made sleep impossible Saturday night. And the note in her Bundt cake box—the handwritten, Sharpied personal one, not the corny, mass-produced card that must have gone to everyone—made it likely she wouldn't get any rest tonight either. It said:

> *I wish I had half your confidence. Every show, I wonder why they picked me for this job. With everyone's eyes on me, I'm sure I'm going to trip*

over my feet and look like an idiot. Not you, though. You're unflappable, a natural on camera and in the kitchen. Good job this week—see you Saturday.

Not only had Kendra dared to slip her another couple of covert compliments, which made Tori's cheeks turn pink, but the chef had also granted Tori a tiny glimpse into her brusque behavior. Kendra was self-conscious, maybe even shy. That could be why she didn't mince words: She didn't want to stand in front of the camera any longer than necessary. Tori also recognized that in sharing something personal with her, Kendra had risked more than a reprimand over contract clauses.

Tori wanted to tell her friends, but she worried about their reactions. Lee Anne would be delighted by the star-crossed-bakers aspect of the flirtation but worried about Tori getting hurt, while Cassie might encourage her to rat on Kendra to the producer and dodge any entanglements that could impact her future on the show. Tori couldn't argue her way out of either option, so she'd decided to stay silent on the subject.

"Sorry," Tori said, realizing she'd been gazing out the window again and shifting her eyes to Lee Anne and Cassie. "I have to work out some recipes this afternoon, plus I need to do my social media homework. The marketing team told us we have to 'create an omnichannel personal brand' ahead of the show's premiere, so I have to set up accounts beyond Facebook."

"Welcome to the twenty-first century." Cassie smirked.

"I hate this," Tori said. "Who's going to want to follow the daily exploits of a teacher who spends most of her summer break in the kitchen?"

"You're so much more than that, sweetie," Lee Anne said. "What's your handle going to be?"

"I don't know. It can't just be my name. There are so many other Tori Moores in the world."

"I have an idea," Cassie said, writing on a piece of scrap paper then pushing it toward her. "How about @MoreToriMoore? You'll be showing more of your life, your baking, your thoughts, your photos—you know, more of you."

"That's a good idea, Cass," Lee Anne said. "Tori, what do you think?"

She nodded. "I could live with that."

Back at her house, following a catnap replete with her cats pinning her to the sofa, Tori spread out her recipe ideas on sticky notes across her kitchen table. The baking brief for the coming week's Cake Challenge instructed the contestants to make sweet and savory cakes "to take to a community picnic." That raised a number of questions. Which community? The Northern California Coastal Association? LGBTQ+ Parents Club? Sequoia High Science Boosters? And what kind of picnic? A PTA potluck? A community baby shower? A cross-country team award ceremony? Who was she baking for this week?

She hoped that, after two weeks of sweet Bake and Switch recipes, they'd co-opt the savory category this time. While Tori had a delicious cornbread muffin recipe with poblanos and Monterey Jack, it wasn't very complicated and would be hard to glam up for the competition. Scanning the table and coming up short on the savory side, she realized she'd have to do some research this week to finalize her decision.

The reverse was true for sweet bakes. She had way too many choices. Tori regularly baked a wide range of cakes, from angel food to devil's food and everything in between. She was the person friends and co-workers would call on to make a celebration cake with flair. She had springform pans in every size to accommodate Baby's First Birthday or a Wedding Reception for two hundred fifty, and she could work wonders in fondant. She was more than ready, if she could just make up her mind.

Maybe it was better to focus on the theme as a filter to narrow the field. Despite the current cookout trends of upscale fare like chili lime shrimp kebobs and kale salad, her childhood memories were deep-fried and sugar-soaked. Picnic desserts conjured brightly colored treats alongside drumsticks and baked beans. Tori remembered how much she loved poke cakes, desserts of convenience that required four ingredients (white cake mix, Jell-O, water to mix them with, and Cool Whip) and four kitchen implements (a mixing bowl, a thirteen-by-nine-inch glass baking pan, a wooden spoon, and a knife to spread the Cool Whip as a frosting). She was able to make them all by herself by the time she was in third grade, which was a relief to her mother, who had little time to cook after working all day and even less desire to do so when they had a school obligation on short notice. When the cake was an hour out of the oven, young Tori would use the end of the wooden spoon handle to drill holes a few inches apart, then pour the liquid Jell-O over the whole business to seep into the crevices. After another hour in the fridge, she'd paint a Cool Whip cloud layer over the stripes of vivid red or orange or green that would be revealed when the cake was cut into squares. Not exactly haute cuisine, but she'd been proud of herself for being a real baker, and she and her classmates had gobbled them up.

This was her community: fellow bakers who got their start as bored kids with distracted parents and an unstoppable sweet tooth. And she thought she might know another person on set who'd be in the group with her.

Tori typed some search criteria into her phone, and up popped an old article she'd stumbled across in her recent googling, titled "My First Desserts." Among the anecdotes from chefs from Lisbon, Tokyo, and New York was a story from "Kendra Campbell, an up-and-coming pastry chef at Rhiannon in Phoenix." Tori enlarged the photo of twenty-eight-year-old Kendra, who was rocking an edgy fade with a long flop of bleached blond hair that skimmed her long black lashes. Scrolling through the article, she found and reread Kendra's contribution:

My mom was a single parent and nurse who worked nights, so my grandmother—we called her Gamma—stayed with my brother, Alden, and me a lot when we were growing up in Vermont.

Gamma was an amazing baker and loved fine dining because she'd lived in Europe as a part of the American diplomatic corps. She also saw the two of us kids as a way to make up for Mom's lack of baking talent. She had us mixing cookie dough and peeling apples before we could see over the kitchen counter, standing on little stools at her side so we could watch and learn.

Gamma's favorite dessert was strawberry shortcake, so when I was eight, I decided to make it for her birthday. It was November, not exactly when the fruit was in season, or even available, in New England. Mom took me grocery shopping on her day off, but we couldn't find fresh strawberries anywhere we went. By the sixth store, she had just had it. I remember Mom, sweaty in her winter coat, standing in the aisle with a bag of frozen strawberries in one hand and a jar of strawberry jam in the other, saying, "Pick one, Julia Child!" I opted for frozen.

I baked a respectable shortcake without a mix, and when Gamma came that evening, I topped it with strawberries and probably half a can of whipped cream since I wasn't allowed to use the standing mixer yet to make it from scratch. Thing was, I hadn't defrosted the strawberries or sliced them, so they were ice-covered rocks. Alden and I sang her "Happy Birthday" and served it to her. Before she took a bite, she asked to speak to the pastry chef—that was me! She asked me to describe the dessert, how I crafted each component, and what drink pairings I recommended for this course. She made me feel like a real hotshot, plus she stalled long enough for some of the berries to defrost enough to eat them without breaking a tooth.

> Her love and respect for baking and bakers is what I try to bring to my work every day.

Tori put her phone down, charmed all over again. This was how the first sparks of Kendra's dream caught fire: A little girl wanted her grandmother to know how much she loved her. Tori was so much like that herself as a kid, baking to take the burden off her single mom, making a small slice of their lives better through sugar and flour. She and Kendra had that in common. Plus, based on her note, Kendra shared some of Tori's imposter syndrome. Tori had no idea why the chef thought she was so calm on camera. Most of the time, she was worried about making a careless mistake and losing Kendra's respect, which would feel worse than being booted off the show.

As delightful as Tori found Kendra, when she let herself imagine actually dating her in some far-off reality, she did have some reservations. There wasn't much evidence that the chef would be a promising match. Kendra wasn't attached, so there had to be a good reason, or reasons, for that to be the case. With all the businesses and projects that popped up in Tori's internet search, the chef was also evidently a workaholic. She wasn't the monster the memes made her out to be, but she wasn't a warm person either. Even though Tori could understand why Kendra acted the way she did, she might not want to accommodate that behavior on a regular basis. And all that came with the wild assumption that Kendra, who had been photographed with so many celebrities, would really find Tori all that interesting. Affirmations via gift boxes were nice, but dating an amateur when you were at the top of your field would likely drive Kendra nuts.

Still, though . . . Tori's arm tingled where Kendra had touched it last week. Who was she to say it couldn't work? It was fun to at least *think* about. But now it was time to get back to the task at hand.

She located her go-to yellow cake recipe. Perhaps she could use this to upgrade the poke cake with higher-quality ingredients, real frosting, and nonsynthetic fruit flavor. Adding up the time she'd need to bake, cool, and slice the cake, she figured she might even have time to candy some citrus slices or shave some chocolate as garnish.

She was onto something. Something fun.

On Saturday, once Liam finished counting down from five, Anika's thousand-watt smile switched on beneath her perky sun hat. "Welcome back to *American Bake-o-Rama*!" she said. "Week number three is our Cake Challenge, and our bakers are creating dishes for a community picnic. We started our day on the savory side with a Bake and Switch full of surprises. Who knew that a lava cake with butternut squash and cheese could be so, so Gouda? Now we are ready for dessert. In true Cake Challenge fashion, we've got chocolate, we've got strawberries. We have ganache and buttercream and all kinds of toppings. I mean, what's not to love?"

Tori was doing all she could to focus on the love, since she was so sick of lemons, she almost had to hold her nose around the mixing bowl. Her morning had gone well—the Gouda in her lava cake oozed on cue during judging, which helped—but the sweet challenge was her best chance to shine a spotlight on her core expertise. Yet she couldn't shake the fact that it could still go south. After all, Brenda had considered herself to be a cookie maven last week, and this week she was sitting at home in New Jersey instead of standing next to Tori in a crisp tan apron.

"Trevor and Kendra, are you ready to visit the first station?" Anika asked.

Tori watched them nod as she stood motionless and barely breathing at Station 1.

Trevor motioned for Anika and Kendra to lead the way. "Ladies frost—I mean, first!"

"Nicely punned, Trevor!" Anika said as she walked toward Tori's workstation. The judges arrived with camera in tow a few seconds later.

"Tori," Trevor began, "tell us about your community and why you chose this cake to share with them."

"I've taught Biochem of Baking at our high school for several years," Tori began. "In addition to giving teenagers a different perspective on science, I also want them to inspire the next wave of students. Every year, we host second graders from the local elementary school to come to our kitchen classroom and make something with their high school 'baking buddies.' We encourage the younger kids to bring a parent or guardian along as well so they can learn a new recipe alongside their kids. That builds our school community, our science community, and our baking community all at once."

"That sounds like such a blast!" Anika said.

"Here is an example of what our baking buddies could make for our picnic," Tori went on. "A strawberry lemon poke cake with zested cream cheese frosting." She gestured toward her entry, cut into twenty-four identical squares with slices of candied lemon on top and displayed on an old-school slate chalkboard as the serving tray. The judges and Anika each took a piece to taste.

"I have never heard of a poke cake before," Trevor admitted between bites.

"You bake a sheet cake then use a wooden spoon handle to poke holes in it while it's still in the pan," Tori explained, miming the technique. "Then you pour the fruit puree over it, and it soaks down into the cake. Kids love poking the holes. It's their favorite part of the whole process."

"This is really bright and refreshing," Trevor said. "The acidity of the lemons balances the strawberries, and the tang of the cream cheese ensures the frosting doesn't get overly sweet."

"I've never had one of these made from scratch," Kendra said, taking another forkful. "Usually, you'd use a box mix and flavored gelatin."

"I tell the parents and students they can make it that way if they want to," Tori said. "I make a point to give them the upscale recipe and alternate versions in case they can't find, or can't afford, the ingredients we use in the classroom. If they can't get fresh berries, they can use frozen ones, or Jell-O, or even something totally different like chocolate pudding. We just want to inspire their love for baking as a family." She looked straight at Kendra. "They need to know they're doing great and can have some fun, you know?"

Without missing a beat, Kendra rewarded her with one of her devastating half smiles. "Well, I wouldn't want them to change a thing about this recipe," she said. "It could inspire a lot of little chefs out there."

"I agree," Trevor said. "Well done, and what a lovely story."

As the team moved on to the next baker, Ted the videographer turned around to throw Tori an enthusiastic okay sign. Tori tossed one back to him as well, giddy and relieved.

Walking from Station 1 to Station 2, Kendra's heart seemed to bounce around her chest like a funky percussion solo. Not only was Tori as fetching and talented as ever, but by the way she looked right at Kendra and smiled, there was no mistaking that *she liked her back*! She couldn't have been more obvious if she had been wearing a huge neon sign around her neck that said MESSAGE RECEIVED! It was all Kendra could do to keep from running behind the counter that separated them to give her a squeeze.

But no, she had some judging to do first. "Hello, Mel," she said—or did she sing? It was hard to tell. "Tell us about your community picnic dessert cake: Who is this for, and what does it represent?"

Mel cut a sharp figure in a black western shirt and black jeans, with lavish silver accents on his Stetson, bolo, belt, and boots. "We Texans go to a lot of barbecues, especially if you're a mariachi," he began. "A lot of times, the party doesn't start until my bandmates and I arrive. There's nothing better than looking out into our audience to see them singing and dancing along with our music, which has been part of their families' lives for generations. The one drawback is that since we're the entertainment, we usually eat last, and sometimes they run out of food before we finish our set. But if there's banana pudding on the buffet, our lead singer Alfonso finds the caterer and begs them to set some aside for him. So, in honor of Alfonso and my fellow Texas mariachis, I have made a banana pudding cake." The camera pulled in tight to take in the tall column of a three-layer, white-frosted cake dusted with crushed walnuts and topped with buttercream rosettes and vanilla wafers.

"Beautiful," Kendra said, her mind still on Station 1. It had been ages since she'd felt the giddy effervescence of a crush being returned. Everything was pretty darn beautiful at the moment.

Trevor cut a slice and divided it for Kendra and Anika. "That is a nice-looking interior," Trevor said. "It looks moist without being underdone."

Kendra had a bite, and as much as Tori's poke cake had transported her, this cake was marvelous as well. "Is that a hint of rum in the caramelized bananas at the top?"

"Smoked tequila," Mel said. "I broke out the good stuff."

"If I had one recommendation," Trevor said, "it would be to reel back the banana flavor. You have banana in the cake itself as well as a lot of fresh slices and the caramelized ones up top. Vanilla or yellow cake would have given our palates a break."

"The frosted decorations are wedding cake quality," Kendra added. "And though I absolutely love buttercream, you would have been better with a whipped frosting so the cake isn't weighed down or overly sweet."

"I see your point," Mel said affably.

"But this is delicious, and I'm sure Alfonso would absolutely love it," Trevor said, smiling. "Thank you, Mel."

"Yes, thank you," Kendra said, her mood as bright as the baker's belt buckle.

The other three bakers had varied levels of success. Halla's Thin Mint Layer Cake, a tribute to her daughters' Girl Scout troop, was eye-poppingly large, ornamented with half a box of the namesake cookies and sweet to the point of toothache. Jayden made the peanut butter cup cupcakes he'd mentioned the week prior to honor his wife's team of NICU nurses. As with Halla, the cupcakes took a back seat to the factory-made treats.

As the team moved on to Natalie at Station 5, Kendra caught a quick glimpse of Tori mouthing *Great job!* to Jayden with a thumbs-up. Kendra, her own hands buried in the pockets of her bomber jacket, gave Tori a clandestine thumbs-up as well.

"Hello, Natalie," Kendra said once everyone was in place. "Tell us about your community and what you've made for their picnic."

"I am a believer in the adage, 'Charity begins at home,'" Natalie said, her eyes somber behind her dark-framed glasses. "I'd like to bake for my parents and my siblings, but they could care less about what they eat. So when I want to create a recipe that's more elevated, I take a Saturday and make something just for myself."

"Yourself?" Trevor asked, baffled.

"Yes," Natalie said firmly. "My community is me, myself, and I. And what 'we' like is opera cake." She stepped aside to reveal two dozen rectangular pieces of the meticulous pastry, featuring thin layers of almond sponge cake cemented together with coffee butter cream and chocolate glaze, fanned out on a mirror with a pair of red roses crossed at one corner.

Had Kendra been chewing gum, she would have swallowed it. She reached over to select a pastry. "These are expertly crafted, as usual, Natalie," she said, wishing her own pastry edges could be that sharp at the restaurant. She took a bite and chewed carefully. "But the coffee's intensity overwhelms the dark chocolate's dense flavor. That makes the overall taste rather bitter."

"Bitter?" Natalie echoed, her expression one of complete disbelief.

Kendra nodded. "In my opinion, yes."

"As Kendra said, this looks impressive," Trevor said, "and given your love for complex recipes, it's no wonder you chose a cake with so many components. I'm not really seeing this as a food you'd find at a picnic, though."

"It's what I'd serve at my picnic," Natalie said flatly.

"No doubt," Trevor said, sounding bemused. "Be sure your form doesn't take priority over your food's function in the future. Thank you, Natalie."

The judging concluded, Kendra followed Trevor offstage as Anika shot her precommercial break wrap-up. He headed to the green room at a fast clip, to the point it was difficult to keep up with him in her chef's clogs. Once in the room, Trevor waved back toward the door. "Close that, will you?"

Once Kendra had secured it, Trevor placed his hand over his mouth and sighed. "That was the only community she could come up with? 'Me, myself, and I?' That poor woman."

Kendra was mystified. "Her family sounds like they don't appreciate her talent, but doesn't she have any friends or co-workers or anyone else to bake for? That's terrible."

There was a loud knock at the door. Kendra answered it and Anika slipped in, closing the door firmly behind her.

"You're talking about Miss 'Charity Begins at Home,' right?" Anika said in a gleeful whisper. "I don't know whether to be sad that she doesn't have any friends or glad no one has to listen to her day in and day out. What is up with that woman?"

"If she wanted to make an opera cake so badly, she could have at least come up with a better backstory," Trevor said. "Something like, she's baking on behalf of all the aged classical music fans who otherwise have no reason to keep living."

"I don't think it's funny," Kendra said, earning a surprised silence from her colleagues. "Whatever Natalie's deal is, I feel for her. She has a lot of talent but not a lot of support, and I can relate, you know . . . one humorless chef to another." She meant what she said, but given Trevor's unreadable expression, worried for a moment that she might have been better off just agreeing with them. Then he smiled and placed a gentle hand on her shoulder.

"You are right," Trevor said quietly. "I was being unfair, and I'm glad you spoke up and put me back on the better path. Now then, let's evaluate her bake. She didn't exactly satisfy the brief."

"That is true," Kendra said, glad to move on and gladder that Trevor had agreed with her, "but Natalie nailed the Bake and Switch as usual, and even though her own recipe was overcaffeinated and bitter, it was better than what Jayden and Halla did this week."

Trevor nodded. "We can't fault her for execution. What about Mel? He is quite the fancy cake man."

"I truly enjoy his baking, and it looked fantastic," Kendra said. "His cake was too banana-y for me, though. It lacked balance, just like Natalie's."

"How about Tori?" Anika asked. "She aced the morning as well as the sweet bake this afternoon."

"And her story was pretty compelling," Trevor said. "She must be a fantastic teacher."

"She must be," Kendra said, her smile rekindling as she brought out the score sheets. "Let's talk through this, Trev, then we can tape our segment while they're on dinner break and get this done by a decent hour."

An hour later, Anika was center stage, as energetic as she'd been at 8:00 A.M. that morning. "My *Bake-o-Rama* friends," she called out, "all the hard work you did today for our challenge was no cakewalk in the park. You all made your communities proud to have you represent them with your amazing skills and talents. Hats off to you!" She tipped the brim of her sun hat and continued. "Our Best Baker this week is someone who can make a butternut lava cake erupt with cheesy deliciousness. And her adaptable take on a picnic favorite can inspire kids of all ages to bake from the heart. Poke, poke! Tori, you're this week's Best Baker! Congratulations!"

Even in shock, Tori was effortlessly attractive. Idly, Kendra imagined striding over to her and elbowing the other contestants out of the way to give her a hug, or perhaps a kiss on the cheek.

Anika's voice rose above the bakers' congratulations, snapping Kendra back to her senses.

"What I have to say next is utterly no fun, because we have gotten so fond of all our bakers over the last three weeks. We have to say goodbye to one of you, and I am sorry to say . . . it's Halla."

As the other bakers gasped, Halla attempted, unsuccessfully, to fend off tears. Tori and the other contestants surrounded her as Anika wrapped the show a few yards away. Kendra knew they'd made the right decision, but for the first time in her *Bake-o-Rama* career, she felt lousy about sending someone home. Halla was such an upbeat person and a thoughtful baker. If only she'd let her own baking take the lead in her cake instead of the Girl Scouts cookies. But she hadn't, and now she was through on *Bake-o-Rama.* Kendra allowed herself to sit with that discomfort for a moment. Tori would be proud of her.

After giving them a few minutes, Kendra and Trevor walked into the fray to congratulate and console. Kendra opted to begin with consolation. "Halla, you are a terrific baker—" was all she could eke out before she was yanked into a tight embrace.

"Kendra, thank you so, so much!" Halla said. "You are an inspiration to me and my girls, and I have learned so much from you. Thank you, thank you, thank you!"

"I'm sure you're the inspiration for your girls," the chef said sincerely. "You have a real gift for food and for people. That's going to get you far, whatever you decide to do next. Great job."

Tearstained and smiling, Halla moved on to Trevor. Kendra turned to find Tori at her elbow. Without a moment's hesitation, she pulled the winner into a congratulatory hug.

"Great job, Tori," she said, wishing she could linger long enough to catch the scent of Tori's shampoo or enjoy the warm arc of her arms. But this wasn't the time or place. She stepped back, her pulse quick and her smile matching Tori's.

"Thank you," Tori said, her hazel eyes gentle. "For everything so far, and for whatever happens next."

"Don't forget your take-home box," Kendra said quickly before

Trevor inserted himself between them for his own hug and conversation. Their special moment was over. Time to make her exit.

After leaving the set, Kendra walked to the far end of the parking lot, where her workhorse of an SUV was parked. The black sky was dusted with an endless swirl of stars stretching over the shadows of broad grape leaves and scrubby hills. The air smelled like warm earth. Her head jerked to the right as a great horned owl called out from the stretch of cedars that lined the vineyard's property. She smiled. Mother Nature was capping a truly marvelous day by showing off.

Kendra had just clicked her seatbelt when her phone buzzed, alerting her to a text from Alden.

Set your alarm, it read. *You're due at our house tomorrow by 11* A.M. *for brunch. No backing out!*

She replied with a Zzz emoji and was putting her phone back into her bag when it buzzed again.

Stella is looking forward to meeting you.

"Who's Stella?" Kendra mumbled. Then the weeks-old conversation she'd had with her matchmaking brother leapt back into her mind. He was following through on his threat to set her up with one of his friends. Tomorrow. Without fail.

If she'd been paying attention, she would have seen, up in the cedars, the great horned owl jerking its head to the left, his acute eardrums picking up a muffled ruckus coming from a woman groaning loudly into her steering wheel.

Kendra had been a critic's darling for more than a decade. Guests had sent her thank-you notes and posted gushing Yelp reviews about her food. She'd even posed with lots of famous folks who insisted on snapping a selfie with her for their social media feeds. But for her, there were no fans better than a two-year-old climbing her leg and a five-year-old leaping in the air to get one of the fresh peach muffins she'd made just for them.

"Peachies! Peachies! Peachies!" they cried.

"Den, they're attacking me!" Kendra yelped.

"That's what I trained them to do," Alden said, taking the cake carrier from her before it got knocked out of her hand. "Jax! Moses! Leave Aunt Kendra alone, guys!"

The towheaded boys, clad in superhero T-shirts and shorts, retreated into the kitchen, where Kendra let each pick his own muffin. Most of Jax's became a second breakfast for the family dachshund. Moses, having had three extra years to master his eating technique, finished every crumb of his before the canine Roomba came his way.

Alden and his wife, Courtney, had given up any hope of their suburban ranch in Concord being an adult dwelling once Jax was born. Their taste in furniture was squishy, easy to spot-clean, and devoid of sharp edges. Noise-making toys inhabited every corner of their living room, and sippy cups outnumbered the stemware in the kitchen. The entire house smelled like Fruit Roll-Ups and stale Cheerios. The chaos was worth it, though. The boys were sticky little balls of affection and wonder, and Kendra was crazy about them. Once they were done eating, she allowed her nephews to drag her into the living room to admire the action figure fortress they'd built out of shipping boxes. She was on her belly helping Spider-Man crawl up a cardboard wall when her sister-in-law came into the room.

"How's it hanging?" she asked.

"Hey, good to see you!" Kendra said, scrambling to her feet for a hug. Courtney's blond hair was pulled back in a scrunchie, and her breezy blue sundress summed up her approach to life: relaxed, unstructured, and cool. "No Sunday concert in the park today?"

"We got the weekend off," she said. "The house is a classical-music-free zone right now."

"Good," Kendra said. "I mean, I'm glad you have time off, not that I don't like trombones."

Courtney rolled her eyes melodramatically, stepping into the kitchen to pour Kendra a cup of coffee. "You're in a safe space, Ken," she said. "You can admit you're not a classical music fan."

"Well, it's only fair," Kendra replied. "You hate rhubarb."

Courtney made a gagging noise then gestured for Kendra to go out to the deck in the backyard while she stayed inside to get the boys situated. Coffee mug in hand, Kendra found her brother sitting in a rattan chair, tucking into an artichoke dip with a toasted slice of a baguette. Next to him was a woman who must be Stella; she had short dark hair and enormous sunglasses. Kendra sighed, but very quietly, so no one else would hear.

She couldn't help feeling that her prospective date was going to have a hard time capturing her interest while her mind was so full of Tori right now. Of course, if she admitted to her brother that she was flirting with a current *Bake-o-Rama* contestant via notes in dessert boxes, he'd probably have a spontaneous aneurysm. Plus, even she had to admit to herself that flirting was a long way from anything more serious, especially given the dozens of practical reasons why that was out of the question. Maybe she should keep an open mind. She hadn't expected to find herself attracted to Tori, after all, so who knew? Stella might be a welcome surprise, too. And since there was really nothing much she could do about Tori, maybe a distraction would be nice.

Walking right up to the woman, she said, "Hello, I'm Kendra," and stuck out her hand.

"Oh, you must be the talented one in the family," Stella said with a grin, standing for a handshake. She was nearly as tall as Kendra with a rangy build, which meant that, for once, Alden had remembered her usual type. She was in a sleeveless black tee, ripstop shorts, and all-terrain sandals that suggested aggressive outdoorsiness. That was a signal, too, that her older brother thought she could use a reason to get some fresh air and sunshine.

"How do you know this guy?" Kendra asked, nabbing a chair next to Courtney, who had just joined them on the deck.

"We work together at the accounting firm," Stella said, settling back in her seat. "When he told me his sister was a chef, I had no idea it was the Cookie Queen."

"Ooh, I should have warned you: She doesn't like that name," her brother said, playfully wagging a finger at his guest.

"It's fine," Kendra said, hoping Alden appreciated her attempt at keeping it cool.

"You earned that title, though," Stella said, taking a sip of tea. "I read that piece on Chippy Chunk in the *Journal* a few weeks ago. That's an impressive empire you've built out of chocolate chips and peanut butter."

Kendra was flattered. "Have you ever dropped by one of our locations?" she asked.

"Not yet," Stella said, crossing her sun-drenched legs. "Your brother has been giving me too much work to do."

"Yeah," Kendra said. "He does that to me, too."

"Are cookies still your favorite thing to make, or have you eaten too many to enjoy them anymore?"

"Eh," Kendra said with a noncommittal shrug. She knew she ought to ask Stella some questions to keep the conversation going, but her resolution from mere moments ago had seemed to evaporate. It wasn't that Kendra didn't appreciate Stella's courteousness and undeniable attractiveness. But today was the day after Kendra had hugged Tori for the first time—for two seconds, under bright lights, and surrounded by peering eyes, but still a hug—and for that reason, Stella just didn't stand a chance.

After a pause, Stella valiantly picked up the conversational baton yet again, saying, "Well, kudos to you. *My* cooking skills start and end with ordering takeout." She dipped a baby carrot into a bowl of ranch dressing. "Besides, cooking for one is the worst kind of depressing."

That hit Kendra harder than she wanted to admit. On Mondays, when Gamma Raye was closed and she had to fend for herself, she often made do with eggs mixed into leftovers she brought home from the restaurant. It was quick and could be eaten standing up, which helped her avoid the kitchen table that seated six for no immediately useful reason.

"Sorry," Stella said, finishing her ranch-and-carrot combo. "I'm sure I just lost all credibility as a human being for saying I don't cook."

"Of course not," Kendra said automatically as her mind went straight to Tori again. She'd never dated someone who was into cooking before . . . not that she was *dating* Tori, but her love of baking definitely caught Kendra's attention. Their shared appreciation meant something to her, she realized. Maybe it should have been obvious, since food was such a big part of Kendra's life, but she was surprised to discover something new about what made someone appeal to her. It wasn't a bad feeling.

"You probably make fabulous meals at home all the time," Stella went on. "Like beef bourguignon."

This was far from the truth. Ask any professional chef what they cook at home, and they'd say, *As little as possible.* Cooking was her day job, and testing recipes, setting menus, and supervising line staff to ensure they were up to her standards was exhausting. It took a lot of resolve to make food on her own time, too, especially just for herself.

Tori would get that.

That was a lot to share with a complete stranger, though, especially one she wasn't planning to see again. Kendra recommitted to keeping things light. "I haven't made that since I was in culinary school," she said. "Do you like that dish? Personally, I've always found the mushrooms to be the most underrated ingredient."

"Mushrooms?" Stella said, shaking her head. "Not for me."

"Why?" Kendra asked, trying not to cringe when she heard a note of arrogance in her voice.

Stella shrugged, taking in Kendra's expression. "Too slimy." She sighed, then said, almost to herself, "I'm guessing that's another mark against me."

Kendra couldn't agree more. Before she could defend fungi any further, however, Alden interjected.

"Don't worry," he said to Stella in a conspiratorial whisper, "the menu at our house centers around two kinds of chicken nuggets, and

Kendra still speaks to me." He turned to his sister. "I need you in the kitchen for a second, Ken. Anyone need a refill while I'm in there?"

"I'm done, thanks," Stella said. It was hard not to miss her meaning, and Kendra felt a stab of guilt. She took Stella's teacup and followed her brother into the house. Once they were in the kitchen, Alden shot her a look.

"Why are you being so unfriendly?" he said. "Even if you're not into her, she is my co-worker. You could at least feign manners. Plus, I thought you said you didn't want to date someone in the industry."

"I— Wait, did I?" Kendra said.

"Just give her a chance," Alden said, pulling an egg casserole out of the oven. "She has a fantastic sense of humor, which means she might be able to put up with you. Plus, she's got plenty of her own money—like, sailboat-docked-in-the-marina kind of money—so you don't have to stress about someone dating you with dollar signs in their eyes. Get the fruit salad out of the fridge, will you?"

Kendra did as she was told, feeling sheepish. "Maybe she's nervous about meeting you," Alden went on. "And given how judgmental you've been during a three-minute conversation, I can see why."

She shot him a look. "What is that supposed to mean?"

"It's like you're trying to find any excuse to push her away," her brother said. "Keep that armor up."

"What armor?" she asked, not sure if she wanted to hear his response.

Looking out to the patio to make sure the women were out of earshot then over to his sons, who were gleefully banging action figures into each other over and over in the living room, Alden asked, "Have you ever wondered why you aren't dating? It may not be the long hours. It may not be that you're not able to meet new people. It may be because you're too scared to let someone get to know you." He looked again toward the patio as Courtney tossed her head back and laughed, making him smile. "You've always said you wanted to have some kind of life with someone, right? How can that ever happen if you never give anyone a chance?"

Kendra wanted so badly to tell him she agreed with him, which was why this connection to Tori was different in a good way. But this wasn't the time. It might never be.

He handed her a pair of well-worn crocheted pot holders. "Now, please take the casserole out and invite everyone to sit down, and if you can't turn on the Campbell charm, at least be civil, okay?"

"Yes, boss," she said, properly chastened.

A couple of hours later, the dirty dishes were piled in the Campbells' sink and Courtney was putting the remainder of the egg casserole and fruit into plastic containers. The boys, full to bursting, were splayed on the couch with a Pixar film lulling them into their afternoon naps. Kendra and Stella were finishing their coffees out on the patio.

She'd obeyed her brother and contributed to the table conversation, which had been a mix of family anecdotes, questions about each other's careers, and interrogation by Moses to confirm that everyone's favorite Avenger was the Hulk. Stella was a great storyteller, with a sardonic worldview Kendra could relate to. She was confident and comfortable in her own skin in a way Kendra liked. After a while, she'd found herself smiling easily as Stella spoke, although she was annoyed to see Alden out of the corner of her eye shooting her a smug "I told you so" look.

And yet, while she had to admit she was enjoying herself, her heart was pulled in another direction. One that was dusted with freckles and framed by waves of strawberry blonde hair.

"It was nice to meet you, Stella," Kendra said, standing and wiping some stray crumbs off her jeans. "But I should probably get going. I have a blog post to edit and a dog who's probably eyeing my kitchen floor as a bathroom if I don't get home soon."

"It was a pleasure," Stella said. "Maybe we can get coffee once the show's in the can." She pulled her phone from her back pocket. "What's your number?"

For a millisecond, Kendra considered giving her a fake number, but then felt a little embarrassed; she wasn't twenty-five anymore. Stella sent her a text to make sure they both had each other's numbers, and then the two headed into the house, where Stella said goodbye to Alden and his family and waved once more to Kendra before leaving. Kendra gathered some sleepy kisses from her nephews then went to the kitchen to wrap things up with her brother and sister-in-law.

"Hey, can we talk before you go?" Alden asked, setting down his dish towel.

She put her keys back into her bag. "Sure."

"Let's go outside," he said. They exited onto the front porch, and Alden motioned her over to a corner away from the door.

"If you're going to grill me about Stella, I will admit she seems to be an interesting person," Kendra said.

"Good to hear," he said with less sly enthusiasm than she expected. "Look, I didn't want to tell you this until after we ate. It's tough news, so I'll just come out and say it. The property owners for Gamma Raye delivered a notice to the office Friday. They're selling the space to a developer who plans to raze the building and build condos. We have to be out by October 1."

"Condos?" Kendra barked, certain there was a mistake. "They can't do that. It's a perfect restaurant space, right in the middle of town on a corner."

"The corner location is what makes it such a valuable piece of real estate," Alden said.

"Can't we make a counteroffer?" she asked.

"We have thirty days to respond, but the price tag is way, way beyond what we could scrape together," Alden said. "We've barely been making rent, Ken."

"We have to counter," Kendra said, her voice rising. "This is the opportunity we've been waiting for: to own the restaurant outright."

"There is no way we can afford it," he said gently. "The owners can get four times what they paid for the lot originally, and they paid a small fortune for it in the first place."

"So we'll get a loan."

"That's a level of mortgage the business wouldn't ever be able to support. Ken, you have to face the fact that either you need to find another location or . . ." His voice trailed off.

"Or what?" Kendra said.

Alden took a deep breath before speaking. "Or you'll have to close."

"There has to be another option," she said, her heart hammering. "I could sell my house."

"I don't think—" Alden started, but Kendra cut him off.

"You could renegotiate my *Bake-o-Rama* contract for a raise or an advance."

"That's not—"

"I could sell Chippy Chunk," she said, her eyes welling up.

"Whoa—"

"This is not just some real estate deal, Alden. This is *my* place we're talking about!" she spat, her tears unstoppable. "We have to do everything we can to save it! Don't you get that?"

"I get how much the restaurant means to you!" he shot back. "It means a lot to me, too. I have been so proud of what you've made of that little corner, and I don't want it shut down any more than you do. But this is a business, and we can't make impulsive decisions. I want you to come to my office tomorrow so we can talk through what the realistic options are." He put a hand on her shoulder. "This will be okay in the end. You will be okay." He stepped a little closer. "Trust me on that, all right?"

Swamped by grief and fear, Kendra was barely able to process what he was saying. She just let him hug her and tried to breathe more slowly until the crying stopped.

"You okay?" he asked after a few minutes.

She nodded. "We'll talk tomorrow."

He reached into his pocket. "Here, Ken, dry your eyes. You look like Frank-n-Furter in the swimming pool."

She looked at what he'd handed her. "Den, this is Jax's Spider-Man sock."

He peered at it. "It's clean. I think."

She giggled in spite of herself. "A sock?"

"Sniff it before you use it."

She rolled her eyes. "Alden Ross, I say this as someone who loves you: You have to up your game in the handkerchief department."

"Handkerchiefs are gross," he said. "I'd use a toddler's sock before one of those."

"I think I have some napkins in the glove compartment," she said, handing it back to him.

He sighed. "Kendra Jane, I say this as someone who loves you: We will get through this. I promise."

She sighed as well. "You had better be right."

15

Across the bay and down the highway in Eucalyptus Point, Tori had a dog-eared copy of Viv Albertine's memoir open on her lap while the Clash screamed out of her stereo speakers as she desperately sought a way to leave the *Bake-o-Rama* drama behind her for one Sunday afternoon. Next week's Custard Challenge was not exactly in her wheelhouse. Puddings, mousses, and pots de crème were not fun to make from scratch. Even though she'd made quite a few crème brûlées in her time—anyone who had ever hosted a sit-down dinner party in the last twenty years probably had—she'd go to a restaurant if she ever had a hankering for one now. Also, savory options seemed uniformly unappetizing, from the molded salmon mousses of the 1950s to the watery foams that trendy chefs squirted on everything from strawberries to sea scallops. There had to be some sort of brunchy take on an egg custard she could throw together, perhaps with mushrooms, shallots, and a couple of drops of truffle oil. To let her ideas marinate for a bit and put off the inevitable research she'd have to do to find recipes she'd be willing to eat much less make, she was taking an official break.

After reading the same page three times, however, she gave up trying to ignore the obvious reason for her inability to relax: Kendra, Kendra, and more Kendra.

Once Anika had announced Tori won the Cake Challenge, she hadn't been able to hear anything else over the blood pounding in her ears. Then she'd felt a quick squeeze on her arm and turned to see Mel whooping, which brought her awareness back to the set and the applause from contestants and judges alike . . . including Kendra, who'd given her that very brief, very public, yet still tantalizing embrace with cameras nearby and the clock ticking. Because of their size difference, Tori's head had rested against Kendra's chest, and she could swear she'd felt her heart beat. She'd replayed that moment in her head dozens of times since.

It had been so, so long since she'd had a meaningful hug that wasn't maternal or platonic. She wished for more time with Kendra, away from the lights and the cameras and so many people. And this week, Kendra's note in her take-home treat box, this one rolled tightly between the handcrafted butterscotch and chocolate pudding cups, was proof that Kendra felt the same way. Tori had left it on the corner of her kitchen counter, where it was daring her to read it for the umpteenth time.

Instead, she pulled up the calendar on her phone and counted the months until her contract restrictions expired, when she and Kendra could grab coffee and sort this out face-to-face. By her calculations, they'd have to wait until a year from Halloween. At that point, both of them would certainly have moved on to other pursuits or, at least in Kendra's case, other people, which made Tori feel even more lonely than she usually did on a summer Sunday afternoon on her own.

Her phone buzzed with an incoming call, startling her and causing her to drop it on the floor. Picking it up and checking the number, she seriously considered stuffing the phone between the sofa cushions until the ringing stopped: It was her ex-wife. But she couldn't. She'd promised she wouldn't ever duck a call from Shelby in case it was an emergency. Being divorced was like the scar she had on her palm from a long-ago bike accident. As soon as she forgot it existed, it would itch, or she'd bump against something sharp, wresting her attention back to an event she deeply wished she could forget.

With a gritty sigh, she pressed the green receiver button on her phone and said hello.

"Hey, Tor," she heard. Shelby's superpower was charm. All this time after she'd cheated on her, the woman's voice still reeked of promises she might keep this time. "How are you doing?"

"Fine," Tori said.

"When the twins were out here, they sounded pretty glad this was the last time they'd be camp counselors," Shelby said conversationally. "How do you think it's going out there for them?"

"What's up?" said Tori. She was in no mood for a social call. She learned through the Cassie-and-Lee-Anne grapevine about her ex's upcoming wedding quite a while ago. If she was finally going to spill the old news, Tori wanted her to get it over with.

"Listen to you cutting to the chase," Shelby said. "Well, I'm guessing you heard about Barb and me."

"About what?" said Tori. As much as she wanted this conversation to end, she wasn't about to make it easy for Shelby by filling in the blanks for her.

"That Barb dumped me."

Tori's mouth fell open in shock. "I thought you were getting married."

"We were," Shelby said.

Tori knew this tactic. Shelby would say very little, waiting for Tori to ask for more details so she'd be roped into caring about what was going on in her ex's life, at the expense of her own feelings. This time, eyeing the note on her kitchen counter, she chose to say nothing. The seconds ticked by.

Finally, Shelby spoke. "I owe you an apology."

"Tell your fiancée that, not me," Tori said.

"Wait, don't hang up," Shelby pleaded. "Milo and Mia told me about *Bake-o-Rama* and what an accomplishment it is to get picked for the show and how much it means to you. I know you'll be terrific. You're an incredible baker and always have been. I should have appreciated that more when we were together. I'm sorry." There was a catch in her voice. "I'm sorry about 'Rocket Blast,' too."

"I don't—" Tori started, but Shelby jumped in again.

"It was a cheap shot during a difficult time, and you deserved better. If I could do it all over—"

Tori ended the call before Shelby could say another word. She dropped her phone on the coffee table and backed away from it like it stank. She went to her stereo, cranked the volume on "Train in Vain," and paced from dining room to living room and back. She went around the same circuit again, yelling over Mick Jones's punkabilly wail.

"It's a little late for apologies, Shelby!" she stormed to the empty air. "What did you want me to do? Cheer? Cry? Take you back? Tell you I adore your awful poetry? *What?*"

When she got tired of pacing, she entered her bedroom and sat on the edge of the bed. It was relatively new; Tori had bought it to replace the one she'd shared with Shelby after her first meeting with a divorce lawyer. Up until that conversation, she had held out a shred of hope that her wife would come to her senses and return home to make the family whole again. But Tori's attorney had put her straight right away: "Infidelity is like black mold: You can't paper over it, it'll poison every other part of your life, and the longer you wait to clean this up and move on, the less you'll be able to salvage for yourself." She'd gone to IKEA on her way home.

Throughout their relationship, Shelby had made it clear that she considered domesticity to be boring, and that anyone who had a passion for that sort of thing—Tori included—was aiming too low in life. Tori never confronted her about that, and so many other slights large and small, in the frail belief their home life with the kids would stay stable and safe that way. What had that gotten her in the end? A divorce.

That was then. *Bake-o-Rama* and Kendra were now: she being praised for what Shelby scorned, and catching the eye of someone who seemed to delight in who she was, just as she was.

Turning the music down, she went back to the kitchen and retrieved Kendra's note from yesterday. As usual, it was much different from the pun of the week that came with the snacks (*When it comes to baking, you're one cool custard!* electronically signed by both judges). This one didn't seem as hastily written as the last one: Kendra's handwriting was neater, and the message was longer and more thought-out:

> Hey, Tori—I think you're right. When you bake for someone in particular, it comes out better. You put more care into it and take more pleasure in making it the best it can be. I have to admit I lost that sense of purpose over the past few years, trying to scale up the cookie business and keep the restaurant running, plus doing this show and all the rest of the promotional stuff. Of course, I want the food to be great, but that hasn't been as important as being a Success lately. I've gotten so worried about slacking off and letting the cracks show because I don't want people to think of me as a failure—a female failure at that. I haven't experienced joy and delight in a long time.
>
> Then when I decided to make my nephews their favorite muffins for brunch on Sunday, I thought about how much I love making those little guys happy by baking for them. Are they the most sophisticated muffins ever? No. Are they my best muffins ever? It doesn't matter, because every time I make them, they plow through them and want more. And I felt good about what I do for a living for the first time in a really long time.
>
> If I could bake you anything at all, what would you like me to make? Figure that out, because I'd love to bake for you someday.
>
> Thanks for inspiring me. Have an amazing week.

Tori pulled a magnet off the side of her fridge and stuck the note in the middle of its door so it could inspire her—and make her blush—as she prepared this week's recipes. Satisfied, she walked over to the picture window in the living room to appreciate her neighbor's calla lilies across the street. Her gaze wandered over to the empty lot down the block, which had been taken over by a blackberry bramble that no one on the street claimed to own. She could see the berries, fat as her thumb and shiny as marcasite in the afternoon sunshine.

Taking a large stainless-steel bowl out of the lower kitchen cabinet, she grabbed a baseball cap and faded flannel shirt off the peg near the back door then strode across the street.

A couple of hours later, Tori was on Lee Anne and Cassie's front porch, her fingernails stained purple. When Lee Anne answered the door, Tori handed her a Ziploc bag full of blackberries.

"You've been productive," Lee Anne said, waving her in. "These look delicious!"

"Urban foraging at its best," Tori said, stepping inside. "Where's Cassie?"

Lee Anne rolled her eyes. "She went to Home Depot to pick up 'just one thing.' That never takes less than an hour."

"Great," Tori said. "Because I need to talk about something without her getting all legal on me."

"Ooh, this sounds intriguing," Lee Anne said with a whistle. "Want a glass of wine?"

It was barely four in the afternoon, but with all Tori had been dealing with that weekend, it seemed overdue. "Absolutely."

Over a glass of nifty pinot grigio in the backyard, Tori brought Lee Anne up to date on the jumble of events from the last few weeks. Just as she did when they were in school together, Lee Anne nodded and uh-huhed then sat back to sum up, counting the main points off on her fingers.

"First up, you did great this week on *Bake-o-Rama*—yay, you!—and you're superpsyched about what that might mean for your future career as a baker. Second, Kendra clearly has feelings for you and is writing you flirty little notes, which is a real boost to your self-esteem after three long years alone but could also get her fired—and third, if you reciprocate, you could get kicked off the show. Fourth, Shelby just cold-called you and sounds like she's trying to get back into your good graces now that she's single again, which is a nonstarter. Did I leave anything out?"

"Fifth," Tori added, "I haven't figured out what I'm going to bake this week, although it's going to use blackberries. That's on me, though."

Lee Anne sat back in her Adirondack chair, every inch the therapist. "If there were no penalties, what would you want to do about Kendra?"

Tori looked skyward and sighed. "Ask her out on a date to see if I can get more than a few cryptic words out of her."

"Why?" Lee Anne asked. "On the show, she seems like she has no filter."

"That's not been my experience," Tori said.

"Because she likes you," said Lee Anne.

Tori shook her head. "Sure, she doesn't hold back in her critiques, but she's always fair, and her tone is a lot less harsh than it used to be. She's even been hugging the winners each week, not just me, and according to the kids, Kendra never hugs anyone. I think that's evidence that she's trying to change." She saw Lee Anne shift in her seat. "What?"

Lee Anne spoke carefully. "Do you think you're making excuses for her since she's interested in you, and you haven't had a date in a couple of decades?"

Tori considered this. Was Lee Anne sensing something she wasn't able to admit to herself? It was a possibility, but her gut told her that wasn't true. "No," she replied.

"This isn't another case of Star Syndrome, is it?" asked Lee Anne.

Tori balked. "What do you mean?"

Lee Anne smirked. "You know exactly what I mean. It's a thrill to catch the eye of the hottest female chef alive, especially after your heart took a beating from your ex." She paused, then spoke again, more gently this time. "But wasn't that a big part of your attraction to Shelby at the beginning? That she was so cool and could have anyone and, still, she chose you?"

Tori's face reddened. "This is not Star Syndrome, Lee Anne. I'm not 'easily awestruck,' no matter what happened with Shelby."

Lee Anne reached over and squeezed her hand. "I believe you, hon. I just had to check." She sat back. "Well then, tell me all about Kendra. What do you like about her, other than the fact that she's a total smoke show?"

Tori smiled. "She's acting like the kids in school who don't fit in and wall themselves off until they click with someone—then the wall comes crashing down. She's relied on this untouchable persona for quite a while, but she's showing some vulnerability in her notes, and she's awkward about it and kind of brave. It's . . . sweet and romantic." She looked at Lee Anne. "Yeah, I'm getting smitten. What's your advice?"

"As a therapist or a friend?"

"As a therapist who is a friend—my best friend."

"Look, I am thrilled you're considering dating again," Lee Anne said. "You're ready to move forward, and you deserve the attention, by the way: You're amazing in more ways than I can count. I really wish it wasn't someone who is off-limits, especially since *Bake-o-Rama* could make your career. But the heart wants what it wants, doesn't it?" Lee Anne let out a long exhale. "My professional advice would be to hold off on reciprocating until you're not bound by the contract; if this is meant to be, you'll find a way. And if you decide to ignore that advice, as a friend, promise me you'll be careful. You're just starting to get to know her, and there's a lot at stake here. I hope it's all worth it."

Just then, the side door rattled, and Cassie came out, carrying a pail of spackle and several beige and orange bags. "Tori!" she said, her face brightening. "I'm starving. You two want to grab some burritos?"

After dinner with her friends, Tori found herself back home, taking stock of the heaping bowl of blackberries on her counter. Fresh fruit opened up new possibilities for the Custard Challenge, but these wouldn't last in the fridge until Saturday. She'd freeze most of them, leaving enough to experiment with over the next couple of days, and do another picking before she drove up to Sonoma on Friday.

Of course, they would never be better than right now. She scooped up a handful, imagining the pleasure of dropping the best ones into Kendra's palm and watching her savor them, one by one.

At 6:00 A.M. on Tuesday, Kendra stepped out the back door of Gamma Raye into the parking lot, where farmers, fishmongers, and butchers bustled around the makeshift farmers' market geared toward the local restaurateurs. Each week, Kendra inspected their wares and confirmed items for the week's menu. One of the glories of operating a restaurant in Sonoma County was access to the country's best produce year-round, not to mention wines, meats, and the rest. She could even get her butter, cream, and eggs directly from one of the best dairies in the state, which was less than a thirty-minute drive from her house. She'd set up shop in the Garden of Eden for foodies.

For the first couple of years of Gamma Raye's operation, the process worked in reverse: Kendra had to get up well before dawn and go to them. She'd drive to farms and warehouses to jockey for supplies alongside more established chefs who had more impressive credentials and fatter wallets. After the five-star reviews in the national press helped establish her credentials, and suppliers started to compete to be included in her purveyor list with their names on the chalkboard over the bar, they'd started to come to her, and she'd invited other locally owned restaurants to take full advantage of the weekly pop-up.

Browsing a stall boasting a variety of leafy greens, Kendra was grateful to focus on a task that required her full attention. It distracted her from fretting over her meeting with Alden the day before. He hadn't presented any easy answers because there were none. To stay in the current location, they would have to win the lottery—not likely. To stay anywhere else in Sonoma, their realtor would have to conjure up a location with similar appeal and accessibility that wasn't more expensive than what they had to float now—also not likely. To move the restaurant to another town, they'd need to figure out how far away from Sonoma they'd be willing to go, with a strong possibility of landing outside the greater Bay Area for affordability's sake. And if none of these could come together in a month's time, she'd have to shutter the restaurant for good by the end of September.

None of these were necessarily wrong moves to make. If this had happened a few years ago, Kendra would have shrugged and moved on; she'd have little to lose and few ties to break. At this point, though, she didn't want to upend her life, especially now that she'd achieved some equilibrium in her crazily demanding career. This was *her* restaurant, and she had thrown all her innovation and ingenuity into it so she could take pride in every meal. She'd chosen each fixture, approved the paint colors, and even created a space in her office for Julia to hang out if Kendra brought her in during off-hours. She evolved the menu so it wouldn't mummify her past glories without veering too far in the other direction and getting too trendy or weird. First and foremost, the food had to satisfy, and there had to be plenty of reasons to leave room for dessert. Gamma Raye embodied her best chef self. It was practically her avatar.

Moving to the fruit growers' stalls, she made her selections and chatted with her kitchen steward, who was standing by to take them to the restaurant pantry. He was eighteen and unafraid of hard work, late nights, or early mornings, points in his favor if Kendra ever needed someone to take on additional responsibility for a bump in pay. She watched him hustle the produce back to Gamma Raye, and her heart broke a little. She hadn't told him or anyone else at the restaurant what was going on, and she was dreading having that conversation, no matter what decision she made. This change would disrupt not just her own life but those of the eighteen people on her payroll. Kendra had built an exceptional team, which was no easy feat in the restaurant business due to the long hours, high pressure, and transient nature of being a server, line cook, or staff member focused on the next, better gig. They were talented, and they were loyal, not just because she paid fairly and respected each person's contribution to Gamma Raye's success but also because they all lived, breathed, and loved the innate pleasure of providing their brand of fine food and hospitality. Just like she did.

Kendra confirmed her orders of beef, pork, and poultry with the butcher, her mind consumed with worry about her team's welfare. Would her sous chef stay with her if she had to relocate to the East Bay, or Oregon? Would she have to lay off the hostess who was a single mom and the pastry baker who had embraced this career after being incarcerated? What about the bartender and the server who fell in love over dozens of shifts and were expecting their first child? What about the steward buzzing back and forth in front of her with their groceries, a kid who showed the same drive and passion she had had when she first picked up that mop at that Italian joint in Vermont? What would happen to him and everyone else?

She walked by flats of strawberries and halted: How would all this impact whatever might happen between her and Tori? How could she even think about dating with all this extra chaos going on? Could this situation get any worse?

Of course, she hadn't mentioned anything on that front to Alden during their conversation yesterday. Especially not after he had warned her that she would have to put her emotions in a lockbox and make an intellectual decision for the good of her career. Kendra wasn't sure that was possible when it came to Gamma Raye, let alone anything—anyone—else. Finishing her shopping, she wished her problems could be cleared away as quickly as the vendors were loading the boxes of unsold food back into their trucks. She waved as the last of them drove off.

"What can I do for you, Chef?" her steward asked, coming back out from the restaurant and pointing at the crates, coolers, and boxes full of her orders. "Pack this up?"

The lot was empty, only a couple of lettuce leaves and a broken egg left at the perimeter. "Uh, sure," she choked out. "Excuse me." She got in her car, drove to an empty parking space on a street well away from Gamma Raye, and started to cry.

Early Friday morning, Tori donned her berry-picking garb, grabbed a bowl, and headed outside. She had found a blackberry pot de crème recipe that won her heart: an updated culinary classic that had the high degree of difficulty she needed to demonstrate at this point in the competition. She'd tried it out and liked the results so much, she'd eaten two after dinner on Monday. She'd then turned her attention to her savory recipe: a mushroom custard served with an asparagus sauce laced with truffle oil. She didn't want to admit how many of those she'd scarfed down on Tuesday: One whiff of truffle oil, and she was ravenous.

But when the bramble came into view, her heart sank. The stretches of nearly ripe berries she'd seen on Sunday had been raided during the week, probably by the blacktail doe and her fawn she'd seen in the neighborhood. The only berries left were way above her head, and it was iffy that she'd be able to get enough for her recipe. She went back to the house, got a step stool, and forged ahead anyway—some were better than none. The results were scant; she'd have to bring some of the frozen berries from the weekend to make up the difference.

Packing the car meant loading up her cooler to keep the berries, eggs, heavy cream, and vegetables on ice. Tori confirmed her list of ingredients, packing twice as much as she'd need in the event she dropped a bowlful of batter or made some irreparable mistake and had to start over. She had some particularly precious cargo this time around, too: a black truffle to shave over the mushroom custard, which would not leave her person until she had to use it. She walked through each recipe to confirm the tools she'd have to haul with her since the *Bake-o-Rama* set didn't always have specialty items like immersion blenders, chinois strainers, or in this case, truffle shavers. Once she was convinced she couldn't gain anything from rechecking her lists one more time, she poured cat food into the automatic feeder and skritched Johnny and Joey, promising to be back soon. Then she hit the road, with Elvis Costello on her car stereo, crooning about his red shoes.

Tori firmly believed this was the world's most awe-inspiring commute, with Highway 1 taking her up the Pacific coast until it merged with Nineteenth Avenue in San Francisco's Sunset District. It then cut through the emerald center of Golden Gate Park and the hilly heart of the Presidio before meeting up with Highway 101 to launch her onto the mighty Golden Gate Bridge, the water of the bay more than two hundred feet below, churning its way out to the Pacific. The fog was thick, and as she drove under the burnt orange arches, she pitied the tourists on the pedestrian walkways, shivering in shorts and impulse-buy sweatshirts, who had been unaware that summer was the coldest time of year to visit this part of California. Once again, Tori couldn't get over the fact she lived and worked in a part of the country that other people dreamed of visiting once during their lifetimes.

Another weekend in Sonoma, another Saturday of intense pressure under the tantalizing gaze of Chef Kendra Campbell. Even though her notes had gotten lengthier and more personal, she couldn't be absolutely certain that Kendra wanted to be more than friends, the result being Tori obsessing over every exchange they'd had . . . and getting more attracted to her by the day.

Tori wrestled with Lee Anne's words of advice as she drove past the exit for Sausalito. What exactly *did* her heart want? Someone who would be patient as she fumbled through dating for the first time since college. A woman whose kisses could go from slow burn to high flame. Certainly someone who was good company, especially as she didn't want to rattle around the house alone once the kids were gone. Hopefully someone who had the potential to become a supportive partner and had a delightful laugh and a devastating way of looking at her across the breakfast table. Most definitely someone who respected and loved her for what she loved to do.

Was any of that possible with Kendra, whose schedule and star status outshone Tori's more mundane dreams? Someone who judged people for a living? Was it worth the risk to attempt to find out?

"Though you try to stop it, she's like a narcotic . . ."

Tori sang along with Mr. Costello through the rest of "Pump It Up."

True that, Elvis.

The cloudless skies and sultry temperatures stayed with her from San Rafael to the gates of Three Vines. When she pulled up to the back kitchen entrance to unload, a welcome voice hailed her.

"Happy Friday, Tori!" Mel said, propping the door open for her. He was dressed in a denim shirt and chinos, saving his western finery for the cameras in the morning.

"Hey there!" she said, giving her friend a hug.

"Need a hand?"

"Sure," she said. Chitchatting about how their week had been while off camera, the two of them carted her cooler and supplies onto the set. Tori looked at each station until she found her apron folded on the stool located in the back right corner facing the judges.

"Station 4?" she said. "I hope that's not telling me something."

"You're not getting superstitious after winning last week, are you?" Mel asked.

"Of course not," she said with a touch of unease.

The schedule for Friday afternoon included yet another social media training session with the Food & Drink TV marketing team dubbed "Influencing the Influencers!" that the four remaining contestants were required to attend. After a few weeks of posting photos of her food and kitchen tips to be ready for when the show started to air, with Lee Anne and Cassie automatically liking and sharing everything so she'd have more than a handful of responses, Tori was getting over her initial worry that she was begging for attention instead of building a "personal brand." She told herself social media was what any good businessperson had to do to connect with customers—especially foodies. After so many years of being in Shelby's shadow, and a few weeks basking in Kendra's attention, she was ready to see if anyone in the online universe cared about who she was or what she thought. If it fell flat, she could go back to what she preferred to focus on: cooking well and cadging more time with Kendra.

Once she'd stowed her ingredients in her refrigerator, Tori went outside to move her car out of the loading zone. She'd just pulled into a spot at the back of the property when a ginormous, battered SUV barreled into a space near the edge of the lot. She gave it no mind until she spied a graphic on the back window of wavy green lines with Hollywood-sign lettering at the center: the Gamma Raye logo. Tori backed out of her spot, casually reparked a few feet down, and waited for Kendra to get out and walk by. No one could fault them for pulling up at the same time, or having a brief chat on the way in before they had to go back to business.

After nearly a minute, Tori couldn't pretend to scroll through her phone any longer and looked over at the SUV. Kendra was motionless, staring out her windshield into the field with a distressed expression. Without a second thought, Tori walked over and tapped on the window. Startled, Kendra recovered with a small smile and rolled down the window.

"Are you okay?" Tori asked.

"Of course," Kendra said, her mask of self-possession back in place.

Tori hesitated, then said, "Are you sure about that?"

Kendra exhaled sharply then scanned the parking lot, probably to confirm that there weren't any other people in view. "Have you ever had your life yanked out from under you?" she said.

"Well, my wife left me for another woman, so yes," she blurted with a blunt laugh, and Kendra's eyes went wide. "You didn't know that," Tori said softly. "I wasn't trying to make light of what you're going through." She'd been so glad to have the chance to speak to Kendra more privately, she'd forgotten how little they knew about each other.

"I am so sorry," Kendra said. "That's way worse than what I'm dealing with."

"It's okay. I've made my peace with it," Tori said. Shelby's recent phone call flickered in her memory for a moment, making Tori glad to focus on Kendra instead. "Why do you ask?"

Kendra rechecked the parking lot before facing Tori, her blue eyes worried. "I'm at a fork-in-the-road moment right now," she said. "I didn't choose to be here, and I feel like no matter what I do, I'll pick the wrong path and ruin my life and a bunch of other people's, too."

This was the kind of conversation Tori had longed to have with Kendra: a deep, introspective dive into what was important to her beyond the show. She was glad that Kendra trusted her enough to talk openly with her. Of course, she'd imagined they'd have their first heart-to-heart over a couple of cocktails at a bistro in a nifty Bay Area neighborhood. Instead, here they were, separated by a car door in a dusty parking lot where anyone could come by and ask pointed questions.

Tori glanced over her shoulder, then back at Kendra. "I know what that feels like, and it's awful," she said. "When I found out Shelby was cheating, I was convinced I had nothing but bad options ahead for me and my kids. What helped me decide was an exercise my therapist gave me. I had to write down every single thing I was worried about, then come up with a positive outcome for each one. Some of them were pretty ridiculous: 'I'll miss coming home to dinner with Shelby . . . but hey, she hated olives, so now I can finally order pizza the way I like it!' But there were other fears that took a lot of soul-searching to understand that I'd be able to handle them, too. The process showed me there's always an upside, even when things seem hopeless."

"So that's how I get out of this trap?" Kendra asked, sounding desperate and a tiny bit hopeful. "Get some paper and write a list?"

Tori shrugged. "It's worth a try. It could prove that this choice you're facing isn't a no-win situation after all." Her mind traveled back to Milo and Mia's pep talk before her final auditions. "Right now, you're seeing everything that's wrong, but you might make a better decision if you're also able to see what's right." She checked her watch. "Sorry, I have to get to class. I hope this helped."

"It did." Kendra unclicked her seatbelt and released the hatchback. "Do you mind giving me a hand? It was my turn to make the goodie boxes."

Tori happily agreed and headed around to the back of Kendra's SUV, which was fitted with shelves. While it was spotless, the interior was dented and scarred from whatever hadn't stayed put over the years. Kendra unhitched two bins, each stacked with a couple dozen small pastry boxes. Tori hefted one and Kendra the other; they weren't heavy but were very full.

Tori nodded toward her car as they passed it on the way toward the building, saying, "Maybe I should just take mine now."

"Well, it needs a logo sticker," Kendra said evenly, "and a note from the judge."

Tori looked over at her. They'd both just been very honest and straightforward with each other, and who knew when they'd have another chance to speak alone. Why not ask? "About those notes," she said.

Kendra kept walking, her eyes forward. "Yeah?"

"You're risking a lot, reaching out to me like that."

"I know," Kendra said. "And I'm okay with that."

"You could lose your job on the show," Tori pressed, her heart starting to race.

The chef chuckled. "Only if they find out."

"Look," Tori said, deciding to just go for it, "I'm flattered . . . and honored . . . and surprised. Why risk all this for me? You're . . . well, you. And I mean, I'm not that special."

Kendra stopped walking and met Tori's eyes. "Yes, you are," she said, her voice low. "You're extraordinary. I hope you know that."

Tori stood motionless, her insides a molten mess. Kendra was probably the last person Tori knew who'd say something she didn't mean—and she'd said she thought Tori was extraordinary. Maybe it was time for her to believe it about herself, too.

A second later, the door to the building opened, and Zak and another production assistant trotted out and took the crates. "You want these in the green room, Kendra?"

"Yep," Kendra said, her judge's demeanor snapping back into place. She turned back to Tori and gave her a small smile. "Good luck this weekend."

"Thanks," Tori replied, still unable to move. "You, too."

The next morning, Tori stood at attention at Station 4, rolling the truffle in her apron pocket between her fingers like a good luck charm. To stay more relaxed, she'd made some adjustments over the last few weeks of competition. For one, she'd found shoe inserts for her Chuck Taylors that gave her some much-needed relief. For another, she stopped worrying about what recipe would be pulled for a Bake and Switch and just accepted what came her way without stressing over it. She also promised herself she'd stop obsessively checking her setup and ingredients right before the cameras rolled, which rattled her nerves more than necessary. She'd taken extra time after dinner the night before to arrange her dry ingredients and utensils on the counter and the berries, veggies, and dairy items in her fridge. Her recipes for the blackberry pots de crème and the mushroom custard with asparagus truffle sauce were on the stand. All was set to go. She was rested and ready.

This week, she was sharing the back benches with Natalie, and, glancing over, saw that the black-clad blonde was thrumming the blade of a butter knife against the edge of the counter and staring straight ahead, her ponytail as tight as her jaw.

"Good morning, Natalie," Tori said. "How's it going?"

"How do you think?" she responded, tapping away.

No matter how irritating and mystifying her behavior was, Tori couldn't help but empathize with her fellow baker. Based on her experience with so many high school students and teachers, Tori saw signs of social anxiety underneath her bravado. Natalie had never joined the others at meal breaks or for a chat in the kitchen while their bakes were in the oven. Once the cameras were off at the end of the weekend, she'd bolt for the parking lot to catch the last flight back to Portland. Natalie was all business all the time, and that had to be exhausting and intensely lonely for her.

"Well, I'm rooting for you," Tori said.

Natalie nodded mechanically. "Me, too."

Tori chose to believe Natalie meant to say she was rooting for her as well.

As Liam called the set to order, Tori spied Kendra just offstage. Drifting off the night before, Tori had wondered what situation Kendra was wrestling with. Was there a death in the family or a serious health diagnosis? Was Julia—such an apt name for a chef's pet—okay? Whatever the issue was, this morning Kendra had put it far enough aside to share a laugh with Trevor in the wings. She looked totally different from the forlorn woman Tori had counseled yesterday afternoon in the parking lot. It looked like her advice had helped . . . and if not, maybe they could park next to each other next weekend and talk some more.

Several minutes went by without any action other than Liam

chatting with Cal and pointing a lot at his tablet. In his sharp madras shirt and khakis, Jayden jogged in place at his station directly in front of Tori's to keep his energy up. Mel caught Tori's attention and mouthed, *You got this!* prompting Tori to mouth *You, too!* back to him. After a particularly vigorous bout of tapping, Natalie's butter knife slipped out of her hand and clattered to the floor. She scrambled to pick it up like a squirrel trying to grab an acorn before a hawk descended.

After a few more agonizing minutes, Anika arrived onstage. Despite the sunniness of her outfit—a kicky kelly-green jumpsuit with a striped belt that coordinated with her headband—she seemed to be in a foul mood. She was hissing something Tori couldn't hear at the sound engineer helping her with her mic, until he turned it on and the whole room caught the end of Anika's tirade: "Let's get this over with!" The host looked up at the stunned faces of the bakers and switched gears. "Hey there, Mel, Jayden, Natalie, and Best Baker Tori!" she said, sweet as pie. "You all look just great! Good luck! Woot woot!"

Cal gave the go-ahead from his director's chair, and once Liam finished the countdown, Anika launched into her introduction as if nothing was amiss. "We have come to the Custard Challenge, dear viewers," she said. "This is a week where you might spot a mousse in the kitchen—a chocolate mousse, that is! There may be puddings of tapioca or rice or bread, and if something goes wrong, our bakers will have to go to Flan B! Our four contestants are ready to present their sweet and savory best for our esteemed judges as we move closer to naming *American Bake-o-Rama*'s overall Best Baker in just a couple of weeks—with the promise of one hundred thousand dollars and a spot on the Food & Drink TV Network roster, too." She stopped and coughed loudly. Collecting herself, she waved toward the director. "Sorry, something got caught in my throat. Do you need me to do that again?"

Liam checked with Cal, then said, "No, just keep going. We'll fix it in post."

Anika rolled her shoulder, reaffixed her smile, and continued, "Let's see what Trevor and Kendra have in store for them today!"

Trevor, decked out in a coral sweater, white linen pants, and dirty bucks, spoke first. "My friends, custards and the like are deceptively difficult. Food meets physics when it comes to steaming, boiling, and chilling your concoctions of cream, eggs, and other delightfully rich ingredients. With that in mind, we will have no Bake and Switch this week. We want to see your best work reflected in your chosen recipes. Do you have anything to add, Kendra?

Kendra made a bold fashion statement of her own in a finely tailored black blazer over a T-shirt with an Escher-inspired graphic of cooks hauling pots around and around an endless staircase. "The further into *Bake-o-Rama* we go," she said, "the less tolerant we'll be of mistakes. Each of you has the skill, experience, and talent to make two dishes that are as delicious as they are flawless. Take your time and stay focused."

"Which one will we start with?" Anika asked.

"Savory," Trevor said.

"And how long do our bakers have?" Anika continued.

"You have two hours," Kendra said. "Plenty of time."

Anika nodded. "Well, we need to stop pudding this off! Bakers: Let's. Get. Started!"

Tori turned on her heel and sprinted to her refrigerator to retrieve the mushrooms and asparagus. But when she opened the door, she was greeted by chaos. Her cartons of eggs and cream were on their sides, crushed and dripping. Her asparagus, which she had stood in containers filled with water to keep fresh, had tipped over, spilling water everywhere and shearing off the tops of most of the spears. And most of her precious blackberries were mashed all over the shelves or falling on the floor through the open door. What was worse was the absence of cold: Everything she touched felt like it had sat on the counter overnight. She looked behind the fridge and saw the plug lying on the floor, well away from the power strip.

"Uh, I need some help here!" Tori shouted. Flooded with adrenaline, she couldn't remember which member of the crew she was supposed to call when there was a mechanical problem, so she started going through any name she could recall. "Cal! Liam! Zak! Ted! Mike! Anyone?" She gingerly opened the freezer and poked a Ziploc bag. Her blackberries were a mushy mess.

Mel rushed over. "Tori, are you hurt? Are you okay?"

"My food—it's ruined," she said in a stunned whisper.

"What do you need?" he said immediately. "I have extra eggs and about a pint of heavy cream." He rushed back to his station. "I have butter galore, too."

Zak arrived. "What's going on?"

"My refrigerator was unplugged, and all my cold ingredients are wrecked." Tori wanted to hold it together and be the no-nonsense problem solver she had to be for her children or students or friends during a crisis. But seeing her blackberries destroyed, her eyes stung with tears, and she could barely hear anything over the sound of her blood pounding in her skull. Ted and Mike came into view, but they were rolling, catching all her misery on camera.

Liam joined Zak to assess the situation, giving updates to Cal over their headsets. Mel was back at her elbow, and Jayden joined them as well.

"What's the recipe you're making right now?" Jayden asked.

"A mushroom custard with an asparagus cream sauce," she said.

"Can you salvage the produce?" Mel asked.

"Yes," she said, her head clearing. "If I can just get a cup of cream, two eggs, and a couple of sticks of butter, I should be able to do this."

"Done," Mel said. "Take them from my fridge."

"If the asparagus can't work, can you use spinach?" Jayden asked. "I have a huge bag of it."

"Maybe," she said, eyeing the number of asparagus tips that had scattered on the floor amid the berries. "Thanks."

"Tori," Liam said, "grab your recipes, and let's go talk this through."

She turned to Mel and Jayden with a full heart. "I can't thank you two enough, but you've got to get back to making your own food. I'll be fine."

"We're in this together," Jayden said, trotting back to his station.

"Yeah, we've got your back," Mel said, his silver hat band glinting under the hot lights. He walked back to his spot past Natalie, who continued to silently sauté her garlic and fennel, peering up at Tori then focusing back on her pan.

Tori followed Liam into the wings, the cameras still in tow. "Here's what you'll do," the assistant director said quickly and quietly. "We want you to keep making your savory recipe and borrow the ingredients from Mel and Jayden just like they offered. We caught them on camera talking with you, which is great footage, too."

"I don't want them to be penalized," she said in a hurried whisper. "They might need that stuff later."

"If they do, we have extra staples in the main kitchen," he assured her.

"Look," Tori said desperately, "this situation wasn't my fault. Can we have extra time on the clock?"

He looked at his watch. "We can give you an extra ten minutes."

"Just me, or everyone?"

"Just you."

"Why not everyone?" she asked. "This wrecked everybody's mojo."

Liam snickered. "Not Natalie's."

Tori had noticed that, but since she'd been so peculiar for so long, Tori didn't want to fault her for it. "Couldn't everyone get more time? That seems fair."

"You're not in a position to negotiate," Liam said sharply. "Keep this up, and you'll only have five minutes extra."

"Understood," Tori said evenly. "But what about the sweet challenge? Nearly all my fruit is unusable."

"We'll talk about that at the lunch break," Liam said. "Now hurry up and get back out there." He clicked a button on his headset. "Cal, she's going back in. I'll talk to Anika in a sec." He turned to Zak. "You need to brief the judges."

Tori rushed back to her spot, cameras tracking her, to find the eggs, butter, cream, and half a bag of spinach her friends promised her.

"Cut, and stop the clock!" Cal bullhorned. The room went quiet. "Bakers, due to an equipment mishap, we are giving Tori ten additional minutes. This means Natalie, Mel, and Jayden will present their dishes while Tori completes her recipe, and she will present her bake last once her time is up. Understood?"

Everyone nodded.

"Anika, are you ready to tape your announcement?" Cal asked, turning to where she stood off to the side with Liam.

"I guess I have to be," Anika said, her tone a note sharper than usual.

"Bakers, we are restarting the clock on Liam's count," Cal said. "When Anika announces the change, you can continue working but please pay attention. Thank you, and over to Liam."

Liam counted down and signaled to Anika, who exhaled then repeated the instructions Cal had just shared for the cameras. Tori looked up occasionally but was too frazzled to listen. She reread her recipe, mouthing the words to get them to stay present in her brain long enough for her to warm the oven, chop and measure the ingredients, and start sautéing. It was going to be a long morning.

Anika entered the green room shaking her head. "That is just some craziness out there."

"What do you mean?" Trevor asked between sips of tea.

Zak slipped in behind the host. "Tori's refrigerator got unplugged, and most of her ingredients spoiled."

"Unplugged?" Kendra asked, setting down her coffee, her pulse skyrocketing. "How did that happen?"

"Don't know," Zak replied. "Some of the other contestants donated supplies, though, so she's making her dish as planned. She'll have ten extra minutes to get it done."

"She shouldn't get any extra time, you know," Anika said, folding her arms. "This show is supposed to test bakers under pressure, and if this happened in a real restaurant, no one would stop the clock and give her a do-over."

"This is television, not real life," Trevor said. "I'm sure it'll play better if we give her a bit of a break here, dear."

"How did her fridge get unplugged?" Kendra asked. "It's not like someone could trip over the cord. Those things are supposed to be taped down."

"Don't know," Zak said again. "I'm sure we'll have a tech debrief over lunch. Anyway, Tori will be judged last." He put his headphones on and headed back to set.

"How odd," Trevor said as Anika sat down at the table with him and Kendra. "We've had plenty of knife wounds and minor burns, and that poor contestant who dropped an entire stack of dessert plates a few years back, but an appliance failure? This is a first."

"Why didn't the crew catch this?" Kendra wondered aloud. "They do a full check of the set an hour before taping. You'd think they would have found it earlier."

"I don't know about that," Anika said with a wry smile. "Have you seen some of those guys first thing in the morning? They look like they sleep in their cars during their week off."

"You don't suppose it's sabotage?" Trevor said with a chuckle of disbelief. Kendra's heart rate doubled.

"Whatever happened, this is on Tori," Anika said. "I hate to say this, but she should have checked everything before the show started."

Trevor nodded, and as she checked in with the hair and makeup crew, Kendra mentally commanded herself to stop worrying. She had faith in Tori's unflappability. She would find a way to rally and get this done. She had to. Kendra wasn't ready to say goodbye.

Two hours later, Kendra stood in front of the bakers as Anika taped the intro to the first round of judging. She watched Tori out of the corner of her eye as she carefully pulled her bain-marie out of the oven, placed it on the stove top, then removed each ramekin out of the pan of hot water to set them on a cooling rack. To Kendra, it seemed she was chugging along as usual, which was a small relief.

"Natalie, please bring your savory custard to the front," Anika said. The baker walked forward with six black ramekins balanced on a tray with a white marble bottom.

"Tell us about your bake," Kendra said, refocusing her attention on Natalie.

"These are fennel thyme custards with crème fraîche and some toasted pistachios," Natalie replied, taking off her oven mitts.

"These look so well executed and presented," Trevor began. "Quite impressive."

"It almost looks like pistachio pudding," Kendra noted with some skepticism. If it looked like dessert yet tasted like quiche, the disconnect could make it difficult to appreciate the dish. Arranging a spoonful with all the major components, she went in for a taste and immediately clapped her hand over her open mouth. "Whoa, that's hot!" she cried out, feeling steam against her fingers. Both the roof of her mouth and tongue were completely singed. "What are those ramekins made of?"

"Stainless steel coated in ceramic," Natalie said defensively.

"Is that a heated tray?" Trevor asked, cautiously waving a hand over his own steaming spoonful.

"Well, yes," the baker admitted. "I put the marble slab into the oven with the custards so they wouldn't get cold."

"Using metal ramekins on a hot surface meant the custards kept cooking after they came out of the oven," Trevor said. "That also made your crème fraîche melt instead of being a cool contrast to the warm custard."

Natalie furrowed her brow and said, "It worked at home."

"Well, it didn't work here," Kendra snapped, accepting a cold glass of water from Zak.

"While the flavors are complementary, it is a bit on the bland side, even with the thyme," Trevor added once his spoon had cooled down enough to taste. "I rarely say this, but it could have used a bit more salt."

Natalie looked at Trevor for a long moment, then turned to

Kendra and asked, "Will you try another bite once they've cooled off?"

"No, thank you," Kendra said, in as neutral a tone as she could muster. She regretted that #TheChopper had reared its angry head at Natalie, of all bakers. "You were right to experiment with new equipment," she added. "You just needed more practice."

"Thank you, Natalie," Trevor said. Kendra watched the baker slink back to her station with a pang of self-recognition. As Anika asked Jayden to come forward, Trevor covered his microphone with his hand and whispered, "Are you all right?"

Kendra covered her mic as well. "I'll live."

"Can you taste anything?" Trevor asked.

She traced the roof of her mouth, which was breaking out in tiny blisters, with her scalded tongue. "We'll see."

As Jayden arrived at the judging table, Kendra could already tell that even despite Natalie's mistake, he would probably lose this round.

"This is a roasted carrot and spinach pot de crème," he said, setting down his tray.

"And where are the pots?" Kendra asked, looking down at a set of very small bowls full of what looked like chunky vegetable mash.

"Here's the thing," Jayden said with a beleaguered smile. "One of my mason jars exploded in the oven and got glass in two of the other ones. I threw those out, but the other jars didn't look too stable, either, so I split up what I had left and put it in bowls."

Kendra touched the outside of a bowl to ensure it wasn't another lump of lava, then took a spoonful. Before she could take a bite, though, Trevor said, "Don't eat that! I just found a piece of glass in my bowl."

"Oh, no!" Jayden said, panicked. "Did you swallow any?"

"Thankfully, no," Trevor replied.

"I am so sorry," Jayden said, collecting the bowls from the judges. "My grandma has used those jars to put up peach jam for years. I didn't realize they were so fragile."

Kendra set down her spoon. "Not being able to taste this is going to make it tough to evaluate beyond presentation," she said. "And I hate to tell you, Jayden, but the presentation isn't great either."

"I have to agree," Trevor said. "Taking the contents out of their jars broke down the custardy consistency. This looks like some sort of vegetable-infused cottage cheese. It's certainly not a pot de crème anymore, and it's not very appetizing."

"Maybe I invented a new dish," Jayden said glumly. "Carrot, spinach, and egg stew with a garnish of glass shards. Dee-licious."

"The lesson here is, when there is a safety concern, it's better to start over than hope everything will turn out okay," Kendra said.

"And when it comes to cookware, function is more important than form," Trevor added.

"Thank you, Jayden," Kendra said. As he slouched back to his station, she gazed over to Station 4 to see how Tori was faring. She was head down over a sauté pan, and the rich scent of truffle oil wafted through the studio. Given how poorly her compatriots had done so far, maybe she still had a chance.

"Mel, please bring your savory dish to the front," Anika called out. He brought forward six small plates, each set with a ramekin, a biscuit, and a rosette of butter.

"Wow, you brought us breakfast by the looks of it," Kendra said. "Tell us about your bake."

"This is fresh corn custard with country ham, Jarlsberg cheese, and jalapeños," he explained. "Then, since I had a couple extra minutes, I rounded off the dish with fresh buttermilk biscuits. Enjoy!"

As soon as Kendra took a bite, she realized Tori would have to be near perfect to beat this dish. "This is really excellent, Mel."

His smile was as bright as the shine of his bolo tie clasp. "Glad you like it!"

"The flavors all line up," she continued, "and the corn makes the consistency creamy and rich without getting heavy or too eggy."

"Yes, when I saw your ingredients, I was concerned this was going to be an omelet in a cup," Trevor added. "What you've done with these ordinary ingredients makes them taste extra special. The biscuit is a lovely bonus, by the way."

"My wife's recipe never fails," Mel said.

By the time he'd arrived back at his station, it was Tori's turn. For the first time in four weeks of competition, Tori looked disappointed; Kendra thought it took her more effort than usual to smile once she'd placed her bake in front of the judges. Her dishes were haphazardly plated and didn't have any finishing touches other than thick slices of truffle. Kendra's warning bells were already sounding.

"Please tell us about your bake, Tori," Trevor said.

"This is mushroom custard with asparagus cream sauce, enhanced with truffle oil and shaved truffles." Tori spoke as if she was trying to convince herself that was actually what she made. Kendra braced herself and took a bite.

She wanted to love it. She knew that some ill force, whether a saboteur or just plain bad luck, had conspired against Tori this round, and she'd had to do her best under strange circumstances. She understood this was not a judgment of her overall worth as a baker, or a person, and Tori could still pull out a save with her second bake if this wasn't her best work. She even mentally compensated for her less sensitive palate following Natalie's scorching hot entry. And yet . . .

"This just doesn't work," Kendra said. "The custard didn't quite set, and the sauce overwhelms instead of enhances the mushroom flavor of the overall dish. Even the asparagus side notes can't cut through the truffle oil; it's too powerful."

"I have to agree," Trevor said. "Truffle oil requires a light touch, since it can dominate other flavors. You could have done without it or used a much thinner shaving of truffle, or both, to focus more on the custard itself."

"I hear you," Tori said, her eyes downcast. "With truffles, less is more."

"Thank you, Tori." Kendra said. The baker took her wares back to her station, turned toward the front, and straightened up. Kendra hoped this meant Tori had already moved on from the morning and could focus on a better road ahead for the afternoon.

"That. Was. Horrendous," Tori said into Ted's camera before recounting the morning's disaster in agonizing detail. She was being forced to relive her anxiety and frustration once more for the *Bake-o-Rama* viewers, which was humiliating enough without the added worry that she was a hair's breadth away from losing this thing. Plus, this interview was all that was standing between her and lunch. She wanted to get it over with so she could drown her sorrows in a raspberry tartlet.

"Say more," the videographer said.

"It was bad enough that my ingredients were wrecked, but on top of that, the judges didn't like my bake anyway. And I understand why: The dish needed more balance."

"Have you met with Cal and Liam yet?" asked Ted. "Do you know how you'll handle your sweet bake?"

"I met with the directors, and I'll be able to get some items from the *Bake-o-Rama* pantry to replace what I lost. But they don't have berries on hand, so I've decided to make a different sweet recipe than I originally planned, since I was only able to salvage a small amount. It's one I've made often, though, and it should work well."

This had been a difficult decision. Without her frozen blackberries, she was missing the one ingredient the dish depended upon, and it simply wouldn't work without it. On the other hand, baking an old recipe from memory was always tricky, especially with her adrenaline running so high.

In answer to Ted's question about what she was making, she said, "I'll keep my recipe a secret for now," and attempted a conspiratorial smile. "Who knows? I may change my mind again before I start baking."

Ted cleared his throat, then said in a quieter voice, "Uh, Zak told me that it looks like someone unplugged your refrigerator on purpose and wrecked your ingredients before taping started today. That kind of thing has never happened before, and the crew is pretty upset about it. Do you, um, have any idea who might have wanted to hurt your chances?"

"Oh." Tori had considered that it was no accident, but hearing someone else say so made it an ugly reality she wasn't ready to sort out on camera. "Uh, no. I don't."

"Does it seem fair that you can't have a complete do-over?" Ted asked.

Based on her earlier conversation with Liam, she knew fairness was not the basis for the directors' decision. They wanted dramatic tension and not a lot of complications offstage. However, she knew on which side her bread was buttered, so she smiled as she replied, "I appreciated getting a little extra time earlier, and I'm ready to move forward to the sweet challenge."

"That's all we need," Ted said, looking at her over the camera. "Thanks, and hey, you did well this morning; I mean, after all that weirdness. You kept your cool. That's awesome."

"Thanks," Tori said. "See you this afternoon." Keeping her cool wasn't exactly making her feel better. She'd lost the morning round on her own lack of merit, and the dish she planned for the afternoon wasn't exactly innovative but was all she could cobble together on short notice with limited options. Plus, with the confirmation that someone was out to scuttle her chances, her mind was swirling with suspects.

She checked her watch. What with her meeting with the directors and the on-camera interview, she barely had enough time to eat and prep her station for the sweet bake.

Tori went to the side patio, grabbed her box lunch, and sat down with Mel and Jayden. As usual, Natalie was nowhere to be found.

"Hey, champ," Mel said as he patted her shoulder. "You doing okay?"

She shrugged and let out a sigh. "I mean, other than blowing my bake and being stalked by someone who wants me to fail so badly they destroyed my stuff, I'm dandy."

"So it wasn't accidental?" Mel asked.

"It wasn't," Tori said between bites.

"That's unreal," Jayden said. "I mean, I want the hundred thousand as much as anyone, but it's only a game, people."

"I agree," Mel said, shaking his head. "Are the producers going to investigate? Do you think they know who did this?"

"I didn't get a chance to talk to them about it," Tori said. "I was focused on what ingredients they had in stock so I could figure out what I could make off the top of my head." She slurped the last of her pesto pasta. "Well, I gotta go prepare to bake something I haven't made in forever and hope the judges don't hate it."

"You changed your dish this late in the process? That's brave," Mel said. "What are you making?"

"I have a couple of ideas," she said. "I'm going to have to wing it."

"My goal this round is to make sure I don't try to kill the judges with ground glass in their food," Jayden added. "What a terrible morning, am I right?"

"The afternoon has to be better," Tori said before pitching her trash and going back to the studio. She went straight to her refrigerator and confirmed it was working and her dairy ingredients were good and cold. She next moved to her station and set up the nonperishables from the show pantry: sugar, salt, cocoa powder, a vanilla bean, and cardamom, along with the remaining blackberries. She had less than a cup that hadn't been damaged, and she was going to make the most of them.

The directors had given her one small accommodation: a piece of paper and a pencil to write out her recipe from memory. "Chocolate Crème Brûlée with Roasted Spiced Blackberries," she wrote at the top. She needed to see it in writing to believe it could be possible.

"How are we going to judge this round?" Kendra whispered through her teeth as she, Trevor, and Anika waited in the wings for their cue to interview the contestants about their sweet bakes. "Jayden nearly killed us, Natalie left me with mouth blisters, and if I was Tori and had just found out someone was out to get me, I wouldn't have done my best work either."

"Look at you, caring about the contestants," Anika joked. "Never thought I'd see the day."

"We'll just have to see what they do this afternoon and factor it all together, as we normally do," Trevor said.

The three of them took their places onstage. During the lunch break, Kendra had skulked around the edges of the set, looking for clues. She was no detective, but if there was a scrap of evidence pointing to who had done this, she'd wanted to find it then personally punish the perp. Tori had been nothing but kind and supportive of each contestant and every crew member—herself included—and she didn't deserve something so mean-spirited. After a few minutes of acting inconspicuous, Kendra had given up. She couldn't see anything in the dark, and the longer she was out there, the weirder it would look if someone asked her what she was doing.

"Friends, we're back for the sweet portion of our competition," Anika said when she got her cue, "after a savory challenge that was, let's face it, pretty challenging for many of you. You'll be baking your own recipes again this time around. Kendra, what's your advice for these frazzled folks?"

"Everyone needs to relax," she replied, her hands moving as if calming the waters, just as Cal had directed her to do. "This afternoon is a fresh opportunity to shine. I'm sure you've double-checked your equipment and ingredients and are ready to go." She caught Tori's eye but quickly diverted her attention to the back wall, just above the camera. "Also, when you're making these sorts of recipes, there's a fine line between creamy and congealed: Watch your timing carefully."

"Right you are, Kendra," Trevor said. "Whatever you make, we want to be able to experience that delightful, custardy mouthfeel along with the rich flavors you incorporate into the dish."

Anika nodded. "So you're saying, 'Don't get flustered—just make great custard?' "

"Something like that," Kendra said, forcing her eyes to twinkle.

With a big smile, Anika snapped to attention facing the bakers. "You have two and a half hours, friends," she called out. "Let's. Get. Started!"

The four bakers immediately got to work. Kendra and Trevor walked toward the back bank of counters along with Ted to tape the bakers' interviews in reverse order this time around, meaning Tori was up first. Liam stopped them a few steps away and motioned to them to cover their microphones with their hands.

"Listen, when you talk to Tori, do not mention anything about this morning's incident at all," he said. "No talking about 'sabotage' or someone trying to 'throw the contest' or 'going after Tori.' None of that has been proven, and I'm sure Buddy would yank the episode if you say anything that hasn't been blessed by Legal. We don't want to see any sympathy or moral support. Nothing overly nice, or that'll come across as favoritism. Just keep things vague. Understand?"

None of this sat well with Kendra. Liam's warning seemed to confirm the likelihood that someone really was after Tori. There was also that word *favoritism.* She had been so careful to judge Tori's work fairly. Had she made a mistake anyway?

"We will be equitable as always, Liam," Trevor said. "Now, may we please get back to work?" The assistant director stepped aside.

When the judges and video team arrived at her station, Tori's ingredients were already measured, and her tools were at the ready.

"Hi there!" Tori said, pouring heavy cream into a saucepan. Worried about showing too much "moral support," Kendra opened her mouth to say hello but stopped herself, immediately feeling silly.

Thankfully, Trevor jumped in. "I see a blowtorch on your counter," he said. "Are you making crème brûlée by any chance?"

"Bingo!" Tori said as she scraped the innards out of a vanilla bean and put them aside. "This is a dessert I made for so many dinner parties back in the day. It's a go-to recipe when I need something elegant on short notice."

"This will be a chocolate version?" Trevor continued, eyeing the cocoa powder.

"Yes, topped with roasted blackberries rolled in cardamom and the seeds from a vanilla bean," she said, gesturing to the tiny black pile on her cutting board.

"Roasting? That's a great idea," Kendra said, hoping Liam wouldn't think it was against the rules for her to be impressed.

"It adds some unexpected, deeper flavors without being too odd," Tori said.

"Just make sure the spices don't overwhelm the dish," Trevor advised.

"Yep, I learned that lesson this morning."

"Have a good bake," Kendra said with a brief smile. She nearly turned to the camera to add, *Hope that's vague enough for you, Liam,* but thought the better of it and moved on to Natalie's station.

The judges interviewed the other bakers in quick succession. Natalie had a bread pudding going that oozed dark chocolate and orange zest, which would be hard to beat if it lived up to how good it smelled already. Mel was tackling a saffron-infused rice pudding with apricot shortbread cookies on the side, and Jayden seemed to be in over his head as he attempted to make mango coconut tapioca.

A half hour later, Kendra was walking around the set, observing each baker anew. This gave her time to ponder over who could have been desperate enough to want to knock Tori out of the way.

She began with Jayden. His station was its usual, well-intentioned disaster area, with tapioca pearls scattered all over the counter and the scent of burning coconut billowing from his oven. As he grabbed the baking sheet out from under the broiler and extinguished some flaming shavings, Kendra considered what his motive could be. The cash prize? With four boys at home, he could certainly use a hundred grand. However, Jayden didn't seem to have a ruthless bone in his body. And if he had thought throwing Tori off her game was going to be a path to victory, it was not working out that way: He was his own worst enemy. He'd had a dangerously inedible morning bake, and his afternoon effort wasn't going much better by the looks of it. Kendra didn't put him high on her list of possible culprits. He was too unorganized to be conniving.

Next was Mel, who was rolling out shortbread dough with a cedar rolling pin that he'd made himself, using a set of silicone guides to ensure the dough was an even quarter-inch thick. Kendra admired his meticulous technique and his reluctance to leave anything to chance. Of the four remaining contestants, Mel was the only one who hadn't yet been named Best Baker. Could that be enough to turn him against Tori, for whom he clearly had a sweet spot? Kendra folded her arms over her clipboard and cocked her head, taking Mel in from a different angle. In all the TV detective shows she'd seen, the bad guy was usually the person no one suspected. Then again, at this point he really didn't need any help to win this challenge. Mel was the only contestant who had produced a savory custard that was delicious *and* didn't almost maim the judges.

She moved to the other side of the stage to hover in Natalie's area. Her bread pudding was in the oven, and Natalie was immobile on the edge of her stool, watching the timer tick down. Her laser-focused intent to win was practically another contestant in this season of *Bake-o-Rama.* Kendra recalled Natalie's response during auditions to the standard question of why she wanted to be on the show: "Because I am the best baker I know, and it's about time someone else agrees with me." That had warmed Buddy's Nielsen-driven soul: Ambitious people created onstage tension and conflict that, in turn, resulted in ratings. For her part, Kendra had found Natalie's frankness refreshing. She knew how good she was and wasn't ashamed to say so. Now, Kendra wondered how far Natalie would go to find the validation she couldn't get elsewhere. Tori's win the previous week might have crushed a piece of Natalie's ego. Could that have snapped something loose in her tightly wound psyche?

Next, it was time to observe Tori. She was rolling individual berries in a mix of spices and sugar and arranging them on a baking sheet one by one with her long, graceful fingers. Their parking lot chat the previous afternoon had been one of the more meaningful conversations Kendra had had in a long time—and had also clarified some important things for her. One, she'd be able to figure out a way to keep Gamma Raye open, she was sure of it. Two, Tori didn't think very highly of herself, maybe because she'd been abandoned in her marriage, and that was a shame. And three, it was totally worth risking *Bake-o-Rama* in order to get closer to her.

Kendra so wanted to tell Tori that she was grateful for her advice, and she didn't deserve to have been treated so badly by her ex, and any time she needed someone to tell her she was extraordinary, she'd be happy to do so. Instead, Kendra silently walked away from Tori's station and back to the green room.

Tori sat alone on the back steps of the patio, her dinner untouched. She'd retreated to lick her wounds after yet another shellacking by the judges. Trevor's words of keen disappointment were swirling in her memory: *Pedestrian. Bland. Unrefined. Average.* What hurt more was the look in Kendra's eyes as she took a bite of Tori's crème brûlée. Hope had flickered then faltered. Having observed her so closely for so many weeks, she could tell Kendra was trying to choose her words instead of being blunt, which she appreciated even though they still made her miserable. "This is a dish that is done so often by so many bakers, it has to be perfect to make an impact," Kendra had finally said. "It's got all the elements of a comforting, warmhearted dessert, but they didn't coalesce completely. The result is less than the sum of its parts." Kendra never said it was bad outright. She may have been trying to spare Tori's feelings, too, which could be another signal that she cared about her. Yet that wasn't enough to avert the inevitable: Tonight, Tori was going to be sent home with no prize money, no TV show, not even a baking sheet . . . nothing.

"Mind if I join you?"

Tori looked up to see Mel. "Sure," Tori said.

"My hip won't let me sit on the ground anymore," he confessed. "I could use a walk, though."

She looked at her watch. There was plenty of time to walk the proverbial green mile before the judges' verdict would be filmed. She tossed her dinner into a trash can and together, she and Mel meandered down the stubbled hillside and headed right. So many people had tramped around the vineyard over the last few weeks that there was an unofficial path in the grass ringing the main building. Tori slowed to keep in line with Mel, who kept a steady pace. They were silent for a few minutes while crickets creaked ahead of sundown in an hour.

"It's times like this I wish my wife was alive to see this," Mel said as he scanned the endless horizon beyond the vineyards.

"Oh, I'm sorry," Tori said. "I didn't realize you were a widower."

"I have been for a long time now," he said. "The girls were in middle school when Sofia passed, and they've got kids about that age now. And don't worry: I'm not alone. Those two are over practically every day, especially now that I've retired."

"That must be nice," Tori said, imagining the twins years from now and hoping they'd still live nearby.

"I wish they'd give me more space, if I can be honest," he said with a fond smile. "They mean so well, but they do everything their way, not my way. Whenever they wash the dishes, I can't find my knives for a week."

"What's making you think of your wife right now?" she asked.

"She always wanted to come to Sonoma for a winery tour," he said, looking off into the distance as they walked. "We'd hoped to make it a twentieth anniversary vacation, but she got so sick so fast, we didn't even have time to take the trip early. She thought California was going to be all sunshine and beaches, like on TV. She would have been so surprised to see how golden the grass is and how big the sky is up here in Northern California. It's breathtaking."

Tori nodded. "It sure is."

"Sofia was the real baker in the family, by the way," he added. "Most of the recipes I use now are ones she used to make all the time. Right after she passed, I decided to keep making the dishes we loved best to keep her memory from fading."

"Your daughters must have loved it," said Tori.

"Not when I started. I was terrible!" Mel said with a laugh. "Man, the faces the girls made when they ate my food! I had no experience. The women in my family did all the cooking growing up, and I had barely touched a stove before Sofia died, but it was important to me that my girls remembered beautiful things about their mom from when she was happy and healthy, not just how she died. And the better I got, the more I knew she would have been proud of me, too. I mean, look at all this," he said, spreading his arms wide. "She wouldn't have believed I could be on a TV show."

"And you'll probably win the whole thing," Tori said, sounding remarkably supportive despite feeling so defeated.

"Anything could happen," Mel said with a shrug. "You still have a shot."

"I don't know about that," Tori said dully. "Neither of my recipes worked at all."

"Someone went out of their way to make things hard for you," Mel said. "That's not your fault. The judges shouldn't hold that against you. Besides, you didn't quit. You did your best anyway. That should be worth something."

"Still, my best was pretty awful. The judges said I'm no better than average," she said, Kendra's disappointed expression looming large in her mind. Tori sighed. "This show was supposed to be a turning point for me. I thought that being on *Bake-o-Rama* could be a sign that I should quit teaching, start a bakery, and do what I truly love for a living."

"You can still start that bakery, whether or not you win, you know," Mel said gently.

"If I don't win, how would I ever afford it?" said Tori.

He shrugged. "It's about more than money. I mean, how much does a dream cost you if you *don't* try to make it come true?"

"You make a good point." For every fear, there was a possibility, just like she'd told Kendra. She exhaled, recalling their conversation. "Anyway, I'm at a fork in the road."

"A dessert fork in the road, maybe?" Mel asked with a nudge to her ribs.

Tori chuckled.

As they neared the patio once more, Mel stopped her and said, "Take direction from your heart, Tori. You're right: You and I are a lot alike. For us, baking is more than just something to do. It connects us to the people we love. It shows we care, and that's why it makes us happy." He leaned in. "Remember that, no matter what the judges say tonight, okay?"

Tori hugged him, making sure she didn't bump into his impressive Stetson as she did so. "You are a wonderful man, Mel," she whispered. "Thank you."

He walked toward the studio. "You coming in?"

Tori hesitated. "I just need to get something out of my car. I'll be right in." Once he was out of sight, she sped out to the parking lot, where Kendra's SUV was still parked next to hers. She hopped in her car, pulled out the spiral notebook and pen she kept in the door, and started writing. A few minutes later, she tore the page out and folded it up so the message wouldn't show. She got out, locked her door, checked over her shoulder, and slipped the note under Kendra's windshield wiper, her heart thumping. Then she turned on her heel and walked quickly back to the studio to freshen up and await her fate.

. . .

Twenty minutes and a fresh application of mascara later, Tori was at Station 4, her apron cinched in place along with her determined expression: She was committed to being graceful in defeat. She looked up front. As usual, there was no way to figure out Kendra's state of mind; she was too skilled at being stone-faced. Trevor was just as impenetrable.

"Today's bakes are in the rearview mirror, my friends," Anika began. "It was a long, hard day for many of you, and you can be proud you made it through, okay? Let's give it up for surviving the Custard Challenge!" She applauded and whooped, ginning up the bakers and crew to join her. Tori clapped along, reluctantly at first, then with genuine relief.

"Now on to the good part first: announcing our Best Baker," Anika said. "I don't want to sound corny, but his savory custard with country ham sure makes breakfast the most delicious meal of the day. And he showed us that with a little saffron, pudding with rice is twice as nice. Mel, you are this week's Best Baker!"

Tori was so happy for him, she almost broke protocol to run over and hug him right then and there. Soon, however, the studio went silent again.

"With every Best Baker, there must also be someone who will not be able to join us next week," Anika intoned somberly. "Accidents happen, and sometimes the bakes just don't work out, especially when food safety is compromised. And that means, as much as we hate to see you go, we must say goodbye to . . . Jayden."

Tori had tuned out once she heard the word *accident,* certain she was the one Anika was talking about. Then Jayden's name broke through her haze, and it was as if she was on an elevator that dropped a floor or two then slammed to a stop. She'd been spared.

"No, that's not right," she whispered to herself. "It should have been me."

"What was that again?" Ted asked, suddenly at her elbow with Mike holding a boom microphone over her head.

"I can't believe they asked Jayden to go," Tori said. "I thought for sure it was my turn after the day I had."

"Can we get you for a debrief after we finish this?" Ted said, motioning toward the crowd.

"Sure." She stayed in place until Anika's close was complete and the judges were walking toward Mel to congratulate him. Knowing it would be a few minutes before she could get to him, she went to Jayden instead.

"I am so sorry," she told him. They both knew they'd been in a race to the bottom all day, and she had survived by the narrowest of margins.

"Hey, it's okay. No hard feelings," he said, motioning her to come on in for a quick hug. "What can I say? I should have started over instead of risking hurting someone. They were right. Safety comes first."

Her tears started to spill. "It wasn't your fault."

"Things happen," Jayden said, staying close enough to exchange whispers. "You know that whatever all that was this morning wasn't your fault either. I hope they figure out who did that to you so you don't have to worry anymore—so you can win this thing!"

Tori nodded and wiped her eyes. "Thanks. Take care of those boys of yours."

"You know I will!" Jayden turned to greet Ted, who had arrived with his camera for a final word.

Tori was wandering toward Mel when Trevor intercepted her. "Glad you're still with us, Tori," he said. "Congratulations!"

"Thank you," Tori said. "I'm lucky to still be here."

"Yes, and another day it might have turned out differently," he said, adjusting his glasses. "But there's no shame in owning this as a win. After all, you rarely have to be the best. You just have to keep showing up."

"That's a good way to think about it," she said. "So, on to bread next week?"

"On to bread indeed," he concurred. "I have a feeling that's more in your comfort zone."

"I'd like to think so."

"Have a good week of practice," Trevor said, trailing off as he moved on to chat with Natalie.

"Let me know if she tells you what happened to my fridge," Tori said under her breath, so quietly no one else could hear. Back on her quest to congratulate Mel, she saw Kendra hugging him and saying something about how "the most delicious food comes from the simplest recipes" before the chef noticed her.

"Hey there!" Kendra looked happy to see her but kept her distance. "You here to congratulate the man of the hour?"

"Yes, I am!" Tori said, basking in Kendra's presence while she could.

"I'll hand him over to you, then. Have a great night, both of you. I have to go tend to Julia."

Once Kendra had left, Mel looked perplexed. "Who is Julia? Her girlfriend?"

"Julia's her dog," Tori said without thinking.

"How'd you know that?" Mel asked, surprised.

"It was in an article somewhere," Tori fibbed. "Mel, I cannot be happier for you. You deserved to win today. It's about time!"

"I'm just happy everything lined up," he said.

She hugged him. "You made Sofia proud, my friend."

"Yes, I think I did," Mel said, looking upward. "And you made your kids proud, too. You didn't give up."

They wished each other good night, and after taping a quick interview with Ted and Mike, Tori secured her spices and other nonperishables in her locker along the back of the stage. She stowed her dishes in her cooler to be washed at home then lugged it down the hallway, stopping at the table of take-home boxes to pick up the one with her name on it. As she did so, she heard someone trotting up behind her. She turned and smiled.

"Hey, I'd appreciate some help with my cooler if—" Tori stopped midsentence.

Instead of a crew member, it was Natalie, speeding for the door.

"I have to get to the airport!" Natalie shouted. The door closed behind her before Tori could say another word.

Hauling her cooler out to the parking lot, Tori thought through every interaction she'd had with Natalie. She had yet to offer Tori or any of the other bakers any friendliness, empathy, or goodwill. Unfortunately, it wasn't hard to imagine her finding her way into the darkened studio then wreaking havoc on her fridge. Tori didn't want to believe that was what actually happened, but who else would have tried to sabotage her?

She popped open the back of her SUV to settle the cooler in place, noticing that Kendra's vehicle was no longer parked in the lot. This meant she'd already gotten Tori's note, the one she'd scribbled frantically as the minutes ticked down before going back on set, the one that said:

Hey . . .

Since this is probably my last week on the show, I want you to know a few things.

First off, about that fork in the road you're facing right now. No matter what you choose to do, it'll be the right choice. You'll do what's best for you and those around you, and it'll all work out. I know that much about you already.

Second, coming off what has to be the weirdest day in Bake-o-Rama history, I'm still trying to figure out whether I have the chops to run my own bakery. On the one hand, I presented some of the sorriest baked goods of my career. On the other, someone out there thinks I'm so good I'm a threat, or else they wouldn't have wrecked my stuff to slow me down. Whatever I decide to do, I know I'm a better baker now than when I started this game, thanks to your feedback.

Third, I get what you're saying about feeling disconnected from a sense of purpose. It's kind of funny that you complimented me last week for focusing on who I'm baking for. This whole stupid day, I wasn't baking anything I like to make or would choose to eat, so on top of having to change up everything on short notice, my heart wasn't in it. I don't want to do that again.

And last off, I really like you. I respect that you expect nothing but our best work. I know you're choosy about who you open up to, and I'm honored to have earned your trust. I'd also like to know where you get your wardrobe—it's a kick!

I hope we'll meet again soon . . . and since you asked what I'd like you to make for me someday, I'll tell you, even though you're going to think I'm completely basic. I'd love your take on a chocolate lava cake. I'm sure most chefs are sick of making that, and you're probably rolling your eyes when you read this, but I don't care. To me, it's the Best. Dessert. Ever. Invented.

T

How would that measure up to today's note from Kendra?

Now in the driver's seat, she flipped on the interior lights and opened her pastry box. Inside were a garlic roll and a currant bun along with a greeting that read *Great bakers always rise to the occasion!* with printed signatures from the judges. Tori tossed it onto the seat and searched the rest of the box for another slip of paper. But there wasn't one. She even broke the buns into pieces in case it had been baked into one of them this time around. Nothing.

"Sugar," Tori said softly. Had Kendra decided it was too risky to write to her anymore—and would her own note to Kendra then be considered a mistake? Then a more horrible thought popped into her mind: Had someone else found the note and removed it? Frantically picking through all the pieces of bun, she realized she hadn't examined the doily at the bottom of the box. Underneath, in familiar handwriting, was a message that was as short as it was torturous:

Whatever happens next will turn out better than we ever imagined.

It already has for me.

I'm so glad you're in my world.

K

"What have you been doing all summer . . . or should I say, *who*?" Della DeMarco asked, taking a long draw on her virgin margarita.

Tori had set up their overdue lunch date at Tio's Tacos with the ulterior motive of picking her colleague's brain. Della's decades of teaching Skills for Living had made her an expert in helping other people sift through their life goals and plot a path forward. Plus, she and Della had built some serious history together. She'd been the one teacher at Sequoia Tori had confided in during her divorce, and as a result, Della and her wife had slipped seamlessly into her wider circle of friends. She was a smart lady, and she cared. However, if they started talking about Tori's love life, they'd never get off the subject.

"Oh, you know me," Tori dodged, squeezing a lemon wedge over her iced tea. "I'm baking my way through the summer."

"Too bad," Della said, the salted rim of the glass imprinted with a crescent of coral lipstick. "I wondered because I heard you were driving back and forth to Sonoma every weekend."

"Who told you that?" Tori asked, wondering who squealed.

"I called Cassie and Lee Anne to see when we could get together for dinner, and they said you weren't available on weekends because you were always in Sonoma," Della said. "I hoped that meant you've found a new lady love."

Tori was unwavering. "No, I'm going up there to bake."

"Oh, are you taking a class?" Della asked. "That must be a pretty amazing course if you're driving all that way."

"Well, it's connected to *American Bake-o-Rama*," Tori said, watching her friend's expression to gauge how much she knew about the show . . . and the judges.

"What's that?" Della asked, looking confused.

"A cooking competition TV show that takes place at Three Vines Winery."

Della shrugged. "Oh. Never heard of it. Well, hope you're enjoying it."

Tori scooped a tortilla chip through the pico de gallo. "I am. A lot. That's why I'd like to talk about something—just between us and not to get out at Sequoia, okay?"

"Absolutely."

"I'm not taking a class in Sonoma," Tori said. "I'm actually a contestant on the next season."

Della put down her forkful of enchilada midbite. "Wow, that's fantastic! You're going to be on TV? When?"

"In October," Tori said.

"Tell me all about it!" Della squealed.

Tori sighed. "I wish I could, but I'm not allowed to say anything until after it airs."

Della nodded, her eyes bright. "Got it. But congrats! This is so exciting!"

"Thanks," Tori said, grateful for Della's support. "Anyway, these past few weeks have been the first time I've gotten to dive deep into baking without any other distractions. I've created some new recipes and gotten so much more efficient. I've watched what works and what doesn't for the other bakers, and I've gotten great feedback from"—she stopped herself before mentioning any names—"a couple of chefs I admire."

"I'm not surprised," Della said. "You're the best cook I know."

Tori beamed. "I've been happier over these last few weeks than I've been in years," she confessed. "I'm more creative and centered and focused, and I get such a sense of satisfaction when it all comes together."

"That's fantast—"

Tori cut in before she could lose her nerve. "Which is why I want to open a bakery—scratch that, I'm *going* to open a bakery." A wave of relief washed over her. This was a definitive statement, a given instead of a possibility, and it was freeing to say that to someone she knew.

Della smiled. "Sounds like a great side hustle."

"No, I want to do this full-time," Tori said, "which would mean I'd have to step away from teaching."

Della was still for a moment, then let out a sigh. "Wow."

Tori began to babble, her words tumbling over one another. "I've been really torn about this, especially since it would mean that we wouldn't be doing Biochem of Baking anymore, and I've loved working with you so much. And as much as I want to do this, I barely know how to start. How do I develop a business plan? Am I too old for this? Will I go broke? Does the world really need another butterscotch brownie?"

Della put her hand over Tori's and squeezed. "Hold up, honey. Take a breath. Maybe two."

As she took a deep breath in, Tori noticed her eyes were wet. "Do you hate me for saying I don't want to teach Biochem of Baking anymore?" she asked.

"Not unless it's because you don't want to teach with me," Della said with a small smirk. "Tori, I totally understand why you want to do something different and challenging after all these years. And hey, teaching is a noble profession, but it's also a job. You're allowed to change jobs, you know."

Tori giggled. "I know."

Della finished her mocktail. "Besides, great minds think alike. Thirty years in, I've decided to retire."

"What?" Tori said, stunned. "That's great news! When did you decide to do that?"

"I always figured I'd be done when I turn sixty in a couple of years," Della said. "Then a few weeks ago, Bettina and I talked it through, and we decided we wanted to start traveling now, before our knees give out, or worse. So I'm meeting with Doug Alonzo next week to work out a transition plan."

Hearing the principal's name brought Tori up short. "I haven't even thought about how I'm going to break the news to Doug," she said. "What would happen if we both left Sequoia? He'll have a coronary. I can't leave!"

Della waved her off. "Tori, he'd survive! Sequoia is a top high school. He shouldn't have too much trouble finding great teachers . . . even though we know full well that the two of us are irreplaceable. We can even meet with him together if you like."

"Thanks," Tori said. "But I haven't figured out a timetable yet. I'll let you know when I do."

Tori felt light-headed. The secret was out, her friend didn't hate her, and there was nothing stopping her from taking this giant step into a whole new career. Except for all the things that could, of course. The many, many things.

"Would I be making a big mistake?" Tori asked.

"Only if you don't think this through, or believe you're doing this alone," Della said. "I'm telling you right now, I'm helping you with your business plan whether you like it or not." She looked at Tori with a furrowed brow. "You know you can do this, right?"

Tori responded with a half nod. "But should I?"

"You don't need my permission," Della said, "but if I can share an observation, you focus so much on what other people expect of you, you push your own desires aside. I know you adore the students, and you love the twins with every piece of your being, and you certainly gave Shelby more support than she deserved. But time moves incredibly fast, and no one is going to live your life but you."

Tori stopped an errant teardrop with the edge of her napkin. "Thanks."

Della peered over her glasses and leaned in. "That's also why I keep bugging you to find someone to enjoy the ride with you . . . but if you're focusing on starting a business, I'll stop. Romance will have to take a back seat for a while."

Tori's stomach clenched.

The waitress dropped the check in a basket on the table between them. As Tori reached for it, Della snapped it up. "Nope, I'm buying. Think of it as an investment in your future bakery. You can pay me back in butterscotch brownies because, to answer your earlier question, yes, the world definitely needs *those*."

Kendra sat sullenly in a low-slung, steel and pleather chair, staring at the clock on the wall as the seconds ticked toward noon. The reception area of her brother's office suite seemed designed to make time pass slowly. The only entertainment was a number of business publications, six months out of date, strewn across a dusty black oval coffee table.

The elevator *bing*ed in the hallway, and Kendra watched her brother walk across the hall and open the glass entry doors of the office, a gym bag over his shoulder. He halted when he saw his sister. "What are you doing here?" he asked.

"I'm here for a lunch meeting," Kendra said.

"With me?" Alden said, confused. "Did I forget we were meeting? Sorry, I was working out."

"No," Kendra said, drawing a slow breath. "It's with a potential investor."

Alden's face was blank. "Who?"

Just then, a voice rang out across the reception area. "Hello, Campbell siblings!" Stella said, striding into the room. In contrast to her rock-climbing attire from brunch a couple of weeks back, she wore a sleek, finely tailored suit and highly polished pumps. She looked like a million bucks: almost literally like stacks of cash. "Ready to go, Kendra?"

"Hey . . . you," Alden stammered, looking from Stella to Kendra. "Can you give me a couple of seconds with my little sister first?"

"Sure," Stella said, slipping her phone out of her purse to turn her attention to scrolling.

Alden waved Kendra into a conference room down the hallway and closed the door. "What is going on here? Is it what I think it is?" His face shone with anticipation, but Kendra couldn't help noticing a slight smugness in his smile, which she found a tad disgusting.

"It's a business discussion," she said flatly.

"Uh-huh," he said, crossing his arms. "Then why didn't you invite me?"

"Because I didn't want this," Kendra said, gesticulating between them.

"This what?"

"Your not-so-secret hope that there was something starting between her and me," she said.

His face fell. "You saw how she was dressed out there? She only looks like that when she's going out for a date after work."

"Well, *I* certainly didn't dress up to meet *her,*" Kendra said, pointing to her ancient biker jacket and faded T-shirt, featuring a cartoon of an angry little girl with black pigtails standing atop the statement, YOU SAID THERE WOULD BE CAKE.

"She probably thinks that's what all the fashionable surly chefs are wearing these days," Alden said. "She'll think it's cute."

"Stella should know this lunch is strictly business," Kendra said. "When I called her, I told her I wanted to continue the conversation we started at your place."

"That sounds flirty, even when you say it," Alden said, his exasperation rising. "Jeez, Kendra, you're terrible at business meetings . . . and dating, apparently."

Kendra glared at the popcorn ceiling. "This is not a date! How many times do I have to tell you that?"

Her brother slapped his palms on either side of his face and groaned. "Why do I have to keep saving you from yourself, Ken?" He dropped his hands to his sides when Kendra didn't deign to respond. "If you really have no romantic intentions, I'll go with you so it's absolutely clear. I just went to the gym and I stink, but we'll just eat someplace sweaty."

"You don't have to come," Kendra said.

"I'm coming."

"I don't want you to come."

"It's not about what you want, it's about what I think is best for the business financially, and—"

Kendra felt as if steam was coming out of her eye sockets. "This is *my* business, Alden—my personal business, and my professional business! You can't tell me what to do with either of them! You might be older, but I'm your client, and I'm the one in charge of my own life—so back off!"

Alden rocked back on his heels. "You're right. I overstepped. Forgive me."

It took Kendra a few breaths before she could say, "You're forgiven."

He looked at the floor. "After forty-some years of looking out for you, it's hard for me to stop sometimes."

"I get it," Kendra said, her voice softer. "Thanks."

"I do want to ask you one thing, as your financial adviser," he said, chancing a glance up. "Why are you asking Stella to invest? She's got a bajillion dollars, but you and I both know she's not a foodie."

"That's exactly why I want her," Kendra said. "This could be a way for her to make another bajillion in a hot industry, and she wouldn't be making suggestions about the menu or anything creative. She could sit back and take her cut of other people's money while eating carrot sticks."

"I see your point," he said, then grinned. "And, as your wingman, can you give me a clue why Stella doesn't ring your bells, beyond her food ignorance? I want to refine my matchmaking skills."

Kendra didn't want to lie, so she didn't. "There's just no chemistry, Den, and I know what that feels like when there is." She put a reassuring hand on her brother's shoulder. "I appreciate you offering to come with us, but trust me. I can handle Stella."

Twenty minutes later, Kendra was seated across from Stella at one of the trendiest seafood restaurants in Berkeley, wishing her brother had come along after all, stinky or not, because Stella seemed oblivious to the fact that they were not having a date.

"That shirt is a gas!" Stella said, pointing toward Kendra's chest from across the table. "Is that crabby little girl supposed to be you?"

Kendra reflexively looked down and back up. "I hope not," she said. "My sous chef gave it to me."

Stella laughed. "Good thing you have a sense of humor."

Kendra, making an effort to look humorous, launched into her opening salvo. "I'm glad you could meet with me on short notice. I'm—"

"How did you get a reservation here?" Stella interrupted, leaning in. "I read that this restaurant has been booked solid since it opened."

"I know the chef, so I called in a favor."

"Wow!" Stella said. "Thanks." Stella sounded genuinely touched, which made Kendra nervous. Why was she having such a hard time communicating that this was not a romantic meal?

Kendra picked up the menu. "What looks good to you?" she asked, immediately regretting her choice of words. "Uh, what are you ordering?"

"I don't know," Stella said, scanning the options. "I don't like much seafood."

"Do you like any fish?"

Stella nodded. "Tuna."

"Great," Kendra said. "They have an amazing sashimi-grade steak with—"

"Um, I like tuna fish," Stella cut in. "Like with mayo and pickle relish."

"They definitely do not have that here," Kendra said, trying to keep her tone light.

Stella kept scanning, a frown on her face. "I'm not feeling the vegetarian option either." After a moment, she set down the menu and looked at Kendra. "It's no problem, though. I'll just order off the menu."

Kendra's jaw tightened. She'd called in a favor to get a table last minute, and this wasn't going to go over well in the kitchen. "That's an insult to the chef," she said.

Stella blinked. "Really?"

"The menu reflects his vision, and the flavors and ingredients are his signature," Kendra said.

"Huh," Stella said. "I thought the customer always comes first."

Kendra tried to think of an analogy. "It's like going to a boat showroom and expecting them to build you a pogo stick."

"Is that how it is at your restaurant?" Stella asked.

Out of the corner of her eye, Kendra saw the server approaching and threw him a look that said now was not the time. The young man turned on his heel. Looking back at Stella, Kendra asked, "What do you mean?"

"Do you get offended if people ask for something they want to eat instead of something you make?" Stella clarified.

"Well, yeah," Kendra said. "We aren't a pizza joint. You don't come to our place to pick toppings."

Her lunch not-date chuckled. "You're offended that we're even talking about this."

"No, of course not," Kendra said quickly.

"Well then, maybe you can answer a question I've had for a long time," Stella said, looking Kendra straight in the eye. "The fact is, we eat because we have to in order to stay alive. So how did we go from caveman times, when a good meal was one that didn't kill us first, to now, when snobby people are willing to drop a car payment so other snobby people can make them dinner?"

"Are you calling me snobby?" Kendra asked, more defensively than she'd intended.

"Of course not, but I'm fascinated by the whole mystique of restaurants," Stella said with a tilt of the head. "There have to be—what? Five thousand places to get a meal in San Francisco alone. Don't take this the wrong way, but what makes a place like this, or Gamma Raye, so special?"

Kendra was flummoxed. "The quality of the food. The innovative menu. The service. The location. Atmosphere. A whole list of reasons."

"But even with all that, you barely make payroll week after week," Stella said. Kendra's eyes widened in surprise. "Look," Stella went on, her tone turning brisk, "Alden told me that your restaurant space is being sold out from under you, and given that we have no chemistry, I assume you were hoping to convince me to be a white knight investor."

Even though Kendra resented being read so easily, she was glad the jig was up. "Yes," she said with a sigh. "That's exactly what I'm hoping."

With a quick nod, Stella went into full business mode. "Alden and I always check each other's work on major clients, so I've looked over your books from the last few years," she said. "All I can say is, good thing so many people are willing to pay six bucks for a cookie at Chippy Chunk when they could get two dozen Chips Ahoy! for half that at Safeway. That part of your business portfolio is healthy. It's ripe for expansion. Gamma Raye, on the other hand, is barely sustainable. You'd be better off if it closed."

"Hey!" Kendra felt as offended as if Stella had called her bulldog ugly.

"I know that's hard to hear," Stella said. "But financially, it's the best move you can make. And I wouldn't be the only potential investor to say so."

Kendra sat back. All around them, guests were digging into their beautifully prepared entrées or sipping from carefully chosen glassware, creating a symphony of clinking and conversation. The air was laced with the comfort of garlic butter and the bracing salt of the raw bar, and out the rear windows, the slate of the bay met the crayon blue of the sky. She'd commiserated with the chef soon after he'd opened this space about how all that effortless elegance cost a fortune. Taking it all in, she knew there was no question: It had been worth it.

"Have you ever loved something other people thought was stupid?" Kendra said at last. "Like a cringey pop band or a sappy movie or a loser baseball team?"

Stella considered the question. "Okay, I'll play," she said. "Yes, I have."

"You can't make sense of why it makes you unbearably happy, but your heart keeps feeding the flame," Kendra said. "Then after years of thinking you're the only idiot out there, you find other people who share your obsession, and you create your place in the world to be with them." Tori popped into her consciousness, and she smiled. "There's no spreadsheet that can justify running a restaurant like Gamma Raye, because that's not how I measure its value."

Stella nodded. "I completely understand how you can feel that way, but at the end of the day, you've got to do what sells. Love doesn't pay the bills, does it?"

"I don't want to waste any more of your time," Kendra said, putting her napkin back on the table. Before she could stand, Stella leaned in.

"It's not a waste of time," she said earnestly. "You have a gift for creating joy through food, and that's a great line of work to be in. I respect your talent and ambition, and you have accomplished a lot already, but the simple truth is, you need to refocus your priorities if you want to continue to grow your business and your brand. So, if you want to talk through your options with someone who isn't related to you, who can give you good advice without trying to make you feel better, I'm free for the next couple of hours. No strings attached."

Kendra thought for a moment. Alden was a shrewd businessman and a sensible adviser, but more than that, he was her protective older brother. Perhaps an outside opinion from someone who had utterly no interest in her was what she needed.

"Okay," Kendra said. "But let's get you some lunch first. There's a deli not far from here that has the best tuna fish sandwiches in Contra Costa County. Sound good?"

Stella smiled. "Sounds good."

Stella slung her purse off the back of her chair and walked toward the valet desk. Following her out, Kendra grabbed their server, handed him a hundred-dollar bill, and told him to send her compliments to the chef.

Tori had spent very little time with Buddy Walters since he'd sat in on her audition so many weeks ago. She'd spot him occasionally standing in the shadows near Cal's director's chair and scanning the set, his hands in the pockets of his fleece vest. Now, as he entered the conference room at Three Vines that Friday afternoon, his overt chumminess was as hard to avoid as his cologne.

"Hey there, Tori Moore," he said. "What's shaking?"

"Hopefully not my refrigerator this week," she said, wincing at her limp attempt at humor.

"Ha! Good one!" Buddy said, sitting in the seat across from her. "Basically, that's what I wanted to meet with you about, so thanks for coming in early today. I know you need to gear up for the Bread Challenge tomorrow."

"I'd like to know what happened," Tori said. "Any leads?"

Buddy frowned. "That, as they say, is a no."

"A 'no'?"

"We talked to every crew member who pulled a shift last weekend to retrace their steps, and we didn't get any new information,"

Buddy said. "We also interviewed each of the contestants to learn what they may have seen or heard, but that was a dead end as well."

His blasé tone made Tori's blood run cold. "Is there security camera footage?" she asked.

"Afraid not," Buddy said, shrugging. "There aren't any focused on the set itself, and the ones in the hallways didn't show anyone who wasn't supposed to be here at the time."

"What about the police?" Tori asked.

"We didn't call them because, basically, unplugging an appliance isn't a crime. Besides, what could they do?"

"I don't know," Tori admitted, thinking through every episode of *CSI* she'd seen. "Dust for prints? Interview suspects?"

He shook his head. "Those fridges have been handled by dozens of people, so prints would be worthless. And as for outsiders talking to the staff, we need to keep what happens on set private. A police report could leak out before we air, and none of us want that, right?"

It was all she could do not to bang her head on the table. "So what am I supposed to do? Just wait for something like this to happen again?"

"Basically, don't worry," Buddy said, leaning back. "We have a security guard patrolling the set and the grounds 24/7. All the appliance cords will be taped down, and Liam will inspect them personally the night before and the morning we shoot. We don't expect any trouble."

"You didn't expect any trouble in the first place, and yet it happened anyway," Tori said in as reasonable a voice as she could, given how much she wanted to grab the lapels of his fleece vest and shake him senseless.

He shrugged again. "Yep, that was a complete and total bummer." Then he leaned forward, his eyes lighting up. "Gotta say, though, you were a pro. I watched your tape from last week, and no one would be able to tell you had any problems. You were mighty, mighty smooth. It was like you've been on television all your life."

"Thanks," she responded, appreciating the compliment in spite of its whiff of creepiness. "Just curious: What would have happened if I'd lost the round?"

He chuckled. "Good thing Jayden crashed and burned, so that's a mute point."

"Moot point," Tori corrected.

"Always the schoolteacher," Buddy said with a smarmy smile. "That's what makes you such a great addition to the show."

"So I'm supposed to go ahead with the taping tomorrow and act like nothing else could possibly go wrong?" Tori asked, knowing the answer.

"I basically see it as leaving the dark past behind to focus on the bright future," he said. "We'll keep our antennae up, but it may be one of life's little mysteries no matter what we do. Now go out there and have a great Bread Challenge, 'kay?"

A few minutes later, Tori walked down the hall to the banquet room for the weekly staff dinner, completely unsettled. On her drive in to the winery, she had been certain Buddy asked to meet because they'd found out who had done this—possibly Natalie, or maybe a disgruntled crew member who chose her at random to air their grievances against the studio—and she'd be able to breathe easy. Instead, some awful person was still on the loose and could strike again at any time.

Tori sighed when she entered the banquet room. Following her heart-to-heart with Della, she wanted to get Mel's perspectives as well since he'd watched her progress on the show. But, to keep a professional distance between cast and crew, a separate table was set for the three remaining contestants. And that was not a conversation she wanted to have in front of Natalie.

She joined the buffet line behind one of the grips and helped herself to a square of vegetarian lasagna and a pile of spinach salad.

As she chose a ciabatta out of a basket lined with a checkerboard napkin, a spasm of self-doubt rippled over her. Was the spinach tomato bread recipe she'd chosen to make too simple for the judges? Did its ribbons of Italian red and green against the white bread come off as tacky? It was too late to do anything but hope that tomorrow's Bake and Switch would be the savory recipe.

"Hey there," Tori said as she sat down at the contestant table, where Mel and Natalie were already digging in. "How was everyone's week?"

"I was just telling Natalie about my granddaughter's soccer tournament," Mel answered. "But you know me: I can yammer on about that for days and not let anyone else get a word in." He turned to Natalie. "No wonder I don't know much about you. But now's as good a time as any to remedy that. What do you do for a living?"

Natalie didn't look up from her salad. For a moment, Tori thought she was going to ignore the question altogether, but then she said, "I work for my family's business."

"That's just wonderful," Mel said. "What industry are they in?"

"Outdoor apparel," Natalie said quietly, spearing another forkful of spinach leaves. "I do product development."

"That sounds like something you'd be great at, with your creative bent," Mel said with genuine warmth. "Do you enjoy your job?"

She chewed carefully, not responding until she had swallowed. "Doesn't matter. A lot of people are relying on me. If it was up to my parents, I'd work there until I die."

"I hear you: Working with family is a blessing and a curse," Mel said, his tone light. "My father and brother had to help me get the tile store up and running. I loved the free labor, but then they started telling me how I should run things, and I had to tell them to stop coming in. And running a small family business can take over your whole life, too."

Natalie put her fork down and pointed to the stitched logo on her black hoodie. "Our family business isn't small."

Tori looked closer at the logo. It was a very familiar pair of long-tailed weasels, one brown and one white: the ubiquitous symbol of a multibillion-dollar clothing company. "Your family owns Overland Sports?" she asked in disbelief.

"Will you look at that!" Mel said with a surprised laugh. "I brought an Overland jacket with me this weekend. Maybe I should get you to autograph it."

Natalie looked miserable, and Tori thought she could intuit why. "What does your family think of your baking?" she asked gently.

"My parents have told me I'm not doing anything special because 'anyone can follow instructions in a cookbook' . . . and nothing's more important than the store, in their opinion." She sat quietly for a moment, her lips tight, before saying something completely unexpected to change the subject. "How are you, Tori?"

"Yeah, did you find out who unplugged your fridge?" Mel asked.

"No," Tori said. "Buddy said their investigation didn't turn up anything."

"One of his staff called me in Austin on Wednesday to interview me," Mel said. "I understand why they had to do it, but it felt awful anyway. I promise you I had nothing to do with it."

"They called me, too," Natalie said. "I was afraid they were going to say we'd have to re-record the Custard Challenge. I hate making custard."

Tori was taken aback: They had something in common after all.

"I just don't get why anyone would do this to anyone, much less me," she said. "I don't think I've done anything that would make someone hold a grudge or get mad."

"I'm sure they'll find who's responsible really soon," Mel said. "There are only so many people who had the access to do something like this. Or the motive."

"I'm going to bed," Natalie announced, standing abruptly. "I'll see you tomorrow."

Mel and Tori watched her beeline out of the room then looked at each other.

"She can't be the one behind all this, right?" Mel whispered.

Tori threw up her hands. "Maybe she is the bad guy, or maybe she's shared enough about her personal life for one day and needs to rest. At this point, I have no idea. So hey, do you have a few minutes for me to fill you in about what's really been going on with me?"

"Of course."

In between bites of the best tiramisu she'd ever experienced, Tori brought him up to speed on questioning her career options, throwing in sprinkles of info about her ex poking around again, and a little about how much she was pining for Milo and Mia even before they were off to college, while keeping the Kendra business tucked safely away.

"Am I crazy or what?" Tori said, once she'd run out of story and dessert.

"No, you're not crazy," Mel said. "You want to be absolutely sure you're making the right decisions as you start a new chapter. I completely understand."

She frowned. "I sense a 'but' coming."

He hesitated before speaking again. "When I decided to open my tile business, I searched for a rule book that would tell me *the* way to run my company. I got advice from family and friends and a few potential customers, and most of them thought it was a stupid idea to go out on my own when I had a steady job with the city at the time. After wrestling with what to do for weeks, Sofia finally said to me, 'By now, you've listened to everyone else on the planet. Have you listened to yourself lately?' She was right: I was letting other people tell me what I had to do to be happy, when the only one who really knew what that was, was me."

Tori considered that. "I'm not someone who likes making mistakes, though," she said.

"Nobody does!" He laughed. "Yet our mistakes tell us more about what we need to do than the successes. I'm sure you'll never use too much truffle oil ever again, for instance."

"You got that right," Tori said with a chuckle. "And I'm not going to leave here tonight without double-checking my setup for tomorrow either."

"I'll do the same in a little while. I need to call my daughter first. If I don't see you ahead of tomorrow, have a good night!"

Tori gave her friend a hug and walked toward the studio. At the door, a security guard wrote down her name then accompanied her on set. Tori opened and closed the refrigerator several times, checked the temperature, tested the lock on her stored supplies, and flicked her appliances on and off. She even poked around on her hands and knees to make sure every cord was taped down and every plug was in a socket. Finally, she stood and dusted off her palms.

"Good to go?" the guard asked.

"Let's hope so," she said.

While Tori was examining every square inch of her station, Kendra sat in the judges' green room reviewing the plan for Saturday's Bread Challenge with Trevor. She read through the Bait and Switch recipe then tossed it onto the conference table. "Are you sure this is a good idea, Trev?"

"I think it's a brilliant idea," Trevor replied. "After all, it's mine."

Kendra wasn't so sure. "The contestants are unsettled enough already after last week, and now we're giving them a recipe that has an intentional mistake."

"This is what separates the bakers who are only good at following instructions from the ones who have the experience to see the error and correct for it," he said, thumping his index finger on the instructions. "At this point in the competition, if they can't figure out how much yeast they need for a set of dinner rolls, they shouldn't move on to next week."

Kendra knew he was right. It wouldn't be the first time they'd altered a recipe for Bake and Switch, like listing baking soda instead of baking powder, to test the bakers' depth of knowledge. That said, the timing was lousy. Especially for Tori.

"I'd be more comfortable about this if they'd found whoever messed up Tori's bake first. She's got to be feeling antsy right now, and if she sees something's off in the recipe, she may think she's being targeted again."

Trevor was unmoved. "Tori will have to find her way through this challenge, just like Mel and Natalie."

"I guess so," she muttered, crossing her arms.

Trevor adjusted his purple-framed reading glasses. "Is something on your mind?" he asked. "You seem more bothered about this than I would have expected."

"I'm fine," she lied, hoping she could deflect attention away from the fact that she wanted nothing more than to find the culprit and personally shove them into a squad car to avenge her lady fair.

Trevor persisted. "How's business these days?"

Relieved he hadn't guessed the prime reason she was out of sorts, Kendra still had to deal with the fact that he'd nailed the secondary one. Ever since Stella had taken her through the raft of reasons Gamma Raye should close, Kendra had been in a funk. As friendly as they'd become lately, she wasn't completely comfortable talking shop with Trevor, though. He had maintained a string of successful restaurants for decades. What would he think of her if he learned she was going to lose her one and only?

Time to find out.

"Not great," she said, relaxing her shoulders. "My restaurant space is being sold out from under me, and unless something changes, I'll have to close by the end of September."

"Oh, dear, that's unfortunate," Trevor said. "Do you have a new location picked out?"

"No," Kendra said. "I'd like to keep the current one."

"Oof, getting into a bidding war can get extraordinarily expensive. Do you think that's wise?"

Clearly, Trevor didn't think so, which made Kendra feel defensive. "It would solve a lot of other problems," she said.

"Like what?"

"The staff won't have to relocate, I wouldn't have to find new suppliers, I could keep my ten-minute commute . . . that sort of thing."

He sized her up. "So your food couldn't possibly be cooked anywhere else?"

"Well—" Kendra started, but Trevor cut in.

"It wouldn't taste as delicious?" he asked, his eyes kind and his smile mischievous.

"That's not what I—"

"People don't go out to eat anywhere else in Northern California?"

"Trevor—"

"And you got into this business so you can have a short commute?"

"Okay, you can stop now!" Kendra said, laughing in spite of herself. "I get it. I may not be looking at this situation in the most rational manner."

He patted her hand fondly. "I understand why. I was just as romantic about my first restaurant."

"Chevalier?"

"Oh, no," Trevor said, "that was my first *successful* restaurant. I'm talking about Candlelight, which I opened not long after I got out of culinary school. A little place with twelve tables in a strip mall in Sausalito. The menu consisted of the popular dishes of the mid-1990s, and there were ferns in the window, brass fixtures, and, of course, lots of candles." He shook his head. "It was dreadful. The menu had no point of view because I'd created a poor copy of what I thought a serious restaurant was supposed to be instead of starting with what I wanted to make. But it was mine, and I was so, so proud."

Kendra was floored. She'd never even heard of Candlelight. "How long was it open?" she asked, a little nervous to hear his answer.

"Thirteen weeks," Trevor said with a rueful smile. "And on top of that, I had to shoulder the remainder of the lease and the cost of storing all my pots and pans while I tried to figure out what to do next. Imogen and I had been married for six months, and her rich father wasn't about to lend money to some deadbeat chef who'd absconded with his daughter, so we had a lot of lean months before Chevalier came together. After that was up and running, and I was cooking the food I wanted to create, I found my audience, and here we are. And surprise, surprise: I didn't miss the ferns so much." He covered his mouth, trying to suppress a massive yawn. "My goodness, I've been talking so long I'm boring myself. I can only imagine what I've done to you."

"You are never dull," Kendra said with a smile.

"Then let me sum up my monologue by saying, Gamma Raye is a passion, not a place. Keep that idea first and foremost, and you'll know what your next step needs to be." He yawned again. "Oh, my! I'm glad I'm sleeping at the hotel this evening. At this rate, I'd nod off driving back to Tiburon. Are you going home tonight?"

"Yep. No reason to get a dog sitter when I live so close." Kendra stood and grabbed her messenger bag. "See you in the morning, and thanks, Trev. You're a gem."

He gave her a hug. "You're gem quality yourself, dear."

The next morning found Kendra back at Three Vines, waiting for her cue to go onstage as Anika greeted the three contestants in front of the cameras.

"Natalie, Mel, and Tori, good morning and congratulations!" Anika said. "You are our *American Bake-o-Rama* semifinalists, ready to tackle what is often the most challenging challenge of all: Bread Week! This is not a time to loaf around, friends. You must crust your instincts, or else your time on the show will be toast!"

"That's a ghastly number of puns, even by Anika's standards," Trevor whispered. Kendra stifled a giggle.

"So let's get *roll*ing, folks. Please help me welcome our lovely and talented judges, Trevor Flynn and Kendra Campbell!"

Kendra strode ahead and took her place to Anika's right. Scanning the stage, she noted that Tori was at the first station this week, practically glowing in a rosy calico shirt with her hair pulled back into a soft bun. Their eyes met for a split second, and Kendra felt a bolt of energy zip between them. Thrown, she turned her attention back to their host.

"Trevor, I understand that our first bread recipe today will be savory, is that right?" Anika asked.

He grinned. "Oh, yes—and it's one of my favorites."

Anika turned back to the contestants with a delighted smile. "You hear that, people? We have a Bake and Switch to start the day off right! Tell us more, Trevor."

"This is a dinner roll recipe my mother used to particularly enjoy," he explained. "She nicknamed it Knitter's Delight, and you'll see why as the bread comes together."

"Ooh, you have me on pins and needles—knitting needles, that is!" Anika turned her attention to Kendra. "Kendra, do you have any advice for our contestants before they turn over the recipe and get started?"

"Trust your instincts, and no matter what, keep baking. That's all I'll say," Kendra said, studiously avoiding looking anywhere near Station 1 in case the electrical spark between them might catch something on fire.

Anika nodded. "Duly noted! Now, is everyone bready? You have three hours, so . . . Let's. Get. Started!"

With that, the contestants turned over the recipes and began reading. Kendra watched their facial expressions to see if the instruction to use two tablespoons of yeast instead of two teaspoons had registered with them yet. Mel and Natalie quickly put their papers down and began prepping their mise en place, dipping their tablespoons into containers of active yeast twice. But Tori had one hand on her hip, the other holding the recipe up to catch more light. Her brow furrowed as she read it aloud to herself, the videographers angling to record it all. On the darkened edge of the set, Kendra moved closer to be in a better position to eavesdrop.

"This can't be right," Tori said, shaking her head. "That's way too much yeast. It should be more like two teaspoons." She paused before continuing to narrate her thoughts for the camera. "It has to be a typo . . . unless . . ." She quickly looked at Mel's workstation then Natalie's. "Well, they both measured out two tablespoons, which is a good thing in a weird way because I'm not being singled out. But it's a bad thing if everyone has the wrong instructions."

She shifted from foot to foot. "Is this some kind of a test?" Standing in the dark, Kendra attempted to send her a one-word telepathic message: *YES!* Whether or not it was received, Tori answered her own question: "Well, Kendra told us to keep baking no matter what and trust our guts, so on we go." Tori put the recipe down and measured out two teaspoons of yeast into a small glass bowl.

Kendra walked away, thrilled that Tori was on the right track . . . and she'd said her name in that honeyed voice of hers.

Once she'd finished her walk-around and observed the other two contestants, Kendra joined Trevor and Anika on the patio to shoot their explainer segment. It was already clear who on the set was doing well and who wasn't.

"The savory challenge today is your recipe for Knitter's Delight rolls, Trevor," Anika began. "What does that name mean, anyway?"

"The finished product should look like balls of yarn." Trevor reached behind him to present a basket of beautifully browned rolls to show the camera.

"How does that work?" Kendra asked as if she didn't already know the answer. "Do they have to roll the dough into ropes?"

"That's what it looks like, but no. Once the dough is divided into six pieces, each one is rolled and stretched to look like a baguette about this big," he explained, measuring the air with his hands. "Then, using a dough scraper, the first half of the oblong is sliced every eighth of an inch. As you can see, those slices bake close together to look like strands of yarn."

"And I've heard there's a surprise when you break them apart," Anika said.

"Exactly," he said, placing a roll on a plate then cutting it with a bread knife. "Before baking, the unsliced part of the dough is flattened to roll up a spoonful of fresh pesto before tucking it under the slices without losing that overall yarn ball shape. When it comes out of the oven, it looks lovely, and when you cut into it, the pesto has infused the flavor of the basic white bread so it's just delightful." Trevor pulled the two halves apart to reveal a dollop of dark green.

"That smells incredible," Kendra said, breathing in deeply. "The presentation is marvelous, too."

"I agree," he said. "You can stuff it with whatever you like: sautéed shallots, chocolate, fruit preserves. It's quite a remarkable bread."

"This was a pretty tricky bake," Anika teased. "And you had to go and make it even trickier, didn't you, Trevor?"

He smiled. "You caught me, Anika. I put an intentional mistake in the ingredient list: Instead of two teaspoons of yeast, the printed recipe said two tablespoons. We wanted to test the bakers' experience to see how well they know their bread making."

"It'll also show us how well they stay cool under pressure and think things through before they start baking," Kendra added.

"Both Mel and Natalie didn't catch the error at first," Trevor said. "From what I saw, though, Mel figured things out early enough to save his bake. I can't say the same about Natalie, I'm afraid."

"But Tori corrected the mistake from the get-go," Kendra said.

"So she's in the clear?" Anika asked.

"We'll have to see what comes out of the oven," Trevor said.

"Cut! Thanks, everyone." Ted came out from behind the camera, and Mike put down the boom microphone to start wrapping up cables.

"Personally, I don't think it's fair to have a mistake in the recipe," Anika told Trevor under her breath.

"It's a challenge they should be able to handle," Trevor replied.

Anika pressed on. "But the bakers trust you. You give them instructions, they're going to follow them."

"Well, sometimes this happens in real life," Kendra said. "There's a misprint or someone copies the instructions wrong. It's a good test of their knowledge and skill."

"Whatever," Anika said with uncharacteristic testiness, straightening her lavender sundress. "Where I come from, you follow the rules and do what's expected of you, but what I think doesn't matter here." She walked out of the green room, leaving Trevor and Kendra looking at each other.

"What was that about?" Trevor asked.

"Clearly she's Team Natalie," Kendra said, mystified.

A few minutes later, Kendra and Trevor were back onstage, ready to judge the results. The studio was redolent with the luxurious scent of butter, garlic, and fresh bread. Anika was in her place and camera ready, radiating good vibes as usual, when the director called "Action!"

"Welcome back to the savory half of our Bread Challenge, where our three bakers did their best to unravel the recipe for Knitter's Delight rolls," Anika said. "Trevor, this was your recipe. What are you looking for in this bake?"

"The same as always: presentation and taste. It needs to look like it's supposed to and taste utterly delicious."

"But will that be possible today, given your mistake?" Anika asked him, doe-eyed.

To Kendra's knowledge, this was the first time Anika had ever gone off script. To her surprise, Cal didn't call "Cut!" but kept the cameras rolling.

"Oh, it was no mistake," Trevor responded evenly, then turned to the contestants. "Bakers, you may have noticed there was an error in the ingredient list when it came to the amount of yeast you were supposed to use. That was intentional: We wanted to get a better sense of your bread-baking experience as well as your familiarity with how to use particular ingredients. Now, we'll see how well you handled this curveball."

That was Anika's cue to call up the first contestant, but she remained silent. Pro that he was, Trevor barreled on. "Very well. Tori, please bring your bake to the judges' table."

Keeping Trevor in her peripheral vision to pick up her cue regardless of what hash Anika was making of the script, Kendra watched Tori stride to the front. She seemed relaxed and confident, and the six rolls in her basket explained why.

"You nailed the presentation part of the challenge," Kendra said. "They are well browned, and the cut marks are even so you get that ball of yarn look."

"Let's see what it looks like inside," Trevor said, cutting one into three pieces. "The pesto stayed put and didn't soak through the dough." He handed Kendra a piece then bit into his. "And the bread is nice and light while the pesto is well balanced."

Kendra finished her sample. "How much yeast did you use?"

"Two teaspoons," Tori said.

"That was the right amount—well done, Tori!" Trevor gave Anika a side-eyed glance, trying to gauge whether or not she was planning to get back on script while continuing to beam at Tori.

Kendra followed his lead and stayed focused on the task at hand. "This was expertly made and looks as delicious as it tastes. Great job, Tori."

"Thank you," Tori said, returning to her station with her head high.

After an awkward couple of seconds, during which Kendra realized Anika wasn't planning on calling up the next contestant, she spoke up herself. "Mel, please bring your bake to the judges' table."

"How much yeast did you put into your rolls?" Trevor asked as Mel presented his basket.

"Two teaspoons."

"Bravo, Mel! Now, let's get a look at these," Trevor said brightly as he turned one of the rolls over in his hand. "They are a little less brown than I'd like, but they look thoroughly baked." He peered closer. "The strands of 'yarn' are consistent, and nothing leaked out the bottom either."

Kendra cut the bread this time, offering the first piece to Anika, who chewed impassively, then taking a taste herself. "The flavor is on the money, and you have the right amount of pesto in there, too," she said. "Very, very good."

"I agree, Mel," Trevor said between chews. "The texture is terrific, and it pulls apart quite nicely. Thank you!"

"My pleasure," Mel said, taking his basket back to his station next to Tori.

Anika finally jumped back in as Mel retreated, saying, "Natalie, please bring your bake forward."

Even from a few feet away, it was obvious that Natalie's bake had not gone well, based on the rolls themselves but also her body language; she was tensed up as if preparing to take a blow.

Trevor picked up a roll, which was small and flat. "Seems you may have had a bit too much yeast," he said.

"I put in two tablespoons per the instructions," Natalie said, looking down at her Doc Martens.

"That's why the bread didn't rise as much as it should," he said.

"Still, it did rise somewhat," Kendra said. "Let's give this a taste."

Trevor took a small bite. "The texture is off, and the yeasty flavor is over-the-top. The pesto is spot-on, however."

Kendra tried it anyway, for fairness' sake. "Yep, I agree with Trevor. It didn't quite overcome the measurement mistake, but it has a good color, and the pesto is fine."

"I understand," Natalie said, peering back up at the judges. Kendra was surprised. Where was the baker's trademark defensiveness? Had she finally learned to take setbacks in stride this late in the game?

"Thank you, Natalie," Anika said. "You did your best under the circumstances."

"Yes, thank you," Kendra echoed.

Once Anika had taped her closing remarks to wrap up the morning, Kendra walked back to the green room to fill out her score sheets while the experience was still fresh. Taking out Tori's form, she scanned the criteria for the three categories: Technique, Taste, and Presentation. She started to award five out of five points for Technique but stopped and sat back. Her pulse was ticking upward.

She did everything right, she told herself. *She deserves full credit. I'd say that even if I didn't . . . like her. This isn't favoritism. It's totally fair. Trevor felt the same way. Right?*

She looked toward Trevor, who sat at the other end of the table filling out his paperwork. She couldn't ask, even offhand, what his thoughts were at this point. They weren't allowed to see each other's scores to ensure their opinions were their own.

Her palms clammy, she reread the criteria, circled 5s across the board then went back to each category to write detailed justifications for each. She was still writing when Trevor stood up to go to lunch.

"I feel like I've eaten an entire head of garlic," he said to Kendra, making smacking noises with his tongue. "Whose fool idea was it to ask them to make pesto, I wonder? Oh, right, that was me. Ready?"

She put a final period on Tori's form. "Not quite. I still have to do Mel's and Natalie's. You don't have to wait for me."

"I don't mind waiting," he said, sitting down on the couch and selecting a shopworn tourism magazine.

Kendra's pulse increased another few beats per minute. Given how much she'd written for Tori's eval, she was going to have to go into similar detail for the others for equity's sake . . . with Trevor hovering nearby. Would he wonder why she was taking more time than normal?

"It might take me a while," she said, hastily filling in her comments about Mel's performance.

Trevor didn't look up from his magazine. "Not to worry. I'm in no hurry."

Several agonizing minutes later, she was done, and the judges sealed their forms in an envelope and handed them to the PA.

"Ready to eat, dear?" Trevor asked.

"Sure," she lied. She was too on edge to be hungry.

25

Tori was feeling good coming into the afternoon, and that made her nervous. She had lucked out that morning, starting with the Bake and Switch that went incredibly well. Catching the error in the recipe off the bat saved a lot of heartache, and she couldn't have been more pleased with how the rolls turned out. Also, Natalie had a higher hill to climb to remain in the competition. If Tori could tie with her during this afternoon's bake, she'd be going to the finals with Mel. Plus, Best Baker was still on the table, her success resting on her delicious, glazed, and occasionally overly moist summer fruit bread.

Knowing there would be no room for error, she'd made a few loaves during the previous week as practice. She'd quickly gotten sick of eating her results, but Cassie and Lee Anne were more than glad to take the leftovers and even declared them flawless. Now onstage, her ingredients and utensils were present and accounted for; she even tasted what were labeled "Salt" and "Sugar" and confirmed they were what they said they were. She was as ready as she could be.

"All right, everyone, it's time to rise to the occasion and get ready for the sweet part of your Bread Challenge!" Anika punned. "You will be baking your own yeasty recipes this afternoon, and as long as you are not using a starter to make your dough, you can make whatever you wish. Brioche, sticky buns, cinnamon bread—no matter how you slice it, the choice is yours! You have four hours to rise and shine! Let's. Get. Started!"

The afternoon sprinted by. Tori's dough rose twice, after which she cut it into pieces and layered them with spoonfuls of blueberries and raspberries before baking. Once it was cool, with plenty of time left, all Tori had to do was take it out of the pan and drizzle it with lemon glaze.

Unfortunately, the fruit bread was all too happy to stay put. She slapped the pan's bottom and sides and tried again, but it wouldn't budge. She ran a knife around the edges, whacked it a second time, and shook it upside down. While some of the blueberries dropped onto the counter, the bread did not budge.

"Of course, this never happens at home," she muttered, aware that Ted had materialized near her station. She searched the racks of utensils at her station and opened a drawer or two. "If I can find a flexible spatula, I may have a way out of this." All she could find was a silicone-coated flipper and a pie server. She huffed air through her nose. "Okay, pie server it is." She worked its blade under the loaf, attempting to unstick it without tearing the soft dough to pieces. After a minute or two, she flipped the pan over into her hand, and the loaf came free. Most of it anyway.

"This is not what I signed up for today!" Tori said into the camera with a pained smile. Setting the loaf on her cooling rack, she picked the shreds out of the pan, arranged it like a jigsaw puzzle on her serving dish, and positioned the rest of the loaf so it would look whole.

"One minute left, bakers!" Anika shouted.

Tori glazed the bejesus out of the bread then placed a beautiful serrated knife with a painted hilt on the platter. She brushed extra sugar off onto her apron and exhaled as Anika declared, "Time is up!"

Tori's heart sank when she looked at her lopsided loaf, but she smiled anyway. From the camera's point of view. she had to be ready for judging, even if her cursed fruit bread was not.

The director called for a thirty-minute break so the contestants could freshen up before Trevor and Kendra weighed in. Tori headed straight for the bathroom. As she walked in, she glanced in the mirror. She noticed a smudge of lemon glaze across her brow, and her hair had become a lank mess. Spot-cleaning her face with a damp paper towel, her prior confidence seemed more like hubris. Her prize money, her future career, and her pride were all riding on a lopsided loaf of breakfast bread melting under the hot lights on her grandmother's cut-glass cake plate. As a Magic 8 Ball would say, *Outlook not so good.*

The door opened, and Natalie entered the bathroom. She locked eyes with Tori in the mirror, turned away quickly, then scooted into a stall without saying a word.

Tori left feeling a little better: Natalie seemed worried, which had to mean Tori had the edge. Then her stomach dipped: Feeling good at Natalie's expense didn't actually feel all that great.

Standing behind Anika and waiting for the crew to assemble, Kendra was mentally reviewing her weekly note to Tori. She'd written it Thursday, taking time with it and restarting twice, wanting it to say a lot without being overwhelming since it could be her last direct communication with Tori until their contracts expired:

> Hey . . . so glad last week wasn't your final week! And thanks for your letter; that meant a lot.
>
> You're right to worry about whether you're ready to open your own place. It's not that you don't make the food people want to eat—you do—or that you don't have the work ethic—you've got that, too, from what I've seen. Hopefully you have enough money socked away to buy your own store so financing's not a problem, or maybe you need to find some investors. (I can give you pointers on what to say to a potential investor . . . and definitely what not to.)
>
> What you have to be ready for is heartbreak. Like when you put every minute into creating the place you've dreamed about your whole life but the customers aren't coming and you have to choose between

buying ingredients and paying staff, or you get slammed by an important critic because of one dish that didn't turn out the night he came by—kind of like Bake-o-Rama with the added threat of having to close your doors. You might die a little inside when you realize your favorite thing to bake is not what people want to buy, or your bestseller is something you only made because it was trendy (my apologies to the world for adding to the pumpkin spice tsunami). It's painful and will make you question why you want to do this to yourself. You'll have to make your peace with it and keep moving forward.

It can also mean you get to a certain age and wonder why you don't have any friends who aren't on your payroll (are they friends then?) and haven't had a relationship that's lasted more than a few months. That may be a "me" problem, though. I've been lousy at making time for other people because I always thought I had to do just one more thing at work to have the kind of success no one could take away from me. I'm realizing that attitude is not all it's cracked up to be, and I want to change that.

The fork in the road I told you about is that I'm about to lose Gamma Raye. It's killing me. More than my cookie stores or being on TV, my restaurant is my baby. It was supposed to be my legacy and crowning achievement, but in a matter of weeks, no matter what I do, it's going to be gone. But on the plus side—the side I wouldn't have considered without you and your little positivity exercise—I'd have my nights and weekends back for the first time in my career. And maybe then I could rejoin the human race.

I hope you'll be there when I do.

Whatever happens on the show, and after the show, I'm so glad I met you.

K

P.S. If your favorite dessert is chocolate lava cake, I'll make you the best one you've ever eaten.

The note was folded in her jacket pocket ready to insert in Tori's take-home box. She had a little less angst about the message, now that she and Trevor had recorded their coy analysis of the three bakers to ratchet up the tension and prompt the viewers to stay tuned after the commercial to find out the results.

Liam called "Action!" and Anika launched into another stream of cheerful, groanworthy bread puns. As she named Mel this week's Best Baker, Kendra applauded. If Tori's bake had stayed in one piece, she could have easily beaten Mel's apricot wreath. Her fruit bread was one of the best Kendra had ever tasted, and Tori had made her laugh by suggesting it deserved extra points for coming out in bite-sized pieces. Mel's braided wreath was flawless, however, with rosettes of cream pastry cushioning brandied apricots.

"But as we all know, not everyone can move forward to the finals," Anika said solemnly. "This baker has had a lot of impressive bakes over the last few weeks, yet today's came up short."

Kendra felt for Natalie. Truth be told, Natalie's pan of cinnamon orange rolls was not far behind Tori's entry in terms of taste, but they were way too fussy. Natalie had twisted them tight and was stingy with the glaze, so there was none of the sloppy, gooey, finger-licking scrumptiousness required of a cinnamon roll. That, plus the problems with her savory bake, meant she just didn't have the points to stay in the game.

Anika continued. "I'm sorry to announce that the baker going home this week is . . . Tori."

Kendra's mouth dropped open. She looked at Trevor, who seemed equally surprised. She tried to catch Anika's eye, but she was finishing her closing speech to wrap the episode. Confused, Kendra looked out to the stage floor. Mel had wrapped a comforting arm around Tori, who was valiantly trying to congratulate him through tears.

Once Cal called "Cut!" Kendra sped over to Trevor and pulled him aside. "What was your score for Natalie?"

"I gave her twenty-four points overall," he replied. "Ten for the first round, and fourteen for the second."

"What about the others?"

"Mel was twenty-nine, and Tori was twenty-eight."

"I rated Natalie the lowest of the three, too," Kendra whispered through her teeth. "So how come Tori was sent home?"

Trevor looked puzzled. "I don't know. I assumed you'd rated Tori much lower than I did."

"We've got to talk to Cal," Kendra said. "This was a mistake."

The judges waded through the crowd of contestants and crew, searching for the director. Kendra found Liam handing off his headset to a sound engineer and waved Trevor over to join them.

"Liam, we have a problem," she said. "Where's Cal?"

"He already left. He had to catch a flight to L.A. right when we finished," the assistant director said.

"Anika announced the wrong loser," she said, controlling her tone as best she could. "We have to call everyone back and reshoot the reveal."

Liam looked nonplussed. "We can't do that."

"What do you mean, 'we can't do that'?" Kendra asked, her temperature rising. "Tori is supposed to come back next week, not Natalie. We have to fix this now."

"Could we at least inform the contestants about the error?" Trevor asked, placing a conciliatory hand on Kendra's and Liam's shoulders.

"We have to leave things as they are for now," Liam said as Kendra loomed over him. "Cal's gone until next week, so we can't reshoot anything tonight. Besides, if you think there was a scoring problem, Buddy's team has to investigate and sign off on the new results. Our hands are tied."

"This is insane!" Kendra said, unable to keep her tone in check any longer. "First, someone wrecked Tori's fridge, and now someone tampered with the voting to make sure she lost. For all we know, she could be in real danger. We have to tell her!"

"Keep it down, Kendra!" Liam shushed. "I'm telling you we can't do anything else right now, and we cannot tell the contestants about this either. The decision on how to fix this is Buddy's. I'm sorry, but this whole thing is above my pay grade."

Kendra scanned the crowd. Anika was hugging Tori, whose face was shiny with tears. Mel was high-fiving some of the crew. Natalie was nowhere to be found.

"Kendra, are you all right?" Trevor asked as she stormed past him down the hallway, stifling a furious groan.

Alone in the green room, Kendra pawed through her messenger bag to find her marker and a packet of Post-its. She scrawled a few words, stuck the note to her folded letter, hoisted her bag over her shoulder, and headed out toward the front entrance. Ensuring the coast was clear, she located Tori's take-home box and popped the lid. Kendra placed her letter on top of the meringue cookies and resealed the box, having made sure the Post-it was impossible to miss:

GAMMA RAYE
MONDAY @ NOON
ENTER THROUGH THE BACK
COME HUNGRY

On Monday, Tori sat in her car in the Gamma Raye parking lot. Over her dashboard speakers, Ian Dury attempted to convince her there were reasons to be cheerful in three parts, and she wanted to believe him.

She had been so wounded by being cut from the competition, she'd taken some solace in the promise of a final hug and a word of comfort from the woman who'd taken up most of her brain's real estate over the last couple of months. Even a flat-out goodbye would have been better than literally nothing, which is what Tori got as she'd dried her tears alonc and collected her ingredients and implements to take home. She'd trudged into the parking lot heartbroken, anxious, and angry. When it had registered that Kendra's SUV was no longer parked next to her own, she'd winced; that meant Kendra had Tori's latest—now final—note in hand, which she'd written before the taping. She'd made it short and flirty, taking a cue from the brevity and boldness of Kendra's previous message:

K,

You might be glad I'm in your world,

but I'm going crazy with you on my mind.

Can't wait until all this nonsense is over and we can chat off camera.

T

She'd been certain she never wanted to see Kendra again . . . until she'd opened her goodie box.

Each time Tori read and reread her latest letter, she fell a little harder for the chef. It wasn't just that Kendra was looking out for her, offering hard-won advice about surviving in the industry. It was that she identified with Kendra's sense of loss and loneliness. Kendra was losing the restaurant she'd built her whole life around at the expense of everything in her personal life. Tori had been in a similar emotional spot when she'd discovered Shelby's infidelity: Her marriage, which had been the center of every choice she'd made, had imploded, taking her professional dreams and self-confidence down with it. Both of them—Kendra and Tori—wanted to balance who they loved and what they loved to do. Neither of them wanted to face life alone. And now that she was off the show, they needed to decide what that meant for them.

Which led Tori to sitting in her car in the Gamma Raye parking lot. In her head, Tori knew that meeting one-on-one with the *Bake-o-Rama* judge, at her restaurant no less, was a bad idea. Sunday, she'd reviewed her contract and did an online search for every meaning of "fraternization" and failed to find a way to frame Kendra's invitation as legally innocent enough to protect them both. She'd even called Cassie for her legal opinion about her having a "hypothetical meeting with a hypothetical judge" and was told that it was better left undone.

In her heart, though, Tori longed to be alone with Kendra with no cameras or rules or expectations. A place where they could hold space for each other for more than a few seconds, and they could hold each other's gaze as long as they wanted. The chance at last, after so many sleepless nights, to talk, and touch. The fact that this could be the last time they'd ever see each other made her ache.

It was worth the risk.

The dashboard clock clicked to 12:01 P.M. Tori stepped out of her car and checked her outfit—a few steps above the casual flair of her *Bake-o-Rama* togs—before walking toward Gamma Raye's rear entrance. With a flutter in her stomach, she walked through a dark hallway and into the dining area. It was warm and inviting, with Craftsman-style dark paneling that gave way to cove ceilings with elegant sconce lighting. Even with the midday sun outside, the curtains across the front windows made the space cozy and private.

Sitting at a centrally located table was a youngish balding man in a trim business suit. He stood and extended his hand. "Tori? I'm Alden Campbell, Kendra's brother and business manager."

"Oh," she said. Her flutter fizzled; meeting Kendra's family was the last thing she'd expected. She shook his hand then sat across from him. "Nice to meet you. Where's Kendra?"

"Whipping up some lunch," he said, taking a seat and hooking his thumb toward the kitchen.

"I know you like mushrooms," shouted a familiar voice. Tori looked toward the back, and there was Kendra in her chef's jacket, visible through the opening in the wall between the kitchen and the restaurant. She was sautéing shallots in a shallow pan on an enormous commercial stove. "And you do nuts and eggs, right? I couldn't remember if you had food restrictions."

"I love it all," Tori said, the flutter back on.

Just then, a burly little dog trotted toward her from the hallway.

"Julia got out of your office, Ken," Alden called to his sister.

"Good thing the health department isn't here," she called back.

"This is Julia?" Tori said, delighted. The dog snuffled her fingers for several seconds, and she leaned down to whisper, "I smell like Johnny and Joey. They're twice as big as you are, but don't worry. They're marshmallows." Whether or not Julia understood, she allowed Tori to pet her suede-soft head.

"No way, Jules," Alden said. "You need to go back to the office." He stood and shooed the dog toward the back. Tori followed to hit the restroom and wash her hands. On her way back, she paused at the kitchen entrance. Kendra turned away from the stove and wiped her hands on her apron. Her eyes were as blue as the gas jets, and her face glowed in the warmth of the kitchen. Tori had always considered Kendra attractive and edgily sexy, but until that moment, she hadn't realized how beautiful she was. Her heart in her throat, Tori took a step toward her then halted, remembering Alden was close by. Kendra had done the same, and her hands dropped to her sides in seeming frustration. As the seconds ticked by, the pan sizzled and steamed on the stove, filling the kitchen with the seductive scent of shallots and butter.

"What would you like to drink?" Kendra asked, breaking the silence.

"Water, please," Tori said. "Sparkling, if you have it."

"Want anything stronger?" Kendra asked with a wry chuckle.

"No, I'm fine," Tori said, relieved they could laugh through the awkwardness. "Nice to meet your brother."

"I invited him because we have some business to cover," Kendra said with a note of apology as she offered her a glass of sparkling water. "I hope you don't mind."

"Not at all." Their fingers touched as she took the glass, and Tori sucked in her breath. Before she made things worse by losing herself in Kendra's gaze, she turned to take in more details of the decor and layout. "This is a gorgeous restaurant," she said. "I'm glad to finally be here. I've heard so much about it."

"Good thing you got to see it before it's gone. Have a seat." Before Tori could say anything more, Kendra yelled out to the dining room, "Hey, Den! Radishes are up."

"Please?" Alden prompted, entering the kitchen.

"You clearly haven't worked in food service," the chef said in mock seriousness.

Alden grabbed a small serving tray set with several small dishes. "You joining us yet?"

"Give me ten minutes," Kendra said. "Start without me."

Soon, Tori was savoring bites of raw radish dipped in whipped butter dotted with flakes of Himalayan salt. The peppery zing of the vegetable coddled by the creamy ease of the butter was so simple and fresh, nothing like the wan, pink-rimmed slices she usually picked out of premade tossed salads.

After the radishes and introductory pleasantries with Alden were done, Kendra came out from the kitchen and placed a bowl in front of each of them. "Today, we have sautéed porcini mushrooms with marjoram and preserved lemon, served over wild rice with poached local eggs and garlic-rubbed toasted baguette slices."

"This looks and smells utterly delicious," Tori said.

"Trust me, it is," Alden said.

Kendra sat down with her own bowl. "I hope you enjoy it."

The next half hour was a blur. Even as she rhapsodized over the food or giggled as the siblings told tales on each other, Tori could not ignore how close she was to Kendra, their hands mere inches apart across the table. Any stray glance or smile gave her a jolt. There was so much electricity in the air, she could swear she could see bolts of lightning speeding between them. And she still didn't know why Alden was there, which nagged at her throughout the main course. She wanted him to state his business as soon as possible . . . then leave.

At last, Kendra cleared the plates onto her tray. "While I get dessert in the oven, how about you tell our guest why we are gathered here."

"Sure," Alden said as Kendra returned to the kitchen. "Look, I wouldn't normally be in favor of Kendra meeting with any of the *Bake-o-Rama* contestants ever, much less while taping is still under way. However, when she told me about what happened on Saturday, and that the producers aren't taking any action to fix things, I was convinced you need to be briefed so you can decide whether you want to take legal action."

"Legal action?" Tori asked, confused. "For losing the semifinal round?"

"No," Kendra said, re-joining them. "For being sent home by mistake."

"What?" Tori wasn't certain she'd heard what she'd just heard.

"You're still supposed to be in the contest," Kendra continued. "Has Buddy talked to you yet?"

"Not since Friday, when he told me to forget that they didn't know who messed up my fridge last week and to focus on the Bread Challenge instead."

Kendra frowned. "That tracks with my conversation with him yesterday."

"Wait—back up," Tori said. "If I qualified, then why wasn't that announced on Saturday night?"

"Trevor and I compared scores after the results were announced," Kendra explained. "Both of us ranked you and Mel higher than Natalie. That means either someone changed the score sheets after we filled them out, or someone gave Anika the wrong information to announce."

"You mean I didn't lose?" Tori said, not quite believing what she was hearing. "I'm still on *Bake-o-Rama*?"

"You should be, but Buddy isn't doing anything," Kendra fumed, her volume rising. "I called him Saturday night, and he said we're taping with Mel and Natalie on Friday as announced because his top priority was keeping the show on schedule!"

"All he really cares about is keeping this mistake under wraps," Alden said with a note of disgust. "Can you imagine what would happen if this got out on social media?"

Tori could barely process this information. "I can't believe someone would change the scores."

"Do you think it was Natalie?" Alden said. "She'd have been sent home otherwise."

"I hope not." Tori thought back to their conversation at dinner on Friday with Mel, how distressed she had seemed—and how abruptly she had left the table. Was that guilt, or something else?

"Someone needs to talk to her," Kendra said, tight-lipped.

"That person will not be you, Ken," Alden warned. "Or you, Tori. At this point, neither of you should be talking to Buddy without representation either." He looked at Tori. "I can check with our lawyer to see if she has anyone to recommend for you."

The fact that she needed a lawyer gave her a chill. "My good friend is a lawyer, and she might know someone if she can't handle this herself."

A timer chimed, and Kendra went into the kitchen to pull dessert out of the oven. Alden looked at Tori empathetically. "I don't know who's responsible for this, but it's probably not personal. It's more likely because of the prize money or a bit of extra fame."

"That doesn't make me feel any better," Tori said.

"I bet."

There was clattering in the kitchen. "Alden!" Kendra called.

"Yes, Chef," he said, scrambling back to the kitchen. He returned with three mugs of coffee, followed by Kendra carrying a tray. Once Alden took his seat, she placed a dessert plate in front of each of them, topped by a ramekin crowned with whipped cream. She turned to Tori, her hands clasped in front of her, a smile on her face.

"Without any eye-rolling, I present to you my chocolate gourmandise with cinnamon whipped cream—which is my nonbasic version of chocolate lava cake. Enjoy!"

Hoping Alden couldn't see her blush, Tori took a bite and was overcome by the warmth of the rich chocolate. "Wow," Tori said for what seemed like the millionth time that afternoon. "This is delicious."

"It's so easy, too," Kendra said. "I'd give you the recipe, but Alden here would probably wrestle it out of your hands for confidentiality reasons."

"Someone has to protect your intellectual property, Ken," he said.

As he was about to go in for another spoonful, his phone buzzed. He glanced at it and stood. "It's Food & Drink TV. I need to take this in your office, Kendra. I'll call you in if you need to be part of the conversation, okay?"

Kendra nodded, and Alden hightailed it down the corridor, closing the office door behind him. Kendra shared an unguarded, almost shy smile. "We're alone," she said.

"For a minute anyway," Tori added with a soft laugh. "Thank you for a great lunch, and for making my favorite dessert."

Kendra smiled back. "It was my pleasure."

"You have a little chocolate at the corner of your mouth."

The tip of Kendra's tongue flickered around her lips, making Tori's breath catch again. "Did I get it?"

"No. It's still there."

Kendra wiped her mouth with her napkin, and Tori wished she could have just kissed it off.

They sat in silence. Tori was aching to ask Kendra if she had longed for a casual afternoon together as much as Tori had, or if she'd had any sleepless nights worrying about what would happen after the show was over. So many questions hung in the air. But with Alden returning any second, she knew it wasn't the right time.

"I'm sorry you have to close the restaurant," she finally said. "That has to be so hard."

"Yeah," Kendra admitted, looking over her shoulder toward the kitchen and back. "We have to be out of here by October 1, and that's coming awfully fast."

"Do you think you'll reopen somewhere else?" Tori asked, nervous that the answer might be somewhere well beyond driving distance.

Kendra shared a crooked smile, which fired up the electricity zapping between them again. "I don't know," she said. "After all, I'm rethinking my priorities."

"Hey, Ken?" Alden called out as he trotted back to the dining area. "The network has called a meeting with the talent at the studio at four o'clock today. You and Trevor are expected to be there in person. Tori, you'll be getting a call shortly to attend in person or by video conference. I didn't tell them you were here; I highly advise you to act surprised when you talk to them."

"Why? What's happened?" Tori asked.

"They've identified who was sabotaging you," he replied.

Kendra settled into an ergonomic chair in the Three Vines conference room next to Alden, ready to rumble. After leaving the restaurant, she'd gone home to drop off Julia and change into jet-black jeans, her leather motorcycle jacket, and a blood-red T-shirt emblazoned with a wreath of kitchen blades and KNIVES TO MEET YOU at its center. If the producers planned on stalling any longer, she wanted them to think there could be a price to pay.

Most of the creative team were already seated around the large oval table. Trevor was to Kendra's left, and his business manager sat at the back of the room, visibly bored, likely because all mobile devices were taken at the door to prevent any leaks to the media. Tori sat a couple of seats over, putting space between herself and Alden, probably to avoid any suspicious chumminess. Kendra had to stop herself from looking her way, and it was excruciating. Just a few hours ago, Tori had been under her roof, yet with her brother there, she'd had to watch her step as much as she did on set. Tori had been so close, and so lovely—but they couldn't even get away with a hug hello. At least she'd been able to watch Tori savor the food she'd made, just for her. Something about their connection had been cemented, even under those frustrating circumstances. That had to be enough for now.

A winery staffer tapped at her laptop until the large monitor on the wall lit up with the faces of those joining the meeting remotely via videoconference. Mel was in the top left box, sitting outdoors on a deck with a view of a large backyard garden behind him. The next box over contained Natalie, who had blotted out her background in a gray blur. After a few minutes of muted chatter, a new face popped onto the screen: a man who looked to be about Trevor's age wearing a dark suit and a short-trimmed mustache that outlined his firmly set mouth and echoed his severe eyebrows.

"Who's that guy?" Kendra whispered to Trevor.

"That's Buddy's boss, the head of the studio," Trevor whispered back. "If he's on the call and Buddy is not, that is not a good sign—for Buddy anyway."

"Good afternoon, everyone," the man said, and the room quieted. "We've got a lot of information to share, and everyone needs to hold their questions for now. I also have to remind everyone of their nondisclosures. Today's discussions must be kept confidential outside these walls or there will be consequences. Severe. Consequences. Got it?" The group nodded. "For those who haven't met me, I'm Ross Chalmers, president of the Food & Drink TV Network. I'm sorry this meeting isn't under more pleasant circumstances, but let's get down to it. To recap what you already know, we have experienced incidents of sabotage targeting one of our bakers that have negatively affected her performance and those of the other contestants. I am glad to say that earlier today we identified the person responsible and removed them from the program."

Kendra held her breath as Ross continued.

"This morning, Anika Charles confessed to purposefully damaging Tori Moore's ingredients and equipment just prior to the Custard Challenge. She also admitted to falsifying the judges' score sheets from last week's Bread Challenge to alter the outcome so that Tori would be sent home even though the judges had awarded her enough points to stay."

The room erupted. Kendra was so stunned, her brain locked up. "Anika? Why would she do something like that?"

"Because she thought Tori was going to take her job!" Natalie blurted over the video link. "That's what she told me before the Bread Challenge."

Tori looked equal parts confused and mortified. "Why would she think I was going to replace her?" she asked.

"Because Buddy said so!" Natalie said. "That's why he got fired. He screwed up big-time."

"He got fired?" Trevor said from Kendra's left.

"Everyone, please settle down. I need to finish," Ross barked, looking over his shoulder to someone off camera. "Rosa, why am I not able to mute Natalie's line?"

A woman appeared next to him on his square of the video call and sized up what was on his screen. "You didn't originate the call, sir," she said quietly. "They have to do it at the winery."

"Don't I just click this button?"

"No, no, no, sir!" she pleaded, her volume rising in alarm. "That's Leave Meeting—" In that instant, Ross disappeared.

"Natalie, tell us the whole story—quick, before he figures out how to call back!" Trevor demanded.

Natalie leaned into her computer's video lens, her image onscreen growing larger and more animated. "Anika pulled me aside before the Bake and Switch on Saturday morning and told me the bread recipe was printed wrong on purpose and that it only needed two teaspoons of yeast. When I asked her why she was telling me this, she said she wanted me to win. I didn't believe her for a second, so I asked what the real reason was. Then she said she overheard Buddy in a conference room telling someone that her contract wasn't going to be renewed because they wanted to go a different direction.

They didn't want some pop culture has-been anymore and intended to hire a *Bake-o-Rama* winner with camera appeal who knew how to bake. Like Tori."

Kendra was relieved that Natalie was in the clear; she respected the Portlander too much to believe she would try to cheat her way to victory. But she also heard a twinge of disappointment in the baker's voice: Buddy wanted to make a star out of someone like Tori . . . not someone like Natalie. That had to sting.

Trevor spoke up. "You knew there was a mistake in the recipe, but you didn't use the correct amount and lost the round. Why?"

"When I told Anika I didn't want to cheat and was going to tell Buddy, she said she'd deny everything and make sure I was kicked off the show," Natalie said. "But I couldn't unhear what she'd told me, so I kept my mouth shut and used too much yeast to look like I didn't know any better. I thought I'd still have a chance to make up for it in my sweet bake, but Mel's and Tori's were so much better than mine. When Anika announced that Tori was going home instead of me, though, I knew I had to say something. I contacted Buddy—who told me to keep quiet and just show up on Friday like normal because this was too big a mess for him to fix. So that's why I contacted Mr. Chalmers's office, and here we are."

Ross reappeared on-screen, his eyebrows furious. "What has she told you?"

"Everything, Ross," Kendra said to the screen. "Anika is a cheat, Buddy is a chicken, and Natalie has more integrity than anyone I've ever met."

Ross pinched the bridge of his nose. "Let's just say, for legal reasons, that's not how I would have put it, but in broad strokes, yes, that's correct."

"So how does this affect the rest of the contest?" Mel asked. "Is it canceled? Do we have to reshoot?"

"We are now going to have separate meetings with the crew, the judges, and the contestants to go over our plan and answer your questions," Ross explained. "Crew will stay here with Cal, the judges and their representatives will go to the small conference room for a meeting with me, and the contestants will need to hang tight in the break room until Cal can see you at the top of the hour. Thank you, and Trevor and Kendra, I'll speak to you in five." Ross disappeared, and soon the entire monitor went blank.

Kendra turned to Alden, dumbfounded. "You don't look surprised that it was Anika."

He nodded. "I'm friends with Buddy's admin, and he told me how Anika was angling for a huge raise and the chance to sing the theme song . . . which doesn't exist."

"Sheesh," Kendra said.

Alden shrugged. "She always struck me as someone whose life goal was to be famous for being famous, but I never thought she'd do something like this." As they stood to file out the door toward the green room, Tori joined them. She looked shaken.

"Hey, are you okay?" Kendra asked, checking her impulse to put a reassuring arm around her.

She offered a wan smile. "I've never been the center of a sabotage plot before, and Anika was always so nice to me during the show. It's a lot to process."

"I never suspected a thing. I guess she's a better actor than we ever gave her credit for," Kendra said.

"This whole situation isn't fair, and none of it was your fault, Tori," Alden said. "Whatever the studio decides to do next, remember that."

"I'll try," Tori said. Alden allowed her to step ahead of them, and Kendra watched her walk down the hall, her head high.

Tori sat in the bakers' break room by herself with Mel and Natalie in their boxes on the wall monitor as they waited for Cal to join them. She was a stew of emotions. She felt awful for ever suspecting Natalie, especially since she'd been the one who stepped forward and risked her own chances of winning. She was angry at Anika yet also felt oddly responsible for sparking her destructive jealousy, even though she knew she couldn't have controlled the situation with Buddy even if she'd known about it.

Plus, she was flattered that Buddy, creep though he was, thought she had TV show potential. She had been concentrating so much on earning *Bake-o-Rama*'s cash prize, she'd nearly forgotten that the winner would be featured on a future Food & Drink TV Network program. Now that she thought about it, she recognized how much she enjoyed bantering with the camera and explaining her methods: like teaching, only to a vast, invisible audience. That hadn't been the case when she'd first auditioned, when her self-esteem was awfully low. Of course, because it was Buddy's idea, it would probably be shelved for good as kind of a fruit-of-the-poisoned-tree situation. She could only hope that Ross might still give her a fighting chance.

"Well, this has been an interesting afternoon," Mel said, throwing his hands in the air. "Who needs to watch telenovelas when you've got *Bake-o-Rama*?"

Tori nodded and looked at Natalie's square of the screen. "Thank you for speaking up. That was really brave and self-sacrificing. You could have just gone to the finals and not said anything."

"I want to win because I'm a great baker, not because I'm a cheater," Natalie said quietly with a small smile. "Besides, I know either of you would have done the same for me."

"Absolutely," Mel said.

"I agree," Tori said.

"What I don't get is *how* Anika did all this," Mel said. "Did Ross's office tell you anything, Natalie?"

"I'm not supposed to say," Natalie said.

Mel nodded. "Understoo—"

"Here's what happened," Natalie interrupted, her dark eyes bright. "Anika told the security guard to let her into the studio the night before the Custard Challenge, saying she'd forgotten something, and he didn't think anything of it because she forgets things all the time. She wrecked everything Friday night and got in early on Saturday to chat up the guy on the crew who was supposed to double-check the setup before we started baking that morning."

"How did they figure out the scores were switched?" Mel asked.

"Anika was a lousy forger. They compared the handwriting to score sheets from previous weeks, and it was easy to see they weren't authentic. When they told her they might dust the pages for fingerprints, she freaked out and confessed. What a loser." Natalie shook her head with a look of disgust.

Cal stepped in and closed the door behind him. "Thanks for waiting for me. The crew conversation took longer than I'd wanted. I'll make this brief." He sat down across from Tori and checked a page of notes. "Let me assure you we plan to air this year's *Bake-o-Rama* season and allow you three to finish the competition. You're all still in the contest, and we still plan to choose a final winner and award the prize money and the TV show contract."

"Good," Natalie said. Tori was relieved.

"I've talked through this with our editing team, and we'll be able to remove Anika's footage and air the first four episodes pretty much as is," Cal said. "We'll have to do the Bread Challenge over again, though, to make sure you each have a fair shot to move forward. No Bake and Switch this time: You'll make a savory and a sweet bread of your choice. Since you've already had your sweet recipes evaluated by the judges, you will have to choose new ones to bake this time though."

"When will we shoot that episode?" Tori asked.

"Day after tomorrow." The bakers gasped and spluttered, and Cal quieted them with his hands. "It's the only way we can stay on schedule for taping the finale this Saturday as planned. Mel, Natalie, we'll fly you out tomorrow and will have staff available to help you source your ingredients so they'll be here when you arrive."

"That's not much notice," Mel said. "If we make it through the semifinals, we'll have to have our bake ready to go for the finale two days later. Can we postpone a week?"

"No," Cal said. "The crew's already assigned to another project. Anyone have any reason they can't do this schedule—work or family commitments you can't change?"

"Do we have a choice?" Natalie said. Tori wondered what she'd have to say to her parents back at the Overland offices about taking more time off.

"Not really," Cal said, exhaling in frustration. "Look, I'm sorry. I know you're all getting the short end of the stick here. The network is having kittens trying to figure out how to announce Anika's departure, much less get the rest ready for broadcast. They don't want to push back the air date for the show, so they aren't going to bend on this."

"Can you two make it work?" Tori asked. "I have nowhere else to be."

"Yep," Mel said. "It's one of the benefits of being retired."

"I'll be there," Natalie said, then added, with a hint of a chuckle. "And you two better be ready."

"Don't worry, I will be," Tori said, smiling at her very weird, very principled new friend.

Wednesday morning arrived sooner than Tori wanted to accept. Her mind hadn't stopped buzzing since that extraordinary meeting on Monday afternoon. *Intrigue! Unexpected rescuers! Second chances!* All that after a delicious, captivating lunch with her favorite celebrity chef, with whom she'd be able to chat on set at least one more time.

She was leaving little to chance for the Bread Challenge redo. She'd baked both of her bread recipes twice in thirty-six hours to make absolutely sure she was ready for any possible unforeseen circumstance. The smell of yeast had seeped into every corner of her kitchen. She'd used so much garlic practicing her tomato spinach bread, the cats had recoiled when she'd tried to pet them. She'd also spent a small fortune on high-end chocolate and made Lee Anne sick and tired of her favorite treat because, yes, she'd decided to go for it: Tori was going to bake the babka. It was her best chance to be selected for the finals, even as it was also her biggest risk for being sent home.

Tori closed her eyes and visualized her bakes: what tasks she would complete while the yeast was blooming, how long she'd leave the dough in the proving drawer, how much filling she'd use so it wouldn't leak out or burn, and so on. She opened her eyes and readjusted to the bright lights of the studio. Mel and Natalie were standing at Stations 1 and 2, with Tori just behind them in the third spot. Their aprons were clean and pressed, and their ingredients were at hand and ready to go. After all the turmoil they'd been through together, they were now a team of friendly rivals. Natalie turned to give her fellow contestants two thumbs-up. It took Tori a moment, after so many weeks of surliness, to realize Natalie was wishing her well and not trying to cast a curse on her or something equally dire. Tori gave her a thumbs-up in return.

"Have fun, ladies!" Mel said. The band on his cowboy hat sported a spray of striped feathers.

"We've got this!" Tori told them. "Whoo-hoo!" The other two "Whoo-hooed" right back. Tori was officially pumped.

Unlike past episodes, Kendra and Trevor were ready at center stage to kick things off at the top of the show. Since the decision had been made not to hire another host to weave into the season, the chefs would now be responsible for opening and closing the show and providing commentary and insights throughout the program in addition to judging the bakes as usual. Trevor looked like he was ready to set sail in a pastel-striped linen shirt and designer boat shoes. Kendra was as fashion forward as ever, edgy in slate-gray jeans with loads of decorative zippers and a long-sleeved ring T-shirt featuring a cartoon of an exhausted-looking loaf of French bread with a speech bubble saying, THUMP ME—I'M DONE. Apparently, the baking puns had survived the week's upheaval.

Liam counted down before pointing to the judges to roll the cameras and start the take. Kendra smiled—something Tori loved to see she was doing more often than she had at the start of the competition—and looked at the center camera.

"Welcome to *American Bake-o-Rama,*" she said, "where the best home cooks in the country get to share their kitchen skills, their family favorites, and their love of all things baked. I'm Kendra Campbell, and I have the great pleasure to stand here with my friend and colleague, Chef Trevor Flynn."

"The pleasure is all mine, Chef," Trevor said. "We are at Week Five, meaning the Bread Challenge is upon us. It is also the semifinal round, and our three incredibly talented bakers are ready to delight us with a savory bread as well as a sweeter recipe later in the day in their quest to move on to next week's final contest."

Kendra looked at each of the bakers. "Natalie, Mel, and Tori, you've impressed us over the last four weeks with your expertise and creativity as you made pies, cookies, cakes, and custards. The Bread Challenge is always a special event at *Bake-o-Rama.* Breaking bread together has been a human tradition for centuries, symbolizing community, family, and friendship. Trevor and I look forward to tasting what you have in store for us today."

"Let's get started, shall we?" Trevor said, clasping his hands in front of him. "As I said, you will start with a savory bread recipe. While it must have yeast, you may not use a starter. You can make whatever you like in whatever shape suits your fancy. Whether it's rolls, loaves, braids, or buns, it has to feature and celebrate rich, delicious flavors."

"You will have four hours for this morning's challenge," Kendra said. "The clock starts now."

Immediately, Tori was in a state of flow, moving effortlessly from one task to another as she'd done so many times over the last few days. Still, any time she looked up to check on the judges' progress as they made their rounds to chat with the contestants, she was startled. Just a glimpse of Kendra—in all her long-limbed, long-lashed, blue-eyed glory—made her knees nearly go out from under her. When Trevor and Kendra finished checking on Mel and Natalie and arrived at her station, Tori's stomach dropped and her cheeks reddened.

"Good morning, Tori," Kendra said. "What are you making for your savory bake?"

She smiled at them both as she collected herself. "Tomato spinach bread," she said as she took a saucepan of warm plum tomato puree, sugar, and yeast off the stove and poured the mixture into a bowl to activate.

"I see garlic and fontina cheese and all sorts of spices here," Trevor said, scanning the ingredients she was setting up in her mise en place. "No spinach, though. Are you making a spinach dough as well as one with tomato?"

"Actually, this bread is a roulade with the tomato dough rolled up around a spinach ricotta filling," Tori explained, mashing garlic cloves with the side of her chef's knife.

"So two kinds of cheese, then?" Kendra asked.

"Three, once I put some Parmesan on the outside of the loaf before baking."

"My ventricles are snapping shut as we speak!" Trevor said, feigning horror.

"It's worth the calories," Tori assured them, moving on to mincing an onion.

"With all that going on, you have to keep the balance of dough, spices, and filling just right," Kendra advised. "It needs to be bread, first and foremost."

"Yep," Tori said. "If it turns into a stuffed crust pizza, then I really blew it."

"That could be delicious, too, though," Kendra said with a touch of wistfulness. "Oh, well, another time. Thank you, Tori."

"Yes, thanks," Trevor said, and they walked offstage. Tori pulled out the mixer, installed thc paddle attachment, and combined her tomato purce with the aromatic ingredients, fontina, and flour, the image of sharing a pizza and a movie on the couch with Kendra clouding her brain.

Once the savory bake was concluded and judged, Tori ate her lunch quickly to have time to walk around the property by herself. She needed a few minutes to focus. The tomato spinach bread had gone flawlessly, the judges were visibly impressed, and while she was ecstatic, the upcoming sweet bake wasn't a slam dunk. She wanted to prepare for the afternoon without psyching herself out or getting cocky. A few minutes appreciating the vineyard view ahead of climbing Mount Babka would do her good.

A little way down the hill from the main building, Tori found a flat patch of ground and took a seat in the cropped grass. The knotty grapevines were planted in even rows that swept down the hillside, their new leaves vivid green, the fruit barely visible. Paint splashes of pink roses bloomed at the opposite ends of every other row. She hugged her knees and breathed deep. If sunshine had a scent, it would be this: warm earth and wildflowers.

She wished she could bring Mia and Milo up for a quick day trip before they went off to college. But they were wrapping up camp counseling and coming home Sunday, so there wouldn't be any time.

Sunday: the day after the final round, if Tori was lucky enough to still be in the mix.

Amid the compressed shooting schedule and all the other upheaval at *Bake-o-Rama,* she hadn't had time to focus on the twins leaving for school in just a few weeks. They'd been firm about wanting to fly to Colorado rather than driving nearly two thousand miles over two major mountain ranges (with Tori crying all the way) to be dropped off at college. To get her to agree, they'd promised to pack and ship what they couldn't take on board and order the rest of their stuff to be delivered directly to their dorm rooms.

They'd be home for a little while, then they'd be gone, and she'd be alone—whether she won or not.

Her mind racing, Tori shut her eyes and took a deep breath.

Nothing you can do about the future right now, she told herself.

Focus on this afternoon's bake.

See the recipe on the stand.

Imagine all the ingredients measured out and ready to go together in the right order.

See the finished babka in the oven then on the serving platter.

Smell the babka.

Be one with the babka.

Her eyes popped open and she stood up, dusting the grass off her backside. It was time to go back in.

30

"Kendra, I am about to swoon. It smells like heaven's chocolate shop in the studio!"

Trevor's delight was contagious. "You're not kidding, Trevor," Kendra agreed. "Lucky us: Each of our three bakers chose a chocolate-themed element for the sweet portion of our Bread Challenge."

"I can't wait any longer," said Trevor. "Mel, please come forward with your bake."

As Trevor waved him forward, Mel placed a black tray on the judges' table festooned with fresh marigolds. "In the tradition of Day of the Dead, I've made you pan de muerto with Mexican hot chocolate. Enjoy!"

Kendra sized up the round loaf of sweet orange bread. "The design represents the body of the departed, right?"

"Yes," Mel said. "The knob on top represents the skull, and the strips coming down the sides are the bones."

"Your sugar skulls are a nice touch," Trevor said, picking up a small white skull decorated with a rainbow of shiny frosting. "They're a little wet, however."

Mel nodded. "Usually, they'd sit out overnight to dry. This time, I baked them in a low-heat oven. I guess it takes more time for the skulls to get completely . . . dead."

Kendra cut the loaf in half. "Hmm. It looks like the bread may not have risen enough before baking. It's pretty dense." She cut a small slice into two pieces and plated it. Trevor washed down his bite with the hot chocolate.

"This is a little bland for my taste," Trevor said. "It's good you have the hot chocolate with that hint of cinnamon and chili to pep it up. That is scrumptious."

"I agree," Kendra said, enjoying a sip. "If there was a bit more orange and even a tad more icing, along with a longer rise, the bread would be perfect. Still, it's quite good. Thank you, Mel."

"No, thank you!" Mel said, returning to his station with his tray and a smile.

Kendra looked at Station 2. "Natalie, please bring your bake forward."

Natalie adjusted her glasses then came up to the judges' table carrying a cedar cutting board bearing a dark brown loaf and two small bowls. "May I present my chocolate peppercorn brioche with a side of strawberry balsamic jam," she said with a smile and a flourish.

All day, Kendra had noticed a change in the idiosyncratic baker. Her shoulders had relaxed, she stood taller, and she'd chatted amicably with the judges whenever they came by her station. When she'd dropped a measuring spoon earlier, Natalie calmly picked it up and set it aside. Only a week before, she would have jumped through the roof. Kendra was proud of her, not only for speaking up when she could have stayed quiet, but also because she was finally confident enough to trust her talent and have fun.

Trevor picked up the brioche, looking it over from every angle before tapping it. "This looks well baked, and it sounds good. Let's take a look inside." He shared a piece with Kendra, and they both put a dollop of jam on their samples.

Kendra took a thoughtful bite. "This is really something," she said between chews. "Brioche is such a luxuriant bread because of all the butter, and I was afraid that with the chocolate, it would be overwhelmingly rich or seem more like a cake. But the texture is perfect, and the bite of the peppercorns reins in the sweetness. That's marvelous."

"The complex flavor of the brioche would stand on its own," Trevor said, wiping his hands with a napkin. "The strawberry jam, with the sweet acidity of the balsamic vinegar, doesn't compete with it at all; it's a great complement to the bread. This is excellent, Natalie."

Her face lit up with a grin. "Thank you both!" she said.

Trevor called Tori to the front, and she came forward, carrying her twisty, sugary loaf as if it were the crown jewels.

"You've made us chocolate babka, I believe," Trevor said with a sparkle in his voice.

"Yes, I have," Tori said, setting it in front of them. "Enjoy!"

Kendra wished she could use a photo of Tori's creation on the cover of her next cookbook: It looked flawless. She took a long, luxurious breath and smiled. "Babka is one of those breads that calls to me when I go into a bakery. That cinnamon and chocolate aroma is irresistible." She picked up the cutting board to examine the loaf. "Let's break into this bad boy." Setting it down and cutting a slice from the center, she poked the interior with the tip of her serrated knife. "It's done all the way through, with the chocolate baked inside without getting overdone."

Trevor was on his second bite and didn't seem to want it to end. "This is just perfect, Tori. It has chocolate everywhere you look, the layers are light and buttery, and the streusel adds a satisfying burst of flavor as well."

Kendra wished he would keep talking so she could keep eating. "I almost never say this, but I'd like a copy of your recipe," she said. "I agree with Trevor: It's perfect. Thank you, Tori."

Tori beamed at each of them in turn. "It's my pleasure. I'm so glad you liked it!"

Kendra's gaze lingered on Tori as she walked back to Station 3 and settled gracefully into her spot, her hazel eyes illuminated by the bright lights of the studio. Kendra took a brief, cleansing breath before speaking. "Bakers, you've earned a break, and it may be a long one. Trevor and I will have a hard time judging this round."

He nodded. "This has been a Bread Challenge for the ages. Great work, all!"

Once the cameras were off and they were freed of their microphones, Kendra and Trevor headed straight for the green room. Trevor closed the door and smiled at his friend and colleague. "You, my dear, are a big fat liar."

"What do you mean?" Kendra said as lightly as she could, worried that he'd caught her mooning over a certain semifinalist.

"You said we'd have a hard time judging this round," he answered. "As much as it breaks my heart, I believe we'd agree that dear Mel came up a hair short. It's a shame. On another day, he'd be a finalist for sure."

"You're right," she said as she plopped with relief onto the squishiest section of the couch. "He is such a nice man and an incredibly talented baker." She was sure Tori would be devastated, even though she'd be tapped for the finale . . . and she had to admit she'd miss having Mel on set, too. Perhaps #TheChopper had moved on at last.

"Ah well, we'll just have to hope the new producers will have an all-star event at some point," Trevor said, sitting on the next squishy cushion over from her. "And it's pretty obvious who our Best Babka Baker is, don't you agree?"

She looked over at her colleague and grinned, a rill of delight coursing through her bloodstream. "One hundred percent."

"Kendra, you ready to talk about Gamma Raye?"

Kendra didn't realize how long she'd been staring out the French doors until her brother tapped her on the shoulder. It was Thursday, with last night's Bread Challenge in the can and the finale shooting in two days, and Alden wanted to take advantage of this brief window of time. She could avoid it no longer.

"Yup." Kendra took a seat at her dining room table, and Alden sat across from her and pulled up a couple of spreadsheets on his laptop. Numbers, other than the ones needed to measure ingredients, rarely interested her. She was a big-picture person, while Alden was happy to sweat the small stuff. Even when business was doing well, talking about profit and loss statements and cash flow was a soul-deadening process. Now that Gamma Raye was breathing its last, she wanted to avoid every detail. It made the situation too real.

"Let's look on the bright side," Alden said. "Without the restaurant, you'll be able to focus more on Chippy Chunk. If you can increase your sales at the stores by even a couple of percentage points, you could feasibly open another location in the next year."

"Uh-huh." Kendra watched a pair of scrub jays get into a screaming match in her backyard.

"Maybe it's time to bring your cookies farther inland. What do you think of Las Vegas? Lots of people want something sweet when they're out partying."

"Uh-huh." She suddenly had a strong urge to go outside and scream with the jays.

Alden frowned. "Come on, you've got to work with me. We need to give a formal reply to the landlord on Monday. I need to know what you want to do."

The jays flew off, and as quiet descended, all the idle ideas and hopes that had swirled around her head the last couple of weeks—the ones she'd written about in her note to Tori the day before—crystallized.

There was a way out of the morass toward something better. She took a deep breath. "Here's what I want to do."

"Please don't say, 'Rob a bank then buy the Sonoma space.'"

"Of course not! I'm serious!" she said, slightly offended. "I am ready to move on from Gamma Raye and do something new."

He drained his coffee mug. "Okay, I'm listening."

"To start, I want to renew my contract with *Bake-o-Rama,* and I want to become an executive producer."

Alden's eyebrows went up. "Really?"

"Why? Do you think it's a stupid idea?"

"No, I think it's a fantastic idea. If you hadn't acted like they were dragging you through hot coals each episode, I would have suggested it from the start. This will be a great way to expand your brand and open up so many other opportunities." He sat back in his chair, folding his arms. "So you like being a judge now? What changed?"

"I guess *I* changed because I took your advice at the start of the season." Her eyes narrowed. "Great, now you have that smug look on your face."

"I do not," Alden said. "I'm just shocked. What did I say?"

"You encouraged me to be more empathetic toward the contestants, so I worked really hard to understand why they were on the show instead of expecting them to disappoint me. I finally figured out that the best contestants don't come on the show for the hype or even the prize money. They love baking for a million different reasons, and they want to share that love with the world. And I have to admit, that helped me reconnect with what's important to me, too."

What she left unsaid was how much of this was inspired by Tori: Her optimism, gentle resolve, and resilience had guided Kendra toward a better version of herself.

Alden snickered. "You admit that I was right? I should buy a lottery ticket—this is my lucky day."

She tossed a balled-up napkin at him with a laugh. "Do not tell anyone about this."

"As an executive producer, what changes would you like to see on the show?"

Kendra leaned in. "I hate how fake the format has become. All Buddy cared about was amping up the drama with a bunch of phony high stakes and candy colors and cliffhangers. Now that it's just Trevor and me up there, we can focus on helping the contestants improve throughout the show. I want to teach them techniques and introduce them to ingredients and cuisines they might not experience otherwise. There's a lot of options here."

"Love it!" Alden said, looking as thrilled as he used to when they were kids building a pillow fort in the living room, creating an adventure. "All right, your first decision is to double down on *Bake-o-Rama.* What else?"

"I liked what you said about expanding the cookie empire," she said, grabbing a cluster of cold green grapes from the bowl on the table. "I agree: Vegas is a great food town. I'm down for making that happen, but I want to go bigger, faster. We'll need an investor."

Alden's eyebrows arched again. "Any investor in particular?"

"Stella seems to think Chippy Chunk has potential. At least she said so when I sent her a couple dozen cookies after our nondate."

His mouth dropped open. "You are really impressing me today. But we still haven't talked about Gamma Raye. Are you ready to step away from owning a restaurant for a while . . . or forever?"

"For a while," she said after enjoying a particularly sweet grape. "When I start again, I can start fresh."

"Okay," Alden said, making notes on a legal pad. "You have to give your team notice, ideally at the start of the month so they have thirty days to find new positions."

Kendra sighed heavily. "I am not looking forward to that conversation. Look, can you do me a huge favor?"

"Sure."

"I'm going to give you a list of chefs around here, and I need you to set up calls so I can introduce them to the staff and place as many of them as possible. I want you to help anyone who needs to apply for unemployment or health insurance or do a résumé, okay? These people gave me their best, and they deserve the best we can give them—especially if I need to hire them again someday."

"Absolutely." He nabbed some grapes for himself. "So much for spinning fewer plates. Sheesh."

"Well, you know me," Kendra said with a glint in her eye. "I need to stay busy to keep out of trouble."

He smiled. "I'm proud of you, Ken. You look happier, more at ease, than you've ever been. That's great to see."

She blushed. "Thanks."

Alden put the naked grape stem on his empty breakfast plate then looked at Kendra for a moment. "You really like Tori, don't you?"

Kendra laughed nervously. "Where is this coming from?" she asked.

"Lunch on Monday."

"That was a business meeting," she retorted.

"That's what I thought it was going to be when you invited me, but thirty seconds in, I felt like a third wheel."

Her ears were getting hot. "That's on you, Den. I was completely professional."

Frowning, he shook his head. "You could have cut the tension between you two with a chef's knife, what with all the furtive looks and overcompensating to stay far apart when I was there. And remember, I've seen you when you're infatuated. I know the signs: You get loud and jokey, like you want to distract me from the fact you like the other person in the room."

Her mind began to spin. "I have no idea what you're talking about. Tori is a contestant, and that's that."

"You two even seemed to have an inside joke about your chocolate gourmandise—and why did you call it chocolate lava cake? I did that once by mistake, and you got all huffy. Level with me, Kendra!"

Kendra cursed under her breath. Alden pushed his chair back and folded his arms in disapproval. "You could have any woman in the Bay Area, and you fall for a contestant? Someone you're judging?"

She threw up her hands. "I swear to you, I'm not giving her any preferential treatment when I evaluate her food. I'm judging her just like anyone else, and if you need proof, Trevor and I score pretty much the same every time."

"I believe you, but the network honchos won't." Alden shot her a stern look. "If you're serious about becoming an executive producer, much less being an impartial judge for the finale, you've got to put some distance between you and Tori. Or, if you want to get serious about her, you'll have to exit *Bake-o-Rama*. You can't have both. You hear me?"

"I hear you," she said, her eyes pricking with tears she was not about to show him. She went to the kitchen to refill her mug. "Want any more coffee?"

"No, I have to get going," he said, stuffing his briefcase with the papers strewn across the dining room table. "Moses starts karate today, and I have to give Courtney a play-by-play later." He stood and met her in the kitchen. "Kendra, I can see how special Tori is, and there's nothing I want more than for you to find someone like that. But you understand why it can't be her, right?"

Those pesky tears were ready to drop, so she smiled as hard as she could. "I understand, loud and clear."

His briefcase in hand, Alden brought her in for a one-armed hug. "Love you. Good luck on the finale this weekend. Can't wait to find out who wins."

"Me, too," she said, knowing that the loser was ultimately going to be herself.

Once Alden left, Kendra pulled a folded piece of paper from her pocket and smoothed it out on the table. She reread the words, written in the purposeful, lilting handwriting of a schoolteacher:

Hey there . . .

Whether I win or lose, American Bake-o-Rama will be over in a matter of days. Since Monday I've spent every waking moment asking myself, what comes next?

One thing's for certain: I have decided to leave teaching to focus on opening my bakery. In fact, I turned in my resignation Tuesday.

I understand why you warned me that I need to prepare to be heartbroken, especially in light of your having to leave Gamma Raye behind. But watching you making lunch, and seeing how delighted you were to be the master of your own kitchen even in its last days, showed me that it's worth going for, even if it doesn't last.

The $100,000 prize money would make this transition a lot easier of course, and my business consultant (Della—you'd love her!) advised me to wait until the show is over before making this decision. I respect her opinion, but a wise man once taught me that I need to be the one who decides what makes me happy, so I quit Sequoia High to follow my passion, starting now. I'm terrified and thrilled and feel stupid and brilliant at the same time.

It sounds a lot like being in love.

Look, I have kids and baggage and, as of a few days ago, a new business that's going to suck up most of my free time for months, if not years. I am probably the last person who should be trying to date. (I'm probably the last person someone would want to date . . .) But if you're willing to try—and you're willing to wait until Bake-o-Rama isn't running our lives—I would love the pleasure of your company.

T

It was 2:00 A.M. on Friday morning, and as bone-tired as she was, Tori knew she had to finish confirming her task list for Saturday before crawling off to bed. With only a few hours to go before the final challenge, every step had to be accounted for.

She'd been going at full speed ever since Wednesday's show wrapped. The outcome had been extremely exhilarating and painful. To come out on top after the chaos of the past two weeks was a thrill, a relief, and a personal point of pride. Now she was going into the finals as the only contestant who'd won Best Baker twice, too, which positioned her well to win. But Mel was not going to be at her side, and that neutralized much of that joy. Tori had nearly sobbed when she'd said goodbye to him on camera that night. His gentle, unwavering friendship had been a key reason she was still in contention, much less able to win. True to form, he'd focused on her even in defeat, helping her pack up her car at the end of the night since he wasn't flying out until the next morning. She'd promised to go to Austin within the year to visit, a vow she knew she'd keep. He'd hugged her a final time then removed his spectacular cowboy hat and placed it on her head. "It's no tiara, but I hope you'll wear it sometimes and know you're the Queen of *Bake-o-Rama* in my book, no matter what happens." Then the bawling began.

Since that night she'd been practicing for the finale with barely any time for a meal or a nap. She was grateful the show was providing all the ingredients, saving her valuable time she'd otherwise have spent shopping. On Saturday, she'd have to bake at least three different types of baked goods to evoke the challenge of the day: "Past, Present, and Future." The presentation and the food had to be innovative, visually appealing, and delicious. Since she signed her contract at the start of the summer, she'd known what the final challenge would be, and she'd decided early on to concentrate on her strongest suits: cake, pie, and bread. She'd refined her concept and practiced the bakes along with the weekly challenges so she wouldn't have to cram at the last minute. Good thing, too, since she'd expended every ounce of energy on Wednesday to win her way into the finals. If she'd started from square one on Thursday, she would have been sunk.

She needed some fresh air to stay alert, so she walked into her backyard and plopped into an Adirondack chair. The fog hadn't materialized this evening, and she had a rare opportunity to stargaze. With her next-door neighbor out of town and her own house lights off, there was less light pollution to cloud the blue-black sky. Her gaze softened, and soon she found the Great Square of Pegasus directly above her. Looking into this corner of the universe, Tori admitted to herself how desperately she wanted to win *Bake-o-Rama*. It would put her on a forward path for months, perhaps years. Doing press as a result of her win, filming her TV show, finalizing her business plan, launching her own bakery: That was a lot to look forward to.

Would her future also include Kendra? Could it?

Kendra certainly seemed to think so, based on the note she'd left under the cream cheese brownie in Tori's goodie box on Wednesday:

T,

I wonder what you're feeling in this moment. Are you excited or scared, or both, because you might just win this thing? Are you still looking forward to opening your own place, or did I scare you off? No matter how the scores come out, you'll be a champion. You're a class act in victory and defeat—another thing I admire about you.

I can't believe we met just a couple of months ago. Even though we've had so little time together, I feel so at ease around you. It's like finding someone in a foreign country who not only speaks your language but knows the slang: I feel understood when I'm with you. I don't know about you, but that hasn't happened to me before. I want to keep this—I don't even know what to call it, but it's more than a friendship, for sure—going.

"This" is coming at the absolute wrong time for both of us. Bake-o-Rama is a key to the next steps in our careers. Even if you don't win, you need the exposure, and I want to renew my contract and become an executive producer. And I know neither of us wants to get fired and go through that kind of PR nightmare.

There has to be a way to work through this, but I'm afraid it'll mean we both would have to give up something really important. I don't know how I feel about that for myself, and I couldn't ask that of you. Yet I don't want to give up on this. We're smart people . . . we'll come up with an answer . . . sometime. Until then, good luck on Saturday.

K

Tori sighed. Kendra was right. She was so close to making her lifelong dream come true, she couldn't get involved with the one person who would scuttle it.

But what if Kendra was her dream come true, too?

A falling star whizzed through the Great Square of Pegasus, startling and delightful. Tori made a wish, one so impossible it couldn't ever become real. Then she went back inside to the kitchen, locking the door behind her, to read that note just one more time.

"Friends in the studio and friends at home, welcome to the final episode of Season 7 of *American Bake-o-Rama.*"

Kendra was grateful that Trevor was leading off for the intro to the finale. It was all she could do to keep it together. Alden's stern advice rang in her ears every time she looked toward Station 1, where Tori was as unavoidably lovely as ever, from her starched apron to her cherry-red Converses.

Off to the left, she could see Ross Chalmers, up from L.A. and standing in the wings. He'd told her and Trevor that he was in Northern California for various production meetings and planned to watch the start and the finish of today's baking as a supportive gesture for Natalie and Tori after all they'd been through. Kendra knew from previous seasons that the last shoot day was often a chance for the head honchos to scout the top bakers for future TV projects. She thought that was unfair, since the two contestants had a long day ahead of them, with all the stress and fatigue of a marathon, and they didn't need to be freaked out of their minds by the presence of the head of the network. Thankfully, he and his beetle brows were deep in the shadows at the edge of the set, and they'd probably never see him.

Of course, *she'd* seen him, and that unsettled her. Now that she was angling for an EP title next season, she couldn't make a false move.

"Natalie and Tori, you have surmounted five culinary challenges thus far with great aplomb, producing ten delicious savory and sweet bakes that have been impressive, and even inspirational," Trevor continued. "Today will be the culmination of your skills and ambition and the ultimate test of how well you work under pressure as you produce what may be the best bakes of your lives."

Kendra spoke up on cue, delivering her lines to the camera positioned between the contestants. "You'll be using your own recipes today—no Bake and Switch to worry about—to create at least three different baked items that together express the theme of our Finale Challenge: 'Past, Present, and Future.' And remember: Your presentation will be as important as the bakes themselves. When you bring your work forward to the judges' table, we want to be wowed."

Trevor nodded. "You have eight hours. Ladies, good luck!"

About an hour into the challenge, Kendra, Trevor, and the camera team arrived at Natalie's station.

Kendra started the conversation. "Hey, Natalie. What are you working on?"

"Everything Christmas," she said, slicing a peeled Granny Smith apple.

"That sounds delightful," Trevor said. "What are you making for us today?"

"I'm making three classic Christmas recipes: stollen, gingerbread people, and plum pudding."

"Those are all pretty traditional," Kendra said. "Are you planning to update the typical ingredients or modernize the presentations?"

"No," Natalie said with a brisk shake of her head. "My family has been using the same recipes for more than a century."

"I am delighted to hear that!" Trevor said. "You're tapping into my childhood holiday memories. How will they represent the present and future?"

The baker slid her apple chunks into a saucepan and grabbed a bottle of rum and a tablespoon. "They are the definition of classic: The recipes were developed eons ago, we make them today, and people will be baking them well into the future, too."

Kendra had to admit that was a brilliant way to approach the Finale Challenge. "I'm sure you'll bring your best work today, Natalie."

"That's the goal," she said brightly, screwing the cap back onto the rum bottle and turning up the heat on the stove.

"Best of luck," Trevor added. "I can't wait to taste the results."

Kendra nodded in agreement then stepped toward Tori's station. Tori was pouring cake batter into three layer cake pans, and there were bags and bags of powdered sugar nearby.

Trevor couldn't mask his amusement. "My goodness, Tori," he said. "I haven't seen this much powder since I went skiing in Gstaad. What are you making, and how will this tie into our theme?"

"Well, baking is the common thread that ties together the best parts of my life, and I'm sure it will continue to do so." She pointed to the bowl behind her. "That dough is for the dinner rolls I used to make with my twins when they were little. I'm using all this confectioners' sugar for a cake representing my current career as a chemistry teacher. It's going to be covered in fondant, which is why I need a ton of confectioner's sugar."

"And what will represent your future?" Kendra asked. The question floated in the air between them.

"An assortment of tarts and pies that will be featured at my bakery—the name of which I will reveal later today."

"How exciting!" Trevor said genially.

Tori looked at him with a blithe smile. "You'll hear it here first."

Kendra knew this was how their futures were supposed to unfold: In a few hours, they'd go their separate ways, with Tori pouring every ounce of attention and energy into her business and Kendra tending some pretty hot irons in the fire, too. Trevor was right—it was exciting. Tori was so talented and had put her life on hold for way too long. Kendra would have some financial breathing room without the restaurant dragging down her P&L, so she could become a bigger player nationally. It was all for the good.

This didn't mean Kendra wasn't feeling utterly lousy, watching every moment tick by as one less she could spend near this spectacular woman.

"It sounds like you've got a lot of work ahead of you," Kendra managed to say. "You have so many individual items to make, you'll have to stay on top of your time every minute of the day."

"And we'll really want to see how all these elements connect in light of today's theme," Trevor said. "It can't just be one thing after the other like a bake sale."

"Yep," Tori said, setting the first cake pan in the oven. "That's the plan."

"Good luck then," Trevor said.

"I'm looking forward to seeing what you come up with," Kendra said.

Tori looked straight at her. "Me, too."

There was that palpable connection between them again, as shocking and brilliant as lightning hitting a lake, which meant that by the time she was safely offstage, Kendra was a wreck. Frustrated and anxious, she headed to the green room to start an hour-long break. Trevor had gone outdoors to take some calls, so she had the space to herself. She contemplated napping, but her mind was too jumbled to sleep. The fog hadn't yet lifted, so going for a walk would be chillier than it was worth. She had to empty her head somehow or else she would spontaneously combust.

Kendra rummaged through her messenger bag to locate her pen and a pad of paper then installed herself in a corner. She wrote and wrote until Zak tapped on the door to take her to the patio to tape the first commentary with Trevor. And throughout the day whenever there was a break, Kendra found a quiet place away from everyone else and poured her heart onto the page.

The hour had come.

Tori watched Kendra address the cameras, bringing the show back from what would be a commercial break to begin judging the finale. Her words didn't register as Tori looked at her display, sitting in a pool of light at her station. She attempted to quiet her mind.

I have done my absolute best today, she reminded herself.

There is nothing I would have done differently.

And if my best isn't good enough, then . . .

Kendra looked toward her. "Tori, please bring your bakes to the judges' table."

"Would you like some help?" Trevor offered.

"Yes, please," Tori said. "It's not heavy; it's just awkward."

Trevor came to her station and positioned himself on the right side of her stair-step display, fully decorated and laden with pastries in a variety of plates and baskets. With a nod, the two of them lifted the structure and brought it forward. Once it was in place, Trevor joined Kendra, and Tori acknowledged her briefly, unwilling to look her in the eye in case she'd forget everything she was planning to say.

Kendra spoke next. "Please tell us your approach to the theme, 'Past, Present, and Future.'"

Mindful of the positioning of the cameras, Tori stood to the side of her display and began her introduction, which she'd recited to herself at every break to make it word-perfect. "I am never happier than when I'm baking. Throughout my life—during the worst and the best of it—baking has brought me joy, comfort, and a true sense of purpose. I entered *American Bake-o-Rama* to find out what I'm capable of, especially compared to so many exceptional bakers." She looked over to Natalie, who answered her smile with a warm one of her own. Tori returned to her script. "Now I'm about to make baking my full-time career. This display is a tribute to my life as a baker: past, present, and future."

She motioned to the basket on her first step. "I first hit my stride as a home baker when my kids were in kindergarten. I got into cooking from scratch for them, and with this dinner roll recipe, they could bake with me, too." She peeled back the tea towel covering the basket. "This is an assortment of what we called Zoo Rolls, using yeasted dough that includes mashed potatoes, because we always had leftovers to use up. The kids started out making little pig faces and bunny rabbits, and as they got more experienced, I showed them how to clip the dough and make these spiky hedgehogs. I also encouraged them to incorporate different flavors, like herbs or cheese. I hope you like them."

Kendra picked up a hedgehog and cooed at it. "Look at that face! What did you use for the eyes and nose?"

"Slices of black olives."

"The expression is priceless," Kendra said, turning it over. "It's also nicely browned without any of the spikes getting singed."

"I particularly like this adorable pig," Trevor said, showing off the ball-shaped roll with the triangle ears and knob of a snout. "It's almost a shame to break it apart, but one must do what one must." He pulled the roll apart and poked its interior. "This looks nice and light, well risen, with the right sort of elasticity. And now for a taste." He tore off a bit including the outside crust, and Kendra did the same with her hedgehog. "Just delicious!"

"If you'd like butter, here you go," Tori said, holding up a small dish.

"No, thanks, this is good on its own," Kendra said. "This has Parmesan in it, right?" Tori nodded. "Nice touch." She finished her bite. "Take us to the present."

Tori brought forward a brightly colored cake. "This chemistry cake represents my career as a teacher. It is a three-layer lemon cake with buttercream frosting covered in marshmallow fondant with fondant test tubes on the sides, topped with a glass flask containing one of my edible chemical experiments. Enjoy!"

"Let's just appreciate the decorating job first off," Kendra said, slowly spinning its dish so the camera could capture all sides. "Your fondant is smooth and even throughout, and the pink contents of the test tubes pop against the light blue and green background. It's very well designed and executed; it looks like a cel from an animated film."

"I'm curious about what could possibly be in that flask," Trevor said. He lifted it off the top and shook some of the ice-blue shards into his hand. "What do I do with these?"

"Put them on your tongue," Tori said.

Once Kendra had a handful, the two of them poured them in their mouths. "These are like Pop Rocks!" Kendra exclaimed through a stifled smile as the candy ricocheted against the back of her teeth. "Did you make them from scratch?"

"Yes," Tori said. "It's one of my students' favorite recipes. The baking soda and citric acid in the hard candy react with the heat and moisture in your mouth, and then the party starts."

"Well, let's hope your cake is just as surprising," Trevor said once the candy had calmed down. He sliced into the cake, lifting a piece out to review. "The fondant is a little thick, and I would have used more frosting between the layers." He divvied up the slice between two small plates and handed one to Kendra. He forked a bite of blue-coated cake into his mouth. "Goodness, the fondant is not just edible. It's actually delicious."

"I agree, and I'm just as surprised as you," Kendra said. "Fondant is often way too sweet or it tastes like old chewing gum. This one is tasty, and the tartness of the lemon cake helps balance the overall bite." Tori nodded even as she obsessed over how thin her fondant should have been.

"So now, on to the future?" Trevor asked, his teeth slightly blue.

"On to the future!" Tori said. She gestured toward the top shelf of her display. "My bakery will offer a variety of breads and pastries, and I want to use whatever is in season, too. To show you what I mean, I've made you peach basil hand pies and a mixed berry tart with mint. Enjoy!"

Kendra started with a hand pie, flipping it in her hands. "This looks underdone. The scoring on the top is sharp, though." Cutting into it, she showed the innards to the camera. "The filling didn't quite fill the whole pastry; there's a gap between the peaches and the crust. Let's give it a taste, though."

As she watched Kendra chew, Tori kept her smile pasted on, certain the camera was capturing the panic dancing in her eyes.

Trevor stepped in. "The flavor of the peach, basil, and, I believe, a splash of bourbon makes this a very sophisticated pie. You might have benefited from cooking down the filling a bit longer, though. That way, the basil would be more incorporated into the flavors instead of being more like a garnish. How about we move on to the tart?" He cut a slice, which promptly fell apart as it hit the plate. "Oh, dear. It looks like we have a slight case of soggy crust syndrome here."

Tori winced like she'd been elbowed in the stomach. "Once I got to making the pies, I was running out of time."

"That explains it, then." Trevor offered the plate to Kendra, who took a spoonful.

"The fruit is quite tasty, but I'm not really getting the fresh mint," she said.

"I didn't want to use too much. A little goes a long way," Tori said, chanting silently in her head, *I have done my absolute best today.*

"With just a few more minutes to pull them together, your tarts would have gone from very good to remarkable." Kendra put her plate down and pointed to several furry figures on her display. "Tell us about these little guys."

"The fondant kitties are stand-ins for my twins, Mia and Milo, who have been part of my baking journey practically since the day they were born seventeen years ago. See here at the first level? When I taught the twins how to make Zoo Rolls, they had more fun making a total mess than they did baking." She pointed out small fondant bags marked FLOUR and SUGAR with striped feline heads popping out of them.

"They're teenagers now, so these days, they laze around the kitchen so they can be right there when the food comes out of the oven, which is why the cats are close to the action on the second shelf." She motioned toward the two languid cats giving the chemistry cake the side-eye.

Kendra looked at the top shelf, and her expression softened. "And what's going on here?"

Tori followed her gaze toward the figures at the center of her pie display, where the two tabbies sat in front of a larger cat positioned next to an object covered by a small cloth napkin. Sitting nearby were several small, happy animals, including a grinning, bat-eared puppy.

"They're here for the grand opening of my bakery." With that, she lifted the napkin to reveal an iced cookie in the shape of a billboard. "Welcome to Elemental, everyone!" She then reached behind the display and clicked a switch. Tiny chaser lights began to flash around the sign.

Natalie started to clap and whistle, and the judges and even some of the crew followed suit. Tori blushed to her toes.

I did it! she told herself. *I'm done!*

"Thank you so much, Tori," Trevor said as the applause wrapped up. "Well done!"

"Yes, thank you, Tori." Kendra's whole face was alight, making Tori turn even more crimson.

"My pleasure," Tori responded, then went back behind her workstation, using the last of her energy to sit down. She was exhausted, exhilarated, anxious, and relieved all at once. She tipped her head back and exhaled as the judges asked Natalie to bring her project to the front. Whatever happened next was out of her hands.

Tori was only half listening as Natalie began telling the judges about her creations. She focused on trying to keep herself calm, but Tori sat up straighter when she saw Kendra walk off abruptly in the direction of the green room. A second later, Cal's voice blasted through his bullhorn, saying, "Everyone, we're going to take a ten-minute break."

Tori craned her neck toward the wings to see what was going on.

"Ten minutes, everyone," Liam echoed. Trevor, looking troubled, headed off in the direction Kendra had gone.

Tori rushed over to Natalie's station. "What's going on?"

"I don't know," Natalie said plaintively. "I started talking about my take on the theme, and a second later, Kendra takes a couple of steps backward, says, 'I'm sorry, I can't do this,' and runs offstage. I hope she's okay."

Tori's blood went cold. "I do, too."

Kendra lay down as soon as she got to the green room, her eyes closed, her long legs hanging over the arm of the couch. Trevor and Liam came in a moment later.

"Are you all right?" Trevor asked, concerned. "Feeling faint?"

"A little," she admitted, wishing the nausea would pass.

"Here's some water if you need it," Liam said, putting a bottle within reach.

"Thanks. Just give me a couple of minutes." She took measured breaths of the comforting, stale air of the green room. Her stomach, and her brain, needed time to reset.

Kendra had two humongous problems to solve in the next eight minutes. First, there was no way she could eat Natalie's food, much less evaluate her work, because every one of her dishes was jam-packed with raisins.

When Kendra was very young, her mother had bought two pounds of raisins to donate to a church nutrition program. Little Kendra had broken into the package while her mom ran an errand, and when she'd returned, the bag was several ounces lighter and

Kendra was groaning on the floor, her face the color of pea soup. These many years later, she knew intellectually there was nothing inherently wrong with raisins. She'd made several efforts to eat them as an adult, especially since they were central to so many dishes, but whenever there were more than a couple, her gut and her gag reflex got in the way. A couple of seasons ago, during her heyday as #TheChopper, she'd reacted poorly when one contestant made a raisin pie as a vegan take on mincemeat, then had to go back on camera to explain her aversion and apologize for saying it "wasn't just beyond meat, it was beyond disgusting!"

Kendra was well aware of Natalie's key ingredient; she'd seen bowls full of them whenever she interviewed the contestant throughout the day. She'd cadged a bottle of antacids from Zak and chewed a few before taping began for the finale, and when she walked over to Natalie's station, she fully intended to push through her disgust and do her job as a judge. Then she got a whiff of plum pudding and nearly lost her lunch. She wouldn't even be able to get close enough to pretend to eat it.

The second dilemma? That fondant Frenchie at the top of Tori's display had to be a sign that the baker wanted to keep Kendra in her life. Even though it was mind-blowingly fantastic news that Tori, too, wanted to defy the odds and find a way forward, Kendra's objectivity as a judge had flown right out the window. The stakes for both of them were way too high to risk Kendra being accused of favoritism. And if anyone found out that their feelings were mutual, Tori would be disqualified, and Kendra would be fired.

No wonder she felt like throwing up.

But suddenly, the queasiness stopped.

"How are you doing there, Chef?" Trevor asked after a couple of minutes.

"I'm better, thanks." she said. And she was—because she figured out that one of her problems solved the other.

Kendra sat up to address the men hovering nearby. "I have to be frank. I can't judge Natalie's entry. Each of her main components uses raisins, and while I can handle a few now and then, that many literally makes me sick. It wouldn't be fair to her to try to evaluate her bakes. I won't be able to appreciate them."

"Swell," Liam muttered, grabbing his walkie-talkie. "Cal, can you come to the green room, please?"

Kendra turned to Trevor. "You know what this means, right?"

"My opinion just got more valuable," he said. He offered her a hand, and she stood up just as Cal arrived.

Liam briefed the director, who turned to Kendra. "You sure you can't continue judging?"

"I'm sure," Kendra said. "Look, it's not Natalie's fault. She can make whatever she wants, and I'm sure her food is terrific. But if I can't eat it, I can't judge it."

"Can you even be on the set," he asked, "or will the smell set you off?"

"I should be okay as long as I can stand a few steps back," she said.

"We can make that work," said Liam.

The director frowned. "Yeah, but this means that Kendra can't judge Tori's work, either, because she couldn't compare the two, and the points would be lopsided."

Trevor chimed in. "And so, as the *Bake-o-Rama* rules dictate, since the other judge is incapacitated, my evaluations alone will determine the winner."

Cal huffed as he folded his arms. "As if this season doesn't have enough drama already. Fine. Here's the plan. We'll brief the contestants and crew then get back on track for the rest of tonight's shoot. Liam, tell Ted and the team to get plenty of footage of Trevor tasting everything. Kendra, take the lead in describing the overall project and comment on the aesthetics as much as you can. We'll be able to edit it together so you're both in the final version commenting on her bakes. We will not broadcast to the viewers that only one of you will score the results. Everyone clear here?"

"Aye, aye, Captain," Trevor said.

"Thank you, Cal. I appreciate all this," Kendra said. She followed them out the door, breathing a lot easier.

Two minutes later, Kendra and Trevor stood at the front of the set, and Natalie stood at the judges' table next to her impressive final bakes. Three slices of a real tree trunk were anchored to the center of the stand at different angles and levels to create shelves. Each dessert rested on a bed of spruce boughs, and little ceramic winter birds were paired up on various branches. The whole display was flecked with snowy powdered sugar, and beautifully decorated cookies shaped like snowflakes ornamented the spaces in between. As she'd promised, it was the epitome of Christmas.

Seeing the camera readying a close-up, Kendra said, "Natalie, please tell us your approach to the theme of our Finale Challenge."

Natalie immediately warmed to the task. "I love traditions, especially during the holidays. It's amazing how some recipes were created hundreds of years ago, and yet we can't imagine Christmas without them today. They are what we look forward to year after year, connecting the past with this year's celebration and setting the table for holiday gatherings for years to come. To celebrate my family's baking customs, I chose three favorites and used the recipes my ancestors brought over from England and Germany. I look forward to sharing them with you now."

"Before we slice up these remarkable desserts, I want to compliment you on your presentation," Kendra said. "Your winter wonderland is simple, tasteful, and unique, and the evergreen boughs set the holiday tone beautifully."

"I also appreciate your precision with the icing on your snowflake cookies," Trevor chimed in. "They look exquisite." Trevor took one off a branch and bit into it. "Very nice flavor; a little bit of peppermint in there, I think. It tastes as good as it looks! But I'm distracting myself. Let's start with the stollen."

As Trevor cut a piece, Kendra asked, "Do you make your stollen with a strip of marzipan inside?"

"Oh, no," said Natalie. "My grandmother believes that's way too decadent."

"That must be why you dust the bread with powdered sugar instead of icing it," Kendra observed.

Natalie stared at her in mock horror. "If Oma had her way, she'd go back to the original recipe from the fifteenth century before the pope allowed bakers to make it with butter." Kendra chuckled.

By now, Trevor was chewing away. "I so love stollen. The rum-soaked fruit and all those warm spices conjure a snowy evening by the fire." He showed the sliced side of the loaf to the camera. "The golden raisins, currants, and candied orange and lemon peel are well distributed and so colorful. And Kendra, I am squarely in Natalie's grandmother's camp. Stollen doesn't need marzipan or glaze to be scrumptious when it's baked as perfectly as this. Beautifully done!"

"Great job, Natalie!" Kendra added, keeping the pace brisk. "Now, let's move on to your gingerbread men."

"Gingerbread *people,*" the baker corrected as she pointed to a cut glass platter laden with a dozen cookies, each decorated with ribbons of royal icing, raisins, and bits of candied red and green cherries.

"I can see that," Trevor said, holding up a couple of examples. "You've got quite the wardrobe on these characters—floral skirts and cherry-encrusted waistcoats and whatnot. Is that a tradition at your house as well?"

Natalie's nostrils flared slightly. "No, that's my own contribution. My nan strictly used only white icing piped to look like rickrack around the wrists and ankles. She wouldn't comprehend this at all."

"It's a good idea to make traditions your own. The bake looks nice and crisp," Kendra commented as Trevor broke a cookie in two. "Just listen to that snap!"

"I prefer a crispy cookie like this to a soft bake," Trevor said after finishing an arm. "If you want soft, go ahead and bake a ginger cake." He set his cookie down and smiled at Natalie. "This is the epitome of what this cookie should be. Well done—and now, is it time for plum pudding?"

"Yes!" Natalie said, lifting a ceramic platter off the top of the display and collecting a small, matching pitcher. She poured the pitcher's contents over the pudding, giving the round ball a white winter cap. As she added a sprig of fake holly and a few fresh, red currants to the top for decoration, she explained, "My nan served her pudding with a vanilla hard sauce instead of flaming it with brandy."

"There we differ. I like my presentation as dramatic as possible," Trevor said with a wink. "Then again, I'm sure the fire marshal is glad we're not setting food on fire in the studio."

He sliced the pudding and showed its interior to the camera as Kendra piped up, "This seems to have set well—do you agree, Trev?"

"This is slightly stodgy but serviceable," Trevor said after tucking away a couple of bites. "As you undoubtedly know, Natalie, the deep flavor only truly comes through after steaming the pudding for hours, then letting it sit."

"I didn't have that kind of time today," Natalie said, slightly stricken. "Don't tell my nan."

Kendra added a final comment. "Natalie, your take on 'Past, Present, and Future' leaned heavily on tradition, and you made your ancestors proud. But your main styles of bakes had very similar flavor profiles, with dried fruit and warm spices in each. Also, even traditional foods can evolve over time. I would have been interested to see how you'd update some of these. Could you add black sesame seeds to your gingerbread for instance, or use tropical dried fruit in the stollen? Those sorts of substitutions could keep the traditions alive while incorporating modern tastes."

Natalie nodded warily. "Maybe at your house. Not at my family's, that's for sure."

Trevor smiled kindly. "Lovely work, Natalie. Thank you."

"Thank you, Natalie," Kendra added, grateful the judging was over.

35

Tori was supposed to sit still and watch Natalie's evaluation, a job that was flatly impossible with her mind doing somersaults. Trevor clapped and cooed throughout the segment, clearly over the moon about her competitor's Dickensian baked goods, eroding Tori's optimism about her own prospects. Questions swirled in her head.

Trevor called Natalie's plum pudding "serviceable"—that's good news for me, right?

What am I going to do if I don't get that prize money?

Do I call Doug Alonzo on Monday and beg for my teaching job back?

What happens next with Kendra if I lose?

Am I about to lose everything, all at once?

Her reverie was interrupted as Natalie walked back to her workstation and Kendra said, "Tori and Natalie, you have done exceptional work today. Trevor and I have one of the best 'worst' jobs in the world right now, because we need to choose who will be the Season 7 *American Bake-o-Rama* Best Baker. So, as we labor away in secret, we wanted to make sure you had some moral support." She turned to the sidelines. "Come on in!"

Seconds later, Mia and Milo ran in from the darkened edges of the set and threw their arms around Tori. She was so surprised, she barely recognized them. "You two! I can't believe you're here! You aren't supposed to be back until tomorrow! I'm so glad you're here! Wait, how did you even get here?"

"Mom, slow down!" Milo said, giving her one more squeeze. "The producers flew us out early so we could be here for the finale."

"Have you been here the whole day?" Tori asked.

"Since lunch," Mia said. "They've had us watching from a conference room and brought us in here a few minutes ago." She pushed back her bangs, which were now several shades of purple. "I hate to tell you, but this is really boring as a live show. I'm glad they edit it before it goes on TV."

"I can't believe you're in the final round—wait, I mean, of *course* I can believe it!" Milo said, grinning. "This is so awesome! Way to go!"

"So, tell us: What's Kendra like?" Mia asked, her blasé tone mixed with fangirl glee. "Any good anecdotes?"

Tori's mouth went dry. She wasn't about to talk about the whole Kendra thing with her children yet, especially with all the cameras wandering around and her microphone still on. Thankfully, Cal shouted "Cut!" over the din, and Zak appeared from the wings to take Tori, Milo, and Mia to a conference room to hang out until the judges were ready. As they were leaving, Tori looked over at Station 2 and spied Natalie chatting up a storm with a tall, lanky guy in a watch cap and denim jacket who was hanging on her every word, nodding and laughing. Tori gave her a mental high five. Whether he was friend, family, or both, she was glad to see Natalie wasn't alone in the world.

The next hour was a joyous jumble of conversation over a basket of high-quality snacks, with Tori grilling the kids for highlights from their summer as camp counselors and them barraging her with questions about the competition. When they asked where Anika was, Tori hesitated.

"Did you have to sign something to be allowed to see the finale?" she asked. "A nondisclosure agreement?"

"Yeah," Mia said. "We had to find a counselor who was over eighteen to witness our signature. We can't blab about anything we see tonight until after the finale airs."

"Like we'd do that," Milo said, frowning as he opened a can of soda. "We respect the integrity of the show too much to spoil it."

Tori tossed each of them a bag of white cheddar popcorn. "Good. Because do I have a story for you!"

She took them through all the drama she'd endured over the past couple of weeks. They were rapt, interjecting "NO WAY!" and "WHOA!" as she recounted Anika's unmasking. They were gearing up for another flood of questions when Zak tapped on the door.

"It's time, folks. Tori, you're needed on set, and you two have seats on the sidelines."

Resuming her spot at Station 1, Tori hugged and kissed the twins before they scurried to their chairs. She adjusted her ponytail and rolled her shoulders in a vain attempt to deactivate the tension creeping back into her body.

"Hey, Tori." She turned to find Natalie standing next to her, her arms out. "Best of luck."

Tori brought her in for a teary-eyed hug. "Good luck to you, too. You're a terrific baker, you know."

"Yes, I know," Natalie said with a giggle. "So are you."

Kendra and Trevor were back in place, ready to be cued in. They had both changed into more festive clothes, with Kendra looking suave in a black tuxedo and a white tee featuring two cookies in cheerleader garb gleefully shaking their pom-poms beneath the phrase CHIP CHIP HOORAY! Tori chuckled to herself as Cal cued the cameras to start rolling.

Trevor began. "My friends, we are at the moment of truth. After six weeks and eleven challenges, we have selected our Best Baker, who will receive our engraved baking sheet." He paused before adding, with a mischievous smirk, "And oh yes, she will also receive one hundred thousand dollars and appear in a future show on the Food & Drink TV Network." Tori laughed along through a forced smile.

Kendra took over, looking straight at the camera as if she couldn't bear to speak to the two contestants directly. "It is my pleasure to announce that the Best Baker for this season of *American Bake-o-Rama* is . . . Natalie."

In a terrible instant, Tori felt as if she had plunged underwater and all movement and sound were warped and slow.

That's it then, she thought. *I lost.*

Just as quickly, Tori came back to the now. She rushed to Natalie's side and hugged her. What else could she do? She wasn't about to fall apart in front of her kids or Kendra—or ultimately the viewing public when this went on the air. She was going to be a gracious loser and congratulate the better baker, keep a stiff upper lip on the long drive home, then spend the rest of the weekend beating herself up.

She stepped away as soon as the lanky man appeared at Natalie's side and found Mia and Milo waiting for her with open arms and huge smiles.

"You are amazing, Mom," Mia said, pulling her close.

Milo hugged her from the other side. "No matter what these people say, we know you're the Best Baker. Ever."

They became a laughing, crying three-headed creature in their own corner of the world when suddenly Natalie's voice cut through the chatter. "Everyone, I want to say something." Tori let the kids go and turned to listen.

With the cameras trained on her, Natalie stood at the center of the set, her baking sheet under one arm, hand in hand with her special guest. She whispered something in his ear, and after he nodded his encouragement, she cleared her throat and stood very straight. "I want to thank everyone so much for all you've done for me throughout *American Bake-o-Rama*. Baking means so much to me, and even though I've been cooking for years, I am not accustomed to this kind of affirmation and support. I am overwhelmed and so grateful."

Tori joined the crowd in a round of applause, but Natalie wasn't finished. "I say that because I don't want anyone here to take this the wrong way, but . . . I don't want the prize money or the show. I want those to go to Tori."

Tori's brain was whirring so fast, all that registered was Cal's geyser of profanity as Ted's camera zoomed in on Natalie.

"Hang on," Liam said. "After all you've gone through, after all these weeks and challenges, you don't want to be Best Baker?"

"No, that's not it!" Natalie said in exasperation, gripping the baking sheet even more tightly. "I am keeping the Best Baker title. I worked hard for it, and I'm very proud to be selected, especially with such tough competition. But I don't want any of the other stuff—the money or the TV show. I don't need them."

"You don't want the money?" Ross Chalmers sputtered from the back of the crowd. "Why not?"

Natalie pursed her lips. "None of your business."

"I run this network, so this is very much my business!" he retorted.

She looked at the ceiling. "It was never about the money. I came on this show for the competition and challenge alone. Plus, the thought of spending one more millisecond on television is giving me hives. And let's face it, Buddy was right: Tori would be a great star of a baking show." She looked at Tori, who had only just closed her mouth. "Tori, will you accept?"

"Of course she will!" Milo blurted out.

Tori shushed him and spun back around to Natalie. "Are you absolutely sure?"

Natalie nodded, squeezing her companion's hand. "There are a lot of other things I'd rather do with my life. Please, it would make me very happy if you accepted."

Tori grabbed Natalie for yet another hug. "Absolutely!" she said into Natalie's shoulder.

After closing interviews were complete, the crowd moved to another part of the winery, which was decorated with balloons, flowers, and swags of fabric printed with the *American Bake-o-Rama* logo. The velvet banner hanging across the main wall had two names crammed into the space after CONGRATULATIONS: TORI AND NATALIE, spelled out in gold letters. Champagne corks popped at regular intervals as servers passed insanely tasty hors d'oeuvres and slices of another massive sheet cake.

Tori made sure the kids had plates of food, informed the banquet manager that they should not get champagne under any circumstances, grabbed a flute for herself, then made the rounds to thank the crew. First up was Cal, whose earlier frustration had dissolved in a glass or two of bubbly. Hugging her like a football coach after a squeaker of a win, he said, "I have no idea how we're going to edit that ending, but that's on me. Fantastic job! See you when you're back for your own show!" As he left to take a call, that piece of her new reality fizzed in her stomach.

My own show . . .

What's it going to be about?

What'll it be called?

Tori's Tortes and Tarts . . .

S'Moores . . .

Please tell me that someone in Marketing is figuring this out . . .

Before she started laughing at her own ridiculousness, Ross Chalmers walked up to her, his hand extended and his brow furrowed. "I'm not sure if I'm supposed to be consoling you or congratulating you right now."

"I'll take either one," Tori said, shaking his hand.

He took a step closer. "Just between you and me, I'm relieved by how this all turned out. I've been in the television business for forty years, and even I couldn't figure out how we were ever going to feature Natalie on her own show. That gal is . . ."

"Uniquely talented?" Tori offered before he could say anything negative about her friend. "I agree—she's one of a kind."

He grunted. "She certainly is. Well, good night, and we'll send over a contract in the next few weeks. I encourage you to run it by your entertainment lawyer before you sign."

As he flagged down a server for another piece of cake, Tori snickered to herself.

I can't wait to tell Cassie that she's an "entertainment lawyer" now.

She spotted Trevor and Kendra off in a corner, saying farewell to Liam. The judges brightened as she approached.

"Well done, Tori!" Trevor said, hugging her carefully so as not to spill his champagne. "I can safely say I could never have anticipated this denouement—and I couldn't be happier. Everybody wins!"

"I agree," Tori said, tipping her glass toward his.

With a clink of their glasses, he continued. "You are a truly marvelous baker, and I'm glad you'll continue to have a television audience."

"This has been a total thrill from beginning to end, and I have been so honored to be on the show with you, Trevor. You've made me a better baker, and I can't thank you enough."

"Oh, you are sweet," he gushed, hugging her again then rearing back with a sorrowful expression. "Oh, drat! I spilled my drink on the floor. Did I splash you?"

Tori checked her outfit. "No, I'm bone dry."

He looked at his glass. "So am I. Anyone else for a refill?"

Tori and Kendra said no, Trevor trooped off in search of a server . . . and at last, the two of them were alone, as much as they could be in the middle of a huge group of people.

"Congratulations," Kendra said, bringing her in for a public-friendly hug that was so brief and so unromantic, Tori wanted to scream.

They stepped apart, and from Kendra's look of surprise, Tori registered they were not alone. Milo and Mia were at Tori's elbows, as dazzled as when they entered the gates of Disneyland as starry-eyed six-year-olds. "Kendra, let me introduce my daughter, Mia, and my son, Milo, who are two of your biggest fans."

"You're not embarrassed to hear her say that?" Kendra asked, extending her hand.

"No! She's right!" Milo said, giving Kendra a solid handshake. "I'm out-of-my-mind happy right now!"

"It's great to meet you, Chef," Mia said with a more mature air, getting a handshake of her own. "We have watched *Bake-o-Rama* from day one, and it only got really good once you became a judge."

"Thanks, and I'm glad Trevor didn't hear you say that." Kendra chuckled, taking their praise in stride. "Do either of you like to bake?"

"He's the better baker," Mia replied, pointing to her brother. "I'm more of an eater. Good thing, too, since Mom is always trying recipes out on us."

"That's a great problem to have," Kendra said, sending a smile Tori's way.

Milo was bouncing on his toes. "I wish they'd let us have our phones so I could get a selfie with you. This is unbelievable!"

"I can fix that," Tori said. "You two hang here while I go get them."

"I have to get mine, too," Kendra said. "I'll go with you."

As they exited the banquet hall into the empty hallway, Kendra asked in a low voice, "Can we go to the green room first? I have something for you."

Tori's heart stopped briefly as her mind raced through the possible reasons for Kendra to want to get her alone . . . on the other side of the building from the party. "It'll have to be quick. They'll be waiting."

They walked purposefully down the corridor, with Tori surreptitiously confirming they were by themselves. Once they were in the green room, Kendra moved to close the door but Tori stopped her.

"No, we need to leave it open."

"What?" Kendra huffed.

Flustered, Tori started a rapid babble. "We made it through these last few weeks without anyone catching on that . . . while we're under contract . . . well, we don't want anyone to think there's any funny business going on . . . what an old-timey term, 'funny business' . . . but . . ."

Kendra pulled the door wide in peeved frustration. "It's open, okay?"

"Are you mad at me?" asked Tori.

Kendra hissed through her teeth. "No, not at you. More like, mad at the universe." As she walked over to her locker, she added, "I really did want to give you something, by the way, although I would be very interested to know what kind of 'funny business' you were imagining." Before Tori could combust from embarrassment, Kendra handed her a well-worn paperback. "Here."

She read the title. "'*Blood, Bones & Butter*?'"

Kendra nodded. "It's the best memoir by a chef I've ever read. Gabrielle Hamilton wrote this while her restaurant, Prune, was still open. Maybe it'll inspire you as you get Elemental off the ground." She pointed at the battered cover. "I've had this copy for years and wanted you to have it: from one chef to another."

"Thank you," Tori said, holding the book to her chest so she wouldn't throw herself at Kendra. They held each other's gaze for a moment, then several, standing too far apart, the air around them warm and buzzing. Fighting back tears, Tori whispered, "Tonight isn't goodbye. I want to see you again. When our contracts are up, a year from October . . ."

"It's already on my calendar," Kendra said, her eyes brimming over as well. With an enormous sigh, she wiped them with the back of her hand, checked her makeup in the mirror next to the door, and walked into the hallway. "So let's get those phones."

After a quick trip to the security desk, they returned to the party to find the twins in an animated conversation with Trevor.

"Tori, kudos to you," Trevor called out once he saw her. "You are an accomplished cook and an exemplary mother, based on what these fine young people have to say about you."

"Glad to see my hype squad is doing their job," Tori said, slinging her arms around them. "But now, I need to get them home. We have all had a long, exciting day."

"First, we need pictures!" Milo said.

"Yeah, Mom, no photo, no proof," Mia said. "May we have our phones, please?"

The kids staged numerous selfies with their idols, and Trevor waved Zak over to take more formal shots of them all. Tori looked around the room and frowned. "Where's Natalie? I want a photo with her, too."

"I saw her leave the set with that strapping gentleman after taping her final comments," Trevor said. "I thought she'd come right back for the party, but now that I think about it, I haven't seen her since."

"Any idea who he was?" Kendra asked.

"No," Tori said with a shrug. "You know how private she is. I can only hope it's someone who truly appreciates her cooking. She deserves that." She checked her watch. "Whoa, I didn't know how late it was. Kids, I need your help to pack up, and then we'll be on our way."

"Yeah, I have to get over to the restaurant," Kendra said. "Need me to call you an Uber, Trev?"

"I only need to toddle over to the hotel," he said after a final swig. "I'm all set."

There was a flurry of hugs and goodbyes, so fast and busy that Tori didn't register the magnitude of the moment as Kendra walked out the door—and literally walked out of her life.

Milo and Mia were a helpful distraction, though, peppering her with questions as they stowed her ingredients and implements in the back of her SUV and throughout the starlit drive back to Eucalyptus Point. But once her children were in their rooms buried in their screens and surrounded by cats, Tori sat down in the silence of her kitchen and finally had that good, long cry that had been brewing all day.

Completely wrung out, she took Kendra's paperback out of her bag and headed upstairs. Once in the bedroom, she opened it to find several pieces of paper folded together. Quickly, she unfolded them and read the Post-it note stuck on the first page:

T,

I took your advice and wrote out all the things I am scared will happen now that the show is over, and then I wrote a positive outcome for each. Now, I'm feeling really optimistic about the future!

See you next October,

K

She read the first sheet of paper:

1. I may never see Tori again . . . but I might, and I can do a lot to make sure that happens.
2. Tori might find someone else . . . but I could change her mind because, hey, who else makes chocolate gourmandise like I do?
3. I may never have a restaurant again . . . and that would mean I'd have more free time to spend with Tori.
4. Tori might love raisins and hate rhubarb . . . so I'll learn how to be more accepting of those who are different from me (even if they're SO WRONG!).

The list went on from there: dozens of problems—some serious, some silly—and somehow, Kendra always saw a way for Tori to be part of their solutions. Not only did it make her laugh, it also helped her see the bright side of this situation, too.

Tori drifted off with the letter in her hand and enjoyed the best night's sleep she'd had in weeks.

. . .

Three weeks later, Tori sat in her kitchen with her laptop, finally taking a stab at systematizing her recipes. For way too long, she'd been rifling through folders full of newspaper clippings, ripped magazine pages, photocopies from her friends' cookbooks, and various handwritten instructions, which made it difficult to find anything. She typed up one recipe after another, updating a spreadsheet to sort and cross-reference them by type, occasion, and Chocolate/Not Chocolate. This project helped her organize her thoughts as she looked for inspiration for her menu at Elemental and revealed holes in her repertory she'd need to fill.

The mindlessness of the task also kept her monkey mind in check as she adjusted to being at home rather than in a classroom—and on her own, now that her newly minted college freshmen were getting used to life in Colorado. It also prevented her from going down too many social media rabbit holes to find out what Kendra might be up to.

Honoring *Bake-o-Rama*'s rules and regs, they had both kept their distance and hadn't made contact since the finale, although Tori had a news alert set to ping her phone with any mention of the Sonoma chef. Lately, there was plenty to ping about. Gamma Raye's October 1 closure had made national news, and every reservation was booked within minutes of Kendra announcing her Last Call menu. The *Chronicle* announced she was becoming an executive producer on *American Bake-o-Rama,* and the piece also set the stage for the upcoming season as "a departure" from their typical format—teasing a "mysterious twist" in the third episode. Frankly, Tori was impressed that the Food & Drink TV honchos had kept the truth about Anika and Buddy locked down for so long. She had a media training session coming up to prepare her for the talk-show circuit once that episode aired so she'd know what she could and couldn't say about the sabotage and saboteur. Hopefully they'd also tell her what she'd need to wear; now that the prize money had arrived in her bank account, she might use a few dollars to get a new pair of red Converses.

Maybe she'd run into Kendra on the media tour . . . but probably not. She shouldn't get her hopes up.

The doorbell rang. Opening her front door, she found a FedEx envelope on the porch. She checked the return address: the office of Ross Chalmers at the Food & Drink TV Network. Her contract had finally arrived.

After texting Cassie to confirm that she was home, Tori tossed the package into the car and sped over to Bernal Heights. Cassie was waiting for her on their deck, with Lee Anne pulling together chips and salsa in the kitchen. Tori handed over the envelope, and Cassie chuckled.

"Wow, you haven't even opened this," her friend said, putting on her glasses. "I admire your restraint."

Lee Anne joined them, bringing out the snacks and three cans of sparkling water. "What will your show be about?"

"I honestly don't know," said Tori. "I'm probably just guesting on another baker's show, or it'll be a half-hour onetime thing. I'm supposed to meet with a producer later this month to go over some concepts."

Lee Anne sat beside Tori. "Well, what would you *want* it to be about?"

Tori smiled. "Glad you asked. I think what'll make me stand apart in the midst of hundreds of other how-to cooking programs is taking the Biochem of Baking approach. And I'm not just talking about sharing the science behind the recipes. I'd also love to have a Baking Buddy segment, teaching parents how to bake with their kids. That could be really fun."

"That's fantastic!" Lee Anne said. "I'd watch you every week. I have to find something else to do with my sister's kids when they visit. I can only go to Alcatraz so many times."

Tori looked over at Cassie. "So what do you make of it?"

Cassie put the document on the table and crossed her arms. "I can answer one question for you: They want you for a six-episode series."

Tori's eyes widened as Lee Anne playfully punched her shoulder. "Look at you, superstar!"

"What else does it say?" Tori said, absorbing the good news.

Cassie scanned the pages. "It's a straightforward talent contract, outlining your per-show compensation structure, residuals, product tie-ins, endorsements, using your likeness . . ."

"You mean, Tori's face could be on spatulas or something?" Lee Anne asked with a giggle.

"That's not out of the question," Cassie said, handing the contract to Tori. "Here, take a look. Fatima in our Entertainment Law division reviewed an advance copy of this, and she said it's more than fair."

As Tori pored over the document, she heard Lee Anne ask Cassie, "How much are they paying her for all this?"

"That's protected by attorney-client privilege," Cassie said dryly.

"Can you keep it down?" Tori said over her shoulder with a grin. "I'm reading here!"

After a few moments, Lee Anne piped up again. "Well, can you give me a general idea? Like, is it beach house money, or a couple of car payments, or what?"

"Maybe not a beach house, but it could float the rent for her new bakery for a while," Cassie answered. "And if they ask her back for another season, she could negotiate for a better deal."

"Good, she more than deserves it," Lee Anne said. "But if they come out with a Tori Moore Spatula Set, I want a cut."

"Shh!" Tori said with a grin. They took the hint, and for a little while, all she could hear was the sound of chips crunching.

About five pages in, Tori found something she didn't quite understand. "What exactly does 'this contract supersedes all past and current agreements' mean?"

"Once you sign this, it'll take precedence over your *Bake-o-Rama* contract," Cassie said. "For instance, under that agreement you were paid zilch for all the episodes you recorded. If you hadn't gotten the prize money from Natalie, you'd have earned nothing more than an apron with your name on it."

Tori's pulse ticked up a notch. "Does it only supersede the *Bake-o-Rama* payment terms?"

Cassie shook her head. "No, it replaces it entirely. New show, new contract, new terms all around."

"When does this go into effect?"

"As soon as you sign it," Cassie said.

"Do you have a pen?" Tori asked, her heart practically doing a jig.

Cassie cocked her head. "You sure you don't want to read it again or take it home or—"

"No, I'm ready to sign."

"Okey doke." Cassie pulled a pen from her front pocket and watched as Tori signed and dated the contract. "And with that, you are officially the next Food & Drink TV Network celebrity cook and the host of *Hour-Long Weekly Show to Be Named Later.* Congratulations!"

"Whoo-hoo!" Lee Anne said, raising her can of sparkling water as a toast. "We still have some champagne in the fridge from New Year's. Want me to open it?"

"No thanks," Tori said, picking up her bag.

"Don't you want to stay for dinner?" Cassie asked.

"No," Tori said. "I have plans."

Once she'd confirmed that Cassie would send the original agreement to the network and make copies for her as well, Tori hugged her friends and sped for the door.

More than two hours and a trip over the Golden Gate Bridge later, Tori was in Sonoma searching for a parking space. Finding a spot in a paid lot, she rushed down the street for a couple of blocks before arriving at the green front door of Gamma Raye.

The place was packed. Every table was full, and bar seating had been installed since she'd visited. Guests stood in clumps near the entrance, and a couple was checking in with a lithe young woman in a tasteful suit at the host stand. Once they left, Tori stepped forward.

"Welcome to Gamma Raye," the woman said warmly. "What time is your reservation?"

Tori immediately felt foolish. "I don't have a reservation."

"I'm terribly sorry, we're booked completely this evening," she said gently. "Would you like to be put on the waiting list for next week?"

"Actually, is there any way I can speak to the chef? I know she has to be superbusy, but it will only take a couple of minutes."

The hostess's brows knitted. "I'm not sure—"

"I can wait," Tori said automatically.

"You may be in for a late night," she hedged, noticing the couple that had come up behind her.

Her heart in her throat, Tori tried another tack. "I work with her at *Bake-o-Rama*. I just need to get a message to her. Is there any chance—"

"Hey."

Tori looked over the hostess's shoulder to see Kendra, stunning in a black tailored chef's jacket, her hair slicked back into a bun, her makeup turning her eyes neon. Tori could not move. Over the past weeks, she'd asked herself if all they'd had was a shared crush made stronger because of it being forbidden. The look on Kendra's face told her it was much different, much deeper than that. Elemental, even.

"Hey," Tori said at last. "Can we talk for a couple of minutes, in your office? I won't keep you long, I promise."

Kendra nodded, and Tori followed her through the crowd toward the hallway where her office was. When they opened the door, Julia raised her head then plopped back down on her bed under the desk with a snort.

Kendra smiled as she closed the door behind them. "So, hi . . . it's so good to see you, and I really want to catch up, but half the state is out there demanding stuffed zucchini blossoms and . . ."

Before Kendra could finish, Tori reached up and guided Kendra's face toward hers, drawing her in for a kiss. For a brief moment, Kendra seemed suspended in surprise, but she quickly pulled Tori closer. Tori let out a moan as Kendra stroked her hair and leaned in to deepen the kiss, holding her in a strong, insistent embrace. In Kendra's arms, Tori felt tender and powerful and glowing and glorious. She was right where she'd wanted to be for ages and didn't want it to end.

Before they could plunge into a full-on make-out session, though, Kendra stepped back, her eyes heavy lidded. "Well, that's one way to get a table without a reservation," she said, slightly out of breath.

Tori burst out laughing. "Glad it worked."

Kendra took Tori's hands in hers. "You can tell I'm happy you came to see me, but, um, weren't we supposed to hold off until next year? That pesky fraternization clause and all that?"

"That is a thing of the past," Tori said, stepping closer. "My new contract with the studio has made it null and void. I can be as wanton as I'd like with celebrity chefs now."

Kendra snorted. "Wonton?"

Tori sighed fondly. "*Wanton.* Loose. Like a trollop."

"Ah, that makes more sense."

Tori cupped Kendra's face, taking in the finer details now that she was up close again: her sharp cheekbones and soft mouth, her lush lashes and thick fringe of bangs, those bottomless eyes and captivating smile. Kendra put her hand over Tori's and brought it to her lips, placing a soft kiss in the middle of her palm. Tori watched as she did so, wanting so much more, but . . .

"You have to go back to the kitchen," Tori said.

"Yeah," Kendra said. "But can you stay, at least for a glass of wine? We can make room at the bar, get you something to eat."

"That would be lovely."

Soon, Tori was savoring a glass of cabernet at the corner of the bar, which was a fine vantage point from which to watch the hubbub of Gamma Raye. Many people were at tables for four or six guests: friends sharing bites from each other's entrées as if they'd never have such a fantastic culinary experience again. Scattered among them were tables for two, with couples bowed over the short space that separated them, their conversations intimate. The food was part of their shared stories now, weaving their lives together a little tighter. Threading through the mix was Kendra, regal and gracious, going from table to table to thank the patrons. Often, they'd offer up a memory or promise to be first in line whenever she opened her next restaurant, and many hugged her and wished her well before walking out into the clear, cool night.

And whenever Kendra came by the bar, she'd whisper in Tori's ear, kiss her lightly on the cheek, and ask the server to bring her another plate of food.

ACKNOWLEDGMENTS

I have loved every element of writing this book, and that was only possible due to the support and encouragement of so many talented, caring people.

My thanks begin with Katy Nishimoto, exceptional senior editor at The Dial Press. I appreciate her insights, direction, and endless enthusiasm, and she was essential to making this story one I can proudly share with the world. Also, thank you to Whitney Frick and Avideh Bashirrad of The Dial Press and Andy Ward of Random House for their warm welcome into their publishing families. I'm grateful to Monique Aimee for bringing Kendra and Tori to visual life through her gorgeous cover artwork. Likewise, I applaud the hard work and creativity of Dial's exceptional team overseeing marketing, publicity, art design and direction, copyediting and manuscript transmission, and production.

I am deeply indebted to my agent, Frances Black of Literary Counsel. Fran is a tireless advocate of writers and writing, and I am blessed to have her looking out for me and my work: She is a gem. Thanks also to Brendan Deneen for representing me in the film, television, and media realms to bring my story to an even larger audience.

I would not have put virtual pen to paper to start this book were it not for Tracy Gardner, aka Jess Sinclair. She is a talented author who is as delightful as her prose, and her persistent praise and reassurance enabled me to write a love story without swear words, which I thought was impossible. I'm so grateful she pestered me in the most gracious way possible, and I'm honored to call her a friend and be her loyal fan.

Many thanks to the members of my writing group: Susan Chaplin, Lynne Golodner, Karen Hildebrandt, Pam Houghton, Jimin Ellie Kim, Kim Kozlowski, Carrie Nantais, Anne Osmer, and the late Debbie Pecis, whose talent, wit, and love of the craft inspired us all. These intrepid ladies waded through so, so many initial drafts and have always been generous with their time and insightful, candid feedback.

My bottomless gratitude goes to my dear friend Gail Nelson, who has put up with my bellyaching for years and pushes me toward better work time and time again.

Thank you to Mara Jaffe for giving me a better understanding of how a restaurant functions and what it takes to be an exceptional chef, being one herself. Also, thank you to Halla Jomaa-Jouney for allowing me to bestow her name and extraordinary personality on one of my characters.

My children have been relentlessly encouraging throughout my writing journey. Thank you, James, Hunter, and Davis, for your love, humor, and exceptional taste in movies and music.

I am a much more experienced eater than I am a baker. Thank goodness my partner, Dani, is an exceptional home cook. She was at the ready with recipes and menu suggestions as I developed my fictional baking challenges, and she answered my incessant questions about technique and timing with clarity and patience. In her hands, food is an expression of pure love. Dani, you're my constant inspiration.

And thank you so much for reading this book. I hope you enjoyed it while eating something incredibly delicious.

LOVE at 350°

LISA PEERS

DIAL DELIGHTS

Love Stories
for the
Open-Hearted

PAPER BAG APPLE PIE

This one-crust, streusel-topped pie is one of my family's all-time favorites. It's easy and so, so satisfying!

CRUST:

- 1 cup plus 1 tablespoon all-purpose flour
- ½ teaspoon salt
- ⅓ cup cold shortening or butter
- 2–4 tablespoons ice water
- 1 egg white, beaten

FILLING:

- ½ cup sugar
- 2 tablespoons flour
- ½ teaspoon nutmeg
- Dash of cinnamon
- 7+ cups of peeled and cored Granny Smith, Jonagold, or Gala apples, cut into 1-inch chunks and placed in a large bowl
- 2 tablespoons lemon juice

TOPPING:

- ½ cup sugar
- ½ cup flour
- ½ cup (1 stick) salted butter

One full-size paper grocery bag

Several large metal paper clips

Place the rack in the middle of the oven and preheat to 425 degrees.

PREPARE THE UNBAKED PIECRUST:

1. In a medium bowl, mix the flour and salt.
2. Using a fork, cut in the shortening or butter until the mixture forms pea-size crumbs.
3. Sprinkle the mixture with the ice water, one tablespoon at a time, tossing it with a fork until all the flour is moistened and the pastry almost leaves the side of the bowl. (You don't have to use all of the water.)
4. With your hands, form the dough into a flattened round. Cover it with plastic wrap and refrigerate for 45 minutes.
5. Using a floured rolling pin on a floured flat surface, roll the dough into a circle about 11 inches in diameter and about ¼ inch thick.
6. Fold the dough into quarters and lay it in a 9-inch glass pie plate. Press the dough down against the bottom and sides of the pie plate, being careful not to stretch or tear it.
7. Trim the extra dough around the edge of the pie plate, leaving enough to pinch into a standing rim.
8. Brush the crust with the beaten egg white.

PREPARE THE FILLING:

1. In a small bowl, combine the sugar, flour, nutmeg, and cinnamon.
2. Sprinkle over the apples in their large bowl and toss until they are well coated.

3. Spoon the apples evenly into the piecrust. It's okay if they are higher than the depth of the pie plate.
4. Drizzle the lemon juice over the apples.

PREPARE THE TOPPING:

1. Combine the sugar and flour in a small bowl.
2. Cut in the butter with a pastry cutter or fork until it looks like coarse meal.
3. Sprinkle over the apples to cover evenly.

BAKING INSTRUCTIONS:

1. Open the paper grocery bag and lay it on its side on a cookie sheet. Slide the pie into the bag, making sure the bag isn't touching it.
2. Fold the edge of the paper bag and close it using large metal paper clips.
3. Place the pie in the center of the center rack and bake for one hour.
4. Once you take it from the oven, split the bag open to remove the pie when it's cool enough to handle with oven mitts.
5. Cool on a wire rack for at least two hours before serving.

AUTHOR Q&A

Q: Tori and Kendra are both in their forties. They're lesbians with life experience who were burned by love before yet are still searching for that one-in-a-million woman with whom they can build a life. Can you talk about your decision to write characters who are a little older than we typically see in romcoms? Why was that important to you? What opportunities or challenges did their ages present?

A: I wholeheartedly believe that happily ever after is possible at any age—so why shouldn't there be more romcoms featuring characters with more lived experience?

As a novelist, I write the kinds of books I'd like to read but haven't seen on the shelves yet. I adore stories about women like my female friends: fully formed adults who are smart and accomplished yet still question what they want to get out of life and love. They have to deal with family obligations and financial issues and careers that are in flux, but they're also hilarious and know how to have a good time.

Especially if it's not the norm for the genre—yet—it's important to me to create romantic stories proving that love and happiness are ageless.

Q: Tori and Kendra have lifelong dreams in both career and love, dreams on which they are (rightfully!) unwilling to compromise, and which require them to confront fear, self-doubt, and real-life obstacles. As you wrote this, your first book, did you find yourself facing similar hopes and concerns?

A: Yeah, I can *definitely* relate to what I put those ladies through. Any self-doubt they experienced had already been well rehearsed in my own head. Their fears of not being good enough—or young enough—to pursue a career based on what they loved to do? Been there, worried about that. And any time Tori gave herself a pep talk, I listened in.

I started focusing on writing novels after turning forty, while a lot of other debut authors are just a few years out of college. I've invested a lot of time and emotional energy into manuscripts that didn't get picked up, and every rejection chipped away at my optimism. I appreciated the support of my family and friends, who saw the good in my work even when I couldn't stand to look at it anymore. More than once I had to tell myself that a bad day of writing might be, well, *awful,* but it was still better than not showing up.

As a writer, my success rests on connecting with folks who don't know me personally. I am incredibly fortunate to hold this book in my hands, and I'm thrilled that it has the potential to find an audience of readers worldwide. I also hope that Tori's and Kendra's experiences, along with mine, might inspire someone to continue to nurture their dreams and define success on their own terms.

Q: You were a professional actor and singer for many years. How did your experience in these fields inform your perspective as you built out the world of *American Bake-o-Rama* and all the ins and outs of bringing a television show to life?

A: With *American Bake-o-Rama* at the center of this story, I had a unique opportunity to cast my characters as judges and contestants, with lines to say and parts to play no matter what else was going on in their lives. As soon as the director called "Action!" stress levels skyrocketed. On top of all that, Tori and Kendra had to be hypervigilant not to drop their guard and let their actual feelings show, because who knows when the mic might be hot, or someone might be watching them. That's familiar territory for me.

Another cool aspect of this story is that after so many years as a stage actor and singer, I finally got to direct, script, and produce a show! I loved delving deep into the experience of creating every aspect of this imaginary televised baking competition: the brightly colored decor, the rules of the game, the wardrobe—and the endless baking puns (I don't know if I should congratulate myself or apologize for that).

Q: You lovingly describe yourself as an experienced eater rather than an experienced baker. How were you able to come up with so many recipes and dishes for the book? Why do you think food is such a connector?

A: Thankfully, my partner, Dani, is one of the best home cooks on the planet. She loves to try out new dishes and identify the absolute best classic recipes: the perfect shortbread cookie, the tastiest berry galette, and on and on. And it's up to me to be the taster: Best. Job. EVER! Our house is full of cookbooks, cooking magazines, and printouts of recipes from chefs of all sorts. No matter what I wanted to feature on *Bake-o-Rama,* Dani had either made it before or knew which resource would have the best ideas.

Food is a love language, and making food for someone is the ultimate romantic gesture. What's more, baking is a sensual endeavor. The rich flavors and aromas, the attentiveness that's required to make sure the recipe turns out well, the pleasure of sharing a few delicious bites: That is so hot!

Q: What do you hope readers will take away from the novel? How do you hope the book will impact their lives, and what do you wish they'll come away feeling?

A: More than anything, I want readers to set their cares aside for a few hours and thoroughly enjoy their time in Northern California with Tori, Kendra, their family and friends, and the *Bake-o-Rama* crew. Reading is one of my favorite ways to take a break, and since folks are carrying so much stress these days, I hope *Love at 350°* will give them a reason to smile—and an excuse to enjoy their favorite dessert.

PHOTO COURTESY OF DAVIS KUREPA-PEERS

LISA PEERS is a writer with a passion for smart, funny love stories with well-deserved happy endings. She has acted professionally in San Francisco, has produced TV and radio programs in Detroit, and is currently a creative director for an international marketing agency. A Harvard graduate with an MFA in Acting from the American Conservatory Theater in San Francisco, Lisa lives in metro Detroit with her partner, Dani, not far from their three grown children, along with their beloved cats and way too much yarn. And plenty of sweets.

Instagram: @lisapeersauthor
Twitter: @lisapeers